RING IN THE DEAD

By J. A. Jance

Joanna Brady Mysteries

Desert Heat
Tombstone Courage
Shoot/Don't Shoot
Dead to Rights
Skeleton Canyon
Rattlesnake Crossing
Outlaw Mountain
Devil's Claw
Paradise Lost
Partner in Crime
Exit Wounds
Dead Wrong
Damage Control
Fire and Ice
Judgment Call

J. P. Beaumont Mysteries

Until Proven Guilty
Injustice for All
Trial by Fury
Taking the Fifth
Improbable Cause
A More Perfect Union
Dismissed with Prejudice
Minor in Possession
Payment in Kind
Without Due Process

Failure to Appear
Lying in Wait
Name Withheld
Breach of Duty
Birds of Prey
Partner in Crime
Long Time Gone
Justice Denied
Fire and Ice
Betrayal of Trust

and

Hour of the Hunter
Kiss of the Bees
Day of the Dead
Queen of the Night

Edge of Evil
Web of Evil
Hand of Evil
Cruel Intent
Trial by Fire
Fatal Error
Left for Dead
Deadly Stakes

Coming Soon in Hardcover
Second Watch

RING IN THE DEAD

A J. P. Beaumont Novella

J. A. JANCE

wm

WILLIAM MORROW
An Imprint of HarperCollinsPublishers

Excerpt from *Second Watch* copyright © 2013 by J. A. Jance.

EPub Edition JULY 2013 ISBN: 9780062291097

Print Edition ISBN: 9780062294821

10 9 8 7 6 5 4 3 2

To John Douglas
for taking a chance on a guy named J.P. Beaumont
all those years ago.

RING IN THE DEAD

IT WAS NEW YEAR'S EVE. Back when I was drinking, New Year's Eve was always a good excuse to tie one on, but now those bad old days were far in the past. Mel was out getting a late-breaking mani-pedi in advance of our surprise (to her) date to walk three blocks up First Avenue for an intimate dinner for two at El Gaucho. Our penthouse condo allows a great view of the Space Needle, three blocks away. That means, at midnight, we'd have ringside seats from the shelter of our bedroom balcony for the Needle's New Year's fireworks display. The weather still hadn't made up its mind if midnight revelers would be greeted by a light sprinkle or pouring rain. It was certain, however, that at least it wouldn't be snowing.

My wife, Mel Soames, and I both work for the Attorney General's Special Homicide Investigation Team, affectionately dubbed S.H.I.T. Yes, I know. The name is a running joke and has been for a very long time, but we've grown to like it over the years. In the brave new world of no-overtime, we both had plenty of comp time available to us, and we had chosen to take it over the holidays, including before and after Christmas. Use it or lose it, as they say.

So I was sitting in my den in solitary splendor, reviewing my life and times and considering a possible list of New Year's resolutions, when the phone rang—the landline, not my cell. Not only do we have a landline, we still have a listed number for it, although it's not one that comes readily to mind since that phone isn't the one I use on a daily basis.

The idea behind keeping a listed number is simple. Being in the directory makes it possible for the people I want to find me—fellow Beaver alums from Ballard High School, for example—to find me. As for the people I don't want finding me? For those—for the ones who want to sell me aluminum siding for my high-rise condo, I answer the phone with an icy, salesman-repelling voice that works equally as well on them and on others, like people making political robo-dials for their favorite candidates and the guys trying to convince me to sign up for the policemen's ball—which is a scam, by the way. For the most part, the spam-type calls come through with the originating number blocked. Those always go unanswered, and if they leave a message, those don't get picked up, either.

This particular call came with a caller ID name: Richard Nolan, and a 503 phone number that meant it was from somewhere in Oregon. Even so, I answered using my pissed-off, ditch-the-sales-pitch voice.

"Detective Beaumont?" a woman's voice asked.

I haven't been Detective Beaumont for years now—

ever since I left Seattle PD. It doesn't mean, however, that I'm no longer that other person.

"I used to be," I said. "Who's asking?"

"My name's Anne Marie Nolan," she said. "I live in Portland, Oregon. Milton Gurkey was my father."

That took my breath away, and it also took me back. When I got promoted to Homicide from Patrol, Milton Gurkey, aka Pickles, was my first partner. We worked together for five years, starting in the spring of 1973. In fact, only months earlier, I had spent time dealing with our first case, which, prior to that, had gone unresolved for almost four decades. Pickles died in 1978. I had long since lost track of his widow, Anna.

"Pickles's daughter?" I replied. "Great to hear from you."

There was a distinct pause on the phone. "No matter how many times I hear it, I can never get used to the idea that that's what you guys all called my dad—Pickles. It seems disrespectful, somehow."

"Sorry," I mumbled. "I didn't mean any disrespect. For the guys who called him that, it was almost a term of endearment. How's your mother, by the way?"

Anne Marie sighed. "Mother passed away a month ago. She was in hospice up here in Seattle when news about that old Wellington case was in the papers. I read the articles to her. She was glad to know that somebody finally solved it. She said that was a case that haunted Daddy until the day he died."

"I'm sorry to hear about your mother," I said. "I wish I had known."

"You and my dad were partners a long time ago," Anne Marie said. "Mom remarried twice after Daddy died. The first guy was a loser who didn't hang around long. The second one, Dan, was great. He died two years ago. Mom took his name, Lawson, when they married, so it's not surprising that you wouldn't have gotten word about her death."

Anne Marie had given me a graceful out. Still, I couldn't help feeling remiss, as if I had been deliberately neglectful. A part of me was glad Anna Gurkey—clearly Anne Marie was her mother's namesake—had known about our finally solving the long cold Monica Wellington case before she died. That case was a loose end left hanging that Pickles and I had dragged around between us the whole time we worked together. Obviously, in the intervening years since Pickles's funeral, Anna Gurkey's life had continued just as mine had, with some good and some bad. Hers was over now, and I regretted that I hadn't made any effort to see her before she died.

"Anyway," Anne Marie continued, resuming her story, "I was here for several weeks while Mom was in hospice. Once she was gone, I had to go home and get caught up on things in Portland. That's where we . . ." She paused, seemed to catch herself, before going on with the story. "That's where I live now," she corrected. "I just left everything in Mother's house as is because I was at the end of my rope. I had expended every bit of energy I could muster, and I simply couldn't face sorting through all that crap by myself. I'm an only child, you see. At the time she died, much preferred being called Beau or J. P. He had come round eventually, but his family must not have gotten the memo.

"I don't much like my given name," I said. "Never have."

After that we fell silent until the elevator door slid open. The penthouse floor of Belltown Terrace is made up of only two units. I showed her to ours, opening and holding the door to let her inside. The attention of first-time visitors is always drawn straight through the dining room to the expanse of windows at the far end of the living room. The glass goes from the upholstered window seat to the crown molding on the ceiling and offers an unobstructed view of Puget Sound on the west and the grain terminal, Seattle Center, and Lower Queen Anne Hill on the north. In the middle of the north-facing windows sat our nine-foot Christmas tree glittering with its astonishing array of lights and decorations.

As I said, most of the time the views through those windows are spectacular with the generally snow-capped Olympic Mountains looming in the far distance. Today, however, in the lashing downpour, the view amounted to little more than variations on a theme of gray on gray. The point where pewter-colored clouds met the gunmetal gray water was somewhere beyond a heavy curtain of rain as a fast-moving storm cell came on shore.

"Sorry about the view," I said. "It's usually a little better than this."

I hoped the quip might help lighten my visitor's mood. It didn't. Her face had been set in a grim expression when I first climbed into her vehicle, and that didn't change. In-

Mom was still living in the house she and Daddy bought when they first got married, the one I was raised in.

"My mother wasn't a hoarder by any means," Anne Marie said, rushing on, "but she didn't throw much away. So I've spent all of Christmas vacation up here sorting through the house, getting ready for an estate sale that I'm planning on holding when the weather clears up in the spring. I'm on my way back to Portland now. I want to be back home before all the drunks hit the streets. The thing is, I found something down in the basement in a cedar chest that I thought you might want to see. I don't know where you are in the city, but I'd be happy to drop it off on my way south."

Pickles and Anna had lived at the north end of Ballard in an area called Blue Ridge. Depending on which route Anne Marie was going to take, she'd be within blocks of my Belltown Terrace condo on her way to I-5 and back out of town.

"I'm at Second and Broad," I said. "In downtown Seattle. You're welcome to stop by to visit."

"I was going to head out right away," she said. "I really don't have much time."

"How about at least stopping long enough for a cup of coffee, then?" I suggested.

"You're sure it's no trouble?"

"We have a machine. It's just a matter of pushing the button."

"All right then," she agreed.

"The building has a doorman," I told her. "Just pull up

out front in the passenger loading zone. I'll come down, meet you, guide you into the parking garage, and let you into the elevator. You can't get into it from the garage without a key."

Once I put down the phone, I stood up and looked around. In the old days the room would have been awash in newspapers, including at least one section folded open to the crossword puzzle page. These days I do the crosswords on my iPad. I closed it up and put it away. Then, leaving the den and my comfortable recliner behind, I went out into the living room, closing the French doors behind me.

Since all the kids had been home for the holidays, the living room and dining room were still decorated for Christmas,. My daughter, Kelly, and son-in-law, Jeremy, had come up from southern Oregon with their two kids. My son, Scott, and his wife, Cherisse, had recently moved back to Seattle from the Bay Area, so we'd had an over-the-top Christmas celebration. Because we'd hired a friend, an interior designer, to come in and do the holiday decorating, the place looked spectacular. I hoped when it came time to put the decorations away, we'd manage to fit all of them back into our storeroom down in the building's basement.

On my way through the kitchen, I made sure the coffee machine was freshly supplied with water and beans. Then I went downstairs to the lobby to wait. I was sitting there, chatting with Bob, the doorman, when a woman in an aging Honda pulled up outside and honked. I went out through the front entrance to meet her. With the wind

blowing and a driving rain falling, I was glad to [...] building's protective canopy overhead as I hurried [...] the car. She opened the passenger-side window.

"I'm Beau," I told her. "If you don't mind, I'll ride and show you where to park."

There was a pause with me standing in the rain w[...] she heaved a stack of assorted junk from the front sea[...] the back. That's what happens when you spend most [...] your driving time in a car all by yourself. The passeng[...] seat morphs into a traveling storage locker.

Once Anne Marie had cleared the seat, I climbed in. By then I was wet, not quite through, but close enough. I directed her around the building on John, into the garage, and over to where the valet parking attendant stood waiting.

"Just leave your keys with him," I instructed.

"Where do I pay?" she asked.

"Don't worry about it," I told her. "I'll have him put it on my tab. They automatically bill me for guest parking at the end of the month."

I used my building key first to enter the elevator lobby, next to call the elevator, and finally to make it work. Once I had done so and punched the PH button, I caught the questioning look Anne Marie sent in my direction.

"Yes," I said in answer to her unasked question. "My wife, Mel, and I live in the penthouse."

It's a long elevator ride. About the time we passed the sixth floor, Anne Marie said, "I always thought your name was Jonas."

When Pickles and I first started working together, he had insisted on calling me by my given name, even though stead, she stopped in the middle of the room and sent a second accusatory stare in my direction.

"If you were a cop, how did you get all this?"

I shrugged. "What can I say?" I quipped. "I married well."

That was the truth. Owning a penthouse suite in Belltown Terrace would never have been possible without the legacy left to me by my second wife, Anne Corley. But my offhand comment about that did nothing to lighten Anne Marie's mood or change her disapproving expression either. She simply turned away and made a beeline for the window seat.

Anne Marie was a relatively tall woman, five-ten or so, squarely built, somewhere in her early fifties. Her graying hair was pulled back in a severe bun, and there was a distinctive hardness about her features that I thought I recognized. Between the time when I'd seen her last—as a teenager at her father's funeral—and now, the woman had done some hard living, and there was nothing in her demeanor to suggest that this was some kind of cheerful holiday visit.

Once Anne Marie sat down, I noticed that instead of putting her purse on the cushion beside her, she kept it on her lap, clutched tightly in her arms like a shield. I wasn't sure if she was holding on to it because it contained something precious or if she was using it as a barrier to help me keep me at bay. I also noticed a light band of pale skin on her ring finger that intimated the relatively recent removal of a wedding ring.

If the poor woman's mother had just died and if her

marriage was coming to an end at the same time, it was no wonder that Anne Marie Gurkey Nolan was a woman under emotional siege. I didn't comment on that deduction aloud, but I tried to take it into consideration as our conversation continued.

"What do you take in your coffee?" I asked.

"Nothing," she said. "Just black."

"Strong or not?" I asked. "My wife gave me a fancy coffee machine for Christmas. It makes individual cups of coffee, and we can adjust the strength for each one by turning the bean control lighter or darker."

"Strong, please," she said. "It's a long drive."

"I don't envy you making that drive in this weather," I commented as I walked away.

She nodded but said nothing.

I was aware of her watching me through the pass-through while I was in the kitchen, gathering coffee mugs; waiting for the beans to grind and the coffee to brew. I couldn't help wondering what this was all about. When I brought the coffee into the living room, she took the mug from the tray with one hand, but she still didn't relinquish her grip on the purse.

Since Anne Marie was clearly so ill at ease, I made no attempt to join her on the window seat. Instead, I sat in one of the armchairs facing her. Hoping to make things better for her, I bumbled along, doing my best to carry on some semblance of polite conversation. In that regard, I was missing Mel in the worst way. She can always smooth out the kinds of difficult situations that turn me into a conversational train wreck.

"I'm so sorry to hear about your mother," I said regretfully. "I'm afraid I lost track of her after your father died."

"I'm not surprised," Anne Marie replied. "Once Daddy was gone, Mother didn't want to have anything to do with Seattle PD."

"Had she been ill long?"

Anne Marie took a tentative sip of coffee and shook her head. "She had a bout with breast cancer several years ago, but she responded well to the treatment. Her doctors said she was in remission. When she got sick again, we thought at first that the breast cancer had returned. It turns out it was a different kind of cancer altogether—pancreatic—and there was nothing anybody could do."

"Losing your mother is always tough," I said.

Anne Marie gave me a challenging look, as though she suspected I had no real understanding of her situation. I could have told her that I had lost my own mother to cancer when I was in my early twenties and much younger than she was now, but I didn't. Still hoping to be a good host, I tried changing the subject, only to land squarely on yet another painful topic.

"I guess the last time I saw you was at your father's funeral."

Anne Marie nodded. "I was only a sophomore in college when Daddy died. I've always hated funerals," she added. "Mother did, too. She told me she wanted to be cremated, and she stated in writing that she didn't want any kind of service. She probably did that for my sake because she knew how much funerals bother me."

My bouncing unerringly from one loaded topic to another didn't do much for putting Anne Marie at ease. Still, it must have worked up to a point, because after a brief pause she pressed forward with the real purpose of her visit.

She straightened her shoulders and took a deep breath before saying, "Mother always blamed you for Daddy's death. So did I."

I was hard-pressed to summon a suitable response for that. I remembered the day Pickles Gurkey died like it was yesterday—in the middle of the afternoon on a rainy Monday. Pickles and I had just placed a homicide suspect under arrest. The guy had turned violent on us, and it had taken both Pickles and me to subdue him. The suspect was in cuffs and safely in the back of the car, when Pickles had suddenly staggered and fallen. At first I thought he'd been punched in the gut or something during the fight, but I soon realized the situation was far worse than that. He'd already had one heart attack by then, and here we were five years later with the same thing happening When I realized this was a second attack—and a massive one at that—I immediately called for help. Seattle's Medic 1 was Johnny-on-the-spot just as they had been the first time around. On this occasion, however, there was nothing they could do; nothing anybody could do.

"I'm sorry," I said. "I did everything I could . . ."

Anne Marie waved aside my attempted apology. "I'm not talking about what you did that day," she said brusquely. "Not when Daddy had his second heart attack. Mother and I blamed you because he went back to work after the first one."

What can you say to something like that? Pickles was a grown man, and grown men get to make their own decisions. We were partners, but I didn't make him come back to work. He wanted to. He insisted on it, in fact, but that was all ancient history. That first had happened back in 1973, almost forty years ago. Even if it had been my fault, what was the point in Anne Marie's bringing it up now? Since I had nothing more to say, I kept quiet. For the better part of a minute an uneasy silence filled the room.

"I'm in a twelve-step program," she explained finally. "Narcotics Anonymous. Do you know anything about them?"

I smiled at that. "Unfortunately I have more than a passing acquaintance as far as twelve steps go," I said. "I'm more into AA than NA, if you know the drill."

Anne Marie nodded. "So I suppose this is what you'd call an eighth step call."

The eighth step in AA and NA is all about making amends to the people we may have harmed. At that moment, I couldn't imagine any reason why Anne Marie Gurkey Nolan would possibly need to make amends to me, but then she continued.

"I did the same thing," she said. "Like Mom, I blamed you. As far as we were concerned, you were the reason Daddy died because you were also the reason he stayed on the job. This week, I found this and discovered we were wrong."

She opened her purse and pulled out a manila envelope. When she handed it over, I could tell from the heft of it that the envelope contained several sheets of paper.

"What is it?" I asked.

"These are some of Daddy's papers. He always said that after he retired, he was going to write a book. Since he never retired, he never completed the book, either, but on his days off, he was always down in the basement, pounding away on an old Smith Corona typewriter. This is the chapter he wrote about you. I thought you might want to see it.

"It was while I was reading this that I finally realized you weren't the reason Daddy kept working. He did it because he was worried about money and about what would happen to Mother if he died. It turns out he had been working a case where some old guy murdered his ailing wife and then took his own life for the same reason—because he didn't think there would be enough money to take care of his widow after he was gone. Daddy wanted to work as long as he could so he could be sure Mother and I wouldn't be left stranded."

I vaguely remembered the case Anne Marie had mentioned, but at that very moment I couldn't recall the exact details or even the names of either victim. What I did remember was that case was the first combination murder-suicide I ever worked. Unfortunately it wasn't the last.

A few minutes later, Anne Marie finished her coffee and abruptly took her leave. After showing her out, I returned to the window seat in the living room, with a brand-new cup of coffee in hand. That's when I finally opened the envelope and removed the yellowing stack of onionskin paper. The keys on the typewriter Pickles had used had been worn and/or broken. Some of the letters in the old-fashioned font had empty spots in them. The ribbon had most likely been far beyond its recommended usage limits as well. The result was something so faded and blurry that it was almost impossible to read.

I expected the piece would focus on the murder-suicide Anne Marie had mentioned earlier. To my surprise, it began with the day Pickles and I first became partners.

IT WAS A big shock to my system to come back from my wife's family reunion in Wisconsin to find out that a new partner had been dropped in my lap. As soon as I clocked in, Captain Tompkins dragged me into the Fishbowl, the glass-plated Public Safety Building's fifth-floor office from which he rules his fiefdom, Seattle PD's Homicide Unit, with a bull-nosed attitude and an iron fist. The powers-that-be are trying to discourage smoking inside the building, but Tommy isn't taking that edict lying down. He smokes thick, evil-smelling cigars that stink to the high heavens. For my money, pipe smoke isn't nearly as bad, but Tommy says pipes are too damned prissy. Prissy is one thing Captain Tompkins is not.

Because he smokes constantly and usually keeps the door to the Fishbowl tightly closed, stepping inside his office is like walking into the kind of smoke-filled room where political wheeling and dealing supposedly gets done. Come to think of it, as far as his office is concerned, that's not as far off the beam as you might think.

As soon as I took a seat in front of Tommy's desk, he slid a file folder across the surface in my direction. There was enough force behind his shove that the file spun off the edge of the desk, spilling the contents and sending loose papers flying six ways to Sunday.

"What's this?" I asked, leaning down to retrieve the scattered bits and pieces. I didn't look at the file folder itself again until I straightened up and had stuffed everything back inside. That's when I saw the name on the outside: Beaumont, Jonas Piedmont.

"Your new partner," Tommy said, leaning back in his chair and blowing a series of smoke rings into the air.

He's a hefty kind of guy, with a wide, flushed face and a bulging, vein-marked nose that hints of too much booze. Sitting there with his jacket off and his tie open at the base of a thick neck, he gazed at me appraisingly through a pair of beady eyes. Looking at him, you might think he'd be clumsy and slow on his feet. You'd be wrong. After years of working for the man, I'm smart enough not to make that mistake. Guys who do don't last long.

"What's this about a new partner?" I asked. "What happened to Eddy?"

Tommy blew another smoke ring and jerked his head to one side. "Guess he finally gathered up enough brown-nosing points to get kicked upstairs," he answered.

Eddy Burnside had been my partner for three years. We got along all right, I guess, but there was no love lost between us, and Eddy's brown-nosing was the least of it. I didn't trust the guy any further than I could throw him, which, in my mind, made him a perfect candidate to move up the ladder. Get him the hell off the streets. If he's upstairs making policy, at least he won't be out in public getting people killed. So even though Eddy

was your basic dud for a partner, being stuck with a brand-new
detective to wean off his mama's tits and potty-train isn't exactly
my idea of a good time, either.

"What the hell kind of a name is Jonas?" I asked.

Calling out someone on account of his name puts me on
pretty thin ice. Milton is the name my mother gave me. It's a good
biblical name, after all, so I don't have a quarrel with it. Milton
may be the name on my badge, but that's not what people call
me. I don't know what my father's people were called in the old
country, but when they came through Ellis Island, the last name
got changed to Gurkey. That word bears only the smallest resemblance to the word "gherkin", one of those little sour pickles my
mother and grandmother used to make. But Gurkey and gherkin
sounded enough alike that the kids at school and later the guys
at the police academy dubbed me Pickles. My family never called
me that, but at school and work, that's who I've always been—
Pickles Gurkey.

In other words, between me and this Jonas guy, I didn't have
a lot of room to talk.

I took a few seconds and scanned through some of the papers
in the folder. This Beaumont guy's job application said he was
a U-Dub graduate who had done a stint in the military. That
probably meant a tour of duty in Vietnam.

"You're sticking me with a college Joe?" I demanded. "Criminal justice? Are you kidding? What does a pack of college profes-
sors know about criminals or justice, either one?"

Captain Tompkins listened to my rant and said nothing.

"That's just what I need," I continued. "Some smart-assed
kid who probably thinks that, since he's got a degree behind his
name, he can run circles around someone like me. All I've got to

brag about is my diploma from Garfield High School. Thanks a whole helluva lot. How'd I get so lucky?"

Tommy blew another cloud of smoke before he answered. "He's not brand-new," he assured me. "Beaumont spent a couple of years on Patrol before they shipped him up here last week. Since you were out of town, he's been working with Larry Powell and Watty Watkins on that dead girl they found over on Magnolia."

"The Girl in the Barrel?" I asked.

The kid who delivers our home newspaper lives next door. Rather than turning our subscription off while we were out of town on vacation, Anna and I had him hold our papers. When we got home from Wisconsin on Friday night, the kid had brought them over, and we'd both gone through the stack. Anna cut out all the coupons she wanted, and I read all the news, just to bring myself back up to speed.

Doing a balancing act to keep from dribbling ashes all over his desk, Tommy managed to park his stogie on the edge of a large marble ashtray that was already overfilled with cigar butts and ashes. I'm sure the cleaning people love dealing with his mess every night.

"That's the one," he said. "As for how you got him? You're the only guy on the fifth floor without a living/breathing partner at the moment. That means your number's up, like it or lump it."

If Tommy had wanted to, I knew he could have moved people around so I wouldn't have been stuck with the new guy, but there was no point in arguing. If I couldn't get Tompkins to change his mind about assigning the new guy to me, maybe I could figure out a way to change the new guy's mind about wanting to be a detective. That was the simplest way to fix the problem—convince *the new detective that what he wanted more than anything was to be an ex-detective.*

"So where is he?" I asked.

"Probably in your cubicle, writing up his first report. Everybody else was tied up with that serial killer workshop this past weekend, so Beaumont ended up going to the girl's funeral up in Leavenworth."

"He went to the funeral by himself?" I asked. "Who was the genius who decided that was a good idea? Shouldn't an experienced detective have handled it?"

Tommy shrugged. "Didn't have a choice. Everybody else had paid to go to the FBI workshop. I figured, how bad could it be? But you might want to look over his paper before he hands it in."

"Great," I sputtered. "Now I'm supposed to haul out a red pencil and correct his spelling and grammar?"

"That's right," Tommy said with wink and a knowing smirk. "If I were you, I'd make sure his report is one hundred percent perfect. Doing it over a time or two or three will be great practice for him, and marking him down will be good for whatever's ailing you at the moment. Go give him hell."

Dismissed, I left the smoky haze of the Fishbowl, doing a slow burn. Next to Larry Powell and Watty, I was one of the most senior guys on the squad. It made no sense to stick me with a newbie who would do nothing but hold me back. Rather than go straight to my cubicle, I beat a path to Larry and Watty's.

"Gee, thanks," I said, standing in the entrance to their five-foot-by-five-foot cell. Which brings me to something else that provokes me to no end. How come prisoners get more room in their cells than we do in our offices? What's fair about that?

"For what?" Larry asked.

"For giving me the new guy."

"He's not brand-new," Larry advised. "We've had to hold his hand for the better part of a week before you came back, so quit your gritching. Besides, you were new once, too."

"Sure you were," Watty said with a grin. "Back when Noah was building that ark, or maybe was it even earlier, back when dinosaurs still roamed the earth?"

"Funny," I grumbled. "So how did he go about getting moved up from Patrol? The last I heard, the word was out that there weren't any openings in Homicide."

"There weren't until Eddy got promoted," Watty said, "but I've heard some talk from other people about this, too. Beaumont's former partner from Patrol, Rory MacPherson, was angling to get into Motorcycles. Beaumont wanted Homicide. A week ago Sunday, the two of them took a dead body call. The next thing you know, voilà! Like magic, they both get the promotions they wanted."

"In other words, something stinks to the high heavens. Are you telling me my new partner is also some bigwig's fair-haired boy?"

"Can't say for sure, but it could be," Larry Powell allowed.

"Sure as hell doesn't make me like him any better."

Unable to delay the inevitable any longer, I stomped off and headed for my lair. As I approached my little corner of Homicide, I heard the sound of someone pounding the hell out of our old Underwood. My mother did me a whale of a favor by insisting I take touch typing in high school. When it comes to writing reports, being able to use all my fingers is a huge help. Obviously this guy's mother hadn't been that smart. Jonas Beaumont was your basic two-fingered typist, plugging away one slow letter key evidence. In fact, we never did solve that particular case. We worked it off and on for a couple of years and finally got shunted away from it entirely.

All this is to say, it wasn't a great start for a partnership. In fact, I'd call it downright grim. I kept the pressure on him, expecting him to go crying to whoever it was who had pulled the strings to move him to Homicide, but that didn't happen, either. He was a smart enough guy who tended to go off half-cocked on occasion.

If he was the hare, I was the tortoise. Jonas had good instincts but he was impatient and wanted to sidestep rules and procedures. I pounded down that tendency every chance I could—made him go through channels, across desks, and up the chain of command. The truth is that with enough practice, he started to get pretty good at it.

I could tell early on that he hit the sauce too much. He and his wife had a couple of little kids at home, and I think they squabbled a lot. I don't mean that the kids squabbled—Jonas and his wife did. I know her name but it's slipped my mind at the moment. It's that old familiar story—the young cop works too hard and can't put the job away when he gets home. Meanwhile the wife is stuck handling everything on the home front. In other words, I understood it, because those were issues Anna and I had put to bed a long time ago, but like I told him that first day, I didn't want any advice on nutrition from him, and I figured he didn't need any marital counseling from me. Fair is fair.

We worked together for several months before the night in early July when everything changed and when our working together morphed from an enforced assignment into a real partnership.

at a time. When I paused in the entrance, he was frowning at the form in the machine with such purpose and concentration that he didn't see me standing there. I noticed right off that he was sitting in the wrong chair.

"I'm Detective Gurkey,, your new partner," I announced by way of introduction. "The desk you're using happens to be mine."

He glanced up at me in surprise. "They told me to use this cubicle," he said. "This is the desk that was empty."

"Maybe so," I told him, "but that was Eddy's desk. He was senior, and he had the window. Eddy's gone now. I'm senior. You're junior. I get the window."

Admittedly, the view from the window is crap. Still, a window is a window. It's a status symbol kind of thing.

"Sorry," he mumbled. "Just let me finish this."

"No," I replied. "I don't think you understand. Like I said, I'm senior. You're junior. That means I don't stand around in the hallway waiting while you get your act together, clear your lazy butt out of my chair, and clean your collection of crap off my desk. Once your stuff is gone, I move into this one. Just because Watty held your hand and treated you with kid gloves all last week doesn't mean I'm going to. Got it?"

"Got it," he answered promptly, pushing his chair away from the desk. "Right away."

I knew I was being a first-class jerk, but that was the whole idea. I wanted the guy gone, and making him miserable was the fastest way to get that job accomplished. I stood there tapping my foot with impatience while he gathered up his coat from the chair and emptied everything he had carefully loaded into Eddy's empty desk drawers back out onto the top of the desk. After that

I took my own sweet time about moving my stuff from one desk to the other. I could tell he was steaming about it while he had to wait, but I didn't let on that I noticed. After all, this was one pissing match I was determined to win.

I left him cooling his heels until I was almost done sorting, then I sent him for coffee. "Two creams, three sugars, and no lectures," I told him. "I get nutritional advice from my wife. I don't need any from you. And if you want coffee for yourself, you'd better get it now. Once we start hitting the bricks, we won't be stopping for coffee and doughnuts. This is Homicide, Jonah; it's not Patrol."

The Jonah bit was a deliberate tweak, and he lunged for the bait.

"Jonas," he corrected. "The name's Jonas, but my friends call me either J. P. or Beau."

"I'm your partner not your friend," I told him. "That means Jonas it is for the foreseeable future."

"Right," he muttered. Then he stalked off to get coffee.

While he was gone, I took it upon myself to read and edit his report. By the time he got back, I had used a red pen to good effect, marking it up like crazy. It turned out Tommy Tompkins was right. Correcting Detective Beaumont's work made me feel better. When Jonas came back with the coffees, I handed him the form.

"Not good enough," I told him. "Not nearly good enough, especially considering you're a hotshot college graduate. Take another crack at this while I find out what we're supposed to be doing today."

I left him there working on that and went looking for the

murder book on the Girl in the Barrel. Tommy had told me that until Jonas and I caught a new case of our own, we'd be doubling up with Larry and Watty Watkins on their ongoing case. I spent some time reviewing the murder book entries. The body of the victim, a girl named Monica Wellington, had been found on Sunday afternoon a week and a day earlier. Beaumont and his Patrol partner, Rory MacPherson, had responded to the 911 call. In the intervening days, Larry and Watty, with Beaumont along for the ride, had done a whole series of initial interviews. The autopsy had revealed that the victim was pregnant at the time of her death, but so far no boyfriend had surfaced.

By the time I'd scanned through the murder book, Jonas had finished the second go-down on his report. He ripped it out of the typewriter, handed it over, and then stood behind me, watching over my shoulder, as I read through it. Unfortunately, there wasn't a damned thing wrong with it.

"I suppose this'll do," I told him dismissively. "Now go down to Motor Pool and get us a car. It's time to hit the road."

And we did, driving all over hell and gone with him at the wheel, doing follow-up interviews with all the people who had been spoken to earlier. Follow-ups aren't fun, by the way. Initial interviews are the real meat and potatoes of the job. The only thing fun about follow-ups is catching people in the lies that they made up on the run the first time around.

Turns out we found nothing—not a damned thing. I was hoping to pull off some little piece of investigative magic to garner some respect and put the new guy in his place, but that didn't happen. Nobody did a Perry Mason–style confession in our presence. We didn't discover some amazing bit of missing

It was an odd week, with the Fourth of July celebration falling on a Wednesday. Jonas and I were at the range doing target practice when we got a call out on the sad case of what, pending autopsies, was being considered murder-suicide. The previous Wednesday, an old guy over in Ballard, a ninety-three-year-old named Farley Woodfield, who had just been given a dire cancer diagnosis, went home from his doctor's office, grabbed his gun, loaded it, and then took out his bedridden wife, the woman for whom he was the primary caregiver. After shooting her dead, he had turned the weapon on himself. Several days after the shootings, the Woodfields' mailman had stepped onto their front porch to deliver a package and had noticed what he termed a "foul odor."

The word "foul" doesn't cover it. Like I said, it was July. The house had been closed up tight. I had been feeling punk over the weekend with something that felt like maybe a summer cold or a case of the flu. I wasn't sick enough to stay home from work, but I can tell you that being called to that ugly crime scene didn't help whatever was ailing me. We found Farley's note on the kitchen table: "With me gone, there goes the pension. Jenny will have nothing to live on and no one to look after her. I can't do that to her. I won't. Sorry for the mess."

He was right about the mess part. It was god-awful. Seeing the crime scene and the note made it clear what had happened, but when you're a homicide detective, that doesn't mean you just fill in the boxes on the report form and call it a job. Once the bodies were transported, Jonas and I spent the day canvassing the neighborhood, talking to people who had lived next to the old couple. From one of the neighbors, we learned that there was a daughter who lived in St. Louis, but there had been some kind of family estrangement, and the daughter had been out of her parents' lives for years.

As for the neighbors? None of them had paid the least bit of attention to the newspapers piling up on the front porch. None of them had noticed that Farley wasn't out puttering in his yard or that the grass he always kept immaculately trimmed with an old-fashioned push mower was getting too long to cut. By the end of the day, I was mad as hell at the neighbors, because I could see that the old guy had a point. With the couple's only child out of the picture, and if Farley wasn't going to be there to look after his wife, who was going to do it? Nobody, that's who!

We had taken the Woodfield call about eleven o'clock in the morning, and it was almost eight o'clock that night when we headed back downtown to file our reports. As usual, Jonas was at the wheel. We were driving east on Denny. When I suggested we take a detour past the Doghouse to grab a bite to eat, he didn't voice any objections. Instead of heading down Second Avenue, he stayed on Denny until we got to Seventh.

The Doghouse is a Seattle institution, started in the thirties by a friend of mine named Bob Murray. It used to be on Denny, but in the early fifties, when the city opened the Battery Street Tunnel to take traffic from the Alaskan Way Viaduct onto Aurora Avenue North, the change in driving patterns adversely affected the restaurant's business. Undaunted, Bob pulled up stakes and moved the joint a few blocks away to a building on Seventh at Battery. The Doghouse has been there ever since. It's one of those places that's open twenty-four hours a day and where you can get breakfast at any hour of the day or night.

It's no surprise that cops go there. In the preceding months,

Jonas and I had been to the Doghouse together on plenty of occasions, grabbing one of the booths that lined the sides of the main dining room. This time, though, when Bob tried to lead us to a booth, I could see we were headed for Lulu McCaffey's station. That's when I called a halt.

Lulu was one of those know-it-all waitresses who was older than dirt. One of the original servers who had made the transition from the "old" Doghouse to the "new" one twenty years earlier, she always acted like she owned the place. Unfortunately and more to the point, this opinionated battle-axe also bore a strong resemblance to my recently departed mother-in-law.

Years ago, I had made the mistake of wising off in front of Lulu. She got even with me by spilling a whole glass of ice water down the front of my menu and into my lap. Ever since, I avoided her station whenever possible. This day in particular, I wasn't prepared to deal with any of her guff, so I asked Bob if we could be seated in the back room.

It turns out that as far as the Doghouse was concerned, Jonas was a back room virgin. There are plenty of restaurant back rooms in Seattle—at the Doghouse, Rosellini's, Vito's, and the Dragon's Head. It's no surprise that many of the people who congregate in those back rooms and play the occasional game of poker are local cops and elected officials who want to keep up appearances as far as the voting public is concerned.

The back room is where Bob delivered us, safely out of Lulu's territory and firing range.

We both ordered burgers.

While we were busy, I had more or less forgotten that I wasn't feeling up to snuff, but sitting still, drinking iced tea, and waiting for our food, it started coming back. The worse I felt, the more I kept remembering everything about that ugly crime scene in Ballard. Farley Woodfield was evidently a World War I vet. There was a framed photo montage hanging over the fireplace. It included several photos of him—a sweet-faced young kid— posing manfully in his brand-new doughboy uniform. The faded cloth matting around the photos was decorated with a collection of miscellaneous pieces that included faded battle ribbons, tarnished medals, and a distinctive sergeant's chevron.

Just thinking about it hit me hard. Here was a poor guy who had given up his youth to go to war and serve his country. Now, seventy years later, he had been left to his own devices with no one to help him or to watch his back.

Our food came. Jonas dove into his; I pushed mine away.

"What's wrong?" he asked.

"Nothing," I said, because I didn't want to talk about what I was thinking. "I need to take a piss is all."

I left the table and the back room, but despite what I'd said, I didn't head for the rest room. I wanted to clear my head, so I went outside and walked around the parking lot for a few minutes. I was thinking about the old guy and wondering what I'd do if I was in his position. If I were gone, would my pension be enough for Anna to be able to get by? If something went wrong with her health, would our daughter come through and take care of her if I wasn't able to do it?

Somewhere along the way, I realized that my arm was hurting—aching like crazy. I kept wondering how I had managed to hurt it that badly without noticing anything had happened. It was hot as hell outside. Even though it was close to nine at night, it wasn't dark outside yet, and it sure as hell wasn't cool. Pretty soon I started feeling light-headed. I went over and stood by the building so I could lean against the wall. That's when all hell broke loose. Two guys came charging out of the restaurant and through the parking lot with Lulu chasing after them, screaming like a banshee.

"You come back here!" she screeched, waving a small piece of paper in the air. "You think you can just walk out on your check, you worthless turds? You think your food's coming out of my paycheck?"

The problem was, as soon as Lulu screamed at them, the two men stopped running and turned on her. At that point, I don't think any of them had seen me, but I saw them. The one guy grabbed Lulu by the arm and swung her around, sending her crashing head first into the trunk of a parked car. That's when things went into slow motion for me. It looked like the other guy was closing in on her. Pushing off from the wall, I drew my Smith & Wesson.

"Okay, you guys," I ordered. "I'm a police officer. Let her go. Get your hands in the air."

Surprised, they all three turned to gawk at me. That's when my body just stopped working, starting with my arm and fingers. The gun fell to the ground and went spinning uselessly away from me across the pavement. I couldn't move and I couldn't breathe because of the crushing pain in my chest. Even while it was happening, I realized I had to be having a heart attack. I had my wits about me enough that I took a step or two back toward the building so that if I fell, I could slide down the wall instead of falling flat on my face or whacking the back of my head on the pavement.

I remember seeing the three other people in the parking lot, standing there frozen in time, staring at me. The one guy was still hanging on to Lulu's arm. Lulu's mouth was open, like she was still screaming although I no longer heard any sound. Her face was red with fury. I more than half expected her to turn around and plant her fist in her attacker's face, but then he dropped out of sight and disappeared from my line of vision for a moment. A second or so later the look on Lulu's face changed. Her eyes widened. In that moment the expression on her face went from utter fury to abject fear. A gun must have gone off then although I don't remember hearing that, either. I saw the blood spray out behind her, saw Lulu stagger backward a step or two, then I blacked out.

When I came to, Jonas was squatting beside me and yelling in my ear. "Pickles! Can you hear me? The ambulance is on its way. What the hell happened?"

He didn't need to tell me about the ambulance. With my hearing back, I could hear the approaching sirens. They were already, in the background, muffled in a load of cotton, but coming closer fast.

"Two guys," I managed. "Lulu. Is she . . . ?"

Jonas shook his head. "She didn't make it," he said. "She's dead. What the hell happened here?"

He reached down then. Putting a pen through the trigger guard of my .38, he carefully pulled the weapon out of my lap and laid it aside, just beyond my reach. I remember wondering: How the hell did my gun get there? But then I figured it out. The guy who shot Lulu must have put it there. A dead woman, my weapon, and my fingerprints. I was screwed.

"There were two guys," I said, gasping around the awful pain in my chest. "They must have taken off. You've got to find them."

"Were they on foot or in a car?"

"On foot, I think. Didn't see a car."

That's the thing. The gun was there in my lap. The assailants were long gone. Jonas knew I hated Lulu's guts, and yet he never doubted me, not for an instant.

"Okay," he said. "Will do, but first I've got to talk to Bob Murray."

A Medic 1 guy appeared over Jonas's shoulder and bodily booted him out of the way. The last thing I remember, as the attendants loaded me onto a gurney, was Jonas striding purposefully back into the restaurant, notebook in hand.

I had other things to think about that night—like living or dying.

I STOPPED READING for a moment, thrown back into that terrible parking lot scene at the Doghouse.

As suddenly as if it were yesterday, it all came crashing back. As soon as Bob Murray told me shots had been fired, I charged out the restaurant's back door, with him at my heels. Out in the parking lot the smell of burned cordite still lingered in the hot, still air. I found Lulu McCaffey's bloody body lying sprawled on the pavement between cars. A green bit of paper that I recognized as the check from someone's table was still clutched in her hand. I checked her pulse first. Finding none and thinking my partner had been shot, too, I turned to Pickles. By then, Bob Murray had raced back inside to call 911.

Pickles was a few feet away from Lulu, slouched against the building. Kneeling next to him, I looked for a wound of some kind, but there wasn't any. Whatever had happened to Pickles, he hadn't been shot. But I did find his gun and I could tell it had been recently fired. He kept trying to talk to me, but all I could make out from his mumble was that there had been two guys and they had taken off on foot.

I knew that if Pickles had taken a potshot at the two fleeing bad guys, there was going to be hell to pay, and I didn't want my fingerprints anywhere on the gun. I used a pen to ease his Smith & Wesson out of his lap and set it down on the pavement. He kept trying to talk to me, but most of what he said was too garbled to understand. Eventually the Medic 1 guys showed up. At the time, Seattle had bragging rights because Medic 1's still relatively new presence in the city had made Seattle the best place in the world to have a heart attack. By the time the ambulance showed up, I was pretty sure that's what we were up against—a heart attack.

As soon as the EMTs took over, I heard the sounds of arriving patrol cars converging on the area. I grabbed an evidence bag from the back of our unmarked car, deposited the gun in that, pocketed both, and hurried back into the restaurant. From the way Pickles looked, I was convinced he was a goner. If his death occurred while he was interrupting someone in the process of committing a crime, that meant that whoever had gunned down Lulu McCaffey would be guilty of two counts of homicide—both his and hers—rather than just one.

Bob Murray was a smart guy. He had come to the same conclusions I had—that the two guys who had skipped out on paying their tab had committed cold-blooded murder in his parking lot. Using chairs from the dining room, he had cordoned off both Lulu's station and the booth where the dine-and-dash bad guys had been sitting. Although the rest of the restaurant had somehow managed to return to some semblance of business as usual, Bob had made sure that none of the tables in Lulu's section had been cleared. He was personally standing guard to see to it that no one ventured anywhere near them.

"Did you see the two guys?" I asked him. "Can you give me any kind of description to pass along to the guys on patrol?"

Bob shook his head. "I was in the kitchen when they came in. Lulu seated them and served them, so she's really the only employee who saw them." He handed me a piece of paper. On it were scribbled several names and phone numbers, written in several distinctly separate styles of handwriting.

"Who are these?" I asked.

"They're the people who were seated at nearby tables," he told me. "I had them write down their names and phone numbers in case you need to get back to them."

"Any of them still here?"

Bob nodded, but his customary grin was missing in action. "All of them," he answered. "I sent them to the bar and told them to have one on me while they wait."

See there? I told you Bob Murray was a smart guy.

I glanced over at the booth. "Nobody's touched it?"

"Nope," he said. "And I aim to keep it that way."

"Great," I said. "When the detectives get here, be sure they get prints off everything. It's hard to find a suspect from an unknown print like that, but once we get the bad guys, having their prints in the system will help put them at the scene of the crime."

"You got it," Bob told me. "I'll see to it."

In the bar, the organ that usually filled the place with sing-along music far into the night was notably silent. The organist was there, but he was sitting alone at the bar quietly having a beer. With Lulu's body still in the parking lot, it wasn't at all surprising that nobody felt like singing. In the darkened room, seated against the far wall at four separate tables, were the other eight people who had been seated in Lulu's station at the time all hell broke loose. Still shocked by what had happened, they huddled together in a subdued group, nursing their drinks and their fear.

Milton Gurkey was my partner. Whether Pickles lived or died, I understood this wouldn't be my case to investigate. Someone else would be doing in-depth interviews of all the potential witnesses, including talking to the poor people currently sheltering in the bar of the Doghouse. All I wanted from them right that moment was a general description of the two suspects—something I could give to the guys out on the streets in patrol cars so officers in the area could be on the lookout for them.

What I ended up with was certainly vague enough. Two guys: one about six feet tall, the other a little shorter. The taller of the two was light-complected with dirty blond hair and maybe/maybe not a mustache. He was wearing yellow and brown plaid Bermuda shorts, a white T-shirt, and tennis shoes with no socks. The other guy, five-ten or so, was both shorter and heavier. He had olive skin—maybe Hispanic. He wore jeans, tennis shoes, and a blue plaid shirt. In other words, neither of these guys were fashion plates, but with the seasonably hot weather, their costumes wouldn't give them away, either, not the way sweatshirts or parkas would have.

By the time I went back outside, the response to the incident made for mayhem on the street. Although the ambulance had already taken off, there were still fire trucks and plenty of patrol cars, marked and unmarked, in attendance. I tracked down the patrol sergeant and gave him what I had gleaned as far as descriptions were concerned. Having done what I could, I drove to Harborview Hospital, where I planted myself in the waiting room of the ER and waited for word on whether or not Pickles Gurkey was going to make it.

I was there when a sergeant from Patrol brought Anna Gurkey to the hospital and dropped her off. Previously, I had never met the woman, but I knew who she was when she walked up to the admitting desk and asked the clerk about her husband, Milton Gurkey. Whatever was going on with the patient right then, he wasn't being allowed visitors. Having been given that information, Anna retreated to one of the straight-backed chairs lining the room. As soon as she was seated, I went up and introduced myself.

Anna Gurkey looked liked she might have stepped out of the movie version of *The Sound of Music*. She reminded me of the homely woman who keeps who bobbing and nodding to the sounds of applause when her group is given its second place award in the talent contest. In other words, Anna wasn't a beauty-queen showstopper. She had a broad face with rough, reddish skin. Her dingy, graying hair was pulled back in a straggly bun. Anna's basic plain-Jane looks were worsened by the reality of where she was and what had happened. She looked the way family members found in ER waiting rooms always look—haggard, terrified, and shell-shocked.

"You're Jonas?" she asked when she heard my name. "Were you there? What happened? The officer who brought me here couldn't tell me a thing."

Wouldn't tell was more likely than couldn't tell, but I was under no such constraints. I told her what I knew. That we'd been working; that we'd stopped off at the Doghouse for a dinner break; that Pickles had excused himself to make a pit stop. After that, for reasons I didn't understand, it had all gone to hell, with Pickles caught up in a shootout in the parking lot.

I had finished telling the story when a doctor emerged from behind closed doors. He sought out Anna, spoke with her in a low, grave voice, and then took her back through the swinging doors with him into the treatment rooms. Anna walked away from me without so much as a backward glance. Considering the seriousness of the situation, I didn't blame her. I waited around awhile longer. When no one came out to give me an update, I finally gave up. On my way home, I stopped by the department to write up my report. That's when I learned that even with the help of timely eyewitness information, Pickles's two assailants had disappeared without a trace.

It was far later than it should have been when I finally

in a cloud of outrage, where I soon discovered I was not alone. Every detective in Homicide was pissed. They all figured like I did that Pickles was getting a bum rap. He was within months of being able to pull the plug and get a pension. If IA somehow made a homicide charge stick against him, he would be out on the street with nothing.

Pickles remained hospitalized for the next ten days. Captain Tompkins found me some inane busywork checking inventories in the Evidence Room. That's what I was doing a week later, when I made it a point to track down the McCaffey murder case file. Among the items in evidence I located the piece of paper—the blank order form—Bob Murray had used to write down the names of potential witnesses in the case. A quick check in the murder book revealed that not one of those folks had been singled out for additional interviews beyond my brief questioning of them in the bar at the Doghouse the day the shooting happened. Unbelievable! Pickles Gurkey was being railroaded fair and square.

It was almost time to go home. I had stopped by Pickles and my cubby on my way out. Pickles's desk was awash in cards and flower and balloons. I was sitting there wondering if I should drag all that stuff up to the hospital before I went home, when my phone rang.

"Hey," Bob Murray said. "I've been calling and calling. How come you never answer your phone?"

"Because I haven't been at my desk," I said curtly. "Did you ever think of leaving a message?"

"Is it true Internal Affairs is out to get Milton?" Bob asked.

Police departments are a lot like families. We can say

drove into the garage at our place on Lake Tapps. The kids were already in bed, and so was Karen. I poured myself a McNaughton's—probably more than one—and sat there waiting for sleep to come. I worried about whether Pickles would make it, but I have to say, not once that day—not one single time—did it ever occur to me that Pickles was the one who shot Lulu McCaffey, but of course, that was just me. I was his partner. What did I know?

When I got to work the following morning, the world had changed. Captain Tompkins called me into his office, where he gave me the welcome news that Pickles was still alive. He was gravely ill and still in Intensive Care, but he was resting comfortably and his condition was listed as stable.

In other words, as far as his health was concerned, Pickles was in better shape than could have been expected. As far as his career was concerned, however, he was not. It turned out that the slug the medical examiner had pulled out of Lulu McCaffey's body had come from Pickles's gun.

As of now, Internal Affairs was on the case. In spades.

The captain sent me straight upstairs to IA, where I spent the next three hours being interviewed by the IA investigator assigned to the case. Lieutenant Gary Tatum was a guy with attitude who was used to throwing his weight around and having people dodge out of the way. We detested each other on sight. I wanted to tell him what Pickles had told me about two guys running away. Tatum didn't want to hear it. He was far more interested in what I knew about the "well-known" feud between Pickles and the dead waitress. I told him about Pickles's water-in-the-crotch experience with Lulu McCaffey, not because I thought it was funny but because it was the truth.

Lieutenant Tatum listened to my version of the story and then nodded. "I've heard that one before." He said it in a bored fashion—as though he hadn't needed to hear it again from me. "But as I understand it, that was a long time ago—a couple of years anyway. There has to be something more recent than that—something more serious—for them to get in this kind of beef."

"There wasn't any beef," I explained. "Detective Gurkey went to take a leak. I'm not sure why he went outside, but he was there when whatever went down went down. He may have been in the parking lot when Lulu was shot, but that doesn't mean he did it."

Tatum gave me his phony Cheshire cat grin complete with an offhand head shake that implied he wasn't buying a word I said and that he thought I was a complete idiot.

"Detective Gurkey's prints are on the gun," Tatum told me. "His are the only prints on the murder weapon. As far as I'm concerned, that means he pulled the trigger. He's also got shot residue on his hands."

"We were at the range yesterday morning," I countered. "We were doing target practice. You can check with them to verify that."

"Oh, we'll be verifying that story, all right," Tatum assured me. "In the meantime, as long as Detective Gurkey is under investigation, you need to know that you're under investigation as well."

"Why?" I demanded. "What did I do? I was sitting

there eating my hamburger and minding my own business when the shots were fired. I don't understand why you're investigating me."

"You know the drill," Tatum said with a shrug. "It's the old what-did-you-know-and-when-did-you-know-it routine. I've told Captain Tompkins to keep you sidelined for the next little while. I wouldn't mind that much if I were you. I got a look at the next week's weather forecast. It's going to be hot as Hades outside. You'll be way better off cooling your heels at a desk job than you will be out tracking bad guys on sidewalks hot enough to fry eggs."

I didn't dignify that statement with a response. Instead, I asked, "What about the two runners—the guys who skipped out on paying their tab, the ones Lulu came outside chasing. What about them? Are you even looking for them?"

"Detective Beaumont," Tatum said with a grim smile. "I don't believe you understand. This matter is not yours to investigate. Internal Affairs is handling it. What we do or do not do is none of your concern. Am I making myself clear?"

The threat was there and so was the message: Stay the hell out of the way or get run over and risk your career in the process.

"Detective Gurkey did not kill that woman," I declared.

Tatum smiled again. "That remains to be seen, doesn't it."

We sat there for a length of time, doing a stare down. "May I go?" I said finally.

"Of course," he said. "Just so long as we understand one another."

We did that! I rode the elevator down to the fifth floor

whatever we like about other people inside the organization, but outsiders aren't allowed the same privilege. I wasn't about to badmouth Lieutenant Tatum or what he was doing.

"Internal Affairs is handling the investigation," I said evenly.

"Yes, I know, and you can take it from me that Lieutenant Gary Tatum is an arrogant asshole," Bob Murray responded. "He came in here for a steak once and sent it back to the kitchen because he said it was too tough to eat. I wouldn't give him the time of day."

That made me laugh outright. The Doghouse menu says right there in black and white that the tenderness of steaks can't be guaranteed.

"So he thought you were what, the Canlis?" I asked.

"Do you want to be cute or do you want me to talk to you?" Bob growled.

"Talk to me," I said. "What have you got?"

"I was talking to my produce guy the other day," he told me. "He says the same thing that happened to Lulu has been happening to a lot of people in different restaurants all over town. Two guys come in, order, eat, and then do the old dine-and-dash bit. One minute they're there. The next minute they're gone without a trace and their bill is still on the table. Nobody ever sees 'em drive off in a vehicle. They just disappear into thin air."

"A tall guy and a short guy?" I asked.

"From what he told me, the tall guy is always there—the one with the light-colored hair. The problem is, he doesn't always seem to hang out with the same guy."

"So the second guy varies?"

"That's my understanding," Bob said.

"Has the produce guy talked to Lieutenant Tatum?"

"Not to my knowledge," Murray said. "Listen, this is my produce guy. I'm the one he talks to."

"And these other dine-and-dash incidents," I said. "Has anyone ever reported it?"

"Probably not. Guys like me don't want to get involved in all that police report crap, and we don't want the names of our restaurants showing up in local police blotters that may be sent along to the media. They figure it's like shoplifting—it's all part of the cost of doing business."

"It is shoplifting," I corrected. "What they're lifting is your food."

"Yes, but the amounts are small enough that it doesn't make sense to make a huge issue of it. Lulu, may she rest in peace, was a hothead, and she always raised absolute hell about it. That's how come she chased those guys out into the parking lot, acting like the price of their meal was going to come out of her hide. I've never once dinged one of my servers because somebody skipped. It's not the waitress's fault if the customer turns out to be a dick, pardon the expression. Why should they take a hit for it?"

Lots of people call detectives dicks. I try not to take it personally.

"Would your produce guy talk to me?" I asked.

"In a heartbeat," Bob Murray said. "Be here tomorrow morning at ten, and I'll see to it."

The next morning at ten o'clock sharp, I entered the Doghouse for the first time since the shooting. The booth where the two killers had sat that fateful afternoon had an OCCUPIED sign on it even though the only thing there was a collection of wilting bouquets, their bedraggled flowers dripping dead petals. Around that small sad memorial, the rest of the Doghouse bustled with business as usual.

Bob Murray met me at the host station and escorted me to a seat at the far end of the counter. "As soon as Alfonso gets here, I'll send him your way."

I was halfway through a plate of ham and eggs when a smallish Mexican man slipped quietly onto the stool beside me.

"You the detective?" he asked.

I held out my hand. "J. P. Beaumont," I said. "And you are?"

"Alfonso Romero of Al's Produce," he said. "I'm Al."

It made sense. In Seattle's white-bread business districts, a Hispanic vegetable delivery guy could pass himself off as white or at least as Italian by plastering the name Al on his truck, and the only people that ruse fooled were the people who needed to be fooled.

"Bob says I should talk to you," he said. "About the skips."

"You think it's a pattern?" I asked.

The waitress brought him coffee and a platter of breakfast that included bacon, eggs over easy, crisp hash browns, whole wheat toast, coffee, and orange juice. It must have been a standing order that was put in place the moment he turned up because Romero hadn't been there nearly long enough for even the fastest short-order cook to deliver a breakfast like that in such a timely fashion.

Romero nodded. "Five different restaurants that I

know about, including this one, but those are only the ones I work with. There are a lot of restaurants out there and a lot of produce guys just like me."

"Do you know some of them?" I asked. "Your competition, I mean."

Romero shrugged. "Of course I know them," he said. "We get our stuff from the same suppliers; we're out on the docks, loading our lettuce and tomatoes at the same time before we head out on our routes."

"Would these other drivers know if the same thing was happening at other restaurants?"

"Sure," Romero said. "Owners talk. Waitresses talk. They're all in the same business, and everybody knows what everybody else is doing."

"If I showed up on the dock at the same time, would the drivers talk to me?"

Alfonso thought about that for a moment before he answered. "Maybe," he said. "But only if I asked 'em."

Which is how, the next morning, I found myself on the loading dock of a huge warehouse off Rainer Avenue at O-dark-thirty in the morning. Having Bob Murray vouch for me was good enough for Alfonso, and having Alfonso making the introductions was good enough for the other drivers. They all knew that Lulu McCaffey had been murdered, and they were eager to help. By the time I left the dock and headed into the department, I was as excited as a kid on his way to see Santa Claus because I knew I was on to something.

There was a pattern here, and over and over it was the same thing. Two guys—customers who have never been there before—show up in a restaurant, order, eat, don't pay, and go. According to the drivers, it happened mostly in the evenings, just at rush hour, at restaurants all over the city—from north to south, east to west, but never the same restaurant twice. I took down the drivers' names and phone numbers. I asked them to keep checking. Back at the department, I had a decision to make. I knew from the scuttlebutt that Lieutenant Tatum was waiting for Pickles to recover enough to be let out of the hospital, at which point he intended to make an arrest and formally charge him in the death of Lulu McCaffey.

If I had thought Tatum was a square shooter, I would have gone straight upstairs with what I had found from Alfonso and the other drivers, but he wasn't, and I didn't.

Cops patronize restaurants. We go to restaurants at every hour of the day and night, so it wasn't necessary to launch an official investigation in order to launch an investigation. I just had to get word out to the beat cops and to the guys on patrol and to the detectives riding around in their unmarked cars that the restaurants in Seattle were suffering from an epidemic of check skippers, and that we needed to be good neighbors and help our friends in the restaurant business find these guys.

That was a cover-your-ass subterfuge, of course. I'm guessing most everybody understood that we were working behind the scenes to give Pickles a helping hand, and they came through. As the produce guys ran their routes and as the cops talked to their contacts, a trickle of information started coming in. The details came in on Post-it notes left on my desk while I was laboring in the Evidence Room; in messages left on my office voice mail; and in some instances, with guys I knew, in phone calls to the house at Lake Tapps.

I finally stapled an oversized map of Seattle to the wallboard in the garage at Lake Tapps and began inserting little plastic beaded straight pins into the map wherever I had a report about another dine-and-dash incident. As the collection of pins grew, it wasn't hard to see the pattern. They ranged all over town, with a gaping hole in the center of the city, from the north end of Columbia City on the south, to Capitol Hill on the east. The Doghouse was the only restaurant with any proximity to downtown.

Everybody on the fifth floor knew what was up, but no one breathed a word of it to Tatum. Instead, we gathered in the break room or in cubicles and talked about it. One of the detectives, who was married to a departmental sketch artist, took her to see the witnesses who had been at the Doghouse the day of the McCaffey shooting and to some of the other restaurants that had been victimized by the check-skipping team. Over time we developed credible composite sketches of the two guys from the Doghouse. Once we had those in hand, we made sure the guys from Patrol had copies with them in their cars; we made sure the beat guys had them, too.

It sounds like this was all straightforward, but it wasn't. For one thing, it was an investigation that wasn't supposed to be happening and had to be invisible. For another, almost everyone had other cases—official cases—that they were supposed to be working. Continuing to toil in the vineyards of the Evidence Room, I was one of two exceptions to that rule. The other one was Pickles Gurkey, who was now officially on administrative leave. Once he got out of the hospital, he was placed under arrest, and then allowed free on bond to await trial after his family posted his immense bail.

I had visited with him in the hospital only once, after he was out of Intensive Care. He told me what he remembered from the crime scene—that he had dropped his gun when the heart attack hit, but that he was sure he hadn't pulled the trigger. Clearly Lieutenant Tatum wasn't buying his story and neither was the King County prosecutor. I wanted to tell him that the guys from Homicide were working the problem and that we hadn't forgotten him, but I didn't dare. And I never went back to the hospital to see him again. I figured if Tatum got wind that there had been any kind of continuing contact between us, he'd be all over me.

They say luck follows the guy who does the work. In that regard we were bound to get lucky eventually. I was down in the Evidence Room one afternoon when the clerk hunted me down and said someone was waiting outside to talk to me. The guy in the hall was a uniformed officer named Richard Vega. He was holding a copy of one of the Doghouse composites—the one of the taller man with the light-colored hair.

"I've seen this guy," he said, waving the sketch in my direction. "My sergeant sent me to Homicide to talk to you, and the clerk up there sent me down here."

"Where have you seen him?" I asked.

"Hanging out down around Pioneer Square," Vega said. "I'm thinking maybe he works somewhere around there."

I thought about the doughnut hole in my circle of pins. Pioneer Square would be well inside it. So maybe, if the guy lived or worked nearby, maybe he didn't want to crap in his own bed or victimize establishments where he might want to be regarded as a regular paying customer.

I knew just where to go. A few years earlier, a Chinese family had bought up a local deli named Bakeman's. The joint was known all over the downtown area for and were doing land-office business selling sandwiches made from fresh turkeys that were roasted on the premises every night.

In regard to restaurant food, pundits often say, "You can get quick, cheap, or good. Pick any two." As far as that was concerned, Bakeman's was in a class by itself because they excelled in all three—quick, cheap, and good! And since they were in the 100 block of Cherry, just down the street from the Public Safety Building, plenty of cops went there for lunch on a daily basis.

Bakeman's was one of the places without a beaded pin on my map, so I rushed there immediately, with a mimeographed copy of the tall guy's composite sketch in hand. It was early, right at the beginning of the lunch rush. The young Asian guy at the cash register took my order: white turkey meat with cranberry sauce on white bread. Mayo and mustard, hold the lettuce and tomato. I handed over my money. When the clerk gave me back my change, he was already eyeing the next customer. That's when I held up the sketch.

"You know this guy?" I asked.

"It's lunch," he replied. "Gotta keep the line moving."

"Have you ever seen him?" I repeated.

He glowered at me. "I'm serving lunch here. I got customers."

I held up my badge next to the sketch. The clerk sighed and shook his head. "You guys," he said wearily in a tone that said he thought all cops were royal pains in the ass.

"Do you know him?" I insisted.

He nodded. "White meat turkey on white, mayo, mustard, cranberry sauce. Almost like you, only he takes lettuce."

"Do you know his name?"

"I don't know names. I know orders. Works construction. Dirty clothes. Who's next?"

"So he comes in after working all day, orders white turkey on white. When does he come in? What time?"

"Afternoons. Before we close. Around two or so. Next?"

"Any day in particular?"

"You want to talk more, order another sandwich."

"Done." I said. "Give me the same as before, both of them to go."

"You didn't say to go for the first one."

"I didn't know I was getting two sandwiches then, either. Now I want them both to go. But tell me, does he come in on a certain day?"

The clerk looked as though he was ready to leap across the counter and strangle me. Instead he glowered at the servers who were putting my sandwiches together. "Both of those turkeys on white are to go," he shouted, and then he glared back at me. "Tuesdays maybe?" he said. "Sometimes Wednesdays, but not every week. Takes his sandwiches to go. Puts them in a lunch pail."

My heart skipped with joy because this happened to be Tuesday.

I gave the clerk my money. He handed me my change. "Next?"

From the way he shouted, I knew better than to press my luck. Without asking any more questions, I took my sandwiches and left. Giddy with excitement, I practically floated back up Cherry to the Public Safety Building, where I rode straight up to the fifth floor, dodged past Captain Tompkins's Fishbowl, and ducked into the cubicle shared by Detectives Powell and Watkins. They were both in. They looked up in surprise when I entered. Surprise turned to welcome when they caught a whiff of the turkey sandwiches.

By two o'clock that afternoon, the three of us had set up shop. Worried that the two guys might have seen me in the Doghouse the day Pickles and I were there at the same time, I stayed across the street, tucked into the shady alcove of a building that let me watch the door to Bakeman's while using the excuse of smoking a cigarette to hang around outside. Watty, who wasn't as fast on his feet as Larry Powell was, stayed in an unmarked car parked at the bottom of Cherry, while Larry went inside and ate a leisurely bowl of soup. I had also contacted Officer Vega and asked him to hang around at the corner of First and Cherry. I was worried that if the suspect was on foot and headed westbound on the eastbound street, Watty wouldn't be able to follow in his vehicle.

At 2:20 I saw the suspect, trudging up Cherry from

First carrying a heavy-duty lunch pail. He certainly looked like the guy in the sketch. He was dressed in grimy clothes and appeared to have put in a hard day of manual labor. I watched him walk past the spot where Watty was waiting at the curb. By the time he turned into Bakeman's, my heart was pounding in my chest. There was nothing to do now but wait.

I checked my watch. The crowd inside the restaurant had died down. With no line, it would take only a couple of minutes for him to order his sandwich, pay, pick up his food, and leave. At 2:26 he appeared again. He stood for a moment at the top of the worn marble steps, then he stepped down, turned right, and headed back down to First. He walked past Watty's vehicle, which was parked at the curb, all right, but it was also pointed in the wrong direction on the one-way street.

I slipped out of my hidey-hole and made my way down the hill. When I got to the corner of First, I waved off Vega. After that, it was up to me. When I turned right onto First, I could see the suspect half a block ahead of me walking uphill. Two blocks later, he turned into a run-down building called the Hargrave Hotel.

In theater circles, SRO means standing room only, and that's considered to be a good thing. In hotel-speak, SRO means single room occupancy, and it's generally not such a good thing. The Hargrave was a flea-bitten flophouse straight out of Roger Miller's "King of the Road." It might have been a lot swankier in an earlier era. Now, though, it was four stories of misery, with ten shoddy rooms, two grim toilets, and one moldy shower per floor. Bring your own towel.

I waited outside until I saw Mr. Lunch Pail get into the creaky elevator and close the brass folding gate behind him. By then, Watty had managed to make it around the block. After flagging him down, I stepped into the building lobby, where a grubby, pockmarked marble countertop served as a front desk. Behind it sat a balding man with a green plastic see-through visor perched on his head.

He looked up at me as I entered. "If you're selling something," he told me, "we ain't buying."

I held up my badge and my composite sketch. As soon as he saw the drawing, the desk clerk glanced reflexively toward the elevator. The dial above the elevator showed that the car had stopped on floor three. Clearly this was a one-elevator building.

"Who's this?" I asked.

"You got a warrant?"

"Not at the moment," I returned mildly, "but I'm wondering how this place would measure up if somebody happened to schedule a surprise inspection from the Health Department?" When he didn't reply, I pressed my advantage. "Who?" I insisted.

"Benjamin Smith."

"How long has he been here?"

The clerk shrugged. "A couple of months, I guess. Pays his rent right on time every week."

"Where does he work?"

"He's a laborer down at that new stadium they're building. The Kingdome, I think it's called. What do you want him for?"

"Girl trouble," I said quickly. "As in underage. Might be better for your relationship with the Health Department if he didn't know that anybody had come by asking about him."

Visor Man nodded vigorously. "My lips are sealed," he said.

I ducked back outside. By then, Larry had caught up and was waiting in the front seat of the car with Watty. I climbed into the back. "The clerk says our guy's name is Benjamin Smith. That may or may not be an alias."

"So if he is our guy," Larry said, "what do we do now? Even if we can get his prints and connect him to the Dog-house crime scene, that still won't be enough to let Pick-les off the hook. It'll be his word against Smith's word. Might be enough for reasonable doubt, but I'm not sure. We need to find a way to corroborate Pickles's version of the story."

I thought about that. Presumably there had been three people present when Lulu McCaffey was gunned down. We had found two of them. Now we needed to locate the third. The blond guy was the one who had usually shown up in the establishments marked by the bead pattern on the map in my garage. When it had become clear that the light-haired guy was doing dine-and-dash with a collection of different pals, I had given up carrying the short guy's sketch and focused instead on the tall one. Now I had a hunch.

"Do either of you have that other Doghouse composite?" I asked.

"I think so," Watty said. "Hand me the notebook there on the backseat." I gave it to him. He rummaged through it for several long minutes before finally handing me what I wanted.

"Wait here," I said. "And open the door so I can get out."

With the new sketch in hand, I hurried back into the lobby. When the desk clerk looked up and saw me, he gave a disgusted sigh. "You again," he said.

I held up the drawing. "Have you ever seen this guy?"

"Sure," he said, "That's Fred—Fred Beman. Everybody called him Cowboy Fred."

"Does he live here, too?" I asked.

"Used to. Left sometime in July."

"Do you know where he went?"

"He's in Walla Walla," the clerk said. "Went back home to the family farm. At least, that's what he said he was going to do when he left here With these guys, you can never tell how much is truth and how much is fiction."

"Did he leave a forwarding address?"

The clerk turned away from me and pulled a long, narrow file box out of the bottom drawer of a file cabinet behind him. Inside the box was a collection of three-by-five cards. After thumbing through them, he pulled out one and handed it to me. All that was on it was a phone number and a P.O. box number in Walla Walla.

It wasn't much, but it was a start.

Detectives Watkins and Powell and I went straight back to the department and looked up Frederick Beman. There were two Frederick Bemans listed. The composite sketch was surprisingly close to the younger one's Department of Licensing photo. His driving record included three DUIs. He'd had a pickup once, but that had been totaled during one of the DUI incidents. The DMV showed no current vehicles listed in his name, although there were several listed for his father, Frederick Beman, Sr., who owned a horse ranch somewhere outside Walla Walla.

"Looks like we're going to Walla Walla," Larry Powell said.

"When?" I asked.

"Right now."

I glanced at my watch. It was after four in the afternoon. "How are we going to do that?"

"We're going to drive," Larry said. "We'll take turns. You go check out a car. Make sure it has a full tank of gas. I'll clear it with the captain."

That's exactly what I did. While the guys at Motor Pool were gassing up the car, I called Karen and told her I wouldn't be home. Since she was stuck there alone with a toddler and a colicky baby, she was not happy to hear that I was off on a cross-state adventure, but there wasn't much she could do about it. Captain Tompkins wasn't thrilled, either, especially with having three members of his Homicide Unit tied up in what he termed a "wild-goose chase," but he relented finally, too. Larry convinced him that this was basically my lead, but that I was too green to chase after it alone. So off we went, all three of us.

Walla Walla is a long way from Seattle—two hundred and fifty miles, give or take. With me sitting in the backseat, I'm sure people who saw us thought I was a crook being hauled off to jail somewhere. We took turns driving. By the time we got into Walla Walla, it was too late to do much of anything but get a room and wait for morning. We opted for one room with two double beds. Not the best arrangement, but bunking with Watty beat sleeping on the floor or out in the car. The next morning, over coffee, we were all complaining about how everyone else snored, so I guess it was pretty even-Steven on that score.

After breakfast we found our way to Beman Arabians. There was a main house and several immense barns with an office complex at the near end of one of them. There were also a number of outbuildings that looked as though they were occupied by workers of one stripe or another. When we asked for Fred Beman, we were directed to the office, where we found a handsome, white-haired, older gentleman seated behind a messy desk. When he stood up and stepped out from behind the desk to greet us, he looked for the all the world as if he had simply emerged, cowboy boots and all, from one of those old Gene Autry movies I loved so much when I was a kid. One look at him was enough to tell us that this might be Fred Beman, but not the one we wanted.

Larry Powell held up his badge. "We're looking for Fred Beman, a younger Fred Beman."

The old man stared at the badge for a moment, then looked back at Larry. "That would be Fred Junior, my son. What's he done now?"

"We're actually interested in a friend of his," Larry said. "A friend from Seattle."

Beman shook his head. "Don't know nothin' about any of those. When Freddie came skedaddlin' back home this summer and begged me to give him another chance, I figured he was in some kind of hot water or other. He's out back shovelin' shit. I told him if he wanted to get back in my good graces and into the family business, he'd be startin' from the bottom."

With that Fred Senior led the way out of his office and into the barn. It was pungent with the smell of horses and hay. We found Fred Junior in one of the stalls, pitchfork in hand. He must have taken after his mother because he didn't look anything like his dad. He didn't smell like his dad, either. His father carried a thick cloud of Old Spice with him wherever he went. The air around Junior reeked of perspiration flavored with something else—vodka most likely. Anyone who thinks vodka doesn't smell hasn't spent any time around a serious drunk. Fred Junior may not have been driving at the moment, but he was most definitely still drinking.

"Someone to see you, Freddie," the old man said, then he turned on the worn heels of his cowboy boots and walked away. It was clear from his posture that whatever problem we represented was his son's problem, and he would have to deal with it on his own.

Fred Junior leaned on the handle of the pitchfork. "What's this about?"

I held up my badge. "It's about your friend Benjamin," I said.

A wary look crossed Fred's face. I had learned at the academy that an assailant with a knife can cut down a guy with a gun before there's time to pull the trigger. I calculated that the wicked metal tines on the long-handled pitchfork could poke holes in my guts faster than any hand-held knife. I was glad I had Watty and Larry Powell there for backup if need be. The problem was, I wanted this guy alive and talking, far more than I wanted him dead.

"What about him?" Fred said.

"He's been telling us some interesting stories," I said casually. "He told us you shot a woman a few weeks ago—shot her in cold blood in the parking lot of the Doghouse Restaurant in Seattle."

The only light in the barn came from the open stall doors along the side of the building and from a few grimy windows up near the roof. Still, even in the relative gloom of the barn, I saw the color drain from his face. The muscles in his jaw clenched.

"I never," he said. "I was there, but I never shot her. I told him, 'Hey, man. I've got the money. Let's just pay the woman.' But Benjy's crazy. He picked up the gun and fired away."

"Maybe you'd like to put down that pitchfork and give us a statement," I suggested.

For a long moment, nobody moved while Fred Junior stood there and considered what he would do. It was quiet enough in the barn that you could have heard a pin drop. Somewhere within hearing distance a fly buzzed.

Finally Fred spoke again. "Can you get me a deal?" he asked.

I shook my head. "I can't promise any deals," I said, "but if you'll help us, I'll do what I can to help you."

It was lame, but it was the best I could do under the circumstances, and it probably wouldn't have worked if Fred Beman hadn't been ready to turn himself in. He didn't need a deal. All you had to do was look at him to see that his conscience was eating him alive. He had run home to Daddy after what happened at the Doghouse. He was half dead from a combination of too much booze and too little sleep. I could tell from the haunted look in his eyes that wherever he went and no matter how much he tried to drink himself into oblivion, Fred could find no escape. Lulu McCaffey in her black uniform and little white apron was still lying there on the hot, dirty pavement, as dead as could be.

"Put down the pitchfork, please," I said quietly. "Place your hands on your head."

There was another long pause. I hadn't drawn my weapon, but I had heard the subtle snap of leather as both Larry and Watty drew theirs. As I said, it was deathly quiet in that barn. I think we were all holding our breaths. When Fred finally moved, it was only to lean over and carefully lower the pitchfork to the floor. Without a word, Watty stepped forward and cuffed him. I read him his rights. By then, Fred was crying his eyes out.

"I couldn't believe it when it happened," he sobbed. "It was just supposed to be fun. He shot her down like she was an animal or something."

We were cops from out of town and were a long way outside our jurisdiction. We also hadn't reported our arrival to any of the local authorities. As a consequence, we needed to get out of Dodge. And since Fred seemed willing enough to talk, we wanted that to happen before he got all lawyered up. Fortunately, Larry Powell had planned ahead. He had brought a battery-powered cassette tape recorder with him. Once the four of us were settled in the car with me riding in back with Fred, we turned on Larry's recorder, read Fred Beman his rights again, and announced into the tape who all was present in the vehicle. Then we began the long drive back to Seattle, listening to his story as we went.

It turned out that skipping out on checks in restaurants was Benjamin Smith's hobby. He did it all the time, whether he had money in his pocket to pay for his dinner or not. He traveled around town on bus passes. That's why he often timed his dine-and-dash events to happen during rush hour when there were plenty of people out and about and lots of buses on the streets. That's how he managed to disappear so readily—by blending in with the crowd.

Gradually, when Fred got a grip on himself, we had him go over the story again, and recount exactly what had happened in the Doghouse parking lot. His story matched Pickles's in every detail, including the fact that none of the three of them—Lulu, Benjamin, or Fred—had seen Pickles Gurkey in the parking lot prior to the moment when he had attempted to intervene in the fight between Lulu and Benjamin. They had stopped their altercation long enough to see him standing there, holding a drawn weapon, and announcing he was a cop. Then he had simply dropped the gun, staggered backward, and fallen against the building.

"I don't know if the guy was drunk or what," Fred continued. "Benjy reached down and picked up the gun. The woman had stopped yelling by then because she was all worried about the guy who had just fallen over. I think she realized at the last moment that Benjy had a gun, but by then it was too late for her to get away. As soon as Benjy shot her, he wiped the gun off with his shirt, put it in the guy's hand, and then dropped it in his lap. The guy on the ground was so out of it, I doubt he had any idea what had just happened. After that, we took off, ran like hell over to Denny, and hopped a bus up to Capitol Hill. Benjy said not to worry, that he was sure both the woman and the cop were dead. Benjy was convinced people would think the cop had done it and that no one would ever find us, but you have," he finished. "You did."

"It turns out Medic 1 showed up in time, and Detective Gurkey didn't die," I told him. "In fact, he's the whole reason we're here today. He's being charged with murder in the death of Lulu McCaffey. He's about to go down for what you did. Our job is to make sure that doesn't happen."

"You still don't understand," Fred insisted. "I'm telling you, I didn't do it. I'm not the one who shot her. Benjy did."

"And then what?"

"And then I had to get out of Seattle. I called my dad and asked if I could come home. Again. He said he'd give me a place to stay and food to eat, but I had to work for it, just like his other hands. And that's what I did."

I looked at my watch. Watty glanced in the rearview

mirror and caught me doing it. "Don't worry," he said. "We'll be there in time."

We drove straight back to Seattle. We dropped by Seattle PD long enough to put Fred Beman in an interrogation room, and then we headed for the Hargrove Hotel. In case Benjamin Smith made a run for it, we stationed two uniformed officers at First and Madison. Watty was parked in a car facing northbound at First and Columbia. Larry Powell and I waited inside the scuzzy lobby of the Hargrave, seated on a pair of swaybacked, cracked leather chairs. The clerk seemed distinctly unhappy to see us. As the moments ticked by, I worried that he might have spilled the beans and Benjamin Smith had already skipped town.

Instead, Benjy—I liked thinking of him that way—showed up right on time, at twenty minutes to three, sauntering along, swinging his lunch pail like he didn't have a care in the world. It was Wednesday. There was no telling if he'd stopped at Bakeman's on his way home. As soon as he pushed open the brass and glass door and started for the elevator, I stood up to head him off.

"Mr. Smith," I said, barring his way and holding my badge up to his face. "Detective Beaumont with Seattle PD. If you don't mind, I'd like to have a word."

I was deliberately in his face, and the man did exactly what I hoped he'd do. He took a swing at me with the lunch pail. Since that's what I was expecting, I blocked it easily. When you need an excuse to take someone into custody, there's nothing like resisting in front of a collection of witnesses to give you a warrantless reason to lock some guy up in a jail cell for the next few hours. On the way to Benjy's interrogation room, I made sure he got a look at Fred, anxious and despairing, sitting in his.

"What's he doing here?" Benjy asked, nodding in Fred's direction.

"What do you think he's doing?" I said. "Mr. Beman is singing like a bird. How do you think we found you?"

MEL CAME IN about then, smiling and waving her freshly manicured, scarlet nails in my face as she kissed me hello. "What were you reading?" she asked, looking down at the scatter of yellowing onionskin paper I had dropped onto the carpet in front of the window seat. I had let the pages fall as I read them. After I had finished reading, I had simply let them be as I sat there recalling that long-ago history.

"It's something Pickles Gurkey wrote before he died," I explained.

"Your old partner?"

I nodded. "His widow, Anna, died a few weeks ago. His daughter, Anne Marie, was cleaning out her mother's house and found this. She dropped it off because she thought I'd want to read it."

"Did you?" Mel asked. "Read it, I mean."

I nodded again.

"May I?"

"Sure," I said. "Help yourself."

So Mel gathered up the pages, settled comfortably on the window seat next to me, and started to read. The

storm had long since ended. The clouds had rolled east-
ward. Outside the sky was a fragile blue, and so was the
water out in the sound, but it was getting on toward evening.

I waited quietly until Mel finished reading. Fortunately
she's a very fast reader.

"So what happened?" she asked, straightening the sheets
of paper and handing them back to me in a neat stack.

"We found the bad guys eventually," I said. "The one
who turned state's evidence got off with two years for in-
voluntary manslaughter. The shooter, Benjamin Smith,
got fifteen years at Monroe for second-degree homicide,
which ended up turning into a life sentence."

"How did that happen?"

"Benjy was an arrogant asshole. That's why he thought
it was great fun to dodge out of restaurants without paying
his bills. As far as he was concerned, the whole thing was
nothing but a lark. Unfortunately for him, prison has a
way of cutting arrogance down to size. Another inmate
stuck a shiv into him. He died ten months into his fifteen-
year sentence."

"The other guy at the restaurant shooting?" Mel asked.

"Fred Beman served his sentence, straightened out his
life, and now he's back home in Walla Walla helping his
father run his horse farm."

"What about Pickles?"

"I was there in the courtroom the day the prosecutor dropped all charges against him. He turned around,
grabbed my hand, shook it like crazy, and said, 'Thanks,
Beau. Thanks a lot.'"

"What about the Jonas bit. Did he ever call you that again?" Mel asked.

"Never. Not once. We worked together for the next five years, and he never called me anything but Beau."

Mel frowned, looking at the papers in her hand.

"Isn't Pickles the guy who ended up dying of another heart attack?" Mel asked.

"Right," I said. "That was Pickles. The second one was five years later."

"So if you saved him from a murder charge, I don't get why his family blamed you when he died of a second heart attack that long after the first."

"They thought he was working to make it up to me— that he owed me somehow—for keeping him out of jail, but it turns out, that wasn't it at all. It was the case."

"What case?"

"The Woodfield case, the one we got called out on that day."

"The old guy who killed his wife and then turned the gun on himself?"

"That's the one. From that day on, I remember whenever we'd go somewhere for lunch or dinner, Pickles would spend most of the time sitting there doing arithmetic on paper napkins or in his notebook, trying to figure out if Anna would be better off if he died while he was still on the job so she'd get a lump sum payment or if she'd end up with more money if she was the joint survivor on his pension."

"Which one would have been better?" Mel asked.

"Pickles opted to work," I said with a shrug. "Anna

probably got a little more money when he died, twenty or thirty thousand more is all. The problem is, she spent the rest of her life mad at him for choosing to work instead of choosing to stay home with her. To her dying day she was convinced that was all my fault."

"Sounds like they both got the short end of the stick," Mel observed.

I looked at her. Mel was beautiful. She loved me, and I loved her. Yes, Pickles Gurkey may have thought he owed me something for saving his bacon on that murder charge, but it turned out that, as of today, I owed him for something even more important.

"Let's not make the same mistake Pickles did," I said. "Whatever time we have,, let's not miss it. Let's spend it together."

Mel smiled back at me and held out her hand. "Deal," she said.

We shook on it.

"So what are we doing for New Year's Eve?" she asked. "Are we going out or staying home?"

I glanced at my watch. The afternoon had disappeared on me. It was almost five o'clock.

"Going out," I said. "Let's go put on our Sunday-go-to-meeting clothes and see what El Gaucho is serving for their blue plate special."

"They don't have a blue plate special," Mel pointed out. "They never have."

"Right," I said. "And it doesn't matter if they do or don't because if there's one lesson Pickles Gurkey taught me today, it's this: Don't worry about the money. Spend the time."

Hours later, when it came time for midnight, we were standing on the balcony of our penthouse when the first volley of fireworks went off from the top of the Space Needle. Mel was holding her flute of real champagne. I had my glass of faux.

On the balcony below ours, someone had turned up their sound system, and "Auld Lang Syne" was blasting out of their speakers at full volume, loud enough to cover the rock and roll coming at us from Seattle Center.

Mel reached over and clinked her glass gently into mine. "Happy New Year," she said.

I nodded. "Thank you," I said. "And to you, and to time spent together."

The fireworks were still blasting skyward when the song from the unit below ended in the familiar refrain, "We'll take a cup o' kindness yet, for auld lang syne."

Maybe I'm just getting sentimental, but a lump caught in my throat. I wiped a stray tear from my eye.

Mel shot me a concerned look. "What?" she asked. "What's going on?"

"Just remembering," I said. Then I raised my glass again. "Here's to Pickles Gurkey," I said. "May he rest in peace."

Next from J. A. Jance:
When memories of J. P. Beaumont's past—
from his early days on the force at Seattle PD
and then, even earlier, to his days in Vietnam—
bombard him, he is reminded
of people and events
he hasn't thought of in years. But
tugging on those long-
ago threads leads to present-day murders,
and soon Beau must face the
fact that some bodies
from the Second Watch just won't stay buried.

Here is a sneak preview of

SECOND WATCH

Coming soon in hardcover
from William Morrow
An Imprint of HarperCollinsPublishers

PROLOGUE

WE LEFT THE P-2 LEVEL of the parking lot at Belltown Terrace ten minutes later than we should have. With Mel Soames at the wheel of her Cayman and with me belted into the passenger seat, we roared out of the garage, down the alley between John and Cedar, and then up Cedar to Second Avenue.

Second is one of those rare Seattle thoroughfares where, if you drive just at or even slightly below the speed limit, you can sail through one green light after another, from the Denny Regrade all the way to the International District. I love Mel dearly, but the problem with her is that she doesn't believe in driving "just under" any speed limit, ever. That's not her style, and certainly not on this cool September morning as we headed for the Swedish Orthopedic Institute, one of the many medical facilities located in a neighborhood Seattle natives routinely call Pill Hill.

Mel was uncharacteristically silent as she drove hell-bent for election through downtown Seattle, zipping through intersections just as the lights changed from yellow to red. I checked to be sure my seat belt was securely fastened and kept my backseat- driving tendencies securely in check. Mel does not respond well to backseat driving.

"Are you okay?" she asked when the red light at Cherry finally brought her to a stop.

The truth is, I wasn't okay. I've been a cop all my adult life. I've been in gunfights and knife fights and even the occasional fistfight. There have been numerous times over the years when I've had my butt hauled off to an ER to be stitched up or worse. What all those inadvertent, spur-of-the-moment ER trips had in common, however, was a total lack of anticipation. Whatever happened happened, and I was on the gurney and on my way. Since I had no way of knowing what was coming, I didn't have any time to be scared to death and filled with dread before the fact. After, maybe, but not before.

This time was different, because this time I had a very good idea of what was coming. Mel was driving me to a scheduled check-in appointment at the Swedish Orthopedic Institute surgical unit Mel and I have come to refer to as the "bone squad." This morning at eight A.M. I was due to meet up with my orthopedic surgeon, Dr. Merritt Auld, and undergo dual knee-replacement surgery. Yes, dual—as in two knees at the same time.

I had been assured over and over that this so-called elective surgery was "no big deal," but the truth is, I had seen the videos. Mel and I had watched them together. I had the distinct impression that Dr. Auld would be more or less amputating both my legs and then bolting them back together with some spare metal parts in between. Let's just say I was petrified.

"I'm fine," I said.

"You are not fine," Mel muttered, "and neither am I." Then she slammed her foot on the gas, swung us into a whiplash left turn, and we charged up Cherry. Given her mood, I didn't comment on her speed or the layer of rubber she had left on the pavement behind us.

I had gimped along for a very long time without admitting to anyone, most of all myself, that my knees were giving me hell. And once I had finally confessed the reality of the situation, Mel had set about moving heaven and earth to see that I did something about it. This morning we were both faced with a heaping helping of "watch out what you ask for."

"You could opt to just do one, you know," she said.

But I knew better, and so did she. When the doctor had asked me which knee was my good knee, I had told him truthfully that they were both bad. The videos had stressed that the success of the surgery was entirely dependent on doing the required postsurgery physical therapy. Since neither of my knees would stand up to doing the necessary PT for the other, Dr. Auld had reluctantly agreed to give me a twofer.

"We'll get through this," I said.

She looked at me and bit her lip.

"Do you want me to drop you at the front door?"

That was a strategy we had used a lot of late. She would

drop me off or pick me up from front doors while she hoofed it to and from parking garages.

"No," I said. "I'd rather walk."

I didn't add "with you," because I didn't have to. She knew it. She also knew that by the time we made it from the parking garage to the building, we would have had to stop to rest three times and my forehead would be beaded with sweat.

"Thank you," she said.

While I eased my body out of the passenger seat and straightened into an upright position, she hopped out and grabbed the athletic bag with my stuff in it out of the trunk. Then she came toward me, looking up at me, smiling.

And the thought of losing that smile was what scared me the most. What if I didn't wake back up? Those kinds of things weren't supposed to happen during routine surgeries, but they did. Occasionally there were unexpected complications and the patient died. What if this was one of those times, and this was the last time I would see Mel or hold her hand? What if this was the end of all of it? There were so many things I wanted to say about how much I loved her and how much she meant to me and how, if I didn't make it, I wanted her to be happy for the rest of her life. But did any of those words come out of my mouth? No. Not one.

"It's going to be okay," she said calmly, as though she had heard the storm of misgivings that was circling around in my head. She squeezed my hand and away we went, limping along, the hare patiently keeping pace with the lumbering tortoise.

I don't remember a lot about the check-in process. I do remember there was a line, and my knees made waiting in line a peculiar kind of hell. Mel offered to stand in line for me, but of course I turned her down. She started to argue, but thought better of it. Instead, she took my gym bag and sat in one of the chairs banked against the wall while I answered all the smiling clerk's inane questions and signed the countless forms. Then, after Mel and I waited another ten minutes, a scrubs-clad nurse came to summon us and take us "back."

What followed was the change into the dreaded backless gown; the weigh-in; the blood draw; the blood pressure, temperature, and pulse checks. Mel hung around for all of that. And she was still there when they stuck me on a bed to await the arrival of my anesthesiologist, who came waltzing into the bustling room with a phony smile plastered on his beaming face. He seemed to be having the time of his life. After introducing himself, he asked my name and my date of birth, and then he delivered an incredibly lame stand-up comic routine about sending me off to never-never land.

Gee, thanks, and how would you like a punch in the nose?

After a second wait of who knows how long, they rolled me into another room. This time Dr. Auld was there, and so were a lot of other people. Again they wanted my name and date of birth. It occurred to me that my name and date of birth hadn't changed in the hour and a half during which I had told four other people the same, but that's evidently part of the program now. Or maybe they do it just for the annoyance factor.

At that point, however, Dr. Auld hauled out a Sharpie

and drew a bright blue letter on each of my knees—R and L.

"That's just so we'll keep them straight," he assured me with a jovial smile.

Maybe he expected me to laugh. I didn't. The quip reminded me too much of the kinds of stale toasts delivered by hungover best men at countless wedding receptions, and it was about that funny, too. I guess I just wasn't up to seeing any humor in the situation.

Neither was Mel. I glanced in her direction and saw the icy blue-eyed stare my lovely wife had leveled in the good doctor's direction. Fortunately, Dr. Auld didn't notice.

"Well," he said. "Shall we do this?"

As they started to roll me away, Mel leaned down and kissed me good-bye. "Good luck," she whispered in my ear. "Don't be long. I'll be right here waiting."

I looked into Mel's eyes and was surprised to see two tears well up and then make matching tracks down her surprisingly pale cheeks. Melissa Soames is not the cry-baby type. I wanted to reach up and comfort her and tell her not to worry, but the anesthesiologist had given me something to "take the edge off," and it was certainly working. Before I could say anything at all, Mel was gone, disappearing from view behind my merry band of scrubs-attired escorts as they wheeled me into a waiting elevator.

I closed my eyes then and tried to remember exactly how Mel looked in that moment before the doors slid shut between us. All I could think of as the elevator sank into what felt like the bowels of the earth was how very much I loved her and how much I wanted to believe that when I woke up, she really would be there, waiting.

CHAPTER 1

EXCEPT SHE WASN'T. WHEN I opened my eyes again, that was the first thing I noticed. The second one was that I was "feeling no pain," as they say, so the drugs were evidently doing what they were supposed to do.

I was apparently in the recovery room. Nurses in flowery scrubs hovered in the background. I could hear their voices, but they were strangely muted, as if somebody had turned the volume way down. As far as my own ability to speak? Forget it. Someone had pushed my mute button; I couldn't say a single word.

In the foreground, a youngish woman sat on a tall rolling stool at the side of the bed. My initial assumption was that my daughter, Kelly, had arrived from her home in southern Oregon. I had told her not to bother coming all the way from Ashland to Seattle on the occasion of my knee-replacement surgery. In fact, I had issued a fatherly decree to that effect, insisting that Mel and I would be fine on our own. Unfortunately, Kelly is her mother's daughter, which is to say she is also headstrong as hell. Since when did she ever listen to a word I said?

So there Kelly sat as big as life, whether I had wanted her at the hospital or not. She wore a maroon-and-gray WSU sweatshirt. A curtain of long blond hair shielded her face from my view while she studiously filed her nails—nails that were covered with bright red polish.

Having just been through several hours of major surgery, I think I could be forgiven for being a little slow on the uptake, but eventually I realized that none of this added up. Even to my drug-befuddled brain, it didn't make sense.

Kelly and I have had our share of issues over the years. The most serious of those involved her getting pregnant while she was still a senior in high school and running off to Ashland to meet up with and eventually marry her boyfriend, a wannabe actor named Jeff. Of course, the two of them have been a couple for years, and my son-in-law is now one of the well-established members of the acting company at the Oregon Shakespeare Festival in Ashland, Oregon.

The OSF offers a dozen or so plays a year, playing in repertory for months at a time, and Jeff Cartwright has certainly paid his dues. After years of learning his trade by playing minor roles as a sword-wielding soldier in one Shakespearian production after another or singing and occasionally tap dancing as a member of the chorus, he finally graduated to speaking roles. This year he was cast as Laertes in *Hamlet* in the Elizabethan theater and, for the first time ever in a leading role, he played Brick in the Festival's retrospective production of *Cat on a Hot Tin Roof* in the Bowmer Theatre. (I thought he did an excellent job, but I may be slightly prejudiced. The visiting theater critic for the *Seattle Times* had a somewhat different opinion.)

It was September, and the season was starting to wind down, but there was no way for Jeff to get away long enough to come up to Seattle for a visit, no matter how brief, and with Kayla and Kyle, my grandkids, back in school, in fourth and first grade, respectively, it didn't seem like a good time for Kelly to come gallivanting to Seattle with or without them in tow just to hover at my sickbed.

In other words, I was both surprised and not surprised to see Kelly there; but then, gradually, a few other details began to sink into my drug-stupefied consciousness. Kelly would never in a million years show up wearing a WSU shirt. No way! She is a University of Oregon Duck, green and yellow all the way. Woe betide anyone who tries to tell her differently, and she has every right to insist on that!

To my everlasting amazement and with only the barest of financial aid from yours truly, this once marginal student got her BA in psychology from Southern Oregon University, and she's now finishing up with a distance-learning master's in business administration from the U of O in Eugene. She's done all this, on her own and without any parental prompting, while running an at-home day care center and looking after her own two kids. When

Kelly turned into a rabid Ducks fan along the way, she got no complaints from me, even though I'm a University of Washington Husky from the get-go.

But the very idea of Kelly Beaumont Cartwright wearing a Cougars sweatshirt? Nope. Believe me, it's not gonna happen.

Then there was the puzzling matter of the very long hair. Kelly's hair used to be about that same length—which is to say more than shoulder length—but it isn't anymore. A year or so ago, she cut it off and donated her shorn locks to a charity that makes wigs for cancer patients. (Karen, Kelly's mother and my ex-wife, died after a long battle with breast cancer, and Kelly remains a dedicated part of the cancer-fighting community. In addition to donating her hair, she sponsors a Relay for Life team and makes certain that both her father and stepfather step up to the plate with cash donations to the cause on a yearly basis.)

As my visitor continued to file her nails with single-minded focus, the polish struck me as odd. In my experience, mothers of young children in general—and my daughter in particular—don't wear nail polish of any kind. Nail enamel and motherhood don't seem to go together, and on the rare occasions when Kelly had indulged in a manicure she had opted for something in the pale pink realm, not this amazingly vivid scarlet, the kind of color Mel seems to favor.

Between the cascade of long blond hair and the bright red nail polish, I was pretty sure my silent visitor wasn't Kelly. If not her, then, I asked myself, who else was likely to show up at my hospital bedside to visit?

Cherisse, maybe?

Cherisse is my daughter-in-law. She has long hair and she does wear nail polish. She and my son, Scott, don't have kids so far, but Cherisse is not a blonde—at least she wasn't the last time I saw her. Besides, if anyone was going to show up unannounced at my hospital bedside, it would be my son, not his wife.

I finally managed to find a semblance of my voice, but what came out of my mouth sounded croaky, like the throaty grumblings of an overage frog.

"Who are you?" I asked.

In answer, she simply shook her head, causing the cascade of silvery blond hair to ripple across her shoulder. I was starting to feel tired—sleepy. I must have blinked. In that moment, the shimmering blond hair and maroon sweatshirt vanished. In their place I saw a woman who was clearly a nurse.

"Mr. Beaumont. Mr. Beaumont," she said, in a concerned voice that was far too loud. "How are you doing, Mr. Beaumont? It's time to wake up now."

"I've already been awake," I wanted to say, but I didn't. Instead, looking up into a worried face topping a set of colorful scrubs, I wondered when it was that nurses stopped wearing white uniforms and white caps and started doing their jobs wearing clothes that looked more like crazed flower gardens than anything else.

"Okay," I managed, only now my voice was more of a whisper than a croak. "My wife?"

"Right here," Mel answered, appearing in the background, just over the nurse's shoulder. "I'm right here."

She looked haggard and weary. I had spent a long time sleeping; she had spent the same amount of time worrying. Unfortunately, it showed.

"Where did she go?" I asked the nurse, who was busy taking my blood pressure reading.

"Where did who go?" she asked.

"The girl in the sweatshirt."

"What girl?" she asked. "What sweatshirt?"

Taking a cue from me, Mel looked around the recovery room, which consisted of a perimeter of several curtained-off patient cubicles surrounding a central nurses' station. The whole place was a beehive of activity.

"I see nurses and patients," Mel said. "I don't see anyone in a sweatshirt."

"But she was right here," I argued. "A blonde with bright red nail polish a lot like yours. She was wearing a WSU sweatshirt, and she was filing her nails with one of those pointy little nail files."

"A metal one?" Mel asked, frowning. "Those are bad for your nails. I haven't used one of those in years. Do they even still sell them?"

That question was directed at the nurse who, busy taking my temperature, simply shrugged. "Beats me," she said. "I'm not big on manicures. Never have been."

That's when I got the message. I was under the influence of powerful drugs. The girl in the sweatshirt didn't exist. I had made her up.

"How're you doing, Mr. B.?" Mel asked. Sidling up to the other side of the bed, she called me by her currently favored pet name and planted a kiss on my cheek. "I talked to the doctor. He said you did great. They'll keep you here in the recovery room for an hour or two, until they're sure you're stable, and then they'll transfer you to your room. I called the kids, by the way, and let everybody know that you came through surgery like a champ."

This was all good news, but I didn't feel like a champ. I felt more like a chump.

"Can I get you something to drink?" the nurse asked. "Some water? Some juice?"

I didn't want anything to drink right then because part of me was still looking for the girl. Part of me was still convinced she had been there, but I couldn't imagine who else she might have been. One of Ron Peters's girls, maybe? Heather and Tracy had both gone to WSU. Of the two, I'd always had a special connection with the younger one, Heather. As a kid she was a cute little blond-haired beauty whose blue-eyed grin had kept me in my place, properly wrapped around her little finger. At fifteen, a barely recognizable Heather, one with hennaed hair and numerous piercings, had gone into full-fledged off-the-rails teenage rebellion, complete with your basic bad-to-the-bone boyfriend.

In the aftermath of said boyfriend's death, unlamented by anyone *but* Heather, her father and stepmother had managed to get the grieving girl on track. She had reenrolled in school, graduated from high school, and gone on to a successful college experience. One thing I did know clearly—this was September. That meant that, as far as I knew, Heather was off at school, too, working on a Ph.D. somewhere in the wilds of New Mexico. So, no, my mysterious visitor couldn't very well be Heather Peters, either.

Not taking my disinterested answer about wanting something to drink for a real no, the nurse handed me a glass with water and a straw bent in my direction. "Drink," she said. I took a reluctant sip, but I was still looking around the room; still searching.

Mel is nothing if not observant. "Beau," she said. "Believe me, there's nobody here in a WSU sweatshirt. And on my way here from the lobby, I didn't meet anybody in the elevator or the hallway who was wearing one, either."

"Probably just dreaming," the nurse suggested. "The stuff they use in the OR puts 'em out pretty good, and I've been told that the dreams that go along with the drugs can be pretty convincing."

"It wasn't a dream," I insisted to the nurse. "She was right here just a few minutes ago—right where you're standing now. She was sitting on a stool."

The nurse turned around and made a show of looking over her shoulder. "Sorry," she said. "Was there a stool here? I must have missed it."

But of course there was no stool visible anywhere in the recovery room complex, and no maroon sweatshirt, either.

The nurse turned to Mel. "He's going to be here for an hour or so, and probably drifting in and out of it for most of that time. Why don't you go get yourself a bite to eat? If you leave me your cell phone number, I can let you know when we're moving him to his room."

of those borderline juvenile delinquent types who ended up being given that old-fashioned bit of legal advice: join the army or go to jail. He had chosen the former and had shipped out for Vietnam after (a) knocking up, and (b) marrying his high school sweetheart. The army had done as promised and made a man out of him. He'd come home to the "baby killer" chorus and had gone to work for the Seattle Police Department because it was a place where a guy with a high school diploma could make enough money to support a wife and, by then, two kids. He had been there ever since, first as a beat cop and now working patrol, but his long-term goal was to transfer over to the Motorcycle unit.

Mac's wife, Melody, stayed home with the kids. From what I could tell from his one-sided version of events, the two of them constantly squabbled over finances. No matter how much overtime Mac worked, there was never enough money to go around. Melody wanted to go to work. Mac was adamantly opposed. Melody was reading too many books and, according to him, was in danger of turning into one of those scary bra-burning feminists.

From my point of view, letting Melody go out and get a job seemed like a reasonable solution. It's what Karen and I had decided to do. She had been hired as a secretary at the Weyerhaeuser corporate headquarters, but we had both regarded her work there as just a job—as a temporary measure rather than a career—because our ultimate goal, once we finally got around to having kids, had been for Karen to stay home and look after them, and that's what she was doing now.

Allowing herself to be convinced, Mel kissed me again. "I am going to go get something," she said.

"You do that," I managed. "I think I'll just nap for a while."

My eyelids were growing heavy. I could feel myself drifting. The din of recovery room noise retreated, and just that quickly, the blonde was back at my bedside, sitting on a rolling stool that seemed to appear and disappear like magic at the same time she did. The cascade of swinging hair still shielded her face, and she was still filing her nails.

I've had recurring dreams on occasion, but not very often. Most of the time it's the kind of thing where something in the dream, usually something bad, jars me awake. When I go back to sleep, the dream picks up again, sometimes in exactly the same place, but a slightly different starting point can lead to a slightly different outcome.

This dream was just like that. I was still in the bed in the recovery room, but Mel was gone and so was my nurse. Everyone else in the room was faded and fuzzy, like from the days before high-def appeared. Only the blonde on the stool stood out in clear relief against everything else.

"Who are you?" I asked. "What are you doing here? What do you want?"

She didn't look up. "You said you'd never forget me," she said accusingly, "but you have, haven't you?"

I was more than a little impatient with all the phony game playing. "How can I tell?" I demanded. "You won't even tell me your name."

"My name is Monica," she answered quietly. "Monica Wellington."

Then she lifted her head and turned to face me. Once the hair was swept away, however, I was appalled to see that there was no face at all. Instead, what peered at me over the neck of the maroon sweatshirt was nothing but a skull, topped by a headful of gorgeous long blond hair, parted in the middle.

"You promised my mother that you'd find out who did it," she said. "You never did."

With that she was gone, plunging me into a strange existence where the boundaries between memory and dream blurred somehow, leaving me to relive that long-ago time in every jarring detail.

CHAPTER 2

WHEN IT COMES TO BORING, nothing beats second watch on a Sunday afternoon. It's a time when nothing much happens. Good guys and bad guys alike tend to spend their Sunday afternoons at home. On a sunny early spring day, like this one, the good guys might be dragging their wintered-over barbecue grills out of storage and giving them a first-of-the-season tryout. The bad guys would probably be nursing hangovers of one kind or another and planning their next illegal exploit.

Rory MacPherson was at the wheel of our two-year-old police-pursuit Plymouth Fury as we tooled around the streets of Seattle's Central West Precinct. We were supposedly on patrol, but with nothing much happening on those selfsame streets, we were mostly out for a Sunday afternoon drive, yakking as we went.

Mac and I were roughly the same age, but we had come to Seattle PD from entirely different tracks. He was one

In that regard, our story was different from Mac and Melody's. The two of us had met in college, where I had snagged Karen away from the clutches of one of my fraternity brothers, a pompous ass named Maxwell Cole. Due to the advent of the pill, we did *not* get "in trouble" before we got married, but it wasn't for lack of trying. My draft number came up at about the same time I graduated from the University of Washington, so I joined up before I was drafted. Karen was willing to get married before I shipped out; I insisted on waiting.

Once I came home, also to the by-then-routine "baby-killer" chorus, Karen and I did get married. I went to work at Seattle PD, while Karen kept the job at Weyerhaeuser she had gotten while I was in the service. It's possible that Karen had a few bra-burning tendencies of her own, but it didn't seem like that big an issue for either one of us at the time, not back when we were dating. For one thing, we were totally focused on doing things the "right way." We put off having kids long enough to buy the house on Lake Tapps. Now that Scott had just turned one, we were both grateful to be settled.

Yes, I admit that driving from Lake Tapps to downtown Seattle is a long commute. That's one of the reasons I drove a VW bug, for fuel economy, but as far as this former city kid is concerned, being able to raise our kids in the country rather than the city makes the drive and the effort worthwhile.

I was raised in Seattle's Ballard neighborhood, where I was one of the few kids around with a single mother. My mom supported us by working at home as a seamstress.

Growing up in poverty was one of the reasons I was determined to raise my own kids with two parents and a certain amount of financial security. I had my eye on being promoted to investigations, preferably Homicide. I had taken the exam, but so far there weren't any openings.

Karen and I had both had lofty and naive ideas about how her stay-at-home life would work. However, with one baby still in diapers and with another on the way, reality had set in in a very big way. From Karen's point of view, her new noncareer path wasn't at all what it was cracked up to be. She was bored to tears and had begun to drop hints about being sold a bill of goods. The long commute meant that my workdays were longer, too. She wanted something more in her life than all Scotty, all the time. She also wanted me to think about some other kind of job where there wouldn't be shift work. She wanted a job for me that would allow us to establish a more regular schedule, one where I could be home on weekends like other people. The big problem for me with that idea was that I loved what I did.

So that's how me and Mac's second-watch shift was going that Sunday afternoon. We had met up at Bob Murray's Doghouse for a hearty Sunday brunch that consisted of steak and eggs, despite the warning on the menu specifying that the tenderness of the Doghouse's notoriously cheap steaks was "not guaranteed." I believe it's possible—make that likely—that we both had some hair of the dog. Mac had a preshift Bloody Mary and I had a McNaughton's and water in advance of heading into the cop shop in downtown Seattle.

Once we checked our Plymouth Fury out of the motor pool, Mac did the driving, as usual. When we were together, I was more than happy to relinquish the wheel. My solitary commutes back and forth from Lake Tapps gave me plenty of "drive time." During Mac's and my countless hours together in cars, we did more talking than anything else.

Mac and I were both Vietnam vets, but we did *not* talk about the war. What we had seen and done there was still too raw and hurtful to talk about, and what happened to us after we came back home was even more so. As a result we steadfastly avoided any discussion that might take us too close to that painful reality. Instead, we spent lots of time talking about the prospects for the newest baseball team in town, the second coming of the Seattle Rainiers, to have a winning season.

Mac was still provoked that the "old" Seattle Rainiers, transformed into the Seattle Pilots, had joined the American League and boogied off to Milwaukee. I didn't have a strong feeling about any of it, so I just sat back and let Mac rant. Finished with that, he went on to a discussion of his son, Rolly, short for Roland. For Mac it was only a tiny step from discussing Seattle's pro baseball team to his son's future baseball prospects, even though Rolly was seven and doing his first season of T-ball, complicated by the unbelievable fact that Melody had signed up to be the coach of Rolly's team.

My eyes must have glazed over about then. At our house, Karen and I were still up to our armpits in diapers. By the way, when I say the word "we" in regard to diapers,

I mean it. I did my share of diaper changing. From where I stood in the process of child rearing, thinking about T-ball or even Little League seemed to be in the very distant future.

What I really wanted right about then was a cigarette break. Mac had quit smoking months earlier. Out of deference to him, I didn't smoke in the patrol car, but at times I really wanted to.

It must have been close to four thirty when a call came in over our two-way radio. Two kids had been meandering around the railroad yard at the base of Magnolia Bluff. Somewhere near the bluff they had found what they thought was an empty oil drum. When they pried off the top, they claimed, they had discovered a dead body inside. I told Dispatch that we were on our way, but Mac didn't exactly put the pedal to the metal.

"I'll bet dollars to doughnuts this is somebody's idea of a great April Fool's joke," he said. "Wanna bet?"

"No bet," I agreed. "Sounds suspicious to me."

We went straight there, not with lights and sirens, but without stopping for coffee along the way, either. We didn't call the medical examiner. We didn't call for the Homicide squad or notify the crime lab because we thought it was a joke. Except it turned out it wasn't a joke at all.

We located the two kids, carrot-topped, freckle-faced twin brothers Frankie and Donnie Dodd, waiting next to a pay phone at the Elliott Bay Marina where they had called 911. They looked to be eleven or twelve years old. The fact that they were both still a little green around the gills made me begin to wonder if maybe Mac and I were wrong about the possibility of this being an April Fool's joke.

"You won't tell our mom, will you?" the kid named Donnie asked warily. "We're not supposed to be down by the tracks. She'll kill us if she finds out."

"Where do you live?" I asked.

"On Twenty-third West," he said, pointing to the top of the bluff. "Up on Magnolia."

"And where does your mother think the two of you are?" I asked.

Frankie, who may have been the ringleader, made a face at his brother, warning Donnie not to answer, but he did anyway.

"She dropped us off at the Cinerama to see *Charlotte's Web*. We tried to tell her that's a kids' movie, but she didn't listen. So after she drove away, we caught a bus and came back here to look around. We've found some good stuff here—a broken watch, a jackknife, a pair of false teeth."

Nodding, Frankie added his bit. "Halfway up the hill we found a barrel. We thought there might be some kind of treasure in it. That's why we opened it."

"It smelled real bad," Donnie said, holding his nose and finishing his brother's thought. "I thought I was going to puke."

"How do you know a body was inside?" I asked.

"We pushed it away from us. When it rolled the rest of the way down the hill, she fell out. She wasn't wearing any clothes."

"That's why we couldn't tell our mother," Donnie concluded, "and that's when we went to the marina to call for help."

"How about if you show us," Mac suggested.

We let the two kids into the back of the patrol car. They were good kids, and the whole idea of getting into our car excited them. Kids who have had run-ins with cops are not thrilled to be given rides in patrol cars. Following their pointed directions, we followed an access road on the far side of Pier 91. There were no gates, no barriers, just a series of NO TRESPASSING signs that they had obviously ignored, and so did we.

The road intersected with the path the barrel had taken on its downhill plunge. Its route was still clearly visible where a gray, greasy film left a trail through the hillside's carpet of newly sprung springtime weeds and across the dirt track in front of us. What looked like a bright yellow fifty-gallon drum had come to a stop some fifteen yards farther on at the bottom of the steep incline. The torso of a naked female rested half inside and half outside the barrel. The body was covered in a grayish-brown ooze that I couldn't immediately identify. The instantly recognizable odor of death wafted into the air, but there was another underlying odor as well. While my nicotine-dulled nostrils struggled to make olfactory sense of that second odor, Mac beat me to the punch.

"Cooking grease," he explained. "Whoever killed her must have shoved her feet-first into a restaurant-size vat of used grease. Restaurants keep the drums out on their loading docks. Once they're full, they haul them off to the nearest rendering plant."

I nodded. That was it—stale cooking grease. The combination of rotten flesh and rotting food was overwhelming. For a time we both stood in a horrified stupor while I fought down the urge to lose my own lunch and wondered if the victim had been dead or alive when she had been sealed inside her grease-filled prison.

Eventually the urgent cawing of a flock of crows wheeling overhead broke our stricken silence. Their black wings flapped noisily against the early April blue sky. I'm a crossword puzzle kind of guy. That gives me access to a good deal of generally useless information. In this instance, I knew that a flock of crows is called a murder, and this noisy bunch, attracted by what they must have expected to be a sumptuous feast, seemed particularly aptly named.

Mac was the first to stir. "I guess it's not a joke," he muttered as he started down the hill toward the body. "I'll keep the damn birds away. You call it in."

Mac was a few years my senior in both regular years and in years on the force. He often issued what sounded like orders. Most of the time I simply went along with the program. In this instance, I was more than happy to comply.

I went back over to the car and leaned inside. Donnie and Frankie were watching, wide eyed, from the backseat. "Did you see her?" Donnie asked. At least I think it was Donnie.

"Yes," I said grimly. "We saw her. While I call this in, I want the two of you to stay right where you are. Got it?"

They both nodded numbly. It wasn't as though they had a choice. There was a web of metal screen between the cruiser's front seat and the backseat. The doors locked from the outside, and there were no interior door handles. Frankie and Donnie Dodd weren't under arrest, but they weren't going anywhere without our permission. They sat there in utter silence while I made the call, letting Dispatch know that they needed to summon the M.E. and detectives from Homicide. When I finished, I hopped out of the car and skidded down the steep incline. Mac was already on his way back up.

"I gave up on the damn birds," he muttered. "She's already dead. How much worse can it be?

"That's all right," I said. "I think I'll go have a look anyway."

"Suit yourself," Mac said with a shrug. "Some people are dogs for punishment."

We had worked together long enough that he knew I wanted a cigarette, but we were both kind enough not to mention it. I waited until I was far enough down the hill to be out of sight before I lit up. I figured out of sight is out of mind and damn the smoke smell later.

Still, smoking was what I was doing when my eyes were inevitably drawn to the body. People passing car wrecks on the highway aren't the only people guilty of rubbernecking. Cops do it, too, and at that time in my career I was enough of a newbie that seeing dead bodies was anything but routine.

I found myself staring at the dead woman—what I could see of her, at least. She lay sprawled facedown on the weedy hillside, half in and half out of the barrel. A tangle of what looked like shoulder-length blond hair spilled out over the ground. A moment later, something red caught my eye, sticking out through the layer of greasy slurry. At first I thought what I was seeing was blood spatter, but that wasn't possible. Clearly the woman had been dead for some time. Once blood is exposed to the air, it oxidizes and goes from red to muddy brown. This was definitely red. Bright red. Scarlet. Inhaling a lungful of smoke, I moved a step or two closer to get a better look.

What I was seeing, of course, was nothing but tiny little patches of bright red nail polish glowing in the sunlight. And that was the single detail that stayed with me from that crime scene—the nail polish. Wanting to look pretty for someone, the victim had gone to the trouble of having a manicure, or else she had given herself one. Had she been going to a dance or a party, maybe? Had she been out on the town for a night of fun?

Whatever it was, when she'd done her nails, she hadn't expected to be dead soon, or that the vivid red nail polish would be the only thing she'd be wearing when someone found her body.

ABOUT THE AUTHOR

J. A. JANCE is the *New York Times* bestselling author of the J. P. Beaumont series, the Joanna Brady series, the Ali Reynolds series, and four interrelated thrillers about the Walker Family. Born in South Dakota and brought up in Bisbee, Arizona, Jance lives with her husband in Seattle, Washington, and Tucson, Arizona.

Visit www.AuthorTracker.com for exclusive information on your favorite HarperCollins authors.

"I wonder how the book got to Guernsey? Perhaps there is some secret sort of homing instinct in books that brings them to their perfect readers."

The Guernsey Literary
and Potato Peel Pie Society

MARY ANN SHAFFER
& ANNIE BARROWS

Dial Press Trade Paperbacks

2009 Dial Press Trade Paperback Edition

Published in the United States by Dial Press Trade Paperbacks,
an imprint of The Random House Publishing Group, a division of
Random House, Inc., New York.

DIAL PRESS and DIAL PRESS TRADE PAPERBACKS are registered trademarks
of Random House, Inc., and the colophon is
a trademark of Random House, Inc.

RANDOM HOUSE READER'S CIRCLE & design is
a trademark of Random House, Inc.

Originally published in hardcover in the United States by The Dial Press,
an imprint of The Random House Publishing Group,
a division of Random House, Inc., in 2008.

Map by George Ward

Library of Congress Cataloging-in-Publication Data
Shaffer, Mary Ann.
The Guernsey Literary and Potato Peel Society / Mary Ann Shaffer
& Annie Barrows.
p. cm.
ISBN: 978-0-385-34100-4 (trade pbk.)
1. Women authors—Fiction. 2. Book clubs (Discussion groups)—Fiction.
3. London (England)—History—20th century—Fiction. 4. Guernsey
(Channel Islands)—Fiction. 5. England—Fiction.
I. Barrows, Annie. II. Title.

PS3619.H3365 G84 2008   2007047869
813/.6 22
Printed in the United States of America

www.randomhousereaderscircle.com

BVG   18 19

Text design by Virginia Norey
Cover design by Roberto de Vicq de Cumptich
Cover image courtesy of Christian Raoul Skrein von Bumbala

Lovingly dedicated to my mother, Edna Fiery Morgan,
and to my dear friend Julia Poppy
—M. A. S.
And to my mother, Cynthia Fiery Barrows
—A. B.

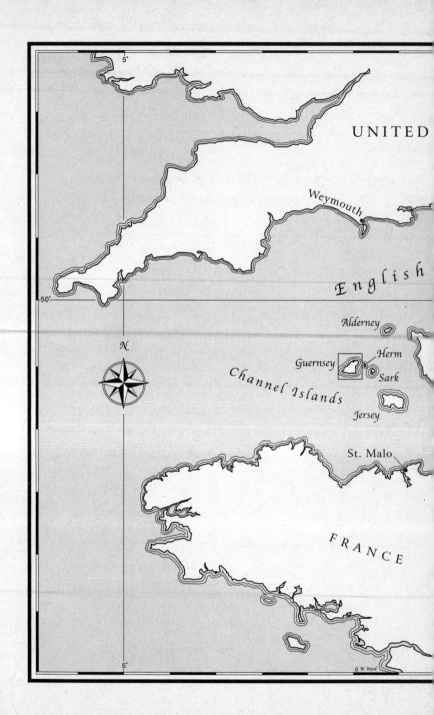

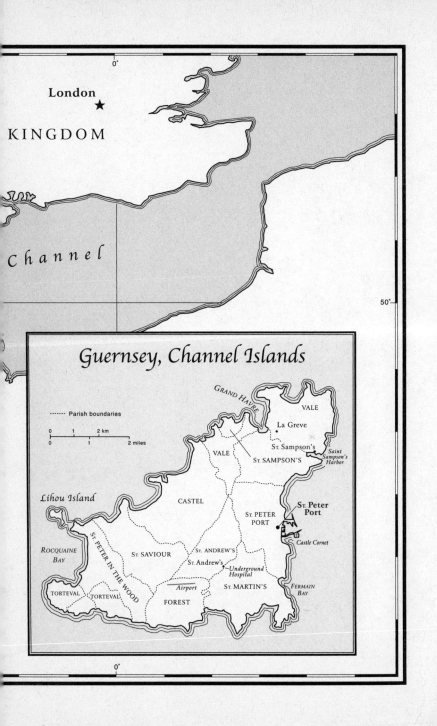

London ★

KINGDOM

Channel

50°

Guernsey, Channel Islands

GRAND HAVRE

VALE

La Greve

------ Parish boundaries

0   1   2 km
0   1   2 miles

VALE

St. Sampson's

St. SAMPSON'S

Saint
Sampson's
Harbor

Lihou Island

CASTEL

St. PETER
PORT

St. Peter
Port

Castle Cornet

ROCQUAINE
Bay

St. SAVIOUR

St. ANDREW'S

St. Andrew's

Underground
Hospital

St. PETER IN THE WOOD

TORTEVAL   TORTEVAL

Airport

FOREST

St. MARTIN'S

FERMAIN
BAY

0°

The Guernsey Literary

and Potato Peel Pie Society

PART ONE

8th January, 1946

Mr. Sidney Stark, Publisher
Stephens & Stark Ltd.
21 St. James's Place
London S.W.1
England

Dear Sidney,

Susan Scott is a wonder. We sold over forty copies of the book, which was very pleasant, but much more thrilling from my standpoint was the food. Susan managed to procure ration coupons for icing sugar and *real eggs* for the meringue. If all her literary luncheons are going to achieve these heights, I won't mind touring about the country. Do you suppose that a lavish bonus could spur her on to butter? Let's try it—you may deduct the money from my royalties.

Now for my grim news. You asked me how work on my new book is progressing. Sidney, it isn't.

English Foibles seemed so promising at first. After all, one should be able to write reams about the Society to Protest the Glorification of the English Bunny. I unearthed a photograph of the Vermin Exterminators' Trade Union, marching down an Oxford street with placards screaming "Down with Beatrix Potter!" But what is there to write about after a caption? Nothing, that's what.

I no longer want to write this book—my head and my heart just aren't in it. Dear as Izzy Bickerstaff is—and was—to me, I don't want to write anything else under that name. I don't want to be considered a light-hearted journalist anymore. I do acknowledge that making readers laugh—or at least chuckle—during the war was no mean feat, but I don't want to do it anymore. I can't seem to dredge up any sense of proportion or balance these days, and God knows one cannot write humor without them.

In the meantime, I am very happy Stephens & Stark is making money on *Izzy Bickerstaff Goes to War*. It relieves my conscience over the debacle of my Anne Brontë biography.

> My thanks for everything and love,
> Juliet

P.S. I am reading the collected correspondence of Mrs. Montagu. Do you know what that dismal woman wrote to Jane Carlyle? "My dear little Jane, everybody is born with a vocation, and yours is to write charming little notes." I hope Jane spat on her.

From Sidney to Juliet

10th January, 1946

Miss Juliet Ashton
23 Glebe Place
Chelsea
London S.W. 3

Dear Juliet:

Congratulations! Susan Scott said you took to the audience at the luncheon like a drunkard to rum—and they to you—

so please stop worrying about your tour next week. I haven't a doubt of your success. Having witnessed your electrifying performance of "The Shepherd Boy Sings in the Valley of Humiliation" eighteen years ago, I know you will have every listener coiled around your little finger within moments. A hint: perhaps in this case, you should refrain from throwing the book at the audience when you finish.

Susan is looking forward to ushering you through bookshops from Bath to Yorkshire. And of course, Sophie is agitating for an extension of the tour into Scotland. I've told her in my most infuriating older-brother manner that It Remains To Be Seen. She misses you terribly, I know, but Stephens & Stark must be impervious to such considerations.

I've just received *Izzy's* sales figures from London and the Home Counties—they are excellent. Again, congratulations!

Don't fret about *English Foibles*; better that your enthusiasm died now than after six months spent writing about bunnies. The crass commercial possibilities of the idea were attractive, but I agree that the topic would soon grow horribly fey. Another subject—one you'll like—will occur to you.

Dinner one evening before you go? Say when.

Love,
Sidney

P.S. You write charming little notes.

From Juliet to Sidney

11th January, 1946

Dear Sidney,

Yes, lovely—can it be somewhere on the river? I want oysters and champagne and roast beef, if obtainable; if not, a chicken will do. I am very happy that *Izzy's* sales are good. Are they good enough that I don't have to pack a bag and leave London?

Since you and S&S have turned me into a moderately successful author, dinner must be my treat.

Love,
Juliet

P.S. I did not throw "The Shepherd Boy Sings in the Valley of Humiliation" at the audience. I threw it at the elocution mistress. I meant to cast it at her feet, but I missed.

From Juliet to Sophie Strachan

12th January, 1946

Mrs. Alexander Strachan
Feochan Farm
by Oban
Argyll

Dear Sophie,

Of course I'd adore to see you, but I am a soul-less, will-less automaton. I have been ordered by Sidney to Bath, Colchester, Leeds, and several other garden spots I can't recall at the moment, and I can't just slither off to Scotland instead. Sidney's brow would lower—his eyes would narrow—he would stalk. You know how nerve-racking it is when Sidney stalks.

I wish I could sneak away to your farm and have you coddle me. You'd let me put my feet on the sofa, wouldn't you? And then you'd tuck blankets around me and bring me tea. Would Alexander mind a permanent resident on his sofa? You've told me he is a patient man, but perhaps he would find it annoying.

Why am I so melancholy? I should be delighted at the prospect of reading *Izzy* to an entranced audience. You know how I love talking about books, and you know how I adore receiving compliments. I should be thrilled. But the truth is that I'm gloomy— gloomier than I ever was during the war. Everything is so *broken,* Sophie: the roads, the buildings, the people. Especially the people.

This is probably the aftereffect of a horrid dinner party I went to last night. The food was ghastly, but that was to be expected. It was the guests who unnerved me—they were the most demoralizing collection of individuals I've ever encountered. The talk was of bombs and starvation. Do you remember Sarah Morecroft? She was there, all bones and gooseflesh and bloody lipstick. Didn't she use to be pretty? Wasn't she mad for that horse-riding fellow who went up to Cambridge? He was nowhere in evidence; she's married to a doctor with grey skin who clicks his tongue before he speaks. And he was a figure of wild romance compared to my dinner partner, who just happened to be a single man, presumably the last one on earth—oh Lord, how miserably mean-spirited I sound!

I swear, Sophie, I think there's something wrong with me. Every man I meet is intolerable. Perhaps I should set my sights lower—not so low as the grey doctor who clicks, but a bit lower. I can't even blame it on the war—I was never very good at men, was I?

Do you suppose the St. Swithin's furnace-man was my one true love? Since I never spoke to him, it seems unlikely, but at least it was a passion unscathed by disappointment. And he had that beautiful black hair. After that, you remember, came the Year of Poets. Sidney's quite snarky about those poets, though I don't see why, since he introduced me to them. Then poor Adrian. Oh, there's no need to recite the dread rolls to you, but Sophie—what *is* the matter with me? Am I too particular? I don't want to be married just to be married. I can't think of anything lonelier than spending the rest of my life with someone I can't talk to, or worse, someone I can't be silent with.

What a dreadful, complaining letter. You see? I've succeeded in making you feel relieved that I won't be stopping in Scotland. But then again, I may—my fate rests with Sidney.

Kiss Dominic for me and tell him I saw a rat the size of a terrier the other day.

> Love to Alexander and even more to you,
> Juliet

12th January, 1946

Miss Juliet Ashton
81 Oakley Street
Chelsea
London S.W. 3

Dear Miss Ashton,

My name is Dawsey Adams, and I live on my farm in St. Martin's Parish on Guernsey. I know of you because I have an old book that once belonged to you—the *Selected Essays of Elia,* by an author whose name in real life was Charles Lamb. Your name and address were written inside the front cover.

I will speak plain—I love Charles Lamb. My own book says *Selected,* so I wondered if that meant he had written other things to choose from? These are the pieces I want to read, and though the Germans are gone now, there aren't any bookshops left on Guernsey.

I want to ask a kindness of you. Could you send me the name and address of a bookshop in London? I would like to order more of Charles Lamb's writings by post. I would also like to ask if anyone has ever written his life story, and if they have, could a copy be found for me? For all his bright and turning mind, I think Mr. Lamb must have had a great sadness in his life.

Charles Lamb made me laugh during the German Occupation, especially when he wrote about the roast pig. The Guernsey Literary and Potato Peel Pie Society came into being because of a roast pig we had to keep secret from the German soldiers, so I feel a kinship to Mr. Lamb.

I am sorry to bother you, but I would be sorrier still not to know about him, as his writings have made me his friend.

> Hoping not to trouble you,
> Dawsey Adams

P.S. My friend Mrs. Maugery bought a pamphlet that once belonged to you, too. It is called *Was There a Burning Bush? A Defense of Moses and the Ten Commandments.* She liked your margin note, "Word of God or crowd control???" Did you ever decide which?

From Juliet to Dawsey

15th January, 1946

Mr. Dawsey Adams
Les Vauxlarens
La Bouvée
St. Martin's, Guernsey

Dear Mr. Adams,

I no longer live on Oakley Street, but I'm so glad that your letter found me and that my book found you. It was a sad wrench to part with the *Selected Essays of Elia.* I had two copies and a dire need of shelf-room, but I felt like a traitor selling it. You have soothed my conscience.

I wonder how the book got to Guernsey? Perhaps there is some secret sort of homing instinct in books that brings them to their perfect readers. How delightful if that were true.

Because there is nothing I would rather do than rummage through bookshops, I went at once to Hastings & Sons upon receiving your letter. I have gone to them for years, always finding the one book I wanted—and then three more I hadn't known I wanted. I told Mr. Hastings you would like a good, clean copy (and *not* a rare edition) of *More Essays of Elia*. He will send it to you by separate post (invoice enclosed) and was delighted to know you are also a lover of Charles Lamb. He said the best biography of Lamb was by E. V. Lucas, and he would hunt out a copy for you, though it may take a while.

In the meantime, will you accept this small gift from me? It is his *Selected Letters*. I think it will tell you more about him than any biography ever could. E. V. Lucas sounds too stately to include my favorite passage from Lamb: "Buz, buz, buz, bum, bum, bum, wheeze, wheeze, wheeze, fen, fen, fen, tinky, tinky, tinky, cr'annch! I shall certainly come to be condemned at last. I have been drinking too much for two days running. I find my moral sense in the last stage of a consumption and my religion getting faint." You'll find that in the *Letters* (it's on page 244). They were the first Lamb I ever read, and I'm ashamed to say I only bought the book because I'd read elsewhere that a man named Lamb had visited his friend Leigh Hunt, in prison for libeling the Prince of Wales.

While there, Lamb helped Hunt paint the ceiling of his cell sky blue with white clouds. Next they painted a rose trellis up one wall. Then, I further discovered, Lamb offered money to help Hunt's family outside the prison—though he himself was as poor as a man could be. Lamb also taught Hunt's youngest daughter to say the Lord's Prayer backward. You naturally want to learn everything you can about a man like that.

That's what I love about reading: one tiny thing will interest you in a book, and that tiny thing will lead you onto another book, and another bit there will lead you onto a third book. It's geometrically progressive—all with no end in sight, and for no other reason than sheer enjoyment.

The red stain on the cover that looks like blood—is blood. I got careless with my paper knife. The enclosed postcard is a reproduction of a painting of Lamb by his friend William Hazlitt.

If you have time to correspond with me, could you answer several questions? Three, in fact. Why did a roast pig dinner have to be kept a secret? How could a pig cause you to begin a literary society? And, most pressing of all, what is a potato peel pie—and why is it included in your society's name?

I have sub-let a flat at 23 Glebe Place, Chelsea, London S.W.3. My Oakley Street flat was bombed in 1945 and I still miss it. Oakley Street was wonderful—I could see the Thames out of three of my windows. I know that I am fortunate to have any place at all to live in London, but I much prefer whining to counting my blessings. I am glad you thought of me to do your *Elia* hunting.

Yours sincerely,
Juliet Ashton

P.S. I never could make up my mind about Moses—it still bothers me.

From Juliet to Sidney

18th January, 1946

Dear Sidney,

This isn't a letter: it's an apology. Please forgive my moaning about the teas and luncheons you set up for *Izzy*. Did I call you a tyrant? I take it all back—I love Stephens & Stark for sending me out of London.

Bath is a glorious town: lovely crescents of white, upstanding houses instead of London's black, gloomy buildings or—worse still—piles of rubble that were once buildings. It is bliss to breathe in clean, fresh air with no coal smoke and no dust. The weather is cold, but it isn't London's dank chill. Even the people on the street look different—upstanding, like their houses, not grey and hunched like Londoners.

Susan said the guests at Abbot's book tea enjoyed themselves immensely—and I know I did. I was able to un-stick my tongue from the roof of my mouth after the first two minutes and began to have quite a good time.

Susan and I are off tomorrow for bookshops in Colchester, Norwich, King's Lynn, Bradford, and Leeds.

Love and thanks,
Juliet

From Juliet to Sidney

21st January, 1946

Dear Sidney,

Night-time train travel is wonderful again! No standing in the corridors for hours, no being shunted off for a troop train to pass, and above all, no black-out curtains. All the windows we passed were lighted, and I could snoop once more. I missed it so terribly during the war. I felt as if we had all turned into moles scuttling along in our separate tunnels. I don't consider myself a real peeper—they go in for bedrooms, but it's families in sitting rooms or kitchens that thrill me. I can imagine their entire lives from a glimpse of bookshelves, or desks, or lit candles, or bright sofa cushions.

There was a nasty, condescending man in Tillman's bookshop today. After my talk about *Izzy*, I asked if anyone had questions. He literally leapt from his seat to go nose-to-nose with me—how was it, he demanded, that I, a mere woman, dared to bastardize the name of Isaac Bickerstaff? "The true Isaac Bickerstaff, noted journalist, nay the sacred heart and soul of eighteenth-century literature: dead now and his name desecrated by you."

Before I could muster a word, a woman in the back row jumped to her feet. "Oh, sit down! You can't desecrate a person who never was! He's not dead because he was never alive! Isaac Bickerstaff was a pseudonym for Joseph Addison's *Spectator* columns! Miss Ashton can take up any pretend name she wants to—so shut up!" What a valiant defender—he left the store in a hurry.

Sidney, do you know a man named Markham V. Reynolds, Jr.? If you don't, will you look him up for me—*Who's Who,* the *Domesday Book,* Scotland Yard? Failing those, he may simply be in the Telephone Directory. He sent a beautiful bunch of mixed spring flowers to me at the hotel in Bath, a dozen white roses to my train, and a pile of red roses to Norwich—all with no message, only his engraved card.

Come to that, how does he know where Susan and I are staying? What trains we are taking? All his flowers have met me upon my arrival. I don't know whether to feel flattered or hunted.

Love,
Juliet

From Juliet to Sidney

23rd January, 1946

Dear Sidney,

Susan just gave me the sales figures for *Izzy*—I can scarcely believe them. I honestly thought everyone would be so weary of the war that no one would want a remembrance of it—and certainly not in a book. Happily, and once again, you were right and I was wrong (it half-kills me to admit this).

Traveling, talking before a captive audience, signing books, and meeting strangers *is* exhilarating. The women I've met have told me such war stories of their own, I almost wish I had my column back. Yesterday, I had a lovely, gossipy chat with a Norwich lady. She has four daughters in their teens, and just last week, the eldest was invited to tea at the cadet school in town. Arrayed in her finest frock and spotless white gloves, the girl made her way to the school, stepped over the threshold, took one look at the sea of shining cadet faces before her—and fainted dead away! The poor child had never seen so many males in one place in her life. Think of it—a whole generation grown up without dances or teas or flirting.

I love seeing the bookshops and meeting the booksellers—booksellers really are a special breed. No one in their right mind would take up clerking in a bookstore for the salary, and no one in his right mind would want to own one—the margin of profit is too small. So, it has to be a love of readers and reading that makes them do it—along with first dibs on the new books.

Do you remember the first job your sister and I had in London? In crabby Mr. Hawke's secondhand bookshop? How I loved him—he'd simply unpack a box of books, hand one or two to us and say, "No cigarette ashes, clean hands—and for God's sake, Juliet, none of your margin notes! Sophie, dear, don't let her drink coffee while she reads." And off we'd go with new books to read.

It was amazing to me then, and still is, that so many people who wander into bookshops don't really know what they're after—they only want to look around and hope to see a book that will strike their fancy. And then, being bright enough not to trust the publisher's blurb, they will ask the book clerk the three questions: (1) What is it about? (2) Have you read it? (3) Was it any good?

Real dyed-in-the-wool booksellers—like Sophie and me—can't lie. Our faces are always a dead giveaway. A lifted brow or curled lip reveals that it's a poor excuse for a book, and the clever customers ask for a recommendation instead, whereupon we frog-march them over to a particular volume and command them to read it. If they read it and despise it, they'll never come back. But if they like it, they're customers for life.

Are you taking notes? You should—a publisher should send not just one reader's copy to a bookshop, but several, so that all the staff can read it, too.

Mr. Seton told me today that *Izzy Bickerstaff* makes an ideal present for both someone you like and someone you don't like but have to give a present to anyway. He also claimed that 30 percent of all books bought are bought as gifts. Thirty percent??? Did he lie?

Has Susan told you what else she has managed besides our tour? Me. I hadn't known her half an hour before she told me my make-up, my clothes, my hair, and my shoes were drab, all drab. The war was over, hadn't I heard?

She took me to Madame Helena's for a haircut; it is now short and curly instead of long and lank. I had a light rinse, too—Susan and Madame said it would bring out the golden highlights in my "beautiful chestnut curls." But I know better; it's meant to cover any grey hairs (four, by my count) that have begun to creep in. I also bought a jar of face cream, a lovely scented hand lotion, a new lipstick, and an eye-lash curler—which makes my eyes cross whenever I use it.

Then Susan suggested a new dress. I reminded her that the Queen was very happy wearing her 1939 wardrobe, so why shouldn't I be? She said the Queen doesn't need to impress strangers—but I do. I felt like a traitor to crown and country; no decent woman has new clothes—but I forgot that the moment I saw myself in the mirror. My first new dress in four years, and such a dress! It is the exact color of a ripe peach and falls in lovely folds when I move. The saleslady said it had "Gallic Chic" and I would too, if I bought it. So I did. New shoes are going to have to wait, since I spent almost a year's worth of clothing coupons on the dress.

Between Susan, my hair, my face, and my dress, I no longer look a listless, bedraggled thirty-two-year-old. I look a lively, dashing, haute-coutuéd (if this isn't a French verb, it should be) thirty.

Apropos of my new dress and no new shoes—doesn't it seem shocking to have more stringent rationing after the war than during the war? I realize that hundreds of thousands of people all over Europe must be fed, housed, and clothed, but privately I resent it that so many of them are Germans.

I am still without any ideas for a book I want to write. It is beginning to depress me. Do you have any suggestions?

Since I am in what I consider to be the North I'm going to place a trunk call to Sophie in Scotland tonight. Any messages for your sister? Your brother-in-law? Your nephew?

This is the longest letter I've ever written—you needn't reply in kind.

Love,
Juliet

From Susan Scott to Sidney

25th January, 1946

Dear Sidney,

Don't believe the newspaper reports. Juliet was not arrested and taken away in handcuffs. She was merely reproved by one of Bradford's constables, and he could barely keep a straight face.

She did throw a teapot at Gilly Gilbert's head, but don't believe his claim that she scalded him; the tea was cold. Besides, it was more of a skim-by than a direct hit. Even the hotel manager refused to let us compensate him for the teapot—it was only dented. He was, however, forced by Gilly's screams to call in the constabulary.

Herewith the story, and I take full responsibility for it. I should have refused Gilly's request for an interview with Juliet. I knew what a loathsome person he was, one of those unctuous little worms who work for *The London Hue and Cry*. I also knew that Gilly and the *LH&C* were horribly jealous of the *Spectator's* success with the Izzy Bickerstaff columns—and of Juliet.

We had just returned to the hotel from the Brady's Booksmith party for Juliet. We were both tired—and full of ourselves—when up popped Gilly from a chair in the lounge. He begged us to have tea with him. He begged for a short interview with "our own wonderful Miss Ashton—or should I say England's very own Izzy Bickerstaff?" His smarm alone should have alerted me, but it didn't—I wanted to sit down, gloat over Juliet's success, and have a cream tea.

So we did. The talk was going smoothly enough, and my mind was wandering when I heard Gilly say, ". . . you were a war widow yourself, weren't you? Or rather—*almost* a war widow—as good as. You were to marry a Lieutenant Rob Dartry, weren't you? Had made arrangements for the ceremony, hadn't you?"

Juliet said, "I beg your pardon, Mr. Gilbert." You know how polite she is.

"I don't have it wrong, do I? You and Lieutenant Dartry *did* apply for a marriage license. You *did* make an appointment to be married at the Chelsea Register Office on 13th December, 1942, at 11:00 A.M. You *did* book a table for luncheon at the Ritz—only you never showed up for any of it. It's perfectly obvious that you jilted Lieutenant Dartry at the altar—poor fellow—and sent him off alone and humiliated, back to his ship, to carry his broken heart to Burma, where he was killed not three months later."

I sat up, my mouth gaping open. I just looked on helplessly as Juliet attempted to be civil: "I didn't jilt him *at the altar*—it was the day before. And he wasn't humiliated—he was relieved. I simply told him that I didn't want to be married after all. Believe me, Mr. Gilbert, he left a happy man—delighted to be rid of me. He didn't slink back to his ship, alone and betrayed—he went straight to the CCB Club and danced all night with Belinda Twining."

Well, Sidney, surprised as Gilly was, he was not daunted. Little rodents like Gilly never are, are they? He quickly guessed that he was on to an even juicier story for his paper.

"OH-HO!" he smirked, "What was it, then? Drink? Other women? A touch of the old Oscar Wilde?"

That was when Juliet threw the teapot. You can imagine the hubbub that ensued—the lounge was full of other people having tea—hence, I am sure, the newspapers learning of it.

I thought his headline, "*IZZY BICKERSTAFF GOES TO WAR—AGAIN! Reporter Wounded in Hotel Bun-Fight,*" was a bit harsh, but not too bad. But "*JULIET'S FAILED ROMEO—A*

FALLEN HERO IN BURMA" was sick-making, even for Gilly Gilbert and the *Hue and Cry.*

Juliet is worried she may have embarrassed Stephens & Stark, but she is literally sick over Rob Dartry's name being slung around in this fashion. All I could get her to say to me was that Rob Dartry was a good man, a very good man—none of it was his fault—and he did not deserve this!

Did you know Rob Dartry? Of course, the drink/Oscar Wilde business is pure rot, but why did Juliet call off the wedding? Do you know why? And would you tell me if you did? Of course you wouldn't; I don't know why I'm even asking.

The gossip will die down of course, but does Juliet have to be in London for the thick of it? Should we extend our tour to Scotland? I admit I'm of two minds about this; the sales there have been spectacular, but Juliet has worked so hard at these teas and luncheons—it is not easy to get up in front of a roomful of strangers and praise yourself and your book. She's not used to this hoopla like I am and is, I think, very tired.

Sunday we'll be in Leeds, so let me know then about Scotland.

Of course, Gilly Gilbert is despicable and vile and I hope he comes to a bad end, but he has pushed *Izzy Bickerstaff Goes to War* onto the Best Seller List. I'm tempted to write him a thank-you note.

Yours in haste,
Susan

P.S. Have you found out who Markham V. Reynolds is yet? He sent Juliet a forest of camellias today.

Telegram from Juliet to Sidney

AM TERRIBLY SORRY TO HAVE EMBARRASSED YOU
AND STEPHENS & STARK. LOVE, JULIET

From Sidney to Juliet

26th January, 1946

Miss Juliet Ashton
The Queens Hotel
City Square
Leeds

Dear Juliet,

Don't worry about Gilly—you did not embarrass S&S; I'm
only sorry that the tea wasn't hotter and you didn't aim lower.
The Press is hounding me for a statement regarding Gilly's latest
muckraking, and I am going to give them one. Don't worry; it's
going to be about Journalism in these degenerate times—not
about you or Rob Dartry.

I just spoke to Susan about going on to Scotland and—
though I know Sophie will never forgive me—decided against it.
Izzy's sales figures are going up—way up—and I think you
should come home.

The *Times* wants you to write a long piece for the supplement—one part of a three-part series they plan to publish in
successive issues. I'll let them surprise you with the subject, but

I can promise you three things right now: they want it written by Juliet Ashton, *not by Izzy Bickerstaff*; the subject is a serious one; and the sum mentioned means you can fill your flat with fresh flowers every day for a year, buy a satin quilt (Lord Woolton says you no longer need to have been bombed out to buy new bed-covers), and purchase a pair of real leather shoes—if you can find them. You can have my coupons.

The *Times* doesn't want the article until late spring, so we will have more time to think up a new book possibility for you. All good reasons to hurry back, but the biggest one is that I miss you.

Now, about Markham V. Reynolds, Junior. I do know who he is, and the *Domesday Book* won't help—he's an American. He is the son and heir of Markham V. Reynolds, Senior, who used to have a monopoly on paper mills in the States and now just owns most of them. Reynolds, Junior, being of an artistic turn of mind, does not dirty his hands in making paper—he prints on it instead. He's a publisher. The *New York Journal,* the *Word, View*—those are all his, and there are several smaller magazines as well. I knew he was in London. Officially, he's here to open the London office of *View,* but rumor has it that he's decided to begin publishing books, and he's here to beguile England's finest authors with visions of plenty and prosperity in America. I didn't know his technique included roses and camellias, but I'm not surprised. He's always had more than his fair share of what we call cheek and Americans call can-do spirit. Just wait till you see him—he's been the undoing of stronger women than you, including my secretary. I'm sorry to say she's the one who gave him your itinerary *and* your address. The silly woman thought he was so romantic-looking, with "such a lovely suit and handmade shoes." Dear God! She couldn't seem to grasp the concept of breach of confidentiality, so I had to sack her.

He's after you, Juliet, no doubt about it. Shall I challenge him to a duel? He would undoubtedly kill me, so I'd rather not. My dear, I can't promise you plenty or prosperity or even butter, but you do know that you're Stephens & Stark's—especially Stark's—most beloved author, don't you?

Dinner the first evening you are home?

Love,
Sidney

From Juliet to Sidney

28th January, 1946

Dear Sidney,

Yes, dinner with pleasure. I'll wear my new dress and eat like a pig.

I am so glad I didn't embarrass S&S about Gilly and the teapot—I was worried. Susan suggested I make a "dignified statement" to the press too, about Rob Dartry and why we did not marry. I couldn't possibly do that. I honestly don't think I'd mind looking like a fool, if it didn't make Rob look a worse one. But it would—and of course, he wasn't a fool at all. But he'd *sound that way*. I'd much prefer to say nothing and look like a feckless, flighty, cold-hearted bitch.

But I'd like *you* to know why—I'd have told you before, but you were off with the Navy in 1942, and you never met Rob. Even Sophie never met him—she was up at Bedford that fall— and I swore her to secrecy afterwards. The longer I put off saying anything, the less important it became for you to know, especially in light of how it made me look—witless and foolish for getting engaged in the first place.

I thought I was in love (*that's* the pathetic part—my idea of being in love). In preparation for sharing my home with a husband, I made room for him so he wouldn't feel like a visiting aunt. I cleared out half my dresser drawers, half my closet, half my medicine chest, half my desk. I gave away my padded hangers and brought in those heavy wooden ones. I took my golliwog off the bed and put her in the attic. Now my flat was meant for two, instead of one.

On the afternoon before our wedding, Rob was moving in the last of his clothes and belongings while I delivered my Izzy article to the *Spectator*. When I was through, I tore home, flew up the stairs, and threw open the door to find Rob sitting on a low stool in front of my bookcase, surrounded by cartons. He was sealing the last one up with gummed tape and string. There were eight boxes—*eight boxes* of my books bound up and ready for the basement!

He looked up and said, "Hello, darling. Don't mind the mess, the porter said he'd help me carry these down to the basement." He nodded toward my bookshelves and said, "Don't they look wonderful?"

Well, there were no words! I was too appalled to speak. Sidney, every single shelf—where my books had stood—was filled with athletic trophies: silver cups, gold cups, blue rosettes, red ribbons. There were awards for every game that could possibly be played with a wooden object: cricket bats, squash racquets, tennis racquets, oars, golf clubs, Ping-Pong paddles, bows and arrows, snooker cues, lacrosse sticks, hockey sticks, and polo mallets. There were statues for everything a man could jump over, either by himself or on a horse. Next came the framed certificates—for shooting the most birds on such and such a date, for First Place in footraces, for Last Man Standing in some filthy tug-of-war against Scotland.

All I could do was scream, "How dare you! What have you DONE?! Put my books back!"

Well, that's how matters started. Eventually, I said something to the effect that I could never marry a man whose idea of bliss was to strike out at little balls and little birds. Rob countered with remarks about damned bluestockings and shrews. And it all degenerated from there—the only thought we probably had in common was, What the hell have we talked about for the last four months? What, indeed? He huffed and puffed and snorted—and left. And I unpacked my books.

Remember the night last year when you met my train to tell me my home had been bombed flat? You thought I was laughing in hysteria? I wasn't—it was in irony—if I'd let Rob store all my books in the basement, I'd still have them, every one.

Sidney, as a token of our long friendship, you do not need to comment on this story—not ever. In fact, I'd far prefer it if you didn't.

Thank you for tracing Markham V. Reynolds, Junior, to his source. So far, his blandishments are entirely floral, and I remain true to you and the Empire. However, I do have a pang of sympathy for your secretary—I hope he sent her some roses for her trouble—as I'm not certain that my scruples could withstand the sight of handmade shoes. If I ever do meet him, I'll take care not to look at his feet—or I'll lash myself to a flagpole first and then peek, like Odysseus.

Bless you for telling me to come home. Am looking forward to the *Times* proposal for a series. Do you promise on Sophie's head it will not be a frivolous subject? They aren't going to ask me to write about the Duchess of Windsor, are they?

Love,
Juliet

From Juliet to Sophie Strachan

31st January, 1946

Dear Sophie,

Thank you for your flying visit to Leeds—there are no words to express how much I needed to see a friendly face just then. I honestly was on the verge of stealing away to the Shetlands to take up the life of a hermit. It was beautiful of you to come.

The *London Hue and Cry*'s sketch of me taken away in chains was overdrawn—I wasn't even arrested. I know Dominic would much prefer a godmother in prison, but he will have to settle for something less dramatic this time.

I told Sidney the only thing I could do about Gilly's callous, lying accusations was to maintain a dignified silence. He said I could do that if I wanted to, but Stephens & Stark could not!

He called a press conference to defend the honor of *Izzy Bickerstaff,* Juliet Ashton, and Journalism itself against such trash as Gilly Gilbert. Did it make the papers in Scotland? If not—here are the highlights. He called Gilly Gilbert a twisted weasel (well, perhaps not in exactly those words, but his meaning was clear) who lied because he was too lazy to learn the facts and too stupid to understand the damage his lies inflicted upon the noble traditions of Journalism. It was lovely.

Sophie, could two girls (now women) ever have had a better champion than your brother? I don't think so. He gave a wonderful speech, though I must admit to a few qualms. Gilly Gilbert is such a snake-in-the-grass, I can't believe he'll just slither away without a hiss. Susan said that, on the other hand, Gilly is also such a frightful little coward, he would not dare to retaliate. I hope she's right.

Love to you all,
Juliet

P.S. That man has sent me another bale of orchids. I'm getting a nervous twitch, waiting for him to come out of hiding and make himself known. Do you suppose this is his strategy?

From Dawsey to Juliet

31st January, 1946

Dear Miss Ashton,

Your book came yesterday! You are a nice lady and I thank you with all my heart.

I have a job at St. Peter Port harbor—unloading ships, so I can read during tea breaks. It is a blessing to have real tea and bread with butter, and now—your book. I like it too because the cover is soft and I can put it in my pocket everywhere I go, though I am careful not to use it up too quickly. And I value having a picture of Charles Lamb—he had a fine head, didn't he?

I would like to correspond with you. I will answer your questions as well as I can. Though there are many who can tell a story better than I can, I will tell you about our roast pig dinner.

I have a cottage and a farm, left to me by my father. Before the war, I kept pigs, and grew vegetables for St. Peter Port markets and flowers for Covent Garden. I often worked also as a carpenter and roofer.

The pigs are gone now. The Germans took them away to feed their soldiers on the continent, and ordered me to grow potatoes. We were to grow what they told us and nothing else. At first, before I knew the Germans as I came to later, I thought I could keep a few pigs hidden—for my own self. But the Agricultural Officer nosed them out and carried them off. Well, that was a blow, but I thought I'd manage all right, for potatoes and turnips were plentiful, and there was still flour then. But it is strange how the mind turns on food. After six months of turnips and a lump of gristle now and then, I was hard put to think about anything but a fine, full meal.

One afternoon, my neighbor, Mrs. Maugery, sent me a note. Come quick, it said. And bring a butcher knife. I tried not to get my hopes high—but I set out for the manor house at a great clip. And it was true! She had a pig, a hidden pig, and she invited me to join in the feast with her and her friends!

I never talked much while I was growing up—I stuttered badly—and I was not used to dinner parties. To tell the truth, Mrs. Maugery's was the first one I was ever invited to. I said yes, because I was thinking of the roast pig, but I wished I could take my piece home and eat it there.

It was my good luck that my wish didn't come true, because

that was the first meeting of the Guernsey Literary and Potato Peel Pie Society, even though we didn't know it then. The dinner was a rare treat, but the company was better. With talking and eating, we forgot about clocks and curfews until Amelia (that's Mrs. Maugery) heard the chimes ring nine o'clock—we were an hour late. Well, the good food had strengthened our hearts, and when Elizabeth McKenna said we should strike out for our rightful homes instead of skulking in Amelia's house all night, we agreed. But breaking curfew was a crime—I'd heard of folks being sent to prison camp for it—and keeping a pig was a worse one, so we whispered and picked our way through the fields as quiet as could be.

We would have come out all right if not for John Booker. He'd drunk more than he'd eaten at dinner, and when we got to the road, he forgot himself and broke into song! I grabbed hold of him, but it was too late: six German patrol officers suddenly rose out of the trees with their Lugers drawn and began to shout—Why were we out after curfew? Where had we been? Where were we going?

I couldn't think what to do. If I ran, they'd shoot me. I knew that much. My mouth was dry as chalk and my mind was blank, so I just held on to Booker and hoped.

Then Elizabeth drew in her breath and stepped forward. Elizabeth isn't tall, so those pistols were lined up at her eyes, but she didn't blink. She acted like she didn't see any pistols at all. She walked up to the officer in charge and started talking. You never heard such lies. How sorry she was that we had broken curfew. How we had been attending a meeting of the Guernsey Literary Society, and the evening's discussion of *Elizabeth and Her German Garden* had been so delightful that we had all lost track of time. Such a wonderful book—had he read it?

None of us had the presence of mind to back her up, but the patrol officer couldn't help himself—he had to smile back at her.

Elizabeth is like that. He took our names and ordered us very politely to report to the Commandant the next morning. Then he bowed and wished us a good evening. Elizabeth nodded, gracious as could be, while the rest of us edged away, trying not to run like rabbits. Even lugging Booker, I got home quick.

That is the story of our roast pig dinner.

I'd like to ask you a question of my own. Ships are coming in to St. Peter Port harbor every day to bring us things Guernsey still needs: food, clothes, seed, plows, feed for animals, tools, medicine—and most important, now that we have food to eat, shoes. I don't believe that there was a fit pair left on the island by the end of the war.

Some of the things being sent to us are wrapped up in old newspaper and magazine pages. My friend Clovis and I smooth them out and take them home to read—then we give them to neighbors who, like us, are eager for any news of the outside world in the past five years. Not just any news or pictures: Mrs. Saussey wants to see recipes; Mme. LePell wants fashion papers (she is a dressmaker); Mr. Brouard reads Obituaries (he has his hopes, but won't say who); Claudia Rainey is looking for pictures of Ronald Colman; Mr. Tourtelle wants to see Beauty Queens in bathing dress; and my friend Isola likes to read about weddings.

There is so much we wanted to know during the war, but we were not allowed letters or papers from England—or anywhere. In 1942, the Germans called in all the wireless sets—of course, there were hidden ones, listened to in secret, but if you were caught listening, you could be sent to the camps. That is why we don't understand so many things we can read about now.

I enjoy the war-time cartoons, but there is one that bewilders me. It was in a 1944 *Punch* and shows ten or so people walking down a London street. The chief figures are two men in bowler hats, holding briefcases and umbrellas, and one man is saying to the other man, "It is ridiculous to say these Doodlebugs have affected people in any way." It took me several seconds to realize that every person in the cartoon had one normal-sized ear and one *very large* ear on the other side of his head. Perhaps you could explain it to me.

Yours sincerely,
Dawsey Adams

Juliet to Dawsey

3rd February, 1946

Dear Mr. Adams,

I am so glad you are enjoying Lamb's letters and the copy of his portrait. He did fit the face I had imagined for him, so I'm glad you felt that way, too.

Thank you very much for telling me about the roast pig, but don't think I didn't notice that you only answered one of my questions. I'm hankering to know more about the Guernsey Literary and Potato Peel Pie Society, and not merely to satisfy my idle curiosity—I now have a professional duty to pry.

Did I tell you I am a writer? I wrote a weekly column for the *Spectator* during the war, and Stephens & Stark publishers collected them together into a single volume and published them under the title *Izzy Bickerstaff Goes to War*. Izzy was the nom-de-plume the *Spectator* chose for me, and now, thank heavens, the poor thing has been laid to rest, and I can write under my own name again. I would like to write a book, but I am having trouble thinking of a subject I could live happily with for several years.

In the meantime, the *Times* has asked me to write an article for the literary supplement. They want to address the practical, moral, and philosophical value of reading—spread out over three issues and by three different authors. I am to cover the philosophical side of the debate and so far my only thought is that reading keeps you from going gaga. You can see I need help.

Do you think your literary society would mind being included in such an article? I know that the story of the society's founding would fascinate the *Times*'s readers, and I'd love to learn more about your meetings. But if you'd rather not, please don't worry—I will understand either way, and either way, would like to hear from you again.

I remember the *Punch* cartoon you described very well and think it was the word *Doodlebug* that threw you off. That was the name coined by the Ministry of Information; It was meant to sound less terrifying than "Hitler's V-1 rockets" or "pilotless bombs."

We were all used to bombing raids at night and the sights that followed, but these were unlike any bombs we had seen before.

They came in the daytime, and they came so fast there was no time for an air-raid siren or to take cover. You could see them; they looked like slim, black, slanted pencils and made a dull, spastic sound above you—like a motor-car running out of petrol. As long as you could hear them coughing and putt-putting, you were safe. You could think "Thank God, it's going past me."

But when their noise stopped, it meant there was only thirty seconds before it plummeted. So, you listened for them. Listened hard for the sound of their motors cutting out. I did see a Doodlebug fall once. I was quite some distance away when it hit, so I threw myself down in the gutter and cuddled up against the curb. Some women, in the top story of a tall office building down the street, had gone to an open window to watch. They were sucked out by the force of the blast.

It seems impossible now that someone could have drawn a cartoon about Doodlebugs, and that everyone, including me, could have laughed at it. But we did. The old adage—humor is the best way to make the unbearable bearable—may be true.

Has Mr. Hastings found the Lucas biography for you yet?

Yours sincerely,
Juliet Ashton

From Juliet to Markham Reynolds

4th February, 1946

Mr. Markham Reynolds
63 Halkin Street
London S.W.1

Dear Mr. Reynolds,

I captured your delivery boy in the act of depositing a clutch of pink carnations upon my doorstep. I seized him and threatened him until he confessed your address—you see, Mr. Reynolds, you are not the only one who can inveigle innocent employees. I hope you don't sack him; he seems a nice boy, and he really had no alternative—I menaced him with *Remembrance of Things Past*.

Now I can thank you for the dozens of flowers you've sent

me—it's been years since I've seen such roses, such camellias, such orchids, and you can have no idea how they lift my heart in this shivering winter. Why I deserve to live in a bower, when everyone else has to be satisfied with bedraggled leafless trees and slush, I don't know, but I'm perfectly delighted to do so.

Yours sincerely,
Juliet Ashton

From Markham Reynolds to Juliet

February 5, 1946

Dear Miss Ashton,

I didn't fire the delivery boy—I promoted him. He got me what I couldn't manage to get for myself: an introduction to you. The way I see it, your note is a figurative hand-shake and the preliminaries are now over. I hope you're of the same opinion, as it will save me the trouble of wangling an invitation to Lady Bascomb's next dinner party on the off-chance you might be there. Your friends are a suspicious lot, especially that fellow Stark, who said it wasn't his job to reverse the direction of the Lend-Lease and refused to bring you to the cocktail party I threw at the *View* office.

God knows, my intentions are pure, or at least, non-mercenary. The simple truth of it is that you're the only female writer who makes me laugh. Your Izzy Bickerstaff columns were the wittiest work to come out of the war, and I want to meet the woman who wrote them.

If I swear that I won't kidnap you, will you do me the honor of dining with me next week? You pick the evening—I'm entirely at your disposal.

Yours,
Markham Reynolds

From Juliet to Markham Reynolds

6th February, 1946

Dear Mr. Reynolds,

I am no proof against compliments, especially compliments about my writing. I'll be delighted to dine with you. Thursday next?

Yours sincerely,
Juliet Ashton

From Markham Reynolds to Juliet

February 7, 1946

Dear Juliet,

Thursday's too far away. Monday? Claridge's? 7:00?

Yours,
Mark

P.S. I don't suppose you have a telephone, do you?

From Juliet to Markham

7th February, 1946

Dear Mr. Reynolds,

All right—Monday, Claridge's, seven.

I do have a telephone. It's in Oakley Street under a pile of rubble that used to be my flat. I'm only sub-letting here, and my landlady, Mrs. Olive Burns, possesses the sole telephone on the premises. If you would like to chat with her, I can give you her number.

Yours sincerely,
Juliet Ashton

From Dawsey to Juliet

7th February, 1946

Dear Miss Ashton,

I'm certain the Guernsey Literary Society would like to be included in your article for the *Times*. I have asked Mrs. Maugery to write to you about our meetings, as she is an educated lady and her words will sound more at home in an article than mine could. I don't think we are much like literary societies in London.

Mr. Hastings hasn't found a copy of the Lucas biography yet, but I had a postcard from him saying, "Hard on the trail. Don't give up." He is a kind man, isn't he?

I'm hauling slates for the Crown Hotel's new roof. The owners are hoping that tourists may want to come back this summer. I am glad of the work but will be happy to be working on my land soon.

It is nice to come home in the evening and find a letter from you.

I wish you good fortune in finding a subject you would care to write a book about.

Yours sincerely,
Dawsey Adams

From Amelia Maugery to Juliet

8th February, 1946

Dear Miss Ashton,

Dawsey Adams has just been to call on me. I have never seen him as pleased with anything as he is with your gift and letter. He was so busy convincing me to write to you by the next post that he forgot to be shy. I don't believe he is aware of it, but Dawsey has a rare gift for persuasion—he never asks for anything for himself, so everyone is eager to do what he asks for others.

He told me of your proposed article and asked if I would write to you about the literary society we formed during—and because of—the German Occupation. I will be happy to do so, but with a caveat.

A friend from England sent me a copy of *Izzy Bickerstaff Goes to War*. We had no news from the outside world for five years, so you can imagine how satisfying it was to learn how England endured those years herself. Your book was as informative as it was entertaining and amusing—but it is the amusing tone I must quibble with.

I realize that our name, the Guernsey Literary and Potato Peel Pie Society, is an unusual one and could easily be subjected to ridicule. Would you assure me you will not be tempted to do so? The Society members are very dear to me, and I do not wish them to be perceived as objects of fun by your readers.

Would you be willing to tell me of your intentions for the article and also something of yourself? If you can appreciate the import of my questions, I should be glad to tell you about the Society. I hope I shall hear from you soon.

Yours sincerely,
Amelia Maugery

From Juliet to Amelia

10th February, 1946

Mrs. Amelia Maugery
Windcross Manor
La Bouvée
St. Martin's, Guernsey

Dear Mrs. Maugery,

Thank you for your letter. I am very glad to answer your questions.

I did make fun of many war-time situations; the *Spectator* felt a light approach to the bad news would serve as an antidote and that humor would help to raise London's low morale. I am very glad *Izzy* served that purpose, but the need to be humorous against the odds is—thank goodness—over. I would never make fun of anyone who loved to read. Nor of Mr. Adams—I was glad to learn one of my books fell into such hands as his.

Since you should know something about me, I have asked the Reverend Simon Simpless, of St. Hilda's Church near Bury St. Edmunds, Suffolk, to write to you. He has known me since I was a child and is fond of me. I have asked Lady Bella Taunton to provide a reference for me too. We were fire wardens together during the Blitz and she wholeheartedly dislikes me. Between the two of them, you may get a fair picture of my character.

I am enclosing a copy of a biography I wrote about Anne Brontë, so you can see that I am capable of a different kind of work. It didn't sell very well—in fact, not at all, but I am much prouder of it than I am of *Izzy Bickerstaff Goes to War*.

If there is anything else I can do to assure you of my good will, I will be glad to do so.

Yours sincerely,
Juliet Ashton

From Juliet to Sophie

12th February, 1946

Dearest Sophie,

Markham V. Reynolds, he of the camellias, has finally materialized. Introduced himself, paid me compliments, and invited me out to dinner—Claridge's, no less. I accepted regally—

Claridge's, oh yes, I *have* heard of Claridge's—and then spent the next three days fretting about my hair. It's lucky I have my lovely new dress, so I didn't have to waste precious fretting time on my clothes.

As Madame Helena said, "The hairs, they are a disaster." I tried a roll; it fell down. A French twist; it fell down. I was on the verge of tying an enormous red velvet bow on the top of my head when my neighbor Evangeline Smythe came to the rescue, bless her. She's a genius with my hair. In two minutes, I was a picture of elegance—she caught up all the curls and swirled them around in the back—and I could even move my head. Off I went, feeling perfectly adorable. Not even Claridge's marble lobby could intimidate *me*.

Then Markham V. Reynolds stepped forward, and the bubble popped. He's dazzling. Honestly, Sophie, I've never seen anything like him. Not even the furnace-man can compare. Tan, with blazing blue eyes. Ravishing leather shoes, elegant wool suit, blinding white handkerchief in breast pocket. Of course, being American, he's tall, and he has one of those alarming American smiles, all gleaming teeth and good humor, but he's not a genial American. He's quite impressive, and he's used to ordering people about—though he does it so easily, they don't notice. He's got that way of believing his opinion is the truth, but he's not disagreeable about it. He's too sure he's right to bother being disagreeable.

Once we were seated—in our own velvet-draped alcove—and all the waiters and stewards and maîtres d'hôtel were finished fluttering about us, I asked him point-blank why he had sent me those scads of flowers without including any note.

He laughed. "To make you interested. If I had written you directly, asking you to meet me, how would you have replied?" I admitted I would have declined. He raised one pointed eyebrow at me. Was it his fault if he could outwit me so easily?

I was awfully insulted to be so transparent, but he just laughed at me again. And then he began to talk about the war and Victorian literature—he knows I wrote a biography of Anne Brontë—and New York and rationing, and before I knew it, I was basking in his attention, utterly charmed.

Do you remember that afternoon in Leeds when we speculated on the possible reasons why Markham V. Reynolds, Junior, was obliged to remain a man of mystery? It's very disappointing, but we were completely wrong. He's not married. He's certainly not bashful. He doesn't have a disfiguring scar that causes him to shun daylight. He doesn't seem to be a werewolf (no fur on his knuckles, anyway). And he's not a Nazi on the lam (he'd have an accent).

Now that I think about it, maybe he *is* a werewolf. I can picture him lunging over the moors in hot pursuit of his prey, and I'm certain that he wouldn't think twice about eating an innocent bystander. I'll watch him closely at the next full moon. He's asked me to go dancing tomorrow—perhaps I should wear a high collar. Oh, that's vampires, isn't it?

I think I am a little giddy.

Love,
Juliet

From Lady Bella Taunton to Amelia

12th February, 1946

Dear Mrs. Maugery,

Juliet Ashton's letter is at hand, and I am amazed at its contents. Am I to understand she wishes me to provide a character reference for her? Well, so be it! I cannot impugn her character—only her common sense. She hasn't any.

War, as you know, makes strange bedfellows, and Juliet and I were thrown together from the very first when we were Fire Wardens during the Blitz. Fire Wardens spent their nights on various London roof-tops, watching out for incendiary bombs that might fall. When they did, we would rush forth with stirrup pump and buckets of sand to stifle any small blaze before it could spread. Juliet and I were paired off to work together. We did not chat, as less conscientious Wardens would have done. I insisted on total vigilance at all times. Even so, I learned a few details of her life prior to the war.

Her father was a respectable farmer in Suffolk. Her mother, I surmise, was a typical farmer's wife, milking cows and plucking chickens, when not otherwise engaged in owning a bookshop in Bury St. Edmunds. Juliet's parents were both killed in a motor accident when she was twelve and she went to live with her great-uncle, a renowned Classicist, in St. John's Wood. There she disrupted his studies and household by running away—twice.

In despair, he sent her to a select boarding school. When she left school, she shunned a higher education, came to London, and shared a studio with her friend Sophie Stark. She worked by day in bookshops. By night, she wrote a book about one of those wretched Brontë girls—I forget which one. I believe the book was published by Sophie's brother's firm, Stephens & Stark. Though it's biologically impossible, I can only assume that some form of nepotism was responsible for the book's publication.

In any event, she began to publish feature articles for various magazines and newspapers. Her light, frivolous turn of mind gained her a large following among the less intellectually inclined readers—of whom, I fear, there are many. She spent the very last of her inheritance on a flat in Chelsea. Chelsea, home of artists, models, libertines, and Socialists—completely irresponsible people all, just as Juliet proved herself to be as a Fire Warden.

I come now to the specifics of our association.

Juliet and I were two of several Wardens assigned to the roof of the Inner Temple Hall of the Inns of Court. Let me say first that, for a Warden, quick action and a clear head were imperative—one had to be aware of *everything* going on around one. *Everything.*

One night in May 1941, a high-explosive bomb was dropped through the roof of the Inner Temple Hall Library. The Library roof was some distance away from Juliet's post, but she was so aghast by the destruction of her precious books that she sprinted *toward* the flames—as if she could single-handedly deliver the Library from its fate! Of course, her delusions created nothing but further damage, for the firemen had to waste valuable minutes in rescuing her.

I believe Juliet suffered some minor burns in the debacle, but fifty thousand books were blown to Kingdom Come. Juliet's name was stricken from the lists of the Fire Wardens, and rightly so. I discovered she then volunteered her services to the Auxiliary Fire Services. On the morning after a bombing raid, the AFS would be on hand to offer tea and comfort to the rescue squads.

The AFS also provided assistance to the survivors: reuniting families, securing temporary housing, clothing, food, funds. I believe Juliet to have been adequate to that daytime task—causing no catastrophe among the teacups.

She was free to occupy her nights however she chose. Doubtless it included the writing of more light journalism, for the *Spectator* engaged her to write a weekly column on the state of the nation in war-time—under the name of Izzy Bickerstaff.

I read one of her columns and canceled my subscription. She attacked the good taste of our dear (though dead) Queen, Victoria. Doubtless you know of the huge memorial Victoria had built for her beloved consort, Prince Albert. It is the jewel in the crown of Kensington Gardens—a monument to the Queen's refined taste as well as to the Departed. Juliet applauded the Ministry of Food for having ordered peas to be planted in the grounds surrounding that memorial—writing that no better scarecrow than Prince Albert existed in all of England.

While I question her taste, her judgment, her misplaced priorities, and her inappropriate sense of humor, she does indeed have one fine quality—she is honest. If she says she will honor the good name of your literary society, she will do so. I can say no more.

Sincerely yours,
Bella Taunton

13th February, 1946

Dear Mrs. Maugery,

Yes, you may trust Juliet. I am unequivocal on this point. Her parents were my good friends as well as my parishioners at St. Hilda's. Indeed, I was a guest at their home on the night she was born.

Juliet was a stubborn but, withal, a sweet, considerate, joyous child—with an unusual bent toward integrity for one so young.

I will tell you of one incident when she was ten years old. Juliet, while singing the fourth stanza of "His Eye Is on the Sparrow," slammed her hymnal shut and refused to sing another note. She told our choir director the lyrics cast a slur on God's character. We should not be singing it. He (the choir director, not God) didn't know what to do, so he escorted Juliet to my office for me to reason with her.

I did not fare very well. Juliet said, "Well, he shouldn't have written, 'His eye is on the sparrow'—what good was that? Did He stop the bird from falling down dead? Did He just say, 'Oops'? It makes God sound like He's off bird-watching, when real people need Him."

I felt compelled to agree with Juliet on this matter—why had I never thought upon it before? The choir did not sing and has not since sung "His Eye Is on the Sparrow."

Juliet's parents died when she was twelve and she was sent to live with her great-uncle, Dr. Roderick Ashton, in London. Though not an unkind man, he was so mired in his Greco-Roman studies he had no time to pay the girl any attention. He had no imagination, either—fatal for one engaged in child-rearing.

She ran away twice, the first time making it only as far as King's Cross Station. The police found her waiting, with a packed canvas carry-all and her father's fishing rod, to catch the train to Bury St. Edmunds. She was returned to Dr. Ashton—and she ran away again. This time, Dr. Ashton telephoned me to ask for my help in finding her.

I knew exactly where to go—to her parents' former farm. I found her opposite the farm's entrance, sitting on a little wooded knoll, impervious to the rain—just sitting there, soaked—looking at her old (now sold) home.

I wired her uncle and went back with her on the train to London the following day. I had intended to return to my parish on the next train, but when I discovered her fool of an uncle had sent his cook to fetch her home, I insisted on accompanying them. I invaded his study and we had a vigorous talk. He agreed a boarding school might be best for Juliet—her parents had left ample funds for such an eventuality.

Fortunately, I knew of a very good school—St. Swithin's. Academically a fine school, and with a headmistress not carved from granite. I am happy to tell you Juliet thrived there—she found her studies stimulating, but I believe the true reason for Juliet's regained spirits was her friendship with Sophie Stark and the Stark family. She often went to Sophie's home for half-term vacation, and Juliet and Sophie came twice to stay with me and my sister at the Rectory. What jolly times we shared: picnics, bicycle rides, fishing. Sophie's brother, Sidney Stark, joined us once—though ten years older than the girls, and despite an inclination to boss them around, he was a welcome fifth to our happy party.

It was rewarding to watch Juliet grow up—as it is now, to know her fully grown. I am very happy she asked me to write to you of her character.

I have included our small history together so you will realize I know whereof I speak. If Juliet says she will, she will. If she says she won't, she won't.

Very truly yours,
Simon Simpless

Susan Scott to Juliet

17th February, 1946

Dear Juliet,

Was that possibly *you* I glimpsed in this week's *Tatler,* doing the rumba with Mark Reynolds? You looked gorgeous—almost as gorgeous as he did—but might I suggest that you move to an air-raid shelter before Sidney sees a copy?

You can purchase my silence with torrid details, you know.

Yours,
Susan

Juliet to Susan Scott

18th February, 1946

Dear Susan,

I deny everything.

Love,
Juliet

From Amelia to Juliet

18th February, 1946

Dear Miss Ashton,

Thank you for taking my caveat so seriously. At the Society meeting last night, I told the members about your article for the *Times* and suggested that those who wished to do so should correspond with you about the books they read and the joy they found in reading.

The response was so vociferous Isola Pribby, our Sergeant-at-Arms, was forced to bang her hammer for order (I admit that Isola needs little encouragement to bang her hammer). I think you will receive a good many letters from us, and I hope they will be of some help in your article.

Dawsey has told you that the Society was invented as a ruse to keep the Germans from arresting my dinner guests: Dawsey, Isola, Eben Ramsey, John Booker, Will Thisbee, and our dear

Elizabeth McKenna, who manufactured the story on the spot, bless her quick wits and silver tongue.

I, of course, knew nothing of their predicament at the time. As soon as they left, I made haste down to my cellar to bury the evidence of our meal. The first I heard about our literary society was the next morning at seven, when Elizabeth appeared in my kitchen and asked, "How many books have you got?"

I had quite a few, but Elizabeth looked at my shelves and shook her head. "We need more. There's too much gardening here." She was right, of course—I do like a good garden book. "I'll tell you what we'll do," she said. "After I'm done at the Commandant's Office, we'll go to Fox's Bookshop and buy them out. If we're going to be the Guernsey Literary Society, we have to look literary."

I was frantic all forenoon, worrying over what was happening at the Commandant's Office. What if they all ended up in the Guernsey jail? Or, worst of all, in a prison camp on the continent? The Germans were erratic in dispensing their justice, so one never knew which sentence would be imposed. But nothing of the sort occurred.

Odd as it may sound, the Germans allowed—and even encouraged—artistic and cultural pursuits among the Channel Islanders. Their object was to prove to the British that the German Occupation was a Model Occupation. How this message was to be conveyed to the outside world was never explained, as the telephone and telegraph cable between Guernsey and London had been cut the day the Germans landed in June 1940. Whatever their skewed reasoning, the Channel Islands were treated much more leniently than the rest of conquered Europe—at first.

At the Commandant's Office, my friends were ordered to pay a small fine and submit the name and membership list of their society. The Commandant announced that he, too, was a lover of literature—might he, with a few like-minded officers, sometimes attend meetings?

Elizabeth told them they would be most welcome. And then she, Eben, and I flew to Fox's, chose armloads of books for our newfound Society, and rushed back to the Manor to put them on my shelves. Then we strolled from house to house—looking as carefree and casual as we could—in order to alert the others to come that evening and choose a book to read. It was agonizing to walk slowly, stopping to chat here and there, when we wanted to scurry! Timing was vital, since Elizabeth feared the Commandant would appear at the next meeting, a bare two weeks away. (He did not. A few German officers did attend over the years but, thankfully, left in some confusion and did not return.)

And so it was that we began. I knew all our members, but I did not know them all well. Dawsey had been my neighbor for over thirty years, and yet I don't believe I had ever spoken to him of anything more than weather and farming. Isola was a dear friend, and Eben, too, but Will Thisbee was only an acquaintance and John Booker was nearly a stranger, for he had only just arrived when the Germans came. It was Elizabeth we had in common. Without her urging, I would never have thought to invite them to share my pig, and the Guernsey Literary and Potato Peel Pie Society would never have drawn breath.

That evening when they came to my house to make their selections, those who had rarely read anything other than Scripture, seed catalogues, and *The Pigman's Gazette* discovered a different kind of reading. It was here Dawsey found his Charles Lamb and Isola fell upon *Wuthering Heights*. For myself, I chose *The Pickwick Papers,* thinking it would lift my spirits—it did.

Then each went home and read. We began to meet—for the sake of the Commandant at first, and then for our own pleasure.

None of us had any experience with literary societies, so we made our own rules: we took turns speaking about the books we'd read. At the start, we tried to be calm and objective, but that soon fell away, and the purpose of the speakers was to goad the listeners into wanting to read the book themselves. Once two members had read the same book, they could argue, which was our great delight. We read books, talked books, argued over books, and became dearer and dearer to one another. Other Islanders asked to join us, and our evenings together became bright, lively times—we could almost forget, now and then, the darkness outside. We still meet every fortnight.

Will Thisbee was responsible for the inclusion of Potato Peel Pie in our society's name. Germans or no, he wasn't going to go to any meetings unless there were eats! So refreshments became part of our program. Since there was scant butter, less flour, and no sugar to spare on Guernsey then, Will concocted a potato peel pie: mashed potatoes for filling, strained beets for sweetness, and potato peelings for crust. Will's recipes are usually dubious, but this one became a favorite.

I would enjoy hearing from you again and learning how your article progresses.

Yours most sincerely,
Amelia Maugery

From Isola Pribby to Juliet

19th February, 1946

Dear Miss Ashton,

Oh my, oh my. You have written a book about Anne Brontë, sister to Charlotte and Emily. Amelia Maugery says she will lend it to me, for she knows I have a fondness for the Brontë girls— poor lambs. To think all five of them had weak chests and died so young! What a sadness.

Their Pa was a selfish thing, wasn't he? He paid his girls no mind at all—always sitting in his study, yelling for his shawl. He never rose up to wait on hisself, did he? Just sat alone in his room while his daughters died like flies.

And their brother, Branwell, he wasn't much either. Always drinking and sicking up on the carpets. They were forever having to clean up after him. Fine work for lady Authoresses!

It is my belief that with two such men in the household and no way to meet others, Emily had to make Heathcliff up out of thin air! And what a fine job she did. Men are more interesting in books than they are in real life.

Amelia told us you would like to know about our book society and what we talk about at our meetings. I gave a talk on the Brontë girls once when it was my turn to speak. I'm sorry I can't send you my notes on Charlotte and Emily—I used them to kindle a fire in my cookstove, there being no other paper in the house. I'd already burnt up my tide tables, the Book of Revelation, and the story about Job.

You will want to know why I admired those girls. I like stories of passionate encounters. I myself have never had one, but now I can picture one. I didn't like *Wuthering Heights* at first, but the minute that specter, Cathy, scrabbled her bony fingers on the window glass—I was grasped by the throat and not let go. With that Emily I could hear Heathcliff's pitiful cries upon the moors. I don't believe that after reading such a fine writer as Emily Brontë, I will be happy to read again Miss Amanda Gillyflower's *Ill-Used by Candlelight*. Reading good books ruins you for enjoying bad books.

I will tell you now about myself. I have a cottage and small holding next to Amelia Maugery's manor house and farm. We are both situated by the sea. I tend my chickens and my goat, Ariel, and grow things. I have a parrot in my keeping too—her name is Zenobia and she does not like men.

I have a stall at Market every week, where I sell my preserves, vegetables, and elixirs I make to restore manly ardor. Kit McKenna—daughter to my dear friend Elizabeth McKenna— helps me make my potions. She is only four and has to stand on a stool to stir my pot, but she is able to whip up big froths.

I do not have a pleasing appearance. My nose is big and was broken when I fell off the hen-house roof. One eyeball skitters up to the top, and my hair is wild and will not stay tamped down. I am tall and built of big bones.

I could write to you again, if you want me to. I could tell you more about reading and how it perked up our spirits while the Germans were here. The only time reading didn't help was after Elizabeth was arrested by the Germans. They caught her hiding one of those poor slave workers from Poland, and they sent her to prison in France. There was no book that could lift my heart then, nor for a long time after. It was all I could do not to slap every German I saw. For Kit's sake, I held myself in. She was only a little sprout then, and she needed us. Elizabeth hasn't come home yet. We are afraid for her, but mind you, I say it's early days yet and she might still come home. I pray so, for I miss her sorely.

Your friend,
Isola Pribby

From Juliet to Dawsey

20th February, 1946

Dear Mr. Adams,

How did you know that I like white lilacs above all flowers? I always have, and now here they are, pluming out over my desk. They are beautiful, and I love having them—the look, the delicious scent and the surprise of them. At first I thought, How on earth did he find these in February, and then I remembered that the Channel Islands are blessed by a warm Gulf Stream.

Mr. Dilwyn appeared at my door with your present early this morning. He said he was in London on business for his bank. He assured me it was no trouble at all to deliver the flowers—there wasn't much he wouldn't do for you because of some soap you gave Mrs. Dilwyn during the war. She still cries every time she thinks of it. What a nice man he is—I am sorry he didn't have time to stop for coffee.

Due to your kind offices, I have received lovely, long letters from Mrs. Maugery and Isola Pribby. I hadn't realized that the Germans permitted *no outside news at all,* not even letters, to reach Guernsey. It surprised me so much. It shouldn't have—I knew the Channel Islands had been occupied, but I never, not once, thought what that might have entailed. Willful ignorance is all I can call it. So, I am off to the London Library to educate myself. The library suffered terrible bomb damage, but the floors are safe to walk on again, all the books that could be saved are back on the shelf, and I know they have collected all the *Times* from 1900 to—yesterday. I shall study up on the Occupation.

I want to find some travel or history books about the Channel Islands too. Is it really true that on a clear day, you can see the cars on the French coast roads? So it says in my Encyclopedia, but I bought it secondhand for 4 shillings and I don't trust it. There I also learned that Guernsey is "roughly seven miles long and five miles wide, with a population of 42,000 inhabitants." Strictly speaking, very informative, but I want to know more than that.

Miss Pribby told me that your friend Elizabeth McKenna had been sent to a prison camp on the continent and has not yet returned. It knocked the wind out of me. Ever since your letter about the roast pig dinner, I had been imagining her there among you. Without even knowing I was doing so, I depended upon one day receiving a letter from her too. I am sorry. I will hope for her early return.

Thank you again for my flowers. It was a lovely thing for you to do.

> Yours ever,
> Juliet Ashton

P.S. You may consider this a rhetorical question if you want to, but why did Mrs. Dilwyn weep over a cake of soap?

From Juliet to Sidney

21st February, 1946

Dearest Sidney,

I haven't heard from you in ages. Does your icy silence have anything to do with Mark Reynolds?

I have an idea for a new book. It's a novel about a beautiful yet sensitive author whose spirit is crushed by her domineering editor. Do you like it?

Love always,
Juliet

From Juliet to Sidney

23rd February, 1946

Dear Sidney,

I was only joking.

Love,
Juliet

From Juliet to Sidney

25th February, 1946

Sidney?

Love,
Juliet

From Juliet to Sidney

26th February, 1946

Dear Sidney,

Did you think I wouldn't notice you were gone? I did. After three notes went unanswered, I made a personal visit to St. James's Place, where I encountered the cast-iron Miss Tilley, who said you were out of town. Very enlightening. Upon pressing, I learned you had gone to Australia! Miss Tilley listened coolly to my exclamations. She would not disclose your exact where-abouts—only that you were scouring the Outback, seeking new authors for Stephens & Stark's list. She would forward any letters to you, at her discretion.

Your Miss Tilley does not fool me. Nor do you—I know ex-actly where you are and what you are doing. You flew to Australia to find Piers Langley and are holding his hand while he sobers up. At least, I hope that's what you are doing. He is such a dear friend—and such a brilliant writer. I want him to be well again and writing poetry. I'd add forgetting all about Burma and the Japanese, but I know that's not possible.

You could have told me, you know. I can be discreet when I really try (you've never forgiven me for that slip about Mrs. Atwater in the pergola, have you? I apologized handsomely at the time).

I liked your other secretary better. And you sacked her for naught, you know: Markham Reynolds and I have met. All right, we've done more than meet. We've danced the rumba. But don't fuss. He has not mentioned *View,* except in passing, and he hasn't once tried to lure me to New York. We talk of higher matters, such as Victorian literature. He's not the shallow dilettante you would have me believe, Sidney. He's an expert on Wilkie Collins, of all things. Did you know that Wilkie Collins maintained two separate households with two separate mistresses and two separate sets of children? The scheduling difficulties must have been shocking. No wonder he took laudanum.

I do think you would like Mark if you knew him better, and you may have to. But my heart and my writing hand belong to Stephens & Stark.

The article for the *Times* has turned into a lovely treat for me— now and ongoing. I have made a group of new friends from the Channel Islands—the Guernsey Literary and Potato Peel Pie Society. Don't you adore their name? If Piers needs distracting, I'll write you a nice fat letter about how they came by their name. If not, I'll tell you when you come home (when are you coming home?).

My neighbor Evangeline Smythe is going to have twins in June. She is none too happy about it, so I am going to ask her to give one of them to me.

Love to you and Piers,
Juliet

From Juliet to Sophie

28th February, 1946

Dearest Sophie—

I am as surprised as you are. He didn't breathe a word to me. On Tuesday, I realized I hadn't heard from Sidney in days, so I went to Stephens & Stark to demand attention and found he'd flown the coop. That new secretary of his is a fiend. To every one of my questions, she said, "I really can't divulge information of a personal nature, Miss Ashton." How I wanted to smack her.

Just as I was concluding that Sidney had been tapped by MI6 and was on a mission in Siberia, horrible Miss Tilley admitted that he'd gone to Australia. Well, it all came clear then, didn't it? He's gone to get Piers. Teddy Lucas seemed quite certain that Piers was going to drink himself steadily to death in that rest home unless someone came and stopped him. I can hardly blame him, after what he's been through—but Sidney won't allow it, thank God.

You know I adore Sidney with all my heart, but there's something terrifically liberating about Sidney *in Australia*. Mark Reynolds has been what your Aunt Lydia would have called persistent in his attentions for the last three weeks, but, even as I've gobbled lobster and guzzled champagne, I've been looking furtively over my shoulder for Sidney. He's convinced that Mark is trying to steal me away from London in general and Stephens & Stark in particular, and nothing I said could persuade him otherwise. I know he doesn't like Mark—I believe aggressive and unscrupulous were the words he used last time I saw him—but really, he was a bit too King Lear about the whole thing. I am a grown woman—mostly—and I can guzzle champagne with whomever I choose.

When not checking under tablecloths for Sidney, I've been having the most wonderful time. I feel as though I've emerged from a black tunnel and found myself in the middle of a carnival. I don't particularly care for carnivals, but after the tunnel, it's delicious. Mark gads about every night—if we're not going to a party (and we usually are), we're off to the cinema, or the theater, or a night club, or a gin house of ill-repute (he says he's trying to introduce me to democratic ideals). It's very exciting.

Have you noticed there are some people—Americans especially—who seem untouched by the war, or at least, un-mangled by it? I don't mean to imply that Mark was a shirker—he was in their Air Corps—but he's simply not sunk under it. And when I'm with him, I feel untouched by the war, too. It's an illusion, I know it is, and truthfully, I'd be ashamed of myself if the war hadn't touched me. But it's forgivable to enjoy myself a little—isn't it?

Is Dominic too old for a jack-in-the-box? I saw a diabolical one in a shop yesterday. It pops out, leering and weaving, its oily black mustache curling above pointed white teeth, the very picture of a villain. Dominic would adore it, after he had got over his first shock.

Love,
Juliet

From Juliet to Isola

28th February, 1946

Miss Isola Pribby
Pribby Homestead
La Bouvée
St. Martin's, Guernsey

Dear Miss Pribby,

Thank you so much for your letter about yourself and Emily Brontë. I laughed when I read that Emily had caught you by the throat the second poor Cathy's ghost knocked at the window. She got me at the *exact same moment.*

Our teacher had assigned *Wuthering Heights* to be read over the Easter holiday. I went home with my friend Sophie Stark, and we whined for two days over the injustice of it all. Finally her brother, Sidney, told us to shut up and *get on with it.* I did, still fuming, until I got to Cathy's ghost at the window. I have never felt such dread as I did then. Monsters or vampires have never scared me in books—but ghosts are a different matter.

Sophie and I did nothing the rest of our holiday but move from bed to hammock to armchair, reading *Jane Eyre, Agnes Grey, Shirley,* and *The Tenant of Wildfell Hall.*

What a family they were—but I chose to write about Anne Brontë because she was the least known of the sisters, and, I think, just as fine a writer as Charlotte. Lord knows how Anne managed to write any books at all, influenced by such a strain of religion as her Aunt Branwell possessed. Emily and Charlotte had the good sense to ignore their bleak aunt, but not poor Anne. Imagine preaching that God meant women to be Meek, Mild, and Gently Melancholic. So much less trouble around the house—pernicious old bat!

I hope you will write to me again.

Yours,
Juliet Ashton

From Eben Ramsey to Juliet

28th February, 1946

Dear Miss Ashton,

I am a Guernsey man and my name is Eben Ramsey. My fathers before me were tombstone-cutters and carvers—lambs a specialty. These are the things I like to do of an evening, but for my livelihood, I fish.

Mrs. Maugery said you would like to have letters about our reading during the Occupation. I was never going to talk—or think, if I could help it—about those days, but Mrs. Maugery said we could trust to your judgment in writing about the Society during the war. If Mrs. Maugery says you can be trusted, I believe it. Also, you had such kindness to send my friend Dawsey a book—and he all but unknown to you. So I am writing to you and hope it will be a help to your story.

Best to say we weren't a true literary society at first. Aside from Elizabeth, Mrs. Maugery, and perhaps Booker, most of us hadn't had much to do with books since our school years. We took them from Mrs. Maugery's shelves fearful we'd spoil the fine papers. I had no zest for such matters in those days. It was only by fixing my mind on the Commandant and jail that I could make myself to lift up the cover of the book and begin.

It was called *Selections from Shakespeare*. Later, I came to see that Mr. Dickens and Mr. Wordsworth were thinking of men like me when they wrote their words. But most of all, I believe that William Shakespeare was. Mind you, I cannot always make sense of what he says, but it will come.

It seems to me the less he said, the more beauty he made. Do you know what sentence of his I admire the most? It is "The bright day is done, and we are for the dark."

I wish I'd known those words on the day I watched those German troops land, plane-load after plane-load of them—and come off ships down in the harbor! All I could think of was *damn them, damn them,* over and over. If I could have thought the words "the bright day is done and we are for the dark," I'd have been consoled somehow and ready to go out and contend with circumstance—instead of my heart sinking to my shoes.

They came here on Sunday, 30th June, 1940, after bombing us two days before. They said they hadn't meant to bomb us; they mistook our tomato lorries on the pier for army trucks. How they came to think that strains the mind. They bombed us, killing some thirty men, women, and children—one among them was my cousin's boy. He had sheltered underneath his lorry when he first saw the planes dropping bombs, and it exploded and caught fire. They killed men in their lifeboats at sea. They strafed the Red Cross ambulances carrying our wounded. When no one shot back at them, they saw the British had left us undefended. They just flew in peaceably two days later and occupied us for five years.

At first, they were as nice as could be. They were that full of themselves for conquering a bit of England, and they were thick enough to think it would just be a hop and a skip till they landed in London. When they found out that wasn't to be, they turned back to their natural meanness.

They had rules for everything—do this, don't do that, but they kept changing their minds, trying to seem friendly, like they were poking a carrot in front of a donkey's nose. But we weren't donkeys. So they'd get harsh again.

For instance, they were always changing curfew—eight at night, or nine, or five in the evening if they felt really mean-minded. You couldn't visit your friends or even tend your stock.

We started out hopeful, sure they'd be gone in six months. But it stretched on and on. Food grew hard to come by, and soon there was no firewood left. Days were grey with hard work and evenings were black with boredom. Everyone was sickly from so little nourishment and bleak from wondering if it would ever end. We clung to books and to our friends; they reminded us that we had another part to us. Elizabeth used to say a poem. I don't remember all of it, but it began "Is it so small a thing to have enjoyed the sun, to have lived light in the spring, to have loved, to have thought, to have done, to have advanced true friends?" It isn't. I hope, wherever she is, she has that in her mind.

Late in 1944, it didn't matter what time the Germans set the curfew for. Most people went to bed around five o'clock anyway to keep warm. We were rationed to two candles a week and then only one. It was mighty tedious, lying up in bed with no light to read by.

After D-Day, the Germans couldn't send any supply ships from France because of the Allied bombers. So they were finally as hungry as we were—and killing dogs and cats to give them-selves something to eat. They would raid our gardens, rooting up potatoes—even eating the black, rotten ones. Four soldiers died eating handfuls of hemlock, thinking it was parsley.

The German officers said any soldier caught stealing food from our gardens would be shot. One poor soldier was caught stealing a potato. He was chased by his own people and climbed up a tree to hide. But they found him and shot him down out of the tree. Still, that did not stop them from stealing food. I am not pointing a finger at those practices, because some of us were doing the same. I figure hunger makes you desperate when you wake to it every morning.

My grandson, Eli, was evacuated to England when he was seven. He is home now—twelve years old, and tall—but I will never forgive the Germans for making me miss his growing-up years.

I must go milk my cow now, but I will write to you again if you like.

My wishes for your health,
Eben Ramsey

From Miss Adelaide Addison to Juliet

1st March, 1946

Dear Miss Ashton,

Forgive the presumption of a letter from a person unknown to you. But a clear duty is imposed upon me. I understand from Dawsey Adams that you are to write a long article for the

Times' literary supplement on the value of reading and you intend to feature the Guernsey Literary and Potato Peel Pie Society therein.

I laugh.

Perhaps you will reconsider when you learn that their founder, Elizabeth McKenna, is not even an Islander. Despite her fine airs, she is merely a jumped-up servant from the London home of Sir Ambrose Ivers, R.A. (Royal Academy). Surely, you know of him. He is a portrait painter of some note, though I've never understood why. His portrait of the Countess of Lambeth as Boadicea, lashing her horses, was unforgivable. In any event, Elizabeth McKenna was the daughter of his housekeeper, if you please.

While Elizabeth's mother dusted, Sir Ambrose let the child putter in his studio, and he kept her in school long after the normal leaving time for one of her station. Her mother died when Elizabeth was fourteen. Did Sir Ambrose send her to an institution to be properly trained for a suitable occupation? He did not. He kept her with him in his home in Chelsea. He proposed her for a scholarship to the Slade School of Fine Art.

Mind you, I do not say Sir Ambrose sired the girl—we know his proclivities too well to admit of that—but he doted upon her in a way that encouraged her besetting sin: lack of humility. The decay of standards is the cross of our times, and nowhere is this regrettable decline more apparent than in Elizabeth McKenna.

Sir Ambrose owned a home in Guernsey—on the cliff tops near La Bouvée. He, his housekeeper, and the girl summered here when she was a child. Elizabeth was a wild thing—roaming unkempt about the island, even on Sundays. No household chores, no gloves, no shoes, no stockings. Going out on fishing boats with rude men. Spying on decent people through her telescope. A disgrace.

When it became clear that the war was going to start in

earnest, Sir Ambrose sent Elizabeth to close up his house. Elizabeth bore the brunt of his haphazard ways in this case, for, in the midst of putting up the shutters, the German army landed on her doorstep. However, the choice to remain here was hers, and, as is proven by certain subsequent events (which I will not demean myself to mention), she is not the selfless heroine that some people seem to think.

Furthermore, the so-called Literary Society is a scandal. There are those of true culture and breeding here in Guernsey, and they will take no part in this charade (even if invited). There are only two respectable people in the Society—Eben Ramsey and Amelia Maugery. The other members: a rag-and-bone man, a lapsed Alienist who drinks, a stuttering swine-herd, a footman posing as a Lord, and Isola Pribby, a practicing witch, who, by her own admission to me, distills and sells potions. They collected a few others of their ilk along the way, and one can only imagine their "literary evenings."

You must not write about these people and their books—God knows what they saw fit to read!

Yours in Christian Consternation and Concern,
Adelaide Addison (Miss)

From Mark to Juliet

March 2, 1946

Dear Juliet,

I've just appropriated my music critic's opera tickets. Covent Garden at 8:00. Will you?

Yours,
Mark

From Juliet to Mark

Dear Mark,

Tonight?

Juliet

From Mark to Juliet

Yes!

M.

From Juliet to Mark

Wonderful! I feel sorry for your critic, though. Those tickets are scarce as hens' teeth.

Juliet

From Mark to Juliet

He'll make do with standing room. He can write about the uplifting effect of opera on the poor, etc., etc.

I'll pick you up at 7.

M.

From Juliet to Eben

3rd March, 1946

Mr. Eben Ramsey
Les Pommiers
Calais Lane
St. Martin's, Guernsey

Dear Mr. Ramsey,

It was so kind of you to write to me about your experiences during the Occupation. At the war's end, I, too, promised myself that I had done with talking about it. I had talked and lived war for six years, and I was longing to pay attention to something—anything—else. But that is like wishing I were someone else. The war is now the story of our lives, and there's no subtracting it.

I was glad to hear about your grandson Eli returning to you. Does he live with you or with his parents? Did you receive no news of him at all during the Occupation? Did all the Guernsey children return at once? What a celebration, if they did!

I don't mean to inundate you with questions, but I have a few more, if you're in an answering frame of mind. I know you were at the roast pig dinner that led to the founding of the Guernsey Literary and Potato Peel Pie Society—but how did Mrs. Maugery come to have the pig in the first place? How does one hide a pig?

Elizabeth McKenna was brave that night! She truly has grace under pressure, a quality that fills me with hopeless admiration. I know you and the other members of the Society must worry as the months pass without word, but you mustn't give up hope. Friends tell me that Europe is like a hive broken open, teeming with thousands upon thousands of displaced people, all trying to get home. A dear old friend of mine, who was shot down in Burma in 1943, reappeared in Australia last month—not in the best of shape, but alive and intending to remain so.

Thank you for your letter.

Yours sincerely,
Juliet Ashton

From Clovis Fossey to Juliet

4th March, 1946

Dear Miss,

At first, I did not want to go to any book meetings. My farm is a lot of work, and I did not want to spend my time reading about people who never was, doing things they never did.

Then in 1942 I started to court the Widow Hubert. When we'd go for a walk, she'd march a few steps ahead of me on the path and never let me take her arm. She let Ralph Murchey take her arm, so I knew I was failing in my suit.

Ralph, he's a bragger when he drinks, and he said to all in the tavern, "Women like poetry. A soft word in their ears and they melt—a grease spot on the grass." That's no way to talk about a lady, and I knew right then he didn't want the Widow Hubert for her own self, the way I did. He wanted only her grazing land for his cows. So I thought—If it's rhymes the Widow Hubert wants, I will find me some.

I went to see Mr. Fox in his bookshop and asked for some love poetry. He didn't have many books left by that time—folks bought them to burn, and when he finally caught on, he closed his shop for good—so he gave me some fellow named Catullus. He was a Roman. Do you know the kind of things he said in verse? I knew I couldn't say those words to a nice lady.

He did hanker after one woman, Lesbia, who spurned him after taking him into her bed. I don't wonder she did so—he did not like it when she petted her downy little sparrow. Jealous of a bitty bird, he was. He went home and took up his pen to write of his anguish at seeing her cuddle the little birdy to her bosom. He took it hard, and he never liked women after that and wrote mean poems about them.

He was a tight one too. Do you want to see a poem he wrote when a fallen woman charged him for her favors—poor lass. I will copy it out for you.

> *Is that battered strumpet in her senses, who asks me*
> *   for a thousand sesterces?*
> *That girl with the nasty nose?*
> *Ye kinsmen to whom the care of the girl belongs,*
> *Call together friends and physicians; the girl is insane.*
> *She thinks she is pretty.*

Those are love tokens? I told my friend Eben I never saw such spiteful stuff. He said to me I had just not read the right poets. He took me into his cottage and lent me a little book of his own. It was the poetry of Wilfred Owen. He was an officer in the First World War, and he knew what was what and called it by its right name. I was there, too, at Passchendaele, and I knew what he knew, but I could never put it into words for myself.

Well, after that, I thought there might be something to this poetry after all. I began to go to meetings, and I'm glad I did, else how would I have read the works of William Wordsworth—he would have stayed unknown to me. I learned many of his poems by heart.

Anyway, I did win the hand of the Widow Hubert—my Nancy. I got her to go for a walk along the cliffs one evening, and I said, "Lookie there, Nancy. The gentleness of Heaven broods o'er the sea—Listen, the mighty Being is awake." She let me kiss her. She is now my wife.

Yours truly,
Clovis Fossey

P.S. Mrs. Maugery lent me a book last week. It's called *The Oxford Book of Modern Verse, 1892–1935*. They let a man named Yeats make the choosings. They shouldn't have. Who is he—and what does he know about verse?

I hunted all through that book for poems by Wilfred Owen or Siegfried Sassoon. There weren't any—nary a one. And do you know why not? Because this Mr. Yeats said—he said, "I deliberately chose NOT to include any poems from World War I. I have a distaste for them. Passive suffering is not a theme for poetry."

Passive Suffering? Passive Suffering! I nearly seized up. What ailed the man? Lieutenant Owen, he wrote a line, "What passing-bells for these who die as cattle? Only the monstrous anger of the guns." What's passive about that, I'd like to know? That's exactly how they do die. I saw it with my own eyes, and I say to hell with Mr. Yeats.

Yours truly,
Clovis Fossey

From Eben to Juliet

10th March, 1946

Dear Miss Ashton,

Thank you for your letter and your kind questions about my grandson, Eli. He is the child of my daughter, Jane. Jane and her new-born baby died in hospital on the day that the Germans bombed us, 28th June, 1940. Eli's father was killed in North Africa in 1942, so I have Eli in my keeping now.

Eli left Guernsey on 20th June, along with the thousands of babies and schoolchildren who were evacuated to England. We knew the Germans were coming and Jane worried for his safety here. The doctor would not let Jane sail with them, the baby's birth being so close.

We did not have any news of the children for six months. Then I got a postcard from the Red Cross, saying Eli was well, but not where he was situated—we never knew what towns our children were in, though we prayed not in a big city. An even longer time passed before I could send him a card in return, but I was of two minds about that. I dreaded to tell him that his mother and the baby had died. I hated to think of my boy reading those cold words on the back of a postcard. But I had to do it. And then a second time, after I got word about his father.

Eli did not come back until the war was over—and they did send all the children home at once. That was a day! More wonderful even than when the British soldiers came to liberate Guernsey. Eli, he was the first boy down the gangway—he'd grown long legs in five years—and I don't think I could have left off hugging him to me, if Isola hadn't pushed me a bit so she could hug him herself.

I bless God that he was boarded with a farm family in Yorkshire. They were very good to him. Eli gave me a letter they had written for me—it was full of all the things I had missed seeing in his growing up. They told of his schooling, how he helped on the farm, how he tried to be steadfast when he got my postcards.

He fishes with me and helps me tend my cow and garden, but carving wood is what he likes best—Dawsey and I are teaching him how to do it. He fashioned a fine snake from a bit of broken fence rail last week, though it's my guess that the broken fence rail was really a rafter from Dawsey's barn. Dawsey just smiled when I asked him of it, but spare wood is hard to find on the island now, as we had to cut down most of the trees—banisters and furniture, too—for firewood when there was no more coal or paraffin left. Eli and I are planting trees on my land now, but it is going to take a long time for them to become grown—and we do all miss the leaves and shade.

I will tell you now about our roast pig. The Germans were fussy over farm animals. Pigs and cows were kept strict count of. Guernsey was to feed the German troops stationed here and in France. We ourselves could have the leavings, if there were any.

How the Germans did favor book-keeping. They kept track of every gallon we milked, weighed the cream, recorded every sack of flour. They left the chickens alone for a while. But when feed and scraps became so scarce, they ordered us to kill off the older chickens, so's the good layers could have enough feed to keep on laying eggs.

We fishermen had to give them the largest share of our catch. They would meet our boats in the harbor to portion out their share. Early in the Occupation, a good many Islanders escaped to England in fishing boats—some drowned, but some made it. So the Germans made a new rule, any person who had a family member in England would not be allowed in a fishing boat— they were afraid we'd try to escape. Since Eli was somewhere in England, I had to lend out my boat. I went to work in one of Mr. Privot's glass houses, and after a time, I got so I could tend the plants well. But my, how I did miss my boat and the sea.

The Germans were especially fractious over meat because they didn't want any to go to the Black Market instead of feeding their own soldiers. If your sow had a litter, the German Agricultural Officer would come to your farm, count the babies, give you a Birth Certificate for each one, and so mark his record book. If a pig died a natural death, you told the AO and out he'd come again, look at the dead body, and give you a Death Certificate.

They would make surprise visits to your farm, and your number of living pigs had better tally up with their number of living pigs. One pig less and you were fined, one time more and you could be arrested and sent to jail in St. Peter Port. If too many pigs went missing, the Germans figured you were selling on the Black Market, and you were sent to a labor camp in Germany. With the Germans you never knew which way they'd blow— they were a moody people.

In the beginning, though, it was easy to fool the Agricultural Officer and keep a secret live pig for your own use. Here is how Amelia came to have hers.

Will Thisbee had a sickly pig who died. The AO came out and wrote a Certificate saying the pig was truly dead and left Will alone to bury the poor animal. But Will didn't—he hied off through the wood with the little body and gave it to Amelia Maugery. Amelia hid her own healthy pig and called the AO saying, "Come quick, my pig has died."

The AO came out right away and, seeing the pig with its toes turned up, never knew it was the same pig he'd seen earlier that morning. He inscribed his Dead Animal Book with one more dead pig.

Amelia took the same carcass over to another friend, and he pulled the same trick the next day. We could do this till the pig turned rank. The Germans caught on finally and began to tattoo each pig and cow at birth, so there was no more dead animal switching.

But Amelia, with a live, hidden, fat, and healthy pig, needed only Dawsey to come kill it quietly. It had to be done quietly because there was a German battery by her farm, and it would not do for the soldiers to hear the pig's death squeal and come running.

Pigs have always been drawn to Dawsey—he could come in a barnyard, and they would rush up to him and have their backs scratched. They'd set up a shindy for anyone else—squealing, snuffling, and plunging about. But Dawsey, he could soothe them down and he knew just the right spot under their chins to slip his knife in quick. There wasn't time for the pigs to squeal; they'd just slide quietly onto the ground sheet.

I told Dawsey they only looked up once in surprise, but he said no, pigs were bright enough to know betrayal when they met it, and I wasn't to try to pretty matters up.

Amelia's pig made us a fine dinner—there were onions and potatoes to fill out the roast. We had almost forgotten how it felt to have full stomachs, but it came back to us. With Amelia's curtains closed against the sight of the German battery, and food and friends at the table, we could make believe that none of it had happened.

You are right to call Elizabeth brave. She is that, and always was. She came from London to Guernsey as a little girl with her mother and Sir Ambrose Ivers. She met my Jane her first summer here, when both were ten, and they were ever staunch to one another since then.

When Elizabeth came back in the spring of 1940 to close up Sir Ambrose's house, she stayed longer than was safe, because she wanted to stand by Jane. My girl had been feeling poorly since her husband, John, went to England to sign up—that was in December of 1939—and she had a difficult time holding on to the baby till her time could come. Dr. Martin ordered her to bed, so Elizabeth stayed on to keep company with Jane and play with Eli. Nothing Eli liked more than to play with Elizabeth.

They were a threat to the furniture, but it was cheerful to hear them laugh. I went over once to collect the two of them for supper and when I stopped in, there they were—sprawled on a pile of pillows at the foot of the staircase. They had polished Sir Ambrose's fine oak banister and come sailing down three floors!

It was Elizabeth who did the needful things to get Eli on the evacuation ship. We Islanders were given only one day's notice when the ships were coming from England to take the children away. Elizabeth worked like a whirl-a-gig, washing and sewing Eli's clothes and helping him to understand why he could not bring his pet rabbit with him. When we set out for the school-yard, Jane had to turn away so as not to show Eli a tearful face at parting, so Elizabeth took him by the hand and said it was good weather for a sea-voyage.

Even after that, Elizabeth wouldn't leave Guernsey when everyone else was trying to get away. "No," she said. "I'll wait for Jane's baby to come, and, when she's fattened up enough, then she and Jane and I will go to London. Then we'll find out where Eli is and go get him." For all her winning ways, Elizabeth was willful. She'd stick out that jaw of hers and you could see it wasn't any use to argue with her about leaving. Not even when we could all see the smoke coming from Cherbourg, where the French were burning up their fuel tanks, so the Germans couldn't have them. But, no matter, Elizabeth wouldn't go without Jane and the baby. I think Sir Ambrose had told her he and one of his yachting friends could sail right into St. Peter Port and take them off Guernsey before the Germans came. To speak the truth, I was glad she did not leave us. She was with me at the hospital when Jane and her new baby died. She sat by Jane, holding on hard to her hand.

After Jane died, Elizabeth and me, we stood in the hallway, numb-like and staring out the window. It was then we saw seven

German planes come in low over the harbor. They were just on one of the reconnaissance flights, we thought—but then they began dropping bombs—they tumbled down the sky like sticks. We didn't speak, but I know what we each were thinking—thank God Eli was safely away. Elizabeth stood by Jane and me in the bad time, and after. I was not able to stand by Elizabeth, so I thank God her daughter, Kit, is safe and with us, and I pray for Elizabeth to come home soon.

I was glad to hear of your friend who was found in Australia. I hope you will correspond with me and Dawsey again, as he enjoys to hear from you such as I do myself.

Yours sincerely,
Eben Ramsey

From Dawsey to Juliet

12th March, 1946

Dear Miss Ashton,

I am happy you liked the white lilacs.

I will tell you about Mrs. Dilwyn's soap. Around about the middle of the Occupation, soap became scarce; families were only allowed one tablet per person a month. It was made of some kind of French clay and lay like a dead thing in the washtub. It made no lather—you just had to scrub and hope it worked.

Being clean was hard work, and we had all got used to being more or less dirty, along with our clothes. We were allowed a tiny bit of soap powder for dishes and clothes, but it was a laughable amount; no bubbles there either. Some of the ladies felt it keenly, and Mrs. Dilwyn was one of those. Before the war, she had bought her dresses in Paris, and those fancy clothes went to ruins faster than the plain kind.

One day, Mr. Scope's pig died of milk fever. Since no one dared eat of it, Mr. Scope offered me the carcass. I remembered my mother making soap from fat, so I thought I could try it. It came out looking like frozen dish water and smelling worse. So I melted it all down and started again. Booker, who had come over to help, suggested paprika for color and cinnamon for scent. Amelia let us have some of each, and we put it in the mix.

When the soap had hardened enough, we cut it into circles with Amelia's biscuit cutter. I wrapped the soap in cheese cloth, Elizabeth tied bows of red yarn, and we gave them as presents to all the ladies at the Society's next meeting. For a week or two, anyway, we looked like respectable folks.

I am working several days a week now at the quarry, as well as at the port. Isola thought I looked tired and mixed up a balm for aching muscles—it's named Angel Fingers. Isola has a cough syrup called Devil's Suck and I pray I'll never need it.

Yesterday, Amelia and Kit came over for supper, and we took a blanket down to the beach afterward to watch the moon rise. Kit loves to do that, but she always falls asleep before it is fully risen, and I carry her home to Amelia's house. She is certain she'll be able to stay awake all night as soon as she's five.

Do you know very much about children? I don't, and although I am learning, I think I am a slow learner. It was much easier before Kit learned to talk, but it was not so much fun. I try to answer her questions, but I am usually behind-hand, and she has moved on to a new question before I can answer the first. Also, I don't know enough to please her. I don't know what a mongoose looks like.

I like having your letters, but I often feel I don't have any news worth the telling, so it is good to answer your rhetorical questions.

Yours,
Dawsey Adams

From Adelaide Addison to Juliet

12th March, 1946

Dear Miss Ashton,

I see you will not be advised by me. I came upon Isola Pribby, whilst in her market stall, scribbling a letter—in response to a letter from you! I tried to resume my errands calmly, but then I came upon Dawsey Adams posting a letter—to you! Who will be next, I ask? This is not to be borne, and I seize my pen to stop you.

I was not completely candid with you in my last letter. In the interests of delicacy, I drew a veil on the true nature of that group and their founder, Elizabeth McKenna. But now, I see that I must reveal all:

The Society members have colluded amongst themselves to raise the bastard child of Elizabeth McKenna and her German Paramour, Doctor/Captain Christian Hellman. Yes, a German soldier! I don't wonder at your shock.

Now, I am nothing if not just. I do not say that Elizabeth was what the ruder classes called a Jerry-bag, cavorting around Guernsey with *any* German soldier who could give her gifts. I never saw Elizabeth wearing silk stockings, clad in silk dresses (indeed, her clothing was as disreputable as ever), smelling of

Parisian scent, guzzling chocolates and wine, or SMOKING CIGARETTES, like other Island hussies.

But the truth is bad enough.

Herewith, the sorry facts: in April of 1942, the UNWED Elizabeth McKenna gave birth to a baby girl—in her own cottage. Eben Ramsey and Isola Pribby were present at the birthing—he to hold the mother's hand and she to keep the fire going. Amelia Maugery and Dawsey Adams (An unmarried man! For shame!) did the actual work of delivering the child, before Dr. Martin could arrive. The putative father? Absent! In fact, he had left the Island a short time before. "Ordered to duty on the continent"— SO THEY SAID. The case is perfectly clear—when the evidence of their illicit connection was irrefutable, Captain Hellman abandoned his mistress and left her to her just deserts.

I could have foretold this scandalous outcome. I saw Elizabeth with her lover on several occasions—walking together, deep in talk, gathering nettles for soup, or collecting firewood. And once, facing each other, I saw him put his hand on her face and follow her cheek-bone down with his thumb.

Though I had little hope of success, I knew it was my duty to warn her of the fate that awaited her. I told her she would be cast out of decent society, but she did not heed me. In fact, she laughed. I bore it. Then she told me to get out of her house.

I take no pride in my prescience. It would not be Christian.

Back to the baby—named Christina, called Kit. A scant year later, Elizabeth, as feckless as ever, committed a criminal act expressly forbidden by the German Occupying Force—she helped shelter and feed an escaped prisoner of the German Army. She was arrested and sentenced to prison on the continent.

Mrs. Maugery, at the time of Elizabeth's arrest, took the baby into her home. And since that night? The Literary Society has raised that child as its own—toting her around from house to house in turn. The principal work of the baby's maintenance was undertaken by Amelia Maugery, with other Society members taking her out—like a library book—for several weeks at a time.

They all dandled the baby, and now that the child can walk, she goes everywhere with one or another of them—holding hands or riding on their shoulders. Such are their standards! You must not glorify such people in the *Times*!

You'll not hear from me again—I have done my best. Let it be on your head.

Adelaide Addison

Cable from Sidney to Juliet

20th March, 1946

DEAR JULIET—TRIP HOME DELAYED. FELL OFF HORSE, BROKE LEG. PIERS NURSING. LOVE, SIDNEY

Cable from Juliet to Sidney

21st March, 1946

OH, GOD, WHICH LEG? AM SO SORRY.
LOVE, JULIET

Cable from Sidney to Juliet

22nd March, 1946

IT WAS THE OTHER ONE. DON'T WORRY—LITTLE
PAIN. PIERS EXCELLENT NURSE. LOVE, SIDNEY

Cable from Juliet to Sidney

22nd March, 1946

SO HAPPY IT WASN'T THE ONE I BROKE. CAN I
SEND ANYTHING TO HELP YOUR CONVALESCENCE?
BOOKS—RECORDINGS—POKER CHIPS—MY LIFE'S
BLOOD?

Cable from Sidney to Juliet

23rd March, 1946

NO BLOOD, NO BOOKS, NO POKER CHIPS. JUST
KEEP SENDING LONG LETTERS TO ENTERTAIN US.
LOVE, SIDNEY AND PIERS

From Juliet to Sophie

23rd March, 1946

Dear Sophie,

I only got a cable, so you know more than I do. But whatever the circumstances, it's absolutely ridiculous for you to consider flying off to Australia. What about Alexander? And Dominic? And your lambs? They'll pine away.

Stop and think for a moment, and you'll realize why you shouldn't fuss. First off, Piers will take excellent care of Sidney. Second, better Piers than us—remember what a vile patient Sidney was last time? We should be glad he's thousands of miles away. Third, Sidney has been stretched as tight as a bow-string for years. He needs a rest, and breaking his leg is probably the only way he'll allow himself to take one. Most important of all, Sophie: *he doesn't want us there.*

I'm perfectly certain Sidney would prefer me to write a new book than to appear at his bedside in Australia, so I intend to stay right here in my dreary flat and cast about for a subject. I do have a tiny infant of an idea, much too frail and defenseless to risk describing, even to you. In honor of Sidney's leg, I'm going to coddle it and feed it and see if I can make it grow.

Now, about Markham V. Reynolds (Junior). Your questions regarding that gentleman are very delicate, very subtle, very much like being smacked in the head with a mallet. Am I in love with him? What kind of a question is that? It's a tuba among the flutes, and I expect better of you. The first rule of snooping is to come at it sideways—when you began writing me dizzy letters about Alexander, I didn't ask if you were in love with him, I asked what his favorite animal was. And your answer told me everything I needed to know about him—how many men would admit that they loved ducks? (This brings up an important point: I don't know what Mark's favorite animal is. I doubt it's a duck.)

Would you care for a few suggestions? You could ask me who his favorite author is (Dos Passos! Hemingway!!). Or his favorite color (blue, not sure what shade, probably royal). Is he a good dancer? (Yes, far better than I, never steps on my toes, but doesn't talk or even hum while dancing. Doesn't hum at all so far as I know.) Does he have brothers or sisters? (Yes, two older sisters, one married to a sugar baron and the other widowed last year. Plus one younger brother, dismissed with a sneer as an ass.)

So—now that I've done all your work for you, perhaps you can answer your own ridiculous question, because I can't. I feel addled around Mark, which might be love but might not. It certainly isn't restful. I'm rather dreading this evening, for instance. Another dinner party, very brilliant, with men leaning across the table to make a point and women gesturing with their cigarette holders. Oh dear, I want to nuzzle into my sofa, but I have to get up and put on an evening dress. Love aside, Mark is a terrible strain on my wardrobe.

Now, darling, don't fret about Sidney. He'll be stalking around in no time.

Love,
Juliet

From Juliet to Dawsey

25th March, 1946

Dear Mr. Adams,

I have received a long letter (two, in fact!) from a Miss Adelaide Addison, warning me not to write about the Society in my article. If I do, she will wash her hands of me forever. I will try to bear that affliction with fortitude. She does work up quite a head of steam about "Jerry-bags," doesn't she?

I have also had a long letter from Clovis Fossey about poetry, and one from Isola Pribby about the Brontë sisters. Aside from delighting me—they gave me brand-new thoughts for my article. Between them, you, Mr. Ramsey, and Mrs. Maugery, Guernsey is virtually writing my article for me. Even Miss Adelaide Addison has done her bit—defying her will be such a pleasure.

I don't know as much about children as I would like to. I am godmother to a wonderful three-year-old boy named Dominic, the son of my friend Sophie. They live in Scotland, near Oban, and I don't get to see him often. I am always astonished, when I do, at his increasing personhood—no sooner had I gotten used to carrying about a warm lump of baby than he stopped being one and started scurrying around on his own. I missed six months, and lo and behold, he learned how to talk! Now he talks to himself, which I find terribly endearing since I do, too.

A mongoose, you may tell Kit, is a weaselly-looking creature with very sharp teeth and a bad temper. It is the only natural enemy of the cobra and is impervious to snake venom. Failing snakes, it snacks on scorpions. Perhaps you could get her one for a pet.

Yours,
Juliet Ashton

P.S. I had second thoughts about sending this letter—what if Adelaide Addison is a friend of yours? Then I decided no, she couldn't possibly be—so off it goes.

From John Booker to Juliet

27th March, 1946

Dear Miss Ashton,

Amelia Maugery has asked me to write to you, for I am a founding member of the Guernsey Literary and Potato Peel Pie Society—though I only read one book over and over. It was *The Letters of Seneca: Translated from Latin in One Volume, with Appendix.* Seneca and the Society, betwixt them, kept me from the direful life of a drunk.

From 1940 to 1944, I pretended to the German authorities that I was Lord Tobias Penn-Piers—my former employer, who had fled to England in a frenzy when Guernsey was bombed. I was his valet and I stayed. My true name is John Booker, and I was born and bred in London.

With the others, I was caught out after curfew on the night of the pig roast. I can't remember it with any clarity. I expect I was tipsy, because I usually was. I recall soldiers shouting and waving guns about and Dawsey holding me upright. Then came Elizabeth's voice. She was talking about books—I couldn't fathom why. After that, Dawsey was pulling me through a pasture at great speed, and then I fell into bed. That's all.

But you want to know about the influence of books on my life, and as I've said, there was only one. Seneca. Do you know who he was? He was a Roman philosopher who wrote letters to imaginary friends telling them how to behave for the rest of their lives. Maybe that sounds dull, but the letters aren't—they're witty. I think you learn more if you're laughing at the same time.

It seems to me that his words travel well—to all men in all times. I will give you a living sample: take the Luftwaffe and their hairdos. During the Blitz, the Luftwaffe took off from Guernsey and joined in with the big bombers on their way to London. They only flew at night so their days were their own, to spend in St. Peter Port as they liked. And how did they spend them? In beauty parlors: having their nails buffed, their faces massaged, their eyebrows shaped, their hair waved and coiffed. When I saw them in their hairnets, walking five abreast down the street, elbowing Islanders off the sidewalk, I thought of Seneca's words about the Praetorian Guard. He'd written—"who of these would not rather see Rome disordered than his hair."

I will tell you how I came to pretend to be my former employer. Lord Tobias wanted to sit out the war in a safe place, so he purchased La Fort manor on Guernsey. He had spent World War I in the Caribbean but had suffered greatly from prickly heat there.

In the spring of 1940, he moved to La Fort with most of his possessions, including Lady Tobias. Chausey, his London butler, had locked himself in the pantry and refused to come. So I, his valet, came in Chausey's stead, to supervise the placing of his furniture, the hanging of his draperies, the polishing of his silver, and *the stocking of his wine cellar*. It was there I bedded each bottle, gentle as a baby to its crib, in its little rack.

Just as the last picture was being hung on the wall, the German planes flew over and bombed St. Peter Port. Lord Tobias, panicking at all the racket, called the captain of his yacht and ordered him to "Redd up the ship!" We were to load the boat with his silver, his paintings, his bibelots, and, if enough room, Lady Tobias, and set sail at once for England.

I was the last one up the gangway, with Lord Tobias screaming, "Hurry up, man! Hurry up, the Huns are coming!"

My true destiny struck me in that moment, Miss Ashton. I still had the key to his Lordship's wine cellar. I thought of all those bottles of wine, champagne, brandy, cognac that didn't make it back to the yacht—and me all alone amongst them. I thought of no more bells, of no more livery, of no more Lord Tobias. In fact, of *no more being in service at all.*

I turned my back on him and quickly walked back down the gangway. I ran up the road to La Fort and watched the yacht sail away, Lord Tobias still screaming. Then I went inside, laid a fire, and stepped down to the wine cellar. I took down a bottle of claret and drew my first cork. I let the wine breathe. Then I returned to the library, sipped, and began to read *The Wine-Lover's Companion.*

I read about grapes, tended the garden, slept in silk pajamas—and drank wine. And so it went until September when Amelia Maugery and Elizabeth McKenna came to call on me. Elizabeth I knew slightly—she and I had chatted several times among the market stalls—but Mrs. Maugery was a stranger to me. Were they going to turn me in to the constable? I wondered.

No. They were there to warn me. The Commandant of

Guernsey had ordered all Jews to report to the Grange Lodge Hotel and register. According to the Commandant, our ID cards would merely be marked "Juden" and then we were free to go home. Elizabeth knew my mother was Jewish; I had mentioned it once. They had come to tell me that I must not, under any circumstances, go to the Grange Lodge Hotel.

But that wasn't all. Elizabeth had considered my predicament thoroughly (more thoroughly than I) and made a plan. Since all Islanders were to have identity cards anyway, why couldn't I declare myself to be Lord Tobias Penn-Piers himself? I could claim that, as a visitor, all my documents had been left behind in my London bank. Amelia was sure Mr. Dilwyn would be happy to back up my impersonation, and he was. He and Amelia went with me to the Commandant's Office, and we all swore that I was Lord Tobias Penn-Piers.

It was Elizabeth who came up with the finishing touch. The Germans were taking over all of Guernsey's grand houses for their officers to live in, and they would never ignore such a residence as La Fort—it was too good to miss. And when they came I must be ready for them as Lord Tobias Penn-Piers. I must look like a Lord at Leisure and act at my ease. I was terrified.

"Nonsense," said Elizabeth. "You have presence, Booker. You're tall, dark, handsome, and all valets know how to look down their noses."

She decided that she would quickly paint my portrait as a sixteenth-century Penn-Piers. So I posed as such in a velvet cloak and ruff, seated against a background of dark tapestries and dim shadows, fingering my dagger. I looked Noble, Aggrieved, and Treasonous.

It was a brilliant stroke, for, not two weeks later, a body of German officers (six in all) appeared in my library—without knocking. I received them there, sipping a Château Margaux '93 and bearing an uncanny resemblance to the portrait of my "ancestor" hanging above me over the mantel.

They bowed to me and were all politeness, which did not prevent them from taking over the house and moving me into the gatekeeper's cottage the very next day. Eben and Dawsey slipped over after curfew that night and helped me carry most of the wine down to the cottage, where we cleverly hid it behind the woodpile, down the well, up the chimney, under a haystack, and above the rafters. But even with all this toting of bottles, I still ran out of wine by early 1941. A sad day, but I had friends to help distract me—and then, then I found Seneca.

I came to love our book meetings—they helped to make the Occupation bearable. Some of their books sounded fine, but I stayed true to Seneca. I came to feel that he was talking to me—in his funny, biting way—but talking to me alone. His letters helped to keep me alive in what was to come later.

I still go to all our Society meetings. Everyone is sick of Seneca, and they are begging me to read someone else. But I'll not do it. I also act in plays that one of our repertory companies puts on—impersonating Lord Tobias gave me a taste for acting, and besides that, I am tall, loud, and can be heard in the last row.

I am happy the war is over, and I am John Booker again.

Yours truly,
John Booker

From Juliet to Sidney and Piers

31st March, 1946

Mr. Sidney Stark
Monreagle Hotel
Broadmeadows Avenue, 79
Melbourne
Victoria
Australia

Dear Sidney and Piers,

No life's blood—just sprained thumbs from copying out the enclosed letters from my new friends on Guernsey. I love their letters and could not bear the thought of sending the originals to the bottom of the earth where they would undoubtedly be eaten by wild dogs.

I knew the Germans occupied the Channel Islands, but I barely gave them a thought during the war. I have since scoured the *Times* for articles and anything I can cull from the London Library on the Occupation. I also need to find a good travel book on Guernsey—one with descriptions, not timetables and hotel recommendations—to give me the feel of the island.

Quite apart from my interest *in their interest* in reading, I have fallen in love with two men: Eben Ramsey and Dawsey Adams. Clovis Fossey and John Booker, I like. I want Amelia Maugery to adopt me; and me, I want to adopt Isola Pribby. I will leave you to discern my feelings for Adelaide Addison (Miss) by reading her letters. The truth is, I am living more in Guernsey than I am in London at the moment—I pretend work with one ear cocked for the sound of the post dropping in the box, and when I hear it, I scramble down the stairs, breathless for the next piece of the story. This must be how people felt when they gathered around the publisher's door to seize the latest installment of *David Copperfield* as it came off the printing press.

I know you're going to love the letters, too—but would you be interested in more? To me, these people and their war-time experiences are fascinating and moving. Do you agree? Do you think there could be a book here? Don't be polite—I want your opinion (both of your opinions) unvarnished. And you needn't worry—I'll continue to send you copies of the letters even if you don't want me to write a book about Guernsey. I am (mostly) above petty vengeance.

Since I have sacrificed my thumbs for your amusement, you should send me one of Piers's latest in return. So glad you are writing again, my dear.

My love to you both,
Juliet

From Dawsey to Juliet

2nd April, 1946

Dear Miss Ashton,

Having fun is the biggest sin in Adelaide Addison's bible (lack of humility following close on its heels), and I'm not surprised she wrote to you about Jerry-bags. Adelaide lives on her wrath.

There were few eligible men left in Guernsey and certainly no one exciting. Many of us were tired, scruffy, worried, ragged, shoeless, and dirty—we were defeated and looked it. We didn't have the energy, time, or money left over for fun. Guernsey men had no glamour—and the German soldiers did. They were, according to a friend of mine, tall, blond, handsome, and tanned—like gods. They gave lavish parties, were jolly and zestful company, possessed cars, had money, and could dance all night long.

But some of the girls who dated soldiers gave the cigarettes to their fathers and the bread to their families. They would come home from parties with rolls, pâtés, fruit, meat patties, and jellies stuffed in their purses, and their families would have a full meal the next day.

I don't think some Islanders ever credited the boredom of those years as a reason to befriend the enemy. Boredom is a powerful reason, and the prospect of fun is a powerful draw—especially when you are young.

There were many folks who would have no dealings with the Germans—if you said so much as good morning, you were abetting the enemy, according to their way of thinking. But circumstances were such that I could not abide by that with Captain Christian Hellman, a doctor in the Occupation forces and my good friend.

In late 1941 there wasn't any salt on the Island, and none was coming to us from France. Root vegetables and soups are listless without salt, so the Germans got the idea of using seawater to supply it. They carried it up from the bay and poured it into a big tanker set in the middle of St. Peter Port. Everyone was to walk to town, fill up their buckets, and carry them home again. Then we were to boil the water away and use the sludge in the bottom of the pan as salt. That plan failed—there wasn't enough wood to waste building up a fire hot enough to boil the pot of water dry. So we decided to cook all our vegetables in the seawater itself.

That worked well enough for flavor, but there were many older people who couldn't make the walk into town or haul heavy buckets home. No one had much strength left over for such chores. I have a slight limp from a badly set leg, and though it kept me from army service, it has never been bad enough to bother me. I was very hale, and so I began to deliver water around to some cottages.

I traded an extra spade and some twine for Mme. LePell's old baby pram, and Mr. Soames gave me two small oak wine casks, each with a spigot. I sawed off the barrel tops to make moveable lids and fitted them into my pram—so now I had transport. Several of the beaches weren't mined, and it was an easy thing to climb down the rocks, fill a cask with seawater, and tote it back up.

The November wind is bleak, and one day my hands were near numb after I climbed up from the bay with the first barrel of water. I was standing by my pram, trying to limber up my fingers, when Christian drove by. He stopped his car, backed up, and asked if I wanted any help. I said no, but he got out of his car anyway and helped me lift the barrel into my pram. Then, without a word, he went down the cliff with me, to help with the second barrel.

I hadn't noticed that he had a stiff shoulder and arm, but between those, my limp, and the loose scree, we slipped coming back up and fell against the hillside, losing our grip on the barrel. It tumbled down, splintered against the rocks, and soaked us. God knows why it struck us both as funny, but it did. We sagged against the cliff-side, unable to stop laughing. That was when Elia's essays slipped from my pocket, and Christian picked it up, sopping wet. "Ah, Charles Lamb," he said, and handed it to me. "He was not a man to mind a little damp." My surprise must have showed, because he added, "I read him often at home. I envy you your portable library."

We climbed back up to his car. He wanted to know if I could find another barrel. I said I could and explained my water-delivery route. He nodded, and I started out with my pram. But then I turned back and said, "You can borrow the book, if you'd like to." You would have thought I was giving him the moon. We exchanged names and shook hands.

After that, he would often help me carry up water, and then he'd offer a cigarette, and we'd stand in the road and talk—about Guernsey's beauty, about history, about books, about farming, but never about the present time—always things far away from the war. Once, as we were standing, Elizabeth rattled up the road on her bicycle. She had been on nursing duty all that day and probably most of the night before, and like the rest of us, her clothes were more patches than cloth. But Christian, he broke off in mid-sentence to watch her coming. Elizabeth drew up to us and stopped. Neither said a word, but I saw their faces, and I left as soon as I could. I hadn't realized they knew each other.

Christian had been a field surgeon, until his shoulder wound sent him from Eastern Europe to Guernsey. In early 1942, he was ordered to a hospital in Caen; his ship was sunk by Allied bombers and he was drowned. Dr. Lorenz, the head of the German Occupation Hospital, knew we were friends and came to tell me of his death. He meant for me to tell Elizabeth, so I did.

The way that Christian and I met may have been unusual, but our friendship was not. I'm sure many Islanders grew to be friends with some of the soldiers. But sometimes I think of Charles Lamb and marvel that a man born in 1775 enabled me to make two such friends as you and Christian.

Yours,
Dawsey Adams

From Juliet to Amelia

4th April, 1946

Dear Mrs. Maugery,

The sun is out for the first time in months, and if I stand on my chair and crane my neck, I can see it sparkling on the river. I'm averting my eyes from the mounds of rubble across the street and pretending London is beautiful again.

I've received a sad letter from Dawsey Adams, telling me about Christian Hellman, his kindness and his death. The war goes on and on, doesn't it? Such a good life—lost. And what a grievous blow it must have been to Elizabeth. I am thankful she had you, Mr. Ramsey, Isola, and Dawsey to help her when she had her baby.

Spring is nearly here. I'm almost warm in my puddle of sunshine. And down the street—I'm not averting my eyes now—a man in a patched jumper is painting the door to his house sky blue. Two small boys, who have been walloping one another with sticks, are begging him to let them help. He is giving them a tiny brush apiece. So—perhaps there is an end to war.

Yours,
Juliet Ashton

From Mark to Juliet

April 5, 1946

Dear Juliet—

You're being elusive and I don't like it. I don't want to see the play with someone else—I want to go with you. In fact, I don't give a damn about the play. I'm only trying to rout you out of that apartment. Dinner? Tea? Cocktails? Boating? Dancing? You choose, and I'll obey. I'm rarely so docile—don't throw away this opportunity to improve my character.

Yours,
Mark

From Juliet to Mark

Dear Mark,

Do you want to come to the British Museum with me? I've got an appointment in the Reading Room at two o'clock. We can look at the mummies afterward.

Juliet

From Mark to Juliet

To hell with the Reading Room and the mummies. Come have lunch with me.

                                        Mark

From Juliet to Mark

You consider that docile?

                                        Juliet

From Mark to Juliet

To hell with docile.

                                        M.

From Will Thisbee to Juliet

                                        7th April, 1946

Dear Miss Ashton,

I am a member of the Guernsey Literary and Potato Peel Pie Society. I am an antiquarian ironmonger, though it pleases some to call me a rag-and-bone man. I also invent labor-saving devices—my latest being an electric clothes-pin that wafts the laundry gently on the breeze, saving the laundress's wrists.

Did I find solace in reading? Yes, but not at first. I'd just go and eat my pie in quietude in a corner. Then Isola got ahold of me and said I had to read a book and talk about it like the others did. She gave me a book called *Past and Present* by Thomas Carlyle, and a tedious thing he was—he gave me shooting pains in my head—until I came to a bit on religion.

I was not a religious man, though not for want of trying. Off I'd go, like a bee among blossoms, from church to chapel to church again. But I was never able to get a grip on Faith— till Mr. Carlyle posed religion to me in a different way. He was walking among the ruins of the Abbey at Bury St. Edmunds, when a thought came to him, and he wrote it down thus:

> Does it ever give thee pause, that men used to have a soul— not by hearsay alone, or as a figure of speech; but as a truth that they knew, and acted upon! Verily it was another world then . . . but yet it is a pity we have lost the tidings of our souls . . . we shall have to go in search of them again, or worse in all ways shall befall us.

Isn't that something—to know your own soul by hearsay, instead of its own tidings? Why should I let a preacher tell me if I had one or not? If I could believe I had a soul, all by myself, then I could listen to its tidings all by myself.

I gave my talk on Mr. Carlyle to the Society, and it stirred up a great argument about the soul. Yes? No? Maybe? Dr. Stubbins yelled the loudest, and soon everyone stopped arguing and listened to him.

Thompson Stubbins is a man of long, deep thoughts. He was a psychiatrist in London until he ran amok at the annual dinner of the Friends of Sigmund Freud Society in 1934. He told me the whole tale once. The Friends were great talkers and their speeches went on for hours—while the plates stayed bare. Finally they served up, and silence fell upon the hall as the psychiatrists bolted their chops. Thompson saw his chance: he beat his spoon upon his glass and shouted from the floor to be heard.

"Did any of you ever think that along about the time the notion of a SOUL gave out, Freud popped up with the EGO to take its place? The timing of the man! Did he not pause to reflect? Irresponsible old coot! It is my belief that men must spout this twaddle about egos, because they fear they have no soul! Think upon it!"

Thompson was barred from their doors forever, and he moved to Guernsey to grow vegetables. Sometimes he rides with me in my cart and we talk about Man and God and all the In-between. I would have missed all this if I had not belonged to the Guernsey Literary and Potato Peel Pie Society.

Tell me, Miss Ashton, what are your views on the matter? Isola thinks you should come to visit Guernsey, and if you do, you could ride in my cart with us. I'd bring a cushion.

Best wishes for your continued health and happiness.

Will Thisbee

From Mrs. Clara Saussey to Juliet

8th April, 1946

Dear Miss Ashton,

I've heard about you. I once belonged to that Literary Society, though I'll wager none of them ever told you about me. I didn't read from any book by a dead writer, no. I read from a work I wrote myself—my book of cookery recipes. I venture to say my book caused more tears and sorrow than anything Charles Dickens ever wrote.

I chose to read about the correct way to roast a suckling pig. Butter its little body, I said. Let the juices run down and cause the fire to sizzle. The way I read it, you could smell the pig roasting, hear its flesh crackle. I spoke of my five-layer cakes—using a dozen eggs—my spun-sugar sweets, chocolate-rum balls, sponge cakes with pots of cream. Cakes made with good white flour—not that cracked grain and bird-seed stuff we were using at the time.

Well, miss, my audience couldn't stand it. They was pushed over the edge, hearing of my tasty recipes. Isola Pribby, that never had a manner to call her own, she cried out I was tormenting her and she was going to hex my saucepans. Will Thisbee said I would burn like my cherries jubilee. Then Thompson Stubbins swore at me, and it took both Dawsey and Eben to get me away safely.

Eben called the next day to apologize for the Society's bad manners. He asked me to remember that most of them had come to the meeting directly from a supper of turnip soup (with nary a bone in it to give pith), or parboiled potatoes scorched on a hot iron—there being no cooking fat to fry them up in. He asked me to be tolerant and forgive them.

Well, I'll not do it—they called me bad names. There wasn't a one of them who truly loved literature. Because that's what my cookery book was—sheer poetry in a pan. I believe they was made so bored, what with the curfew and other nasty Nazi laws, they only wanted an excuse to get out of an evening, and reading is what they chose.

I want the truth of them told in your story. They'd never have touched a book, but for the OCCUPATION. I stand by what I say, and you can quote me direct.

My name is—Clara S-A-U-S-S-E-Y. Three esses, in all.

Clara Saussey (Mrs.)

From Amelia to Juliet

10th April, 1946

My dear Juliet,

I, too, have felt that the war goes on and on. When my son, Ian, died at El Alamein—side by side with Eli's father, John—visitors offering their condolences, thinking to comfort me, said "Life goes on." What nonsense, I thought, of course it doesn't. It's death that goes on; Ian is dead now and will be dead tomorrow and next year and forever. There's no end to that. But perhaps there will be an end to the sorrow of it. Sorrow has rushed over the world like the waters of the Deluge, and it will take time to recede. But already, there are small islands of—hope? Happiness? Something like them, at any rate. I like the picture of you standing upon your chair to catch a glimpse of the sun, averting your eyes from the mounds of rubble.

My greatest pleasure has been in resuming my evening walks along the cliff tops. The Channel is no longer framed in rolls of barbed wire, the view is unbroken by huge *VERBOTEN* signs. The mines are gone from our beaches, and I can walk when, where, and for as long as I like. If I stand on the cliffs and turn out to face the sea, I don't see the ugly cement bunkers behind me, or the land naked without its trees. Not even the Germans could ruin the sea.

This summer, gorse will begin to grow around the fortifications, and by next year, perhaps vines will creep over them. I hope they are soon covered. For all I can look away, I will never be able to forget how they were made.

The Todt workers built them. I know you have heard of Germany's slave workers in camps on the continent, but did you know that Hitler sent over sixteen thousand of them here, to the Channel Islands?

Hitler was fanatic about fortifying these islands—England was never to get them back! His generals called it Island Madness. He ordered large-gun emplacements, anti-tank walls on the beaches, hundreds of bunkers and batteries, arms and bomb depots, miles and miles of underground tunnels, a huge underground hospital, and a railroad to cross the island to carry materials. The coastal fortifications were absurd—the Channel Isles were better fortified than the Atlantic Wall built against an Allied invasion. The installations jutted out over every bay. The Third Reich was to last one thousand years—in concrete.

So, of course, he needed thousands of slave workers; men and boys were conscripted, some were arrested, and some were just picked up off the streets—out of cinema queues, from cafés, from the country lanes and fields of any German

Occupied territory. There were even political prisoners from the Spanish Civil War. The Russian prisoners of war were treated the worst, perhaps because of their victory over the Germans on the Russian Front.

Most of these slave workers came to the islands in 1942. They were kept in open sheds, dug-out tunnels, in pens, some of them in houses. They were marched all over the island to their work sites: thin to the bone, dressed in ragged trousers with bare skin showing through, often no coats to protect them from the cold. No shoes or boots, their feet tied up in bloody rags. Young lads, fifteen and sixteen, were so weary and starved they could scarcely put one foot in front of another.

Guernsey Islanders would stand by their gates to offer them what little food or warm clothing they could spare. Sometimes the Germans guarding the Todt work columns would let the men break ranks to accept these gifts—other times they would beat them to the ground with rifle butts.

Thousands of those men and boys died here, and I have recently learned that their inhuman treatment was the intended policy of Himmler. He called his plan Death by Exhaustion, and he implemented it. Work them hard, don't waste valuable food-stuffs on them, and let them die. They could, and would, always be replaced by new slave workers from Europe's Occupied countries.

Some of the Todt workers were kept down on the Common, behind a wire fence—they were white as ghosts, covered in cement dust; there was only one water standpipe for over a hundred men to wash themselves.

Children sometimes went down to the green to see the Todt workers behind the wire fences. They would poke walnuts and apples, sometimes potatoes, through the wire for them. There was one Todt worker who did not take the food—he came to see the children. He would put his arm through the wire just to hold their faces in his hands, to touch their hair.

The Germans did give the Todt workers one-half day a week off—on Sunday. That was the day when the German Sanitary Engineers emptied all the sewage into the ocean—by way of a big pipe. Fish would swarm for the offal, and the Todt workers would stand in that feces and filth up to their chests—trying to catch the fish in their hands, to eat them.

No flowers or vines can cover over such memories as these, can they?

I have told you the most hateful story of the war. Juliet, Isola thinks you should come and write a book about the German Occupation. She told me she did not have the skill to write such a book herself, but, as dear as Isola is to me, I am terrified she might buy a notebook and begin anyway.

Yours ever,
Amelia Maugery

From Juliet to Dawsey

11th April, 1946

Dear Mr. Adams,

After promising never to write to me again, Adelaide Addison has sent me another letter. It is devoted to all the people and practices she deplores, and you are one of them, along with Charles Lamb.

It seems she called on you to deliver the April issue of the parish magazine—and you were nowhere to be found. Not milking your cow, not hoeing your garden, not washing your house, not doing anything a good farmer should be doing. So she entered your barnyard, and lo—what did she see? You, lying up in your hay-loft, reading a book by Charles Lamb! You were "so enraptured with that drunkard," you failed to notice her presence.

What a blight that woman is. Do you happen to know why? I lean toward a malignant fairy at her christening.

In any event, the picture of you lolling in the hay, reading Charles Lamb, pleased me very much. It made me recall my own childhood in Suffolk. My father was a farmer there, and I helped out at the farm; though admittedly all I did was jump out of our car, open the gate, close it and jump back in, gather eggs, weed our garden, and flail at the hay when I was in the mood.

I remember lying in our hay-loft reading *The Secret Garden* with a cowbell beside me. I'd read for an hour and then ring the bell for a glass of lemonade to be brought to me. Mrs. Hutchins, the cook, finally grew weary of this arrangement and told my mother, and that was the end of my cowbell, but not my reading in the hay.

Mr. Hastings found the E. V. Lucas biography of Charles Lamb. He decided not to quote a price to you, but just to send it along to you at once. He said, "A lover of Charles Lamb ought not to have to wait."

Yours ever,
Juliet Ashton

11th April, 1946

Dear Sidney,

I'm as tender-hearted as the next girl, but dammit, if you don't get back here soon, Charlie Stephens is going to have a nervous breakdown. He's not cut out for work; he's cut out for handing over large wads of cash and letting you do the work. He actually turned up at the office *before ten o'clock* yesterday, but the effort annihilated him. He was deathly white by eleven, and had a whiskey at eleven-thirty. At noon, one of the innocent young things handed him a jacket to approve—his eyes bulged with terror and he began that disgusting trick with his ear—he's going to pull it right off one day. He went home at one, and I haven't seen him yet today (it's four in the afternoon).

In other depressing developments, Harriet Munfries has gone completely berserk; she wants to "color-coordinate" the entire children's list. Pink and red. I kid you not. The boy in the mail-room (I don't bother learning their names anymore) got drunk and threw away all letters addressed to anyone whose name started with an S. Don't ask why. Miss Tilley was so impossibly rude to Kendrick that he tried to hit her with her telephone. I can't say I blame him, but telephones are hard to come by and we can't afford to lose one. You must sack her the minute you come home.

If you need any further inducement to buy an aeroplane ticket, I can also tell you that I saw Juliet and Mark Reynolds looking very cozy at Café de Paris the other night. Their table was behind the velvet cordon, but from my seat in the slums, I could spy all the telltale signs of romance—he murmuring little nothings in her ear, her hand lingering in his beside the cocktail glasses, his touching her shoulder to point out an acquaintance. I considered it my duty (as your devoted employee) to break it up, so I elbowed my way past the cordon to say hello to Juliet. She seemed delighted and invited me to join them, but it was apparent from Mark's smile that he didn't want company, so I retreated. He's not a man to cross, that one, with his thin smile, no matter how beautiful his ties are, and it would break my mum's heart if my lifeless body was found bobbing in the Thames.

In other words, get a wheelchair, get a crutch, get a donkey to tote you, but come home *now.*

Yours,
Susan

From Juliet to Sidney and Piers

12th April, 1946

Dear Sidney and Piers,

I've been ransacking the libraries of London for background on Guernsey. I even got a ticket to the Reading Room, which shows my devotion to duty—as you know, I'm petrified of the place.

I've found out quite a lot. Do you recall a wretched, goofy series of books in the 1920s called *A-Tramp in Skye* . . . or *A-Tramp in Lindisfarne* . . . or *in Sheepholm*—or whatever port the author happened to sail his yacht into? Well, in 1930 he sailed into St. Peter Port, Guernsey, and wrote a book about it (with day trips to Sark, Herm, Alderney, and Jersey, where he was mauled by a duck and had to return home).

Tramp's real name was Cee Cee Meredith. He was an idiot who thought he was a poet, and he was rich enough to sail any-where, then write about it, then have it privately printed, and then give a copy to any friend who would take it. Cee Cee didn't trouble himself with dull fact: he preferred to scamper off to the nearest moor, beach, or flowery field, and go into transports with his Muse. But bless him anyhow; his book *A-Tramp in Guernsey* was just what I needed to get the feel of the island.

Cee Cee went ashore at St. Peter Port, leaving his mother, Dorothea, to bob about the adjacent waters, retching in the wheel-house. In Guernsey, Cee Cee wrote poems to the freesias and the daffodils. Also to the tomatoes. He was agog with admi-ration for the Guernsey cows and the blooded bulls, and he com-posed a little song in honor of their cowbells ("tinkle, tinkle, such a merry sound . . ."). Directly beneath the cows, in Cee Cee's estimation, were "the simple folk of the country parishes, who still speak the Norman patois and believe in fairies and witches." Cee Cee entered into the spirit of the thing and saw a fairy in the gloaming.

After carrying on about the cottages and hedgerows and the shops, Cee Cee at last reached the sea, or, as he has it, "*The SEA! It* is everywhere! The waters: azure, emerald, silver-laced, when they are not as hard and dark as a bag of nails.*"*

Thank God *Tramp* had a co-author, Dorothea, who was made of sterner stuff and loathed Guernsey and everything about it. She was in charge of delivering the history of the island, and she was not one to gild the lily:

. . . As to Guernsey's history—well, the least said, soonest mended. The Islands once belonged to the Duchy of Normandy, but when William, Duke of Normandy, became William the Conqueror, he

took the Channel Islands along with him in his back pocket and he gave them to England—with special privileges. These privileges were later increased by King John, and added to yet again by Edward III. WHY? What did they do to deserve the preference? Nary a thing! Later, when that weakling Henry VI managed to lose most of France back to the French, the Channel Islands elected to stay a Crown Possession of England, as who would not?

The Channel Islands freely owe their allegiance and love to the English Crown, but heed this, dear reader—*THE CROWN CANNOT MAKE THEM DO ANYTHING THEY DO NOT WANT TO DO!*

. . . Guernsey's ruling body, such as it is, is named the States of Deliberation but called the States for short. The real head of everything is the President of the States, who is elected by the *STATES*, and called the Bailiff. In fact, everyone is elected, not appointed by the King. Pray, what is a monarch for, if *NOT TO APPOINT PEOPLE TO THINGS?*

. . . The Crown's only representative to this unholy mélange is the Lieutenant Governor. While he is welcome to attend the meetings of the States, and he may talk and advise all he wants, he does *NOT HAVE A VOTE.* At least he is allowed to live in Government House, the only mansion of any note on Guernsey—if you don't count Sausmarez Manor, which I don't.

. . . The Crown cannot impose Taxes on the Islands—or Conscription. Honesty forces me to admit the Islanders don't need Conscription to make them go to war for dear, dear England. They volunteered and made very respectable, even heroic, soldiers and sailors against Napoleon and the Kaiser. But be advised—these selfless acts do not make amends for the fact *THAT THE CHANNEL ISLANDS PAY NO INCOME TAX TO ENGLAND. NOT ONE SHILLING. IT MAKES ONE WANT TO SPIT!*

Those are her kindest words—I will spare you the rest, but you get her general drift.

One, or better yet, both of you write to me. I want to hear how both the patient and the nurse are doing. What does your doctor say about your leg, Sidney—I swear you've had time to grow a new one.

XXXXXX,
Juliet

From Dawsey to Juliet

15th April, 1946

Dear Miss Ashton,

I don't know what ails Adelaide Addison. Isola says she is a blight because she likes being a blight—it gives her a sense of destiny. Adelaide did me one good turn, though, didn't she? She told you, better than I could, how much I was enjoying Charles Lamb.

The biography came. I've read fast—too impatient not to. But I'll go back and start over again—reading more slowly this time, so I can take everything in. I did like what Mr. Lucas said about him—"he could make any homely and familiar thing into something fresh and beautiful." Lamb's writings make me feel more at home in his London than I do here and now in St. Peter Port.

But what I cannot imagine is Charles, coming home from work and finding his mother stabbed to death, his father bleeding, and his sister Mary standing over both with a bloody knife. How did he make himself go into the room and take the knife away from her? After the police had taken her off to the madhouse, how did he persuade the Judge in Court to release her to his care and his care alone? He was only twenty-one years old then—how did he talk them into it?

He promised to take care of Mary for the rest of her life—and, once he put his foot on that road, he never stepped off it. It is sad he had to quit writing poetry, which he loved, and instead write criticism and essays, which he did not honor much, to make money.

I think of all his life, working as a clerk at the East India Company, so he could save money for the day, and it always came, when Mary would grow mad again, and he would have to place her in a private home.

And even then he did seem to miss her—they were such friends. Picture them: he had to watch her like a hawk for the awful symptoms, and she herself could tell when the madness was coming on and could do nothing to stop its coming—that must have been worst of all. I imagine him sitting there, watching her on the sly, and her sitting there, watching him watching her. How they must have hated the way the other one was forced to live.

But doesn't it seem to you that when Mary was sane there was no one saner—or better company? Charles certainly thought so, and so did all their friends: Wordsworth, Hazlitt, Leigh Hunt, and, above all, Coleridge. On the day Coleridge died they found a note he had scribbled in the book he was reading. It said, "Charles and Mary Lamb, dear to my heart, yes, as it were, my heart."

Perhaps I've written over-long about him, but I wanted you

and Mr. Hastings to know how much your books have given me to think about and the pleasure I find in them.

I like the story from your childhood—the bell and the hay. I can see it in my mind. Did you like living on a farm—do you ever miss it? You are never really away from the countryside in Guernsey, not even in St. Peter Port, so I cannot imagine the difference living in a big city like London would make.

Kit has taken against mongooses, now she knows they eat snakes. She is hoping to find a boa constrictor under a rock. Isola stopped by this evening and said to tell you hello—she will write to you as soon as she gets her crops in—rosemary, dill, thyme, and henbane.

Yours,
Dawsey Adams

From Juliet to Dawsey

18th April, 1946

Dear Dawsey,

I am so glad you want to talk about Charles Lamb on paper. I have always thought Mary's sorrow made Charles into a great writer—even if he had to give up poetry and clerk for the East India Company because of it. He had a genius for sympathy that not one of his great friends could touch. When Wordsworth chided him for not caring enough about nature, Charles wrote, "I have no passion for groves and valleys. The rooms where I was born, the furniture which has been before my eyes all my life, a book case which has followed me about like a faithful dog wherever I have moved—old chairs, old streets, squares where I have sunned myself, my old school—have I not enough, without your Mountains? I do not envy you. I should pity you, did I not know, that the Mind will make friends of any thing." A Mind that can make friends of any thing—I thought of that often during the war.

By chance, I came upon another story about him today. He often drank too much, far too much, but he was not a sullen drunk. Once, his host's butler had to carry him home, slung over his shoulder in a fireman's hold. The next day Charles wrote his host such a hilarious note of apology, the man bequeathed it to his son in his will. I hope Charles wrote the butler too.

Have you ever noticed that when your mind is awakened or drawn to someone new, that person's name suddenly pops up everywhere you go? My friend Sophie calls it coincidence, and Mr. Simpless, my parson friend, calls it Grace. He thinks that if one cares deeply about someone or something new one throws a kind of energy out into the world, and "fruitfulness" is drawn in.

> Yours ever,
> Juliet

From Isola to Juliet

18th April, 1946

Dear Juliet,

Now that we are corresponding friends, I want to ask you some questions—they are highly personal. Dawsey said it would not be polite, but I say that's a difference twixt men and women, not polite and rude. Dawsey's never asked me a personal question in fifteen years. I'd take it kindly if he would, but Dawsey's got quiet ways. I don't expect to change him, nor myself either. I see it that you cared to know about us, so I guess you would like us to know about you—only you just didn't happen to think of it first.

First of all, I saw a picture of you on the dust jacket of your book about Anne Brontë, so I know you are below forty years of age—how far below? Was the sun in your eyes, or does it happen that you have a squint? Is it permanent? It must have been a windy day because your curls are blowing all about. I couldn't quite make out the color of your hair, though I can tell it isn't blonde—for which I am glad. I don't like blondes very much.

Do you live by the river? I hope so, because people who live near running water are much nicer than people who don't. I'd be mean as a scorpion if I lived inland. Do you have a serious suitor? I do not.

Is your flat cozy or grand? Be fulsome, as I want to be able to picture it in my mind. Do you think you would like to visit us on Guernsey? Do you have a pet? What kind?

Your friend,
Isola

From Juliet to Isola

20th April, 1946

Dear Isola,

I am glad you want to know more about me and am only sorry I didn't think of it myself, and sooner.

Present-day first: I am thirty-three years old, and you were right—the sun was in my eyes. In a good mood, I call my hair Chestnut with Gold Glints. In a bad mood, I call it mousy brown. It wasn't a windy day; my hair always looks that way. Naturally curly hair is a curse, and don't ever let anyone tell you different. My eyes are hazel. While I am slender, I am not tall enough to suit me.

I don't live by the Thames anymore and that is what I miss the most about my old home—I loved the sight and sound of the river at all hours. I live now in a borrowed flat in Glebe Place. It is small and furnished within an inch of its life, and the flat owner won't be back from the United States until November, so I have the run of his house until then. I wish I had a dog, but the building management does not allow pets! The Kensington Gardens aren't so very far, so if I begin to feel cooped up I can walk to the park, rent a deck chair for a shilling, loll about under the trees, watch the passers-by and children play, and I am soothed—somewhat.

Eighty-one Oakley Street was demolished by a random V-1 just over a year ago. Most of the damage was to the row of houses behind mine, but three floors of Number 81 were sheared off, and my flat is now a pile of rubble. I hope Mr. Grant, the owner, will rebuild—for I want my flat, or a facsimile of it, back again, just as it was—with Cheyne Walk and the river outside my windows.

Luckily, I was away in Bury when the V-1 hit. Sidney Stark, my friend and now publisher, met my train that evening and took me home, and we viewed the huge mountain of rubble and what was left of the building.

With part of the wall gone, I could see my shredded curtains waving in the breeze and my desk, three-legged and slumped on the slanting floor that was left. My books were a muddy, sopping pile and although I could see my mother's portrait on the wall—half gouged out and sooty—there was no safe way to recover it. The only intact possession left was my large crystal paper-weight—with *Carpe Diem* carved across its top. It had belonged to my father—and there it sat, whole and unchipped, atop a pile of broken bricks and splintered wood. I could not do without it so Sidney clambered over the rubble and retrieved it for me.

I was a fairly nice child until my parents died when I was twelve. I left our farm in Suffolk and went to live with my great-uncle in London. I was a furious, bitter, morose little girl. I ran away twice, causing my uncle no end of trouble—and at the time, I was very glad to do so. I am ashamed now when I think about how I treated him. He died when I was seventeen so I was never able to apologize.

When I was thirteen, my uncle decided I should go away to boarding school. I went, mulish as usual, and met the Head-mistress, who marched me into the Dining Room. She led me to a table with four other girls. I sat; arms crossed, hands tucked under my armpits, glaring like a molting eagle, looking around for someone to hate. I hit upon Sophie Stark, Sidney's younger sister.

Perfect, she had golden curls, big blue eyes, and a sweet, sweet smile. She made an effort to talk with me. I didn't answer until she said, "I hope you will be happy here." I told her I wouldn't be staying long enough to find out. "As soon as I find out about the trains, I am gone!" said I.

That night I climbed out onto the dormitory roof, meaning to sit there and have a good brood in the dark. In a few minutes, Sophie crawled out—with a railway timetable for me.

Needless to say, I never ran away. I stayed—with Sophie as my new friend. Her mother would often invite me to their house for holidays, which was where I met Sidney. He was ten years older than me and was, of course, a god. He later changed into a bossy older brother, and later still, one of my dearest friends.

Sophie and I left school and—wanting no more of academic life, but LIFE instead—we went to London and shared rooms Sidney had found for us. We worked together for a while in a bookshop, and I wrote—and threw away—stories at night.

Then the *Daily Mirror* sponsored an essay contest—five hundred words on "What Women Fear Most." I knew what the *Mirror* was finagling for, but I'm far more afraid of chickens than I am of men, so I wrote about that. The judges, thrilled at not having to read another word about sex, awarded me first prize. Five pounds and I was, at last, in print. The *Daily Mirror* received so many fan letters, they commissioned me to write an article, then another one. I soon began to write feature stories for other newspapers and magazines. Then the war broke out, and I was invited to write a semi-weekly column for the *Spectator,* called "Izzy Bickerstaff Goes to War." Sophie met and fell in love with an airman, Alexander Strachan. They married and Sophie moved to his family's farm in Scotland. I am godmother to their son, Dominic, and though I haven't taught him any hymns, we did pull the hinges off his cellar door last time I saw him—it was a Pictish ambush.

I suppose I do have a suitor, but I'm not really used to him yet. He's terribly charming and he plies me with delicious meals, but I sometimes think I prefer suitors in books rather than right in front of me. How awful, backward, cowardly, and mentally warped that will be if it turns out to be true.

Sidney published a book of my Izzy Bickerstaff columns and I went on a book tour. And then—I began writing letters to strangers in Guernsey, now friends, whom I would indeed like to come and see.

Yours ever,
Juliet

From Eli to Juliet

21st April, 1946

Dear Miss Ashton,

Thank you for the blocks of wood. They are beautiful. I could not believe what I saw when I opened your box—all those sizes and shades, from pale to dark.

How did you happen to find the different kinds and shapes of wood? You must have gone to so many places to find them all. I'll bet you did and I don't know how to thank you for that. They came at just the right time too. Kit's favorite animal was a snake she saw in a book, and he was easy to carve, being so long and thin. Now she's gone on ferrets. She says she won't ever touch my whittling knife again if I'll carve her a ferret. I don't think it will be too hard to make one, for they are pointy, too. Because of your gift, I have wood to practice with.

Is there an animal you would like to have? I want to carve a present for you, but I'd like it to be something you'd favor. Would you like a mouse? I am good with mice.

Yours truly,
Eli

From Eben to Juliet

22nd April, 1946

Dear Miss Ashton,

Your box for Eli came Friday—what a kindness of you. He sits and studies the blocks of wood—as if he sees something hidden inside them, and he can make it come out with his knife.

You asked if all the Guernsey children were evacuated to England. No—some stayed, and when I missed Eli, I looked at the little ones around me and was glad he had gone. The children here had a bad time, for there was no food to grow on. I remember picking up Bill LePell's boy—he was twelve but weighed no more than a child of seven.

It was a terrible thing to decide—send your kiddies away to live among strangers, or let them stay with you? Maybe the Germans wouldn't come, but if they did—how would they behave to us? But, come to that, what if they invaded England, too—how would the children manage without their own families beside them?

Do you know the state we were in when the Germans came? Shock is what I'd call it. The truth is, we didn't think they'd want us. It was England they were after, and we were of no use to them. We thought we'd be in the audience like, not up on the stage itself.

Then in the spring of 1940 Hitler got himself going through Europe like a hot knife through butter. Every place fell to him. It was so fast—windows all over Guernsey shook and rattled from the explosions in France, and once the coast of France was gone, it was plain as day that England could not use up her men and ships to defend us. They needed to save them for when their own invasion began in earnest. So we were left to ourselves.

In the middle of June, when it became pretty certain we were in for it, the States got on the telephone to London and asked if they would send ships for our children and take them to England. They could not fly, for fear of being shot down by the Luftwaffe. London said yes, but the children had to be ready at once. The ships would have to hurry here and back again while there was still time. It was such a desperate time for folks and there was such a feel of Hurry, Hurry.

Jane had no more strength than a cat then, but she knew her mind. She wanted Eli to go. Other ladies were in a dither—go or stay?—and they were wild to talk it over, but Jane told Elizabeth to keep them away. "I don't want to hear them fuss," she said. "It's bad for the baby." Jane had an idea that babies knew everything that happened around them, even before they were born.

The time for dithering was soon over. Families had one day to decide, and five years to abide with it. School-age children and babies with their mothers went first on the 19th and 20th of June. The States gave out pocket money to the kiddies, if their parents had none to spare. The littlest children were all excited about the sweets they could buy with it. Some thought it was like a Sunday School outing, and they'd be back by nightfall. They were lucky in that. The older children, like Eli, knew better.

Of all the sights I saw the day they left, there is one picture I can't get out of my mind. Two little girls, all dressed up in pink party dresses, stiff petticoats, shiny strap shoes—like their Ma thought they'd be going to a party. How cold they must have been crossing the Channel.

All the children were to be dropped off at their school by their parents. It was there we had to say our good-byes. Buses came to take the children down to the pier. The boats that had just been to Dunkirk came back across the Channel for the children. There was no time to get a convoy together to escort them. There was no time to get enough lifeboats on board—or life jackets.

That morning we stopped first at the hospital for Eli to bid his mother good-bye. He couldn't do it. His jaw was clamped shut so tight, he could only nod. Jane held him for a bit, and then Elizabeth and me walked him down to the schoolyard. I hugged him hard and that was the last time I saw him for five years. Elizabeth stayed because she had volunteered to help get the children inside ready.

I was walking back to Jane in the hospital, when I recalled something Eli had once said to me. He was about five years old, and we were walking down to La Courbière to see the fishing boats come in. There was an old canvas bathing shoe left lying right in the middle of the path. Eli walked around it, staring. Finally, he said, "That shoe is all alone, Grandpa." I answered that yes it was. He looked at it some more, and then we walked on by. After a bit, he said, "Grandpa, that's something I never am." I asked him, "What's that?" And he said, "Lonesome in my spirits."

There! I had something happy to tell Jane after all, and I prayed it would stay true for him.

Isola says she wants to write you herself of the doings inside the school. She says she was witness to a scene you will want to know about as an authoress: Elizabeth smacked Adelaide Addison in the face and made her leave. You do not know Miss Addison, and you are fortunate in that—she is a woman too good for daily wear.

Isola told me you might come to visit Guernsey. I would be glad to offer you hospitality with me and Eli.

Yours,
Eben Ramsey

Telegram from Juliet to Isola

DID ELIZABETH REALLY SLAP ADELAIDE
ADDISON? IF ONLY I HAD BEEN THERE! PLEASE
SEND DETAILS. LOVE, JULIET

From Isola to Juliet

24th April, 1946

Dear Juliet,

Yes, she did—slapped her right across the face. It was lovely.

We were all at the St. Brioc School to help the children get ready for the buses to take them down to the ships. The States didn't want the parents to come into the school itself—too crowded and too sad. Better to say good-byes outside. One child crying might set them all off.

So it was strangers who tied up shoelaces, wiped noses, put a nametag around each child's neck. We did up buttons and played games with them until the buses could come.

I had one bunch of kiddies trying to touch their tongues to their noses, and Elizabeth had another bunch playing that game that teaches them how to lie with a straight face—I forget what it's called—when Adelaide Addison came in with that doleful mug of hers, all piety and no sense.

She gathered a circle of children around her and commenced singing "For Those in Peril on the Sea" over their little heads. But no, "safety from storms" *wasn't enough* for her. God had to keep them from being blown up too. She set about ordering the poor things to pray for their parents every night—who knew what the German soldiers might do to them? Then she said to be especially good little boys and girls so that Mama and Daddy could look down on them from Heaven and BE PROUD OF THEM.

I tell you, Juliet, she had those children crying and sobbing fit to die. I was too shocked to move, but not Elizabeth. No, quick as an adder's tongue, she had ahold of Adelaide's arm and told her to SHUT UP.

Adelaide cried, "Let me go! I am speaking the Word of God!"

Elizabeth, she got a look on her that would turn the devil to stone, and then she slapped Adelaide right across the face—nice and sharp, so her head wobbled on her shoulders—and hauled her over to the door, shoved her out, and locked it. Old Adelaide kept a-pounding on the door, but no one paid her any heed. I lie—silly Daphne Post did try to open it, but I got her round the neck and she stopped.

It is my belief that the sight of a good fight shocked the fear right out of those babies, and they stopped crying, and the buses all came and we loaded the children on. Elizabeth and me, we didn't go home, we stood in the road and waved till the buses was out of sight.

I hope I never live to see another such day, even with Adelaide getting slapped. All those little children bereft in the world—I was glad I did not have any.

Thank you for your life story. You have had such sadness with your Ma and Pa and your home by the river, for which things I am sorry. But me, I am glad you have dear friends like Sophie and her Ma and Sidney. As to that Sidney, he sounds a very fine man—but bossy. It's a failing common in men.

Clovis Fossey has asked if you would send the Society a copy of your prize-winning essay on chickens. He thinks it would be nice to read aloud at a meeting. Then we could put it in our archives, if we ever have any.

I'd like to read it too, chickens being the reason I fell off a hen-house roof—they'd chased me there. How they all came at me—with their razor lips and back-to-back eyeballs! People don't know how chickens can turn on you, but they can—just like mad dogs. I didn't keep hens until the war came—then I had to, but I am never easy in their company. I would rather have Ariel butt me on my bottom—that's open and honest and not like a sly chicken, sneaking up to jab you.

I would like it if you would come to see us. So would Eben and Amelia and Dawsey—and Eli, too. Kit is not so sure, but you needn't mind that. She might come round. Your newspaper article will be printed soon, so you could come here and rest up. It may be that you could find a story here you'd like to tell about.

Your friend,
Isola

From Dawsey to Juliet

26th April, 1946

Dear Juliet,

My temporary job at the quarry is over, and Kit is staying with me for a bit. She is sitting beneath the table I'm writing upon, whispering. What's that you're whispering, I asked, and there was a long quiet. Then she commenced whispering again, and I can make out my own name mixed into the other sounds. This is what generals call a war of nerves, and I know who is going to win.

Kit doesn't resemble Elizabeth very much, except for her grey eyes and a look she gets when she is concentrating hard. But she is like her mother inside—fierce in her feelings. Even when she was a tiny creature, it was so. She howled until the glass shivered in the windows, and when she gripped my finger in her little fist, it turned white. I knew nothing of babies, but Elizabeth made me learn. She said I was fated to be a father and she had a responsibility to make sure I knew more than the usual run of them. She missed Christian, not just for herself, for Kit, too.

Kit knows her father is dead. Amelia and I told her that, but we didn't know how to speak of Elizabeth. In the end, we said that she'd been sent away and we hoped she'd return soon. Kit looked from me to Amelia and back, but she didn't ask any questions. She just went out and sat in the barn. I don't know if we did right.

Some days I wear myself out with wishing for Elizabeth to come home. We have learned that Sir Ambrose Ivers was killed in one of the last bombing raids in London, and, as Elizabeth inherited his estate, his solicitors have begun a search for her. They must have better ways to find her than we have, so I am hopeful that Mr. Dilwyn will get some word from her—or about her—soon. Wouldn't it be a blessed thing for Kit and for all of us if Elizabeth could be found?

The Society is having an outing on Saturday. We are attending the Guernsey Repertory Company's showing of *Julius Caesar*—John Booker is to be Marc Antony and Clovis Fossey is going to play Caesar. Isola has been reading Clovis his lines, and she says we will all be astonished at his performance, especially when, after he's dead, he hisses, "Thou shalt see me at Philippi!" Just thinking of the way Clovis hisses it has kept her awake for three nights, she says. Isola exaggerates, but only enough to enjoy herself.

Kit's stopped whispering. I've just peered under the table, and she's asleep. It's later than I thought.

Yours ever,
Dawsey

From Mark to Juliet

April 30, 1946

Darling,

Just got in—the entire trip could have been avoided if Hendry had telephoned, but I smacked a few heads together and they've cleared the whole shipment through customs. I feel as though I've been away for years. Can I see you tonight? I need to talk to you.

Love,
M.

From Juliet to Mark

Of course. Do you want to come here? I have a sausage.

Juliet

From Mark to Juliet

A sausage—how appetizing.
Suzette, at 8:00?

Love,
M.

From Juliet to Mark

Say please.

J.

From Mark to Juliet

Pleased to see you at Suzette at 8:00.

Love,
M.

From Juliet to Mark

1st May, 1946

Dear Mark,

I didn't refuse, you know. I said I wanted to think about it. You were so busy ranting about Sidney and Guernsey that perhaps you didn't notice—I only said I wanted time. I've known you *two months*. It's not long enough for me to be certain that we should spend the rest of our lives together, even if you are. I once made a terrible mistake and almost married a man I hardly knew (perhaps you read about it in the papers)—and at least in that case, the war was an extenuating circumstance. I won't be such a fool again.

Think of it: I've never seen your home—I don't even know where it is, really. New York, but which street? What does it look like? What color are your walls? Your sofa? Do you arrange your books alphabetically? (I hope not.) Are your drawers tidy or messy? Do you ever hum, and if so, what? Do you prefer cats or dogs? Or fish? What on earth do you eat for breakfast—or do you have a cook?

You see? I don't know you well enough to marry you.

I have one other piece of news that may interest you: Sidney is not your rival. I am not now nor have I ever been in love with Sidney, nor he with me. Nor will I ever marry him. Is that decisive enough for you?

Are you absolutely certain you wouldn't rather be married to someone more tractable than I?

Juliet

From Juliet to Sophie

1st May, 1946

Dearest Sophie,

I wish you were here. I wish we still lived together in our lovely little studio and worked in dear Mr. Hawke's shop and ate crackers and cheese for supper every night. I want so much to talk to you. I want you to tell me whether I should marry Mark Reynolds.

He asked me last night—no bended knee, but a diamond as big as a pigeon egg—at a romantic French restaurant. I'm not certain he still wants to marry me this morning—he's absolutely furious because I didn't give him an unequivocal yes. I tried to explain that I hadn't known him long enough and I needed time to think, but he wouldn't listen to me. He was certain that I was rejecting him because of a secret passion—for Sidney! They really are obsessed with one another, those two.

Thank God we were at his flat by then—he began shouting about Sidney and godforsaken islands and women who care more about a passel of strangers than men who are right in front of them (that's Guernsey and my new friends there). I kept trying to explain and he kept shouting until I began to cry from frustration. Then he felt remorseful, which was so unlike him and endearing that I almost changed my mind and said yes. But then I imagined a lifetime of having to cry to get him to be kind, and I went back to no again. We argued and he lectured and I wept a bit more because I was so exhausted, and eventually he called his chauffeur to take me home. As he shut me into the back seat, he leaned in to kiss me and said, "You're an idiot, Juliet."

And maybe he's right. Do you recall those awful, awful Cheslayne Fair novels we read the summer we were thirteen? My favorite was *The Master of Blackheath*. I must have read it twenty times (and so did you, don't pretend you didn't). Do you remember Ransom—how he manfully hid his love for the girlish Eulalie so that she could choose freely, little knowing that she had been mad for him ever since she fell off her horse when she was twelve? Here's the thing, Sophie—Mark Reynolds is exactly like Ransom. He's tall and handsome, with a crooked smile and a chiseled jaw. He shoulders his way through the crowd, careless of the glances that follow him. He's impatient and magnetic, and when I go to powder my nose, I overhear other women talking about him, just like Eulalie did in the museum. People notice him. He doesn't try to make them—they can't help it.

I used to get shivers about Ransom. Sometimes I do about Mark, too—when I look at him—but I can't get over the nagging feeling that I'm no Eulalie. If I were ever to fall off a horse, it would be lovely to be picked up by Mark, but I don't think I'm likely to fall off a horse any time soon. I'm much more likely to go to Guernsey and write a book about the Occupation, and Mark can't abide the thought. He wants me to stay in London and go to restaurants and theaters and marry him like a reasonable person.

Write and tell me what to do.

Love to Dominic—and you and Alexander as well.
Juliet

From Juliet to Sidney

3rd May, 1946

Dear Sidney,

I may not be as distraught as Stephens & Stark is without you, but I do miss you and want you to advise me. Please drop everything you are doing and write to me at once.

I want to get out of London. I want to go to Guernsey. You know I've grown very fond of my Guernsey friends, and I'm fascinated by their lives under the Germans—and afterward. I've visited the Channel Islands Refugee Committee and read their files. I have read the Red Cross reports. I've read all I can find on Todt slave workers—there hasn't, so far, been much. I've interviewed some of the soldiers who liberated Guernsey and talked to Royal Engineers who removed the thousands of mines from their beaches. I've read all of the "unclassified" government reports on the state of the Islanders' health, or lack of it; their happiness, or lack of it; their food supplies, or lack of them. But I want to know more. I want to know the stories of the people who were there, and I can never learn those by sitting in a library in London.

For example—yesterday I was reading an article on the liberation. A reporter asked a Guernsey Islander, "What was the most difficult experience you had during the Germans' rule?" He made fun of the man's answer, but it made perfect sense to me. The Islander told him, "You know they took away all of our wireless sets? If you were caught having a hidden radio, you'd get sent off to prison on the continent. Well, those of us who had secret radios, we heard about the Allies landing in Normandy. Trouble was, we weren't supposed to know it had happened! Hardest thing I ever did was walk around St. Peter Port on June 7, not grinning, not smiling, not doing anything to let those Germans know that I KNEW their end was coming. If they'd caught on, someone would be in for it—so we had to pretend. It was very hard to pretend not to know D-Day had happened."

I want to talk to people like him (though he's probably off writers now) and hear about their war, for that's what I'd like to read, instead of statistics about grain. I'm not sure what form a book would take, or if I could even write one at all. But I would like to go to St. Peter Port and find out.

Do I have your blessing?

> Love to you and Piers,
> Juliet

Cable from Sidney to Juliet

10th May, 1946

HEREWITH MY BLESSING! GUERNSEY IS A
WONDERFUL IDEA, BOTH FOR YOU AND FOR
A BOOK. BUT WILL REYNOLDS ALLOW IT?
LOVE, SIDNEY

Cable from Juliet to Sidney

11th May, 1946

BLESSING RECEIVED. MARK REYNOLDS IS NOT IN A
POSITION TO FORBID OR ALLOW. LOVE, JULIET

From Amelia to Juliet

13th May, 1946

My dear,

It was a delight to receive your telegram yesterday and learn
that you are coming to visit us!

I followed your instructions and spread the news at once—

you have sent the Society into a whirlwind of excitement. The members instantly offered to provide you with anything you might need: bed, board, introductions, a supply of electric clothes-pins. Isola is over the moon that you are coming and is already at work on behalf of your book. Though I cautioned her that it was only an idea as yet, she is bound and determined to find material for you. She has asked (perhaps threatened) everyone she knows in the market to send you letters about the Occupation; she thinks you'll need them to persuade your publisher that the subject is book-worthy. Don't be surprised if you are inundated with mail in the next weeks.

Isola also went to see Mr. Dilwyn at the bank this afternoon and asked him to offer you the rental of Elizabeth's cottage for your visit. It is a lovely site, in a meadow below the Big House, and it is small enough for you to manage easily. Elizabeth moved there when the German officers confiscated the larger house for their use. You would be very comfortable there, and Isola assured Mr. Dilwyn that he need only stir himself to draw up a lease for you. She herself will tend to everything else: airing out rooms, washing windows, beating rugs, and killing spiders.

I hope you won't feel burdened by all these arrangements, as Mr. Dilwyn had planned to assess the property soon for its rental possibilities. Sir Ambrose's solicitors have begun an inquiry into Elizabeth's whereabouts. They have found there is no record of her arrival in Germany, only that she was put on a transport in France, with Frankfurt as the intended destination of the train. There will be further investigations, and I pray that they will lead to Elizabeth, but in the meantime, Mr. Dilwyn wants to rent the property left to Elizabeth by Sir Ambrose, to provide income for Kit.

I sometimes think that we are morally obliged to begin a

search for Kit's German relations, but I cannot bring myself to do it. Christian was a rare soul, and he detested what his country was doing, but the same cannot be true for many Germans, who believed in the dream of the Thousand-Year Reich. And how could we send our Kit away to a foreign—and destroyed—land, even if her relations could be found? We are the only family she's ever known.

When Kit was born, Elizabeth kept her paternity a secret from the authorities. Not out of shame, but because she was afraid that the baby would be taken from her and sent to Germany to be raised. There were dreadful rumors of such things. I wonder if Kit's heritage could have saved Elizabeth if she had made it known when she was arrested. But as she didn't, it is not my place to do so.

Excuse my unburdening myself. My worries travel about my head on their well-worn path, and it is a relief to put them on paper. I will turn to more cheerful subjects—such as last evening's meeting of the Society.

After the uproar about your visit had subsided, the Society read your article about books and reading in the *Times*. Everyone enjoyed it—not just because we were reading about ourselves, but because you brought us views we'd never thought to apply to our reading before. Dr. Stubbins pronounced that you alone had transformed "distraction" into an honorable word—instead of a character flaw. The article was delightful, and we were all so proud and pleased to be mentioned in it.

Will Thisbee wants to have a welcome party in your honor. He will bake a Potato Peel Pie for the event and has devised a cocoa icing for it. He made a surprise dessert for our meeting last night—Cherries Flambé, which fortunately burned down to the pan, so we did not have to eat it. I wish Will would leave cookery alone and go back to ironmongery.

We all look forward to welcoming you. You mentioned that you have to finish several reviews before you can leave London— but we will be delighted to see you whenever you come. Just let us know the date and time of your arrival. Certainly, an aeroplane flight to Guernsey would be faster and more comfortable than the mail boat (Clovis Fossey said to tell you that air hostesses give gin to passengers—and the mail boat doesn't). But unless you are bedeviled by sea-sickness, I would catch the afternoon boat from Weymouth. There is no more beautiful approach to Guernsey than the one by sea—either with the sun going down, or with gold-tipped, black storm clouds, or the Island just emerging through the mist. This is the way I first saw Guernsey, as a new bride.

> Fondly,
> Amelia

From Isola to Juliet

14th May, 1946

Dear Juliet,

I have been getting your house all ready for you. I asked several of my friends at Market to write to you of their experiences, so I hope they do. If Mr. Tatum writes and asks for money for his recollections, don't pay him a penny. He is a big fat liar.

Would you like to know of my first sight of the Germans? I will use adjectives to make it more lively. I don't usually—I favor stark facts.

Guernsey seemed quiet that Tuesday—but we knew they were there! Planes and ships carrying soldiers had come in the day before. Huge Junkers thumped down, and after unloading all their men, they flew off again. Being lighter now and more frolicsome, they hedgehopped, swooping up and swooping down, all over Guernsey, scaring the cows in the fields.

Elizabeth was at my house, but we couldn't summon up the spirit to make hair tonic, even though my yarrow was in. We just drifted around like a couple of ghouls. Then Elizabeth gathered herself up. "Come on," she says. "I'm not going to sit inside waiting for them. I'm going to town to seek out my enemy."

"And what are you going to do after you've found him?" I asks, sort of snappish.

"I'm going to look at him," she says. "We're not animals in a cage—they are. They're stuck on this island with us, same as we're stuck with them. Come on, let's go stare."

I liked that idea, so we put on our hats and went. But you would never believe the sights we saw in St. Peter Port.

Oh, there were hundreds of German soldiers—and they were SHOPPING! Arm in arm they went strolling along Fountain Street—smiling, laughing, peering into store windows, going in shops and coming out with their arms filled with packages, calling out to one another. North Esplanade was filled with soldiers too. Some were just lolling about, others touched their caps to us and bowed, polite-like. One man said to me, "Your island is beautiful. We will be fighting in London soon, but now we have this—a holiday in the sun."

Another poor idiot actually thought he was in Brighton. They were buying ice lollies for the streams of children following them. Laughing and having a fine time they were. If it weren't for those green uniforms, we'd have thought the tour boat from Weymouth was in!

We started to go by Candie Gardens, and there everything changed—carnival to nightmare. First, we heard noise—the loud steady rhythm of boots coming down heavy on hard stones. Then a troop of goose-stepping soldiers turned onto our street; everything about them gleamed; buttons, boots, those metal coal-scuttle hats. Their eyes didn't look at anyone or anything— just stared straight ahead. That was scarier than the rifles slung over their shoulders, or the knives and grenades stuck in their boot-tops.

Mr. Ferre, who'd been in back of us, grabbed my arm. He'd fought on the Somme. Tears were running down his face, and not knowing it, he was twisting my arm, wringing it, saying, "How can they be doing this again? We beat them and here they are again. How did we let them do this again?"

Finally, Elizabeth said, "I've seen enough. I need a drink."

I keep a good supply of gin in my cupboard, so we came on home.

I will close now, but I will be able to see you soon and that gives me joy. We all want to come meet you—but a new fear has struck me. There could be twenty other passengers on the mail boat, and how will I know which one is you? That book photo is a blurry little thing, and I don't want to go kissing the wrong woman. Could you wear a big red hat with a veil and carry lilies?

Your friend,
Isola

From An Animal Lover to Juliet

Wednesday evening

Dear Miss,

I too am a member of the Guernsey Literary and Potato Peel Pie Society—but I never wrote to you about my books, because I only read two—kiddies' tales about dogs, loyal, brave, and true. Isola says you are coming to maybe write about the Occupation, and I think you should know the truth of what our States did to animals! Our own government, mind, not the dirty Germans! They would be ashamed to tell of it, but I am not.

I don't much care for people—never have, never will. I got my reasons. I never met a man half so true as a dog. Treat a dog right and he'll treat you right—he'll keep you company, be your friend, never ask you no questions. Cats is different, but I never held that against them.

You should know what some Guernsey folks did to their pets when they got scared the Germans was coming. Thousands of them quit the island—flew off to England, sailed away, and left their dogs and cats behind. Deserted them, left them to roam the streets, hungry and thirsty—the swine!

I took in as many dogs as I could gather up, but it wasn't enough. Then the States stepped in to take care of the problem— and did worse, far worse. The States warned in the newspapers that, because of the war, there might not be enough food for humans, much less for animals. "You may keep one family pet," they said, "but the States will have to put the rest to sleep. Feral cats and dogs, roaming the island, will be a danger to the children."

And that is what they did. The States gathered them animals

into trucks, and took them to St. Andrews Animal Shelter, and those nurses and doctors put them all to sleep. As fast as they could kill one truck load of pets, another truck load would arrive.

I saw it all—the collecting, the unloading at the shelter, and the burying.

I saw one nurse come out of the shelter and stand in the fresh air, gulping it down. She looked sick enough to die herself. She had herself a cigarette and then she went back on in to help with the killing. It took two days to kill all the animals.

That's all I want to say, but put it in your book.

An Animal Lover

From Sally Ann Frobisher to Juliet

15th May, 1946

Dear Miss Ashton,

Miss Pribby told me you would be coming to Guernsey to hear about the war. I hope we will meet then, but I am writing now because I like to write letters. I like to write anything, really.

I thought you'd like to know how I was personally humiliated during the war—in 1943, when I was twelve. I had scabies.

There wasn't enough soap on Guernsey to keep clean—not our clothes, our houses, or ourselves. Everyone had skin diseases of one sort or another—scales or pustules or lice. I myself had scabies on top of my head—under my hair—and they wouldn't go away.

Finally, Dr. Ormond said I must go to Town Hospital and have my head shaved, and cut the tops of the scabs off to let the pus out. I hope you will never know the shame of a seeping scalp. I wanted to die.

That is where I met my friend Elizabeth McKenna. She helped the nurses on my floor. The nurses were always kind, but Miss McKenna was kind *and* funny. Her being funny helped me in my darkest hour. When my head had been shaved, she came into my room with a basin, a bottle of Dettol, and a sharp scalpel.

I said, "This isn't going to hurt, is it? Dr. Ormond said it wouldn't hurt." I tried not to cry.

"He lied," Miss McKenna said, "it's going to hurt like hell. Don't tell your mother I said 'hell.' "

I started to giggle at that, and she made the first slice before I had time to be afraid. It did hurt, but not like hell. We played a game while she cut the rest of the tops off—we shouted out the names of every woman who had ever suffered under the blade. "Mary, Queen of Scots—Snip-snap!" "Anne Boleyn—Whap!" "Marie Antoinette—Thunk!" And we were done.

It hurt, but it was fun too because Miss McKenna had turned it into a game.

She swabbed my bald head with Dettol and came in to visit me that evening—with a silk scarf of her own to wrap round my head as a turban. "There," she said, and handed me a mirror. I looked in it—the scarf was lovely, but my nose looked too big for my face, just as it always did. I wondered if I'd ever be pretty, and asked Miss McKenna.

When I asked my mother the same question, she said she had no patience with such nonsense and beauty was only skin-deep. But not Miss McKenna. She looked at me, considering, and then she said, "In a little more time, Sally, you're going to be a stunner. Keep looking in the mirror and you'll see. It's bones that count, and you've got them in spades. With that elegant nose of yours, you'll be the new Nefertiti. You'd better practice looking imperious."

Mrs. Maugery came to visit me in hospital and I asked her who Nefertiti was, and if she was dead. It sort of sounded like it. Mrs. Maugery said she was indeed dead in one way, but immortal in another way. Later on, she hunted up a picture of Nefertiti for me to see. I wasn't exactly sure what imperious was, so I tried to look like her. As yet, I haven't grown into my nose, but I'm sure it will come—Miss McKenna said so.

Another sad story about the Occupation is my Aunt Letty. She used to have a big, gloomy old house out on the cliffs near La Fontenelle. The Germans said it lay in their big guns' line of fire and interfered with their gun practice. So they blew it up. Aunt Letty lives with us now.

> Yours sincerely,
> Sally Ann Frobisher

From Micah Daniels to Juliet

15th May, 1946

Dear Miss Ashton,

Isola gave me your address because she is sure you would like to see my list for your book.

If you was to take me to Paris today, and set me down in a fine French restaurant—the kind of place what has white lace tablecloths, candles on the walls, and silver covers over all the plates—well, I tell you it would be nothing, nothing compared to my *Vega* box.

In case you don't know of it, the *Vega* was a Red Cross ship that come first to Guernsey on 27 December, 1944. They brought food to us then, and five more times—and it kept us alive until the end of the war.

Yes, I do say it—kept us alive! Food had not been so plentiful for several years by then. Except for the devils in the Black Market, not a spoonful of sugar was left on the Island. All the flour for bread had run out about the first of December of '44. Them German soldiers was as hungry as we was—with bloated bellies and no body warmth from food.

Well, I was tired to death of boiled potatoes and turnips, and I would have soon turned up my toes and died, when the *Vega* came into our port.

Mr. Churchill, he wouldn't let the Red Cross ships bring us any food before then because he said the Germans would just take it, and eat it up themselves. Now that may sound like smart planning to you—to starve the villains out! But to me it said he just didn't care if we starved along with them.

Well, something shoved his soul up a notch or two, and he decided we could eat. So in December, he says to the Red Cross, "Oh, all right, go ahead and feed them."

Miss Ashton, there were TWO BOXES of food for every man, woman, and child on Guernsey—all stored up in the *Vega*'s hold. There was other stuff too: nails, seed for planting, candles, oil to cook with, matches to light a fire, some clothing, and some shoes. Even a few layettes for any new babies around.

There was flour and tobacco—Moses can talk about manna all he wants, but he never seen anything like this! I am going to tell you everything in my box, because I wrote it all down to paste in my memory book.

Six ounces of chocolate	*Twenty ounces of biscuits*
Four ounces of tea	*Twenty ounces of butter*
Six ounces of sugar	*Thirteen ounces of Spam*

Two ounces of tinned milk *Eight ounces of raisins*
Fifteen ounces of marmalade *Ten ounces of salmon*
Five ounces of sardines *Four ounces of cheese*
Six ounces of prunes *One ounce of pepper*
One ounce of salt *A tablet of soap*

I gave my prunes away—but wasn't that something? When I die I am going to leave all my money to the Red Cross. I have written to tell them so.

There is something else I should say to you. It may be about those Germans, but honor due is honor due. They unloaded all those boxes of food for us from the *Vega,* and they didn't take none, not one box of it, for themselves. Of course, their Commandant had told them, "That food is for the Islanders, it is not yours. Steal one bit and I'll have you shot." Then he gave each man unloading the ship a teaspoon, so's he could scrape up any flour or grain that spilled on the roadway. They could eat that.

In fact, they were a pitiful sight—those soldiers. Stealing from gardens, knocking on doors asking for scraps. One day I saw a soldier catch up a cat, and slam its head against a wall. Then he cut it off, and hid the cat in his jacket. I followed him—till he come to a field. That German skinned that cat and boiled him up in his billy can, and ate it right there.

That was truly, truly a sorrowful sight to see. It made me sick, but underneath my sick, I thought, "There goes Hitler's Third Reich—dining out," and then I started laughing, fit to die. I am ashamed of that now, but that is what I did.

That is all I have to say. I wish you well with your book writing.

Yours truly,
Micah Daniels

From John Booker to Juliet

16th May, 1946

Dear Miss Ashton,

Amelia told us you are coming to Guernsey to gather stories for your book. I will welcome you with all my heart, but I won't be able to tell you about what happened to me because I get the shakes when I talk about it. Maybe if I write it down, you won't need me to say it out loud. It isn't about Guernsey anyway— I wasn't here. I was in Neuengamme Concentration Camp in Germany.

You know how I pretended I was Lord Tobias for three years? Peter Jenkins's daughter, Lisa, was dating German soldiers. Any German soldier, so long as he would give her stockings or lipsticks. This was so until she took up with Sgt. Willy Gurtz. He was a mean little runt. The two of them together benasties the mind. It was Lisa who betrayed me to the German Commandant.

In March of 1944, Lisa was having her hair done in an upsweep at the beauty parlor, where she found an old, pre-war copy of *Tatler* magazine. There, on page 124, was a colored picture of Lord and Lady Tobias Penn-Piers. They were at a wedding in Sussex— drinking champagne and eating oysters. The words under the picture told all about her gown, her diamonds, her shoes, her face, and his money. The magazine mentioned that they were owners of an estate, called La Fort, on the island of Guernsey.

Well, it was pretty plain—even to Lisa, who's thick as a post—that Lord Tobias Penn-Piers was not me. She did not wait for her hair to be combed out, but left at once to show the picture to Willy Gurtz, who took it straight to the Commandant.

It made the Germans feel like fools, bowing and scraping all that time to a servant—so they were extra spiteful and sent me to the camp at Neuengamme.

I did not think I would live out the first week. With other prisoners, I was sent out to clear unexploded bombs during air raids. What a choice—to run into a square with the bombs raining down or to be killed by the guards for refusing. I ran and scuttled like a rat and tried to cover myself when I heard bombs whistle past my head and somehow I was alive at the end of it. That's what I told myself—Well, you're still alive. I think all of us said the same each morning when we woke up—Well, I'm still alive. But the truth is, *we weren't.* What we were—it wasn't dead, but it wasn't alive either. I was a living soul only a few minutes a day, when I was in my bunk. Those times, I tried to think of something happy, something I'd liked—but not something I loved, for that made it worse. Just a small thing, like a school picnic or bicycling downhill—that's all I could stand.

It felt like thirty years, but it was only one. In April of '45, the Commandant at Neuengamme picked out those of us who were still fit enough to work and sent us to Belsen. We rode for several days in a big, open truck—no food, no blankets, no water, but we were glad we weren't walking. The mud-puddles in the road were red.

I imagine you already know of Belsen and what happened there. When we got off the truck, we were handed shovels. We were to dig great pits to bury the dead. They led us through the camp to the spot, and I feared I'd lost my mind because everyone I saw was dead. Even the living looked like corpses, and the corpses were lying where they'd dropped. I didn't know why they were bothering to bury them. The fact was, the Russians were coming from the east, and the Allies were coming from the west—and those Germans were terrified of what they'd see when they got there.

The crematorium could not burn the bodies fast enough—so after we dug long trenches, we pulled and dragged the bodies to the edges and threw them in. You'll not believe it, but the SS forced the prisoners' band to play music as we lugged the corpses—and for that, I hope they burn in hell with polkas blaring. When the trenches were full, the SS poured petrol over the bodies and set fire to them. Afterwards, we were supposed to cover them with dirt—as if you could hide such a thing.

The British got there the next day, and dear God, but we were glad to see them. I was strong enough to walk down the road, so I saw the tanks crash down the gates and I saw the British flag painted on their sides. I turned to a man sitting against a fence nearby and called out "We're saved! It's the British!" Then I saw he was dead. He had only missed it by minutes. I sat down in the mud and sobbed as though he'd been my best friend.

When the Tommies came down out of the tanks, they were weeping, too—even the officers. Those good men fed us, gave us blankets, saw us to hospitals. And bless them, they burned Belsen to the ground a month later.

I read in the newspaper that they've put up a war refugee camp in its place now. It gives me the shivers to think of new barracks being built there, even for a good purpose. To my mind, that land should be a blank forever.

I'll write no more of this, and I hope you'll understand if I do not care to speak of it. As Seneca says, "Light griefs are loquacious, but the great are dumb."

I do recall something you might like to know for your book. It happened in Guernsey, when I was still pretending to be Lord Tobias. Sometimes of an evening Elizabeth and I would walk up to the headlands to watch the bombers flying over—hundreds of them, on their way to bomb London. It was terrible to watch and know where they were headed and what they meant to do.

The German radio had told us London was leveled—flattened, with nothing left but rubble and ashes. We didn't quite believe them, German propaganda being what it was, but still—

We were walking through St. Peter Port on one such night when we passed the McLaren House. That was a fine old house taken over by German officers. A window was open and the wireless was playing a beautiful piece of music. We stopped to listen, thinking it must be a program from Berlin. But, when the music ended, we heard Big Ben strike and a British voice said, "*This is the BBC—London.*" You can never mistake Big Ben's sound! London was still there! Still there. Elizabeth and I hugged, and we started waltzing up the road. That was one of the times I could not think about while I was in Neuengamme.

Yours sincerely,
John Booker

From Dawsey to Juliet

16th May, 1946

Dear Juliet,

There's nothing left to do for your arrival except wait. Isola has washed, starched, and ironed Elizabeth's curtains, looked up the chimney for bats, cleaned the windows, made up the beds, and aired all the rooms.

Eli has carved a present for you, Eben has filled your woodshed, and Clovis has scythed your meadow—leaving, he says, the clumps of wildflowers for you to enjoy. Amelia is planning a supper party for you on your first evening.

My only job is to keep Isola alive until you get here. Heights make her giddy, but nevertheless she climbed to the roof of Elizabeth's cottage to stomp for loose tiles. Fortunately, Kit saw her before she reached the eaves and ran for me to come talk her down.

I wish I could do more for your welcome—I hope it may be soon. I am happy you are coming.

> Yours,
> Dawsey

Juliet to Dawsey

19th May, 1946

Dear Dawsey,

I'll be there the day after tomorrow! I am far too cowardly to fly, even with the inducement of gin, so I shall come by the evening mail boat.

Would you give Isola a message for me? Please tell her that I don't own a hat with a veil, and I can't carry lilies—they make me sneeze—but I do have a red wool cape and I'll wear that on the boat.

Dawsey, there isn't one thing you could do to make me feel more welcome in Guernsey than you already have. I'm having trouble believing that I am going to meet you all at last.

> Yours ever,
> Juliet

From Mark to Juliet

May 20, 1946

Dear Juliet,

You asked me to give you time, and I have. You asked me not to mention marriage, and I haven't. But now you tell me that you're off to bloody Guernsey for—what? A week? A month? Forever? Do you think I'm going to sit back and let you go?

You're being ridiculous, Juliet. Any half-wit can see that you're trying to run away, but what nobody can understand is why. We're right together—you make me happy, you never bore me, you're interested in the things I'm interested in, and I hope I'm not deluded when I say I think the same is true for you. We belong together. I know you loathe it when I tell you I know what's best for you, but in this case, I do.

For God's sake, forget about that miserable island and marry me. I'll take you there on our honeymoon—if I must.

Love,
Mark

From Juliet to Mark

20th May, 1946

Dear Mark,

You're probably right, but even so, I'm going to Guernsey tomorrow and *you can't stop me.*

I'm sorry I can't give you the answer you want. I would like to be able to.

Love,
Juliet

P.S. Thank you for the roses.

From Mark to Juliet

Oh for God's sake. Do you want me to drive you down to Weymouth?

Mark

From Juliet to Mark

Will you promise not to lecture me?

Juliet

From Mark to Juliet

No lectures. However, all other forms of persuasion will be employed.

Mark

From Juliet to Mark

Can't scare me. What can you possibly do while driving?

Juliet

From Mark to Juliet

You'd be surprised. See you tomorrow.

M.

PART TWO

From Juliet to Sidney

22nd May, 1946

Dear Sidney,

There's so much to tell you. I've been in Guernsey only twenty hours, but each one has been so full of new faces and ideas that I've reams to write. You see how conducive to working island life is? Look at Victor Hugo—I may grow prolific if I stay here for any length of time.

The voyage from Weymouth was ghastly, with the mail boat groaning and creaking and threatening to break to pieces in the waves. I almost wished it would, to put me out of my misery, except I wanted to see Guernsey before I died. And as soon as we came in sight of the island, I gave up the notion altogether because the sun broke beneath the clouds and set the cliffs shimmering into silver.

As the mail boat lurched into the harbor, I saw St. Peter Port rising up from the sea on terraces, with a church on the top like a cake decoration, and I realized that my heart was galloping. As much as I tried to persuade myself it was the thrill of the scenery, I knew better. All those people I've come to know and even love a little, waiting to see—me. And I, without any paper to hide behind. Sidney, in these past two or three years, I have become better at writing than living—and think what you do to my writing. On the page, I'm perfectly charming, but that's just a trick I learned. It has nothing to do with me. At least, that's what I was thinking as the mail boat came toward the pier. I had a cowardly impulse to throw my red cape overboard and pretend I was someone else.

When we drew right alongside the pier, I could see the faces of the people waiting—and then there was no going back. I knew them by their letters. There was Isola in a mad hat and a purple shawl pinned with a glittering brooch. She was smiling fixedly in the wrong direction and I loved her instantly. Next to her stood a man with a lined face, and at his side, a boy, all height and angles. Eben and his grandson, Eli. I waved to Eli and he smiled like a beam of light and nudged his grandfather—and then I got shy and lost myself in the crowd that was pushing down the gangplank.

Isola reached me first by leaping over a crate of lobsters and grabbed me up in a fierce hug that swung me off my feet. "Ah, lovey!" she cried while I dangled.

Wasn't that dear? All my nervousness was squeezed right out of me along with my breath. The others came toward me more quietly, but with no less warmth. Eben shook my hand and smiled. You can tell he was broad and hardy once, but he is too thin now. He somehow looks both grave and friendly at the same time. How does he manage to do that? I found myself wanting to impress him.

Eli swung Kit up on his shoulders, and they came forward together. Kit has chubby little legs and a stern face—dark curls, big grey eyes—and she did not take to me one bit. Eli's jersey was speckled in wood shavings, and he had a present for me in his pocket—an adorable little mouse with crooked whiskers, carved from walnut. I gave him a kiss on the cheek and survived Kit's malevolent glare. She has a very forbidding way about her for a four-year-old.

Then Dawsey held out his hands. I had been expecting him to

look like Charles Lamb, and he does, a little—he has the same even gaze. He presented me with a bouquet of carnations from Booker, who couldn't be present; he had concussed himself during a rehearsal and was in hospital overnight for observation. Dawsey is dark and wiry, and his face has a quiet, watchful look about it—until he smiles. Saving a certain sister of yours, he has the sweetest smile I've ever seen, and I remembered Amelia writing that he has a rare gift for persuasion—I can believe it. Like Eben—like everyone here—he is too thin, though you can tell he was more substantial once. His hair is going grey, and he has deep-set brown eyes, so dark they look black. The lines around his eyes make him seem to be starting a smile even when he's not, but I don't think he's over forty. He is only a little taller than I am and limps slightly, but he's strong—he hefted all my luggage, me, Amelia, and Kit into his wagon with no trouble.

I shook hands with him (I can't remember if he said anything) and then he stepped aside for Amelia. She's one of those ladies who is more beautiful at sixty than she could possibly have been at twenty (oh, how I hope someone says that about me someday!). Small, thin-faced, lovely smile, with grey hair in coronet braids, she gripped my hand tightly and said, "Juliet, I am glad you are here at last. Let's get your things and go home." It sounded wonderful, as though it really were my home.

As we stood there on the pier, some glint of light kept flashing in my eyes, and then around the dock. Isola snorted and said it was Adelaide Addison, at her window with opera glasses, tracking every move we made. Isola waved vigorously at the gleam and it stopped.

While we were laughing about that, Dawsey was seeing to my bags and making sure that Kit didn't fall off the pier and generally making himself useful. I began to see that this is what he does—and that everyone depends upon him to do it.

The four of us—Amelia, Kit, Dawsey, and I—rode to Amelia's farm in Dawsey's cart, while everyone else walked. It wasn't far except in terms of landscape, for we moved from St. Peter Port out into the countryside. There are rolling pasture-lands, but they end suddenly at cliffs, and all around is the moist salt smell of the sea. As we drove, the sun set and the mist rose. You know how sounds become magnified in the fog? Well, it was like that—every bird's chirp was weighty and symbolic. Clouds boiled up over the cliff-sides, and the fields were swathed in grey by the time we reached the manor house, but I saw ghostly shapes that I think were the cement bunkers built by the Todt workers.

Kit sat beside me in the wagon and sent me many sideways glances. I was not so foolish as to try to talk to her, but I played my severed-thumb trick—you know, the one that makes your thumb look like it has been sliced apart.

I did it over and over, casually, not looking at her, while she watched me like a baby hawk. She was intent and fascinated but not gullible enough to break into giggles. She just said at last, "Show me how you do that."

She sat across from me at supper and turned down her spinach with a thrust-out arm, hand straight up like a policeman. "Not for me," she said, and I, for one, would not care to disobey her. She pulled her chair close to Dawsey's and ate with one elbow planted firmly on his arm, pinning him in his place. He didn't appear to mind, even if it did make cutting his chicken difficult, and when supper was over, she immediately climbed into his lap. It is obviously her rightful throne, and though Dawsey seemed to be attending to the conversation, I spied him poking out a napkin-rabbit while we talked of food-shortages during the Occupation. Did you know that the Islanders ground bird-seed for flour until they ran out of it?

I must have passed some test I didn't know I was being given, because Kit asked me to tuck her into bed. She wanted to hear a story about a ferret. She liked vermin, did I? Would I kiss a rat on the lips? I said "Never" and that apparently won her favor—I was plainly a coward, but not a hypocrite. I told her a story and she presented her cheek an infinitesimal quarter of an inch to be kissed.

What a long letter—and it only contains the first four hours of the twenty. You'll have to wait for the other sixteen.

Love,
Juliet

From Juliet to Sophie

24th May, 1946

Dearest Sophie,

Yes, I'm here. Mark did his best to stop me, but I resisted him mulishly, right to the bitter end. I've always considered dogged-ness one of my least appealing characteristics, but it was valuable last week.

It was only as the boat pulled away, and I saw him standing on the pier, tall and scowling—and somehow wanting to marry *me*—that I began to think maybe he was right. Maybe I am a complete idiot. I know of three women who are mad for him—he'll be snapped up in a trice, and I'll spend my declining years in a grimy bed-sit, with my teeth falling out one by one. Oh, I can see it all now: No one will buy my books, and I'll ply Sidney with tattered, illegible manuscripts, which he'll pretend to publish out of pity. Doddering and muttering, I'll wander the streets carrying my pathetic turnips in a string bag, with newspaper tucked into my shoes. You'll send me affectionate cards at Christmas (won't you?) and I'll brag to strangers that I was once nearly engaged to Markham Reynolds, the publishing tycoon. They'll shake their heads—The poor old thing's crazy as a bedbug, of course, but harmless.

Oh God. This way lies insanity.

Guernsey is beautiful and my new friends have welcomed me so generously, so warmly, that I haven't doubted I've done right to come here—until just a moment ago, when I started thinking about my teeth. I'm going to stop thinking about them. I'm going to step into the meadow of wildflowers right outside my door and run to the cliff as fast as I can. Then I'm going to fall down and look at the sky, which is shimmering like a pearl this afternoon, and breathe in the warm scent of grass and pretend that Markham V. Reynolds doesn't exist.

I've just come back indoors. It's hours later—the setting sun has rimmed the clouds in blazing gold and the sea is moaning at the bottom of the cliffs. Mark Reynolds? Who's he?

Love always,
Juliet

27th May, 1946

Dear Sidney,

Elizabeth's cottage was plainly built for an exalted guest to stay in, because it's quite spacious. There is a big sitting room, a bathroom, a larder, and a huge kitchen downstairs. There are three bedrooms and a bath upstairs. And best of all, there are windows everywhere, so the sea air can sweep into every room.

I've shoved a writing table by the biggest window in my sitting room. The only flaw in this arrangement is the constant temptation to go outside and walk over to the cliff's edge. The sea and the clouds don't stay the same for five minutes running and I'm scared I'll miss something if I stay inside. When I got up this morning, the sea was full of sun pennies—and now it all seems to be covered in lemon scrim. Writers ought to live far inland or next to the city dump, if they are ever to get any work done. Or perhaps they need to be stronger-minded than I am.

If I needed any encouragement to be fascinated by Elizabeth, which I don't, her possessions would do it for me. The Germans arrived to take over Sir Ambrose's house and gave her only six hours to remove her belongings to the cottage. Isola said Elizabeth brought only a few pots and pans, some cutlery and kitchen china (the Germans kept the good silver, crystal, china, and wine for themselves), her art supplies, an old wind-up phonograph, some records, and the rest were armloads of books. So many books, Sidney, that I haven't had time to really look at them—they fill the living-room shelves and overflow into the kitchen hutch. She even set a stack at the end of the sofa to use for a table—wasn't that brilliant?

In every nook, I find little things that tell me about her. She was a noticer, Sidney, like me, for all the shelves are lined with shells, bird feathers, dried sea grasses, pebbles, eggshells, and the skeleton of something that might be a bat. They're just bits that were lying on the ground, that anyone else would step over or on, but she saw they were beautiful and brought them home. I wonder if she used them for still-lifes? I wonder if her sketch-books are here somewhere? There's prowling to be done. Work first, but the anticipation is like Christmas Eve seven days a week.

Elizabeth also carried down one of Sir Ambrose's paintings. It is a portrait of her, painted I imagine when she was about eight years old. She is sitting on a swing, all ready to pump up and away—but having to sit still for Sir Ambrose to paint. You can tell by her eyebrows that she doesn't like it. Glares must be inheritable, because she and Kit have identical ones.

My cottage is right inside the gates (honest three-barred farm gates). The meadow surrounding the cottage is full of scattered wildflowers until you get to the cliff's edge where rough grass and gorse take over.

The Big House (for want of a better name) is the one that Elizabeth came to close up for Ambrose. It is just up the drive from the cottage and is a wonderful house. Two-storied, L-shaped, and made of beautiful blue-grey stone. It's slate-roofed with dormer windows and a terrace stretching from the crook of the L down its length. The top of the crooked end has a windowed turret and faces the sea. Most of the huge old trees had to be cut down for firewood, but Mr. Dilwyn has asked Eben and Eli to plant new trees—chestnuts and oaks. He is also going to have peach trees espaliered next to the brick garden walls—as soon as they are rebuilt too.

The house is beautifully proportioned with wide tall windows that open straight out onto the stone terrace. The lawn is growing green and lush again, covering up the wheel ruts of German cars and trucks.

Escorted at different times by Eben, Eli, Dawsey, or Isola, I have quartered the island's ten parishes in the past five days; Guernsey is very beautiful in all its variety—fields, woods, hedgerows, dells, manors, dolmens, wild cliffs, witches' corners, Tudor barns, and Norman cottages of stone. I have been told stories of her history (very lawless) with almost every new site and building.

Guernsey pirates had superior taste—they built beautiful homes and impressive public buildings. These are sadly dilapidated and in need of repair, but their architectural beauty shows through anyway. Dawsey took me to a tiny church—every inch of which is a mosaic of broken china and smashed pottery. One priest did this all by himself—he must have made pastoral calls with a sledgehammer.

My guides are as various as the sights. Isola tells me about cursed pirate chests bound with bleached bones washing up on the beaches and what Mr. Hallette is hiding inside his barn (he says it's a calf, but we know better). Eben describes how things used to look, before the war, and Eli disappears suddenly and then returns with peach juice and an angelic smile on his face. Dawsey says the least, but he takes me to see wonders—like the tiny church. Then he stands back and lets me enjoy them as long as I want. He's the most un-hurrying person I've ever met. As we were walking along the road yesterday, I noticed that it cut very close to the cliffs and there was a trail leading down to the beach below. "Is this where you met Christian Hellman?" I asked. Dawsey looked startled and said yes, this was the spot. "What did he look like?" I asked, for I wanted to picture the scene. I expected it was a futile request, given that men cannot describe each other, but Dawsey knew how. "He looked like the German you imagine—tall, blond hair, blue eyes—except he could feel pain."

With Amelia and Kit, I have walked to town several times for tea. Cee Cee was right in his raptures over sailing into St. Peter Port. The harbor, with the town traipsing straight up and steeply to the sky, must be one of the most beautiful in the world. Shop windows on High Street and the Pollet are sparkling clean and are beginning to fill up with new goods. St. Peter Port may be essentially drab right now—so many buildings need refurbishing—but it does not give off the dead-tired air poor London does. It must be because of the bright light that flows down on everything and the clean, clear air and flowers growing everywhere—in fields, on verges, in crannies, between paving stones.

You really have to be Kit's height to see this world properly. She's grand at pointing out certain things I would otherwise miss—butterflies, spiders, flowers growing tiny and low to the ground—they're hard to see when you are faced with a blazing wall of fuchsias and bougainvillea. Yesterday, I came upon Kit and Dawsey crouched in the brush beside the gate, quiet as thieves. They weren't stealing, though; they were watching a blackbird tug a worm out of the ground. The worm put up a good fight, and the three of us sat there in silence until the blackbird finally got it down his gullet. I'd never really seen the entire process before. It's revolting.

Kit carries a little box with her sometimes when we go to town—a cardboard box, tied up tight with cord and a red yarn handle. Even when we have tea, she holds it on her lap and is very protective of it. There are no air holes in the box, so it can't be a ferret. Or, oh Lord, maybe it's a dead ferret. I'd love to know what's in it, but of course I can't ask.

I do like it here, and I'm settled in well enough to start work now. I will, as soon as I come back from fishing with Eben and Eli this afternoon.

> Love to you and Piers,
> Juliet

From Juliet to Sidney

30th May, 1946

Dear Sidney,

Do you remember when you sat me down for fifteen sessions of the Sidney Stark School of Perfect Mnemonics? You said writers who sat scribbling notes during an interview were rude, lazy, and incompetent and you were going to make sure I never disgraced you. You were unbearably arrogant and I loathed you, but I learned your lessons well—and now you can see the fruits of your hard work:

I went to my first meeting of the Guernsey Literary and Potato Peel Pie Society last night. It was held in Clovis and Nancy Fossey's living room (with spill-over into the kitchen). The speaker of the evening was a new member, Jonas Skeeter, who was to talk about *The Meditations of Marcus Aurelius*.

Mr. Skeeter strode to the front of the room, glared at us all, and announced he didn't want to be there and had only read Marcus Aurelius's silly book because his oldest, his dearest, and his *former* friend, Woodrow Cutter, had shamed him into it. Everyone turned to look at Woodrow, and Woodrow sat there, obviously shocked and his mouth agape.

"Woodrow," Jonas Skeeter went on, "came across my field where I was busy, building up my compost. He was holding this little book in his hands and he said he'd just finished reading it. He'd like me to read it too, he said—it was very *profound*.

"'Woodrow, I've got no time to be *profound*,' I said.

"He said, 'You should make time, Jonas. If you'd read it, we'd have better things to talk about at Crazy Ida's. We'd have more fun over a pint.'

"Now, that hurt my feelings, no good saying it didn't. My childhood friend had been holding himself above me for some time—all because he read books for you people and I didn't. I'd let it pass before—to each his own, as my Mum always said. But now he had gone too far. He had insulted me. *He put himself above me in conversation.*

"'Jonas,' he said, 'Marcus was a Roman emperor—and a mighty warrior. This book is what he thought about, down there among the Quadi. They were barbarians who was waiting in the woods to kill all the Romans. And Marcus, hard-pressed as he was by those Quades, he took the time to write up this little book of his thoughts. He had long, long thoughts, and we could use some of those, Jonas.'

"So I pushed down my hurt and took the damned book, but I came here tonight to say before all, Shame, Woodrow! Shame on you, to put a book above your boyhood friend!

"But I did read it and here is what I think. Marcus Aurelius was an *old woman*—forever taking his mind's temperature—forever wondering about what he had done, or what he had not done. Was he right—or was he wrong? Was the rest of the world in error? Could it be him instead? No, it was everybody else who was wrong, and he set matters straight for them. Broody hen that he was, he never had a tiny thought that he couldn't turn into a sermon. Why, I bet the man couldn't even take a piss—"

Someone gasped, "Piss! He said piss in front of ladies!"

"Make him apologize!" cried another.

"He doesn't have to apologize. He's supposed to say what he thinks, and that's what he thinks. Like it or not!"

"Woodrow, how could you so hurt your friend?"

"For shame, Woodrow!"

The room fell quiet when Woodrow stood up. The two men met in the middle of the floor. Jonas held out his hand to Woodrow, and Woodrow clapped Jonas on the back, and the two of them left, arm in arm, for Crazy Ida's. I hope that's a pub and not a woman.

Love,
Juliet

P.S. Dawsey was the only Society member who seemed to find last night's meeting at all funny. He's too polite to laugh out loud, but I saw his shoulders shaking. I gathered from the others that it had been a satisfying but by no means extraordinary evening.

Love again,
Juliet

From Juliet to Sidney

31st May, 1946

Dear Sidney,

Please read the enclosed letter—I found it slipped under my door this morning.

Dear Miss Ashton,

Miss Pribby told me you wanted to know about our recent Occupation by the German Army—so here is my letter.

I am a small man, and though Mother says I never had a prime, I did. I just didn't tell her about it. I am a champion whistler. I have won contests and prizes for my whistling. During the Occupation, I used this talent to unman the enemy.

After Mother was asleep, I would creep out of the house. I'd make my silent way down to the Germans' brothel (if you'll pardon the term) on Saumarez Street. I'd hide in the shadows until a soldier emerged from his tryst. I do not know if ladies are aware of this, but men are not at their peak of fitness after such an occasion. The soldier would start walking back to his quarters, often whistling. I'd start slowly walking, whistling the same tune (but much better). He'd stop whistling, but I *would not stop whistling.* He'd pause a second, thinking that what he had taken for an echo was *actually another person in the dark—following him. But who?* He would look back, I'd have slipped into a doorway. He'd see no one—he'd start on his way again, but not whistling. I'd start to walk again and to whistle again. He'd stop—I'd stop. He'd hurry on, but I'd still whistle, following him with hard footsteps. The soldier would rush toward his quarters, and I'd return to the brothel to wait for another German to stalk. I do believe I made many a soldier unfit to perform his duties well the next day. Do you see?

Now, if you'll pardon me, I will speak more about brothels. I do not believe those young ladies were there because they wanted to be. They were sent from the Occupied territories of Europe, same as the Todt slave workers. It could not have been nice work. To the soldiers' credit, they demanded the German authorities give the women an extra food allowance, same as given to the island's heavy workers. Furthermore, I saw some of these same ladies share their food with the Todt workers, who were sometimes let out of their camps at night to hunt for food.

My mother's sister lives on Jersey. Now that the war is over, she can come visit us—more's the pity. Being the sort of woman she is, she told a nasty story.

After D-Day the Germans decided to send their brothel ladies back to France, so they put them all on a boat to St. Malo. Now those waters are very wayward, broiled-up, and ugly. Their boat was swept onto the rocks and all aboard were drowned. You could see those poor drowned women—their yellow hair (bleached hussies, my aunt called them) spread out in the water, washing against the rocks. "Served them right, the whores," my aunt said—she and my mother laughed.

It was not to be borne! I jumped up from my chair and knocked the tea table over on them deliberately. I called them dirty old bats.

My aunt says she will never set foot in our house again, and Mother hasn't spoken to me since that day. I find it all very peaceful.

Yours truly,
Henry A. Toussant

From Juliet to Sidney

6th June, 1946

Mr. Sidney Stark
Stephens & Stark Ltd.
21 St. James's Place
London S.W.1

Dear Sidney,

I could hardly believe it was you, telephoning from London last night! How wise of you not to tell me you were flying home; you know how planes terrify me—even when they aren't dropping bombs. Wonderful to know you are no longer five oceans away, but only across the Channel. Will you come to see us as soon as you can?

Isola is better than a stalking horse. She has brought seven people over to tell me their Occupation stories—and I have a growing packet of interview notes. But for now, notes are all they are. I don't know yet if a book is possible—or, if possible, what form it should take.

Kit has taken to spending some of her mornings here. She brings rocks or shells and sits quietly—well, moderately quietly—on the floor and plays with them while I work. When I am finished, we take a picnic lunch down to the beach. If it's too foggy, we play indoors; either Beauty Parlor—brushing each other's hair until it crackles—or Dead Bride.

Dead Bride is not a complicated game like Snakes and Ladders; it's quite simple. The bride veils herself in a lace curtain and stuffs herself into the laundry hamper, where she lies as though dead while the anguished bridegroom hunts for her. When he finally discovers her entombed in the laundry hamper, he breaks into loud wails. Then and only then does the bride jump up, yell "Surprise!" and clutch him to her. Then it is all joy and smiles and kisses. Privately, I don't give that marriage much of a chance.

I knew that all children were gruesome, but I don't know whether I'm supposed to encourage them in it. I'm afraid to ask Sophie if Dead Bride is too morbid a game for a four-year-old. If she says yes, we'll have to stop playing, and I don't want to stop. I love Dead Bride.

So many questions arise when you are spending your days with a child. For instance, if one likes to cross one's eyes a lot, might they get stuck that way forever—or is that a rumor? My mother said they would, and I believed her, but Kit is made of sterner stuff and doubts it.

I am trying hard to remember my parents' ideas about child-raising, but, as the child raised, I'm scarcely a good judge. I know I got spanked for spitting my peas across the table at Mrs. Morris, but that's all I can recall. Perhaps she deserved it. Kit seems to show no ill-effects from having been brought up piece-meal by Society members. It certainly hasn't made her fearful and retiring. I asked Amelia about it yesterday. She smiled and said there was no hope that a child of Elizabeth's would be fearful and retiring. Then she told me a lovely story about her son, Ian, and Elizabeth when they were children. He was to be sent to school in England, and he was not at all happy about it, so he decided to run away from home. He consulted Jane and Elizabeth, and Elizabeth persuaded him to buy her boat for his escape. The trouble was, she had no boat—but she didn't tell him that. Instead, she built one herself in three days. On the appointed afternoon, they hauled it down to the beach, and Ian set off, with

Elizabeth and Jane waving their hankies from the shore. About half a mile out, the boat began to sink—fast. Jane was all for running to get her father, but Elizabeth said there wasn't time and since it was all her fault, she would have to save him. She took off her shoes, dove into the waves, and swam out to Ian. Together, they pulled the wreckage to shore, and she brought the boy to Sir Ambrose's house to dry off. She returned his money, and as they sat steaming before the fire, she turned to him and said gloomily, "We'll just have to steal a boat, that's all." Ian told his mother that he decided it would be simpler to go to school after all.

I know it will take a prodigious amount of time to catch up on your work. If you do have a moment to spare, could you find a book of paper dolls for me? One full of glamorous evening gowns, please.

I know Kit is growing fond of me—she pats my knee in passing.

Love,
Juliet

From Juliet to Sidney

10th June, 1946

Dear Sidney,

I've just received a wonderful package from your new secretary. Is her name really Billee Bee Jones? Never mind, she's a genius anyway. She found Kit two books of paper dolls—and not just any old paper dolls either. She found Greta Garbo and *Gone with the Wind* paper dolls—pages of lovely gowns, furs, hats, boas—oh, they are wonderful. Billee Bee also sent a pair of snub-nosed scissors, a piece of thoughtfulness that would never have occurred to me. Kit is using them now.

This is not a letter, but a thank-you note. I'm writing one to Billee Bee, too. However did you find such an efficient person? I hope she's plump and motherly, because that's how I'm imagining her. She enclosed a note saying eyes do not stay crossed permanently—it's an old wives' tale. Kit is thrilled and plans to cross her eyes until supper.

> Love to you,
> Juliet

P.S. I would like to point out that contrary to certain insinuating remarks in your last, Mr. Dawsey Adams makes no appearance in this letter. I haven't seen Mr. Dawsey Adams since Friday afternoon, when he came to pick up Kit. He found us decked in our finest jewels and marching about the room to the stirring strains of *Pomp and Circumstance* on the gramophone. Kit made him a dishtowel cape, and he marched with us. I think he has an aristocrat lurking in his genealogy; he can gaze benevolently into the middle distance just like a duke.

Letter received in Guernsey on 12th June, 1946

To: "Eben" or "Isola" or Any Member of a Book Society
on Guernsey, Channel Islands, Great Britain
(Delivered to Eben 14th June, 1946)

Dear Guernsey Book Society,

I greet you as those dear to my friend Elizabeth McKenna. I write to you now so that I may tell you of her death in Ravensbrück Concentration Camp. She was executed there in March of 1945.

In those days before the Russian Army arrived to free the camp, the SS carried truck loads of papers to the crematorium and burned them in the furnaces there. Thus I feared you might never learn of Elizabeth's imprisonment and death.

Elizabeth spoke often to me of Amelia, Isola, Dawsey, Eben, and Booker. I recall no surnames but believe the names Eben and Isola to be unusual Christian names and thus hope you may be found easily on Guernsey.

I know also that she cherished you as her family, and she felt gratitude and peace that her daughter, Kit, was in your care. Therefore, I write so you and the child will know of her and the strength she showed to us in the camp. Not strength only, but a métier she had for making us forget where we were for a small while. Elizabeth was my friend, and in that place friendship was all that aided one to remain human.

I reside now at the Hospice La Forêt in Louviers in Normandy. My English is yet poor, so Sister Touvier is improving my sentences as she writes them down.

I am now twenty-four years of age. In 1944, I was caught by

the Gestapo at Plouha in Brittany, with a packet of forged ration cards. I was questioned, beaten only, and sent to Ravensbrück Concentration Camp. I was put in Block Eleven, and it was here I met Elizabeth.

I will tell you how we met. One evening she came to me and said my name, Remy. I had a joy to hear my name spoken. She said, "Come with me. I have a wonderful surprise to show you." I did not understand her meaning, but I ran with her to the back of the barracks. A broken window there was stuffed with papers, and she pulled them out. We climbed out and ran toward the Lagerstrasse.

There I saw fully what she had meant by a wonderful surprise. The sky showing above the walls looked to be on fire—low-flying clouds of red and purple, lit from below with dark gold. They changed shapes and shades as they raced together across the sky. We stood there, hand in hand, until the darkness came.

I do not think that anyone outside such a place could know how much that meant to me, to spend such a quiet moment together.

Our home, Block Eleven, held almost four hundred women. In front of each barracks was a cinder path where roll call was held twice a day, at 5:30 A.M., and in the evening after work. The women from each barracks stood in squares of one hundred women each—ten women in ten rows. The squares would stretch so far to the right and left of ours, we could often not see the end of them in the fog.

Our beds were on wooden shelves, built in platforms of three. There were pallets of straw to sleep upon, sour smelling and alive with fleas and lice. There were large yellow rats which ran over our feet at night. This was a good thing, for the overseers hated the rats and stench, so we would have freedom from them in the late nights.

Then, Elizabeth told me about your island of Guernsey and your book society. These things seemed like Heaven to me. In the bunks, the air we breathed was weighted with sickness and filth, but when Elizabeth spoke, I could imagine the good, fresh sea air and the smell of fruit in the hot sun. Though it cannot be true, I do not remember the sun shining one day on Ravensbrück. I loved to hear, too, about how your book society came to be. I almost laughed when she told of the roasted pig, but I didn't. Laughter made trouble in the barracks.

There were several standpipes with cold water for us to wash in. Once a week we were taken for showers and given a piece of soap. This was necessary for us, for the thing we feared most was to be dirty, to fester. We dared not become ill, for then we could not work. We would be of no further use to the Germans and they would have us put to death.

Elizabeth and I walked with our group each morning at 6:00, to reach the Siemens factory where we worked. It was outside the walls of the prison. Once there, we pushed handcarts to the railroad siding and unloaded heavy metal plates onto the carts. We were given wheat paste and peas at noon, and returned to camp for roll call at 6:00 P.M. and a supper of turnip soup.

Our duties changed according to need, and one day we were ordered to dig a trench to store potatoes in for winter. Our friend Alina stole a potato but dropped it on the ground. All digging stopped until the overseer could discover the thief.

Alina had ulcerated corneas, and it was necessary that the overseers not notice this—for they might think her to be going blind. Elizabeth said quickly she had taken the potato, and was sent to the punishment bunker for one week.

The cells in this bunker were very small. One day, while Elizabeth was there, a guard opened the door to each cell and turned high-pressure water hoses on the prisoners. The force of the water pushed Elizabeth to the floor, but she was fortunate that the water never reached her folded blanket. She was eventually able to rise and lie under her blanket until the shivering stopped. But a young pregnant girl in the next cell was not so fortunate or so strong as to get up. She died that night, frozen to the floor.

I am perhaps saying too much, things you do not wish to hear. But I must do this to tell you how Elizabeth lived—and how she held on hard to her kindness and her courage. I would like her daughter to know this also.

Now I must tell you the cause of her death. Often, within months of being in camp, most women stopped menstruation. But some did not. The camp doctors had made no provision for the prisoners' hygiene during this time—no rags, no sanitary towels, no soap. The women who were menstruating just had to let the blood run down their legs.

The overseers liked this, this oh so unsightly blood, it gave them the excuse to scream, to hit. A woman named Binta was the overseer for our evening roll call and she began to rage at a bleeding girl. Rage at her, and threaten her with her upraised rod. Then she began to beat the girl.

Elizabeth broke out of our line fast—so fast. She grabbed the rod from Binta's hand and turned it upon her, hitting her over and over. Guards came running and two of them struck Elizabeth to the ground with their rifles. They threw her into a truck and took her again to the punishment bunker.

One of the guards told me that on the next morning soldiers formed a guard around Elizabeth and took her from her cell. Outside the camp walls there was a grove of poplar trees. The branches of the trees formed an allée and Elizabeth walked down this by herself, unaided. She knelt on the ground and they shot her in the back of her head.

I will stop now. I know that I often felt my friend beside me when I was ill after the camp. I had fevers, and I imagined that Elizabeth and I were sailing to Guernsey in a little boat. We had planned this in Ravensbrück—how we would live together in her cottage with her baby, Kit. It helped me to sleep.

I hope you will come to feel Elizabeth by your side as I do. Her strength did not fail her, nor her mind, not ever—she just saw one cruelty too many.

Please accept my best wishes,
Remy Giraud

Note from Sister Cecile Touvier,
placed in the envelope with Remy's letter

Sister Cecile Touvier, Nurse, writing to you. I have made Remy go to rest now. I do not approve of this long letter. But she insisted on writing it.

She will not tell you how sick she has been, but I will. In the few days before the Russians arrived at Ravensbrück, those filthy Nazis ordered anyone who could walk to leave. Opened the gates and turned them loose upon the devastated countryside. "Go," they ordered. "Go—find any Allied troops that you can."

They left those exhausted, starving women to walk miles and miles without any food or water. There were not even any gleanings left in the fields they walked past. Was it any wonder their walk became a death march? Hundreds of the women died on the road.

After several days, Remy's legs and body were so swollen with famine edema, she could not continue to walk. So she just laid herself down in the road to die. Fortunately, a company of American soldiers found her. They tried to give her something to eat, but her body would not receive it. They carried her to a field hospital, where she was given a bed and quarts of water were drained from her body. After many months in hospital, she was well enough to be sent to this hospice in Louviers. I will tell you she weighed less than sixty pounds when she arrived here. Otherwise, she would have written you sooner.

It is my belief that she will get her strength back properly once she has written this letter and she can set about laying her friend to rest. You may, of course, write to her, but please do not ask her questions about Ravensbrück. It will be best for her to forget.

Yours truly,
Sister Cecile Touvier

From Amelia to Remy Giraud

16th June, 1946

Mlle. Remy Giraud
Hospice La Forêt
Louviers
France

Dear Mlle. Giraud,

How good you were to write to us—how good and how kind. It could not have been an easy task to call up your own terrible memories in order to tell us of Elizabeth's death. We had been praying that she would return to us, but it is better to know the truth than to live in uncertainty. We were grateful to learn of your friendship with Elizabeth and to think of the comfort you gave to one another.

May Dawsey Adams and I come visit you in Louviers? We would like to, very much, but not if you would find our visit too disturbing. We want to know you and we have an idea to propose. But again, if you'd prefer that we didn't, we will not come.

Always, our blessings for your kindness and courage.

Sincerely,
Amelia Maugery

From Juliet to Sidney

16th June, 1946

Dear Sidney,

How comforting it was to hear you say "God damn, oh God damn." That's the only honest thing to say, isn't it? Elizabeth's death is an abomination and it will never be anything else.

It's odd, I suppose, to mourn so for someone you've never met. But I do. I have felt Elizabeth's presence all along; she lingers in every room I enter, not just in the cottage, but in Amelia's library, which she stocked with books, and Isola's kitchen, where she stirred up potions. Everyone always speaks of her—even now—in the present tense, and I had convinced myself that she would return. I wanted so much to know her.

It's worse for everyone else. When I saw Eben yesterday, he seemed older than ever before. I'm glad he has Eli by him. Isola has disappeared. Amelia says not to worry; she does that when she's sick at heart.

Dawsey and Amelia have decided to go to Louviers to try to persuade Mlle. Giraud to come to Guernsey. There was a heartrending moment in her letter—Elizabeth used to help her go to sleep in the camp by planning their future in Guernsey. She said it sounded like Heaven. The poor girl is due for some Heaven; she has already been through Hell.

I am to take care of Kit while they are gone. I am so sad for her—she will never know her mother—except by hearsay. I wonder about her future, too, as she is now—officially—an orphan. Mr. Dilwyn told me there is plenty of time to make a decision. "Let us leave well enough alone at the moment." He doesn't sound like any other banker or trustee I've ever heard of, bless his heart.

All my love,
Juliet

From Juliet to Mark

17th June, 1946

Dear Mark,

I'm sorry that our conversation ended badly last night. It's very difficult to convey shades of meaning while roaring into the telephone. It's true—I don't want you to come this weekend. But it has nothing whatever to do with you. My friends have just been dealt a terrible blow. Elizabeth was the center of the circle here, and the news of her death has shaken us all. How strange—

when I picture you reading that sentence, I see you wondering why this woman's death has anything to do with me or you or your plans for the weekend. It does. I feel as though I'd lost someone very close to me. I am in mourning.

Do you understand a little better now?

Yours,
Juliet

From Dawsey to Juliet

21st June, 1946

Miss Juliet Ashton
Grand Manoir, Cottage
La Bouvée
St. Martin's, Guernsey

Dear Juliet,

We are here in Louviers, though we have not been to see Remy yet. The trip has tired Amelia very much and she wants to rest for a night before we go to the hospice.

It was a direful journey across Normandy. Piles of blasted stone walls and twisted metal line the roads in towns. There are big gaps between buildings, and the ones left look like black, broken-off teeth. Whole fronts of houses are gone and you can see in, to the flowered wallpaper and the tilted bedsteads clinging somehow to the floors. I know now how fortunate Guernsey really was in the war.

Many people are still in the streets, hauling away bricks and stone in wheelbarrows and carts. They've made roads of heavy wire netting placed over rubble, and tractors are moving along them. Outside the towns are ruined fields with huge craters and torn-up land and hedges.

It is grievous to see the trees. No big poplars, elms, and chestnuts—what's left is pitiful, charred black, and stunted—sticks without shade.

Mr. Piaget, the innkeeper here, told us that the German engineers ordered hundreds of soldiers to chop down trees—whole woods and coppices. Then they stripped off the branches, smeared the trunks with creosote, and stuck them upright in holes they had dug in the fields. The trees were called Rommel's Asparagus and were meant to keep Allied gliders from landing and soldiers from parachuting.

Amelia went to bed right after supper, so I walked through Louviers. The town is pretty in spots, though much of it was bombed and the Germans set fire to it when they retreated. I cannot see how it will become a living town again.

I came back and sat on the terrace till full dark, thinking about tomorrow.

Give Kit a hug from me.

Yours ever,
Dawsey

From Amelia to Juliet

23rd June, 1946

Dear Juliet,

We met Remy yesterday. I felt unequal somehow to meeting her. But not, thank Heavens, Dawsey. He calmly pulled up lawn chairs, sat us down under a shade tree, and asked a nurse if we could have tea.

I wanted Remy to like us, to feel safe with us. I wanted to learn more about Elizabeth, but I was frightened of Remy's fragility and Sister Touvier's admonitions. Remy is very small and is far too thin. Her dark curly hair is cut close to her head, and her eyes are enormous and haunted. You can see that she was a beauty in better times, but now—she is like glass. Her hands tremble a good deal, and she is careful to hold them down in her lap. She welcomed us as much as she was able, but she was very reserved until she asked about Kit—had she gone on to Sir Ambrose in London?

Dawsey told her of Sir Ambrose's death and how we are raising Kit. He showed her the photograph of you and Kit that he carries. She smiled then and said, "She is Elizabeth's child. Is she strong?" I couldn't speak, thinking of our lost Elizabeth, but Dawsey said yes, very strong, and told her about Kit's passion for ferrets. That made her smile again.

Remy is alone in the world. Her father died long before the war; in 1943, her mother was sent to Drancy for harboring enemies of the government and later died in Auschwitz. Remy's two brothers are missing; she thought she saw one of them in a German train station as she was on her way to Ravensbrück, but he did not turn when she screamed his name. The other she has not seen since 1941. She believes that they, too, must be dead. I was glad Dawsey had the courage to ask her questions—Remy seemed to find relief in speaking of her family.

I finally broached the subject of Remy coming to stay awhile with me in Guernsey. She grew reserved again and explained that she was going to leave the hospice very soon. The French government is offering pensions to concentration-camp survivors: for time lost in camps, for permanent injuries, and for recognition of suffering. They also give a small stipend to those who wish to resume their education.

In addition to the government stipend, the Association Nationale des Anciennes Déportées et Internées de la Résistance will help Remy pay the rent of a room or share a flat with other survivors, so she has decided to go to Paris and seek an apprenticeship in a bakery.

She was adamant about her plans, so I left the matter there, but I don't believe Dawsey is willing to do so. He thinks that sheltering Remy is a moral debt we owe to Elizabeth—perhaps he is right, or perhaps it is simply a way to relieve our sense of helplessness. In any case, he has arranged to go back tomorrow and take Remy for a walk along the canal and to visit a certain patisserie he saw in Louviers. Sometimes, I wonder where our old, shy Dawsey has gone.

I feel well, though I am unusually tired—perhaps it is seeing my beloved Normandy so devastated. I will be glad to be home, my dear.

A kiss for you and Kit,
Amelia

From Juliet to Sidney

28th June, 1946

Dear Sidney,

What an inspired present you sent Kit—red satin tap shoes covered with sequins. Wherever did you find them? Where are mine?

Amelia has been tired since her return from France, so it seems best for Kit to stay with me, especially if Remy decides to come to Amelia's when she leaves the hospice. Kit seems to like the idea too—Heaven be thanked. Kit knows her mother is dead now; Dawsey told her. I'm not sure what she feels about it. She hasn't said anything, and I wouldn't dream of pressing her. I try not to hover unduly or make her special treats. After Mother and Father died, Mr. Simpless's cook brought me huge slices of cake and then stood there, watching me mournfully while I tried to swallow. I hated her for thinking that cake would somehow make it up to me for losing my parents. Of course, I was a wretched twelve-year-old, and Kit is only four—she would probably like some extra cake—but you understand what I mean.

Sidney, I am in trouble with my book. I have much of the data from the States' records and a slew of personal interviews to start the story of the Occupation—but I can't make them come together in a structure that pleases me. Straight chronology is too tedious. Shall I pack my pages up and send them to you? They need a finer and more impersonal eye than mine. Would you have time to look them over now or is the backlog from your Australian trip still so heavy?

If it is, don't worry—I am working anyway and something brilliant may yet come to me.

Love,
Juliet

P.S. Thank you for the lovely clipping of Mark dancing with Ursula Fent. If you were hoping to send me into a jealous rage, you failed. Especially as Mark had already telephoned to tell me that Ursula follows him about like a lovesick bloodhound. You see? The two of you *do* have something in common: you both want me to be miserable. Perhaps you could start a club.

From Sidney to Juliet

1st July, 1946

Dear Juliet,

Don't pack up your pages—I want to come to Guernsey myself. Will this weekend suit you?

I want to see you, Kit, and Guernsey—in that order. I have no intention of reading your pages while you pace up and down in front of me—I'll bring the ms back to London.

I can arrive Friday afternoon on the five o'clock plane and stay until Monday evening. Will you book a hotel room for me? Can you also manage a small supper party? I want to meet Eben, Isola, Dawsey, and Amelia. I'll bring the wine.

Love,
Sidney

From Juliet to Sidney

Wednesday

Dear Sidney,

Wonderful! Isola won't hear of you staying at the inn (she hints of bedbugs). She wants to put you up herself and needs to know if noises at dawn are apt to bother you? That is when Ariel, her goat, arises. Zenobia, the parrot, is a late sleeper.

Dawsey and I and his cart will meet you at the airfield. May Friday hurry up and get here.

Love,
Juliet

From Isola to Juliet (left under Juliet's door)

Friday—close to dawn

Lovey, I can't stop, I must hurry to my Market stall. I am glad your friend will be staying with me. I've put lavender sprigs in his sheets. Is there one of my elixirs you'd like me to slip in his coffee? Just nod to me at Market and I'll know which one you mean.

XXX
Isola

From Sidney to Sophie

6th July, 1946

Dear Sophie,

I am, at last, on Guernsey with Juliet and am ready to tell you three or four of the dozen things you asked me to find out.

First and foremost, Kit seems as fond of Juliet as you and I are. She is a spirited little thing, affectionate in a reserved way (which is not as contradictory as it sounds) and quick to smile when she is with one of her adoptive parents from the Literary Society.

She is adorable, too, with round cheeks, round curls, and round eyes. The temptation to cuddle her is nearly overwhelming, but it would be a slight upon her dignity, and I am not brave enough to try it. When she sees someone she doesn't like, she has a stare that would shrivel Medea. Isola says she reserves it for cruel Mr. Smythe, who beats his dog, and evil Mrs. Guilbert, who called Juliet a Nosy Parker and told her she ought to go back to London where she belonged.

I'll tell you one story of Kit and Juliet together. Dawsey (more about him later) came by to pick Kit up and go see Eben's fishing boat come in. Kit said good-bye, flew out, then flew back in, ran up to Juliet, lifted her skirt a quarter of an inch, kissed her knee-cap, and flew back out again. Juliet looked dumbfounded—and then as happy as you or I have ever seen her.

I know you think Juliet seemed tired, worn, frazzled, and pale when you saw her last winter. I don't think you realize how harrowing those teas and interviews can be; she looks as healthy as a horse now and is full of her old zest. So full, Sophie, I think she may never want to live in London again—though she doesn't realize it yet. Sea air, sunshine, green fields, wildflowers, the ever-changing sky and ocean, and most of all, the people seem to have seduced her from City life.

I can easily see how they could. It's such a homey, welcoming place. Isola is the kind of hostess you always wished you'd come across on a country visit—but never do. She rousted me out of bed the first morning to help her dry rose petals, churn butter, stir up something (God knows what) in a big pot, feed Ariel, and go to the fish market to buy her an eel. All of this with Zenobia the parrot on my shoulder.

Now, about Dawsey Adams. I have inspected him, as per instructions. I liked what I saw. He's quiet, capable, trustworthy—oh Lord, I've made him sound like a dog—and he has a sense of humor. In short, he is completely unlike any of Juliet's other swains—praise indeed. He did not say much at our first meeting—nor at any of our meetings since, come to think of it—but let him walk into a room, and everyone in it seems to breathe a little sigh of relief. I have never in my life had that effect on anyone, can't imagine why not. Juliet seems a bit nervous around him—his silence *is* slightly daunting—and she made a dreadful mess of the tea things when he came by for Kit yesterday. But Juliet has always shattered teacups—remember what she did to Mother's Spode?—so that may not signify. As for him, he watches her with dark, steady eyes—until she looks at him and then he glances away (I do hope you're appreciating my observational skills).

One thing I can say unequivocally: he's worth dozens of Mark Reynoldses. I know you think I'm unreasonable about Reynolds, but you haven't met him. He's all charm and oil, and he gets what he wants. It's one of his few principles. He wants Juliet because she's pretty and "intellectual" at the same time, and he thinks they'll make an impressive couple. If she marries him, she'll spend the rest of her life being shown to people at theaters and clubs and weekends and she'll never write another book. As her editor, I'm dismayed by that prospect, but as her friend, I'm horrified. It will be the end of our Juliet.

It's hard to say what Juliet is thinking about Reynolds, if anything. I asked her if she missed him, and she said, "Mark? I suppose so," as if he were a distant uncle, and not a favorite one at that. I'd be delighted if she forgot all about him, but I don't think he'll allow it.

To return to minor topics like the Occupation and Juliet's book, I was invited to accompany her on calls to several Islanders this afternoon. Her interviews were to be about Guernsey's Day of Liberation on May 9 last year.

What a morning that must have been! The crowds were lined up along St. Peter Port's harbor. Silent, absolutely silent, masses of people looking at the Royal Navy ships sitting just outside their harbor. Then when the Tommies landed and marched ashore, all hell broke loose. Hugs, kisses, crying, yelling.

So many of the soldiers landing were Guernseymen themselves. Men who hadn't seen or heard a word from their families in five years. You can imagine their eyes searching the crowds for family members as they marched—and the joy of their reunions.

Mr. LeBrun, a retired postman, told us the most unusual story of all. Some British ships took leave of the fleet in St. Peter Port and sailed a few miles north to St. Sampson's Harbor. Crowds had gathered there, waiting to see the landing craft crash through the German anti-tank barriers and come up onto the beach. When the bay doors opened, out came not a platoon of uniformed soldiers, but one lone man, got up as a caricature English gent in striped trousers, a morning coat, top hat, furled umbrella, and a copy of yesterday's *Times* clasped in his hand. There was a split-second of silence before the joke sank in, and then the crowd roared—he was mobbed, clapped on the back, kissed, and put up on the shoulders of four men to be marched down the street. Someone screamed, "News—news from London herself," and snatched the *Times* out of his hand! Whoever that soldier was, he was brilliant and deserves a medal.

When the rest of the soldiers emerged, they were carrying chocolates, oranges, cigarettes, tea bags to toss to the crowd. Brigadier Snow announced that the cable to England was being repaired, and soon they could be talking to their evacuated children and families in England. The ships also brought in food, tons of it, and medicines, paraffin, animal feed, clothes, cloth, seeds, and shoes!

There must be enough stories to fill three books—it may be a matter of culling. But don't worry if Juliet sounds nervous from time to time—she should. It's a daunting task.

I must stop now and get dressed for Juliet's supper party. Isola is swathed in three shawls and a lace dresser scarf—and I want to do her proud.

Love to you all,
Sidney

From Juliet to Sophie

7th July, 1946

Dear Sophie,

Just a note to tell you Sidney is here and we can stop worrying about him—and his leg. He looks wonderful: tanned, fit, and without a noticeable limp. In fact, we threw his cane in the ocean—I'm sure it's half-way to France by now.

I had a small supper party for him—cooked by me alone, and edible, too. Will Thisbee gave me *The Beginner's Cook-Book for Girl Guides*. It was just the thing; the writer assumes you know nothing about cookery and writes useful hints—"When adding eggs, break the shells first."

Sidney is having a grand time as Isola's houseguest. They apparently sat up late talking last night. Isola doesn't approve of small talk and believes in breaking the ice by stomping on it.

She asked him if we were engaged to be married. If not, why not? It was plain to everyone that we doted on one another.

Sidney told her that indeed he did dote on me; always had, always would, but we both realized we could never marry—he was a homosexual.

Sidney told me that Isola neither gasped, fainted, nor blinked—just gave him her good old fish eye and asked, "And Juliet knows?"

When he told her yes, I had always known, Isola jumped up, swooped down, kissed his forehead, and said, "How nice—just like dear Booker. I'll not tell a soul; you can rely on me."

Then she sat back down and began to talk about Oscar Wilde's plays. Weren't they a stitch? Sophie, wouldn't you have loved to be a fly on the wall? I would.

Sidney and I are going shopping now for a hostess gift for Isola. I said she would love a warm, colorful shawl, but he wants to get her a cuckoo clock. Why???

Love,
Juliet

P.S. Mark doesn't write, he telephones. He rang me up just last week. It was one of those terrible connections that forced us perpetually to interrupt one another and bellow "WHAT?" but I managed to get the gist of the conversation—I should come home and marry him. I politely disagreed. It upset me much less than it would have a month ago.

From Isola to Sidney

8th July, 1946

Dear Sidney,

You are a very nice house guest. I like you. So did Zenobia, else she would not have flown onto your shoulder and cuddled there so long.

I'm glad you like to sit up late and talk. I favor that myself of an evening. I am going to go to the manor now to find the book you told me about. How is it that Juliet and Amelia never made mention of Miss Jane Austen to me?

I hope you will come visit Guernsey again. Did you like Juliet's soup? Wasn't it tasty? She will be ready for pie crust and gravy soon—you must go at cooking slowly, else you'll just make slops.

I was lonesome for company after you left, so I invited Dawsey and Amelia to take tea yesterday. You should have seen how I didn't utter a word when Amelia said she thought you and Juliet were going to marry. I even nodded and slitted my eyes, like I knew something they didn't, to throw them off the scent.

I do like my cuckoo clock. How cheery it is! I run in the kitchen to watch it. I am sorry Zenobia bit the little bird's head off, she has a jealous nature—but Eli said he could carve me another one, as good as new. His little perch still pops out on the hour.

> With fondness, your hostess,
> Isola Pribby

From Juliet to Sidney

9th July, 1946

Dear Sidney,

I knew it! I knew you'd love Guernsey. The next-best thing to being here myself was having you here—even for such a short visit. I'm happy that you know all my friends now, and they you. I'm particularly happy you enjoyed Kit's company so much. I regret to tell you that some of her fondness for you is due to your present, *Elspeth the Lisping Bunny*. Her admiration for Elspeth has caused her to take up lisping, and I am sorry to say, she is very good at it.

Dawsey just brought Kit home—they have been visiting his new piglet. Kit asked if I was writing to Thidney. When I said yes, she said, "Thay I want him to come back thoon." Do you thee what I mean about Elspeth?

That made Dawsey smile, which pleased me. I'm afraid you didn't see the best of Dawsey this weekend; he was extra-quiet at my supper party. Perhaps it was my soup, but I think it more likely that he is preoccupied with Remy. He seems to think that she won't get better until she comes to Guernsey to recuperate.

I am glad you took my pages home to read. God knows I am

at a loss to divine just *what exactly* is wrong with them—I only know something is.

What on earth did you say to Isola? She stopped in on her way to pick up *Pride and Prejudice* and to berate me for never telling her about Elizabeth Bennet and Mr. Darcy. Why hadn't she known there were better love stories around? Stories not riddled with ill-adjusted men, anguish, death, and graveyards! What else had we kept from her?

I apologized for such a lapse and said you were perfectly right, *Pride and Prejudice* was one of the greatest love stories ever written—and she might actually die of suspense before she finished it.

Isola said Zenobia is saddened by your leaving—she's off her feed. So am I, but I'm so grateful you could come at all.

Love,
Juliet

From Sidney to Juliet

12th July, 1946

Dear Juliet,

I've read your chapters several times, and you are right—they won't do. Strings of anecdotes don't make a book.

Juliet, your book needs a center. I don't mean more in-depth interviews. I mean one person's voice to tell what was happening all around her. As written now, the facts, as interesting as they are, seem like random, scattered shots.

It would hurt like hell to write this letter to you, except for one thing. You already have the core—you just don't know it yet.

I am talking about Elizabeth McKenna. Didn't you ever notice how everyone you interviewed sooner or later talked about Elizabeth? Lord, Juliet, who painted Booker's portrait and saved his life and danced down the street with him? Who thought up the lie about the Literary Society—and then made it happen? Guernsey wasn't her home, but she adapted to it and to the loss of her freedom. How? She must have missed Ambrose and London, but she never, I gather, whined about it. She went to Ravensbrück for sheltering a slave worker. Look how and why she died.

Juliet, how did a girl, an art student who had never held a job in her life, turn herself into a nurse, working six days a week in the hospital? She did have dear friends, but in reality she had no one to call her own at first. She fell in love with an enemy officer and lost him; she had a baby alone during war time. It must have been fearful, despite all her good friends. You can only share re-sponsibilities up to a point.

I'm sending back the ms and your letters to me—read them again and see how often Elizabeth is spoken of. Ask yourself why. Talk to Dawsey and Eben. Talk to Isola and Amelia. Talk to Mr. Dilwyn and to anyone else who knew her well.

You live in her house. Look around you at her books, her be-longings.

I think you should write your book around Elizabeth. I think Kit would greatly value a story about her mother—it would give her something to hang on to, later. So, either quit altogether—or get to know Elizabeth well.

Think long and hard and tell me if Elizabeth could be the heart of your book.

Love to you and Kit,
Sidney

From Juliet to Sidney

15th July, 1946

Dear Sidney,

I don't need more time to think about it—the minute I read your letter, I knew you were right. So slow-witted! Here I've been, wishing that I had known Elizabeth, missing her as if I had—why did I never once think of writing about her?

I'll begin tomorrow. I want to talk to Dawsey, Amelia, Eben, and Isola first. I feel that she belongs to them more than the others, and I want their blessing.

Remy wants to come to Guernsey, after all. Dawsey has been writing to her, and I knew he could persuade her to come. He could talk an angel out of Heaven if he chose to speak, which is not often enough to suit me. Remy will stay with Amelia, so I get to keep Kit with me.

Undying love and gratitude,
Juliet

P.S. You don't suppose Elizabeth kept a diary, do you?

From Juliet to Sidney

17th July, 1946

Dear Sidney,

No diary, but the good news is she did draw while her paper and pencil lasted. I found some sketches stuffed into a large art folio on the bottom shelf of the sitting-room bookcase. Quick line drawings that seem marvelous portraits to me: Isola caught unaware, hitting at something with a wooden spoon; Dawsey digging in a garden; Eben and Amelia with their heads together, talking.

As I sat on the floor, turning them over, Amelia dropped by for a visit. Together we pulled out several large sheets of paper, covered with sketch after sketch of Kit. Kit asleep, Kit on the move, on a lap, being rocked by Amelia, hypnotized by her toes, delighted with her spit bubbles. Maybe every mother looks at her baby that way—with that intense focus—but Elizabeth put it on paper. There was one shaky drawing of a wizened little Kit, made the day after she was born, according to Amelia.

Then I found a sketch of a man with a good, strong, rather broad face; he's relaxed and appears to be looking over his shoulder, smiling at the artist. I knew at once it was Christian—he and Kit have a cowlick in exactly the same place. Amelia took the paper into her hands; I had never heard her speak of him before and asked if she had liked him.

"Poor boy," she said. "I was so set against him. It seemed insane to me that Elizabeth had chosen him—an enemy, a German—and I was frightened for her. For the rest of us, too. I thought that she was too trusting, and he would betray her and us—so I told her that I thought she should break off with him. I was very stern with her.

"Elizabeth just stuck out her chin and said nothing. But the next day, he came to visit me. Oh, I was appalled. I opened the door and there was an enormous, uniformed German standing before me. I was sure my house was about to be requisitioned and I began to protest when he thrust forward a bunch of flowers—limp from being clutched. I noticed he was looking very nervous, so I stopped scolding and demanded to know his name. 'Captain Christian Hellman,' he said, and blushed like a boy. I was still suspicious—what was he up to?—and asked him the purpose of his visit. He blushed more and said softly, 'I've come to tell you my intentions.'

" 'For my house?' I snapped.

" 'No. For Elizabeth,' he said. And that's what he did—just as if I were the Victorian father and he the suitor. He perched on the edge of a chair in my drawing room and told me that he intended to come back to the Island the moment the war was over, marry Elizabeth, raise freesias, read, and forget about war. By the time he was finished speaking, I was a little in love with him myself."

Amelia was half in tears, so we put the sketches away and I made her some tea. Then Kit came in with a shattered gull's egg she wanted to glue together, and we were thankfully distracted.

Yesterday Will Thisbee appeared at my door with a plate of cakes iced with prune whip, so I invited him to tea. He wanted to consult with me about two different women; and which one of the two I'd marry if I were a man, which I wasn't. (Do you have that straight?)

Miss X has always been a ditherer—she was a ten-month baby and has not improved in any material way since then. When she heard the Germans were coming, she buried her mother's silver teapot under an elm tree and now can't remember which tree. She is digging holes all over the Island, vowing she won't stop till she finds it. "Such determination," said Will. "Quite unlike her." (Will was trying to be subtle, but Miss X is Daphne Post. She has round vacant eyes like a cow's and is famous for her trembling soprano in the church choir.)

And then there is Miss Y, a local seamstress. When the Germans arrived, they had only packed one Nazi flag. This they needed to hang over their headquarters, but that left them with nothing to run up a flag pole to remind the Islanders they'd been conquered.

They visited Miss Y and ordered her to make a Nazi flag for them. She did—a black, nasty swastika, stitched onto a circle of dingy puce. The surrounding field was not scarlet silk, but baby-bottom-pink flannel. "So inventive in her spite," said Will. "So forceful!" (Miss Y is Miss Le Roy, thin as one of her needles, with a lantern jaw and tight-folded lips.)

Which did I think would make the best companion for a man's nether years, Miss X or Miss Y? I told him that if one had to ask which, it generally meant neither.

He said, "That's exactly what Dawsey said—those very words. Isola said Miss X would bore me to tears, and Miss Y would nag me to death.

"Thank you, thank you—I shall keep up my search. *She* is out there somewhere."

He put on his cap, bowed, and left. Sidney, he may have been polling the entire Island, but I was so flattered to have been included—it made me feel like an Islander instead of an Outlander.

Love,
Juliet

P.S. I was interested to learn that Dawsey has opinions on marriage. I wish I knew more about them.

From Juliet to Sidney

19th July, 1946

Dear Sidney,

Stories of Elizabeth are everywhere—not just among the Society members. Listen to this: Kit and I walked up to the churchyard this afternoon. Kit was off playing among the tombstones, and I was stretched out on Mr. Edwin Mulliss's tombstone—it's a table-top one, with four stout legs—when Sam Withers, the cemetery's ancient groundskeeper, stopped beside me. He said I reminded him of Miss McKenna when she was a young girl. She used to take the sun right there on that very slab—brown as a walnut she'd get.

I sat up straight as an arrow and asked Sam if he had known Elizabeth well.

Sam said, "Well—not as to say real well, but I liked her. She and Eben's girl, Jane, used to come up here together to that very tombstone. They'd spread a cloth and eat their picnic—right on top of Mr. Mulliss's dead bones."

Sam went on about what catbirds those two little girls were, always up to some mischief—they tried to raise a ghost one time and scared the daylights out of the vicar's wife. Then he looked over at Kit, who'd reached the church gate by then and said, "That's surely a sweet little girl of hers and Captain Hellman's."

I pounced on that. Had he known Captain Hellman? Had he liked him?

He glared at me and said, "Yes, I did. He was a fine fella, for all he was a German. You're not going to throw off on Miss McKenna's little girl because of that, are you?"

"I wouldn't dream of it!" I said.

He waggled a finger at me. "You'd better not, missy! You'd best learn the truth of certain matters, before you go trying to write any book about the Occupation. I hated the Occupation, too. Makes me mad to think of it. Some of those blighters was purely mean—come right into your house without knocking—push you around. They was the sort to like having the upper hand, never having had it before. But not all of them was like that—not all, by a long shot."

Christian, according to Sam, was not. Sam liked Christian. He and Elizabeth had come upon Sam in the churchyard once, trying to dig out a grave when the ground was ice-hard and as cold as Sam himself. Christian picked up the shovel and threw his back into it. "He was a strong fella, and he was done as soon as he started," Sam said. "Told him he could have a job with me anytime, and he laughed."

The next day, Elizabeth came out with a thermos jug full of hot coffee. Real coffee from real beans Christian had brought to her house. She gave him a warm sweater too that had belonged to Christian.

Sam said, "Truth to tell, as long as the Occupation was to last, I met more than one nice German soldier. You would, you know, seeing some of them as much as every day for five years. Greetings were bound to happen.

"You couldn't help but feel sorry for some of them—there at the last—stuck here and knowing their folks back home were being bombed to pieces. Didn't matter then who started it in the first place. Not to me, anyway.

"Why, there'd be soldiers riding guard in the back of potato lorries going to the army's mess hall—children would follow them, hoping potatoes would fall off into the street. Soldiers would look straight ahead, grim-like, and then flick potatoes off the pile—on purpose.

"They did the same thing with oranges. Same with lumps of coal—my, those were precious when we didn't have no fuel left. There was many such incidents. Just ask Mrs. Godfray about her boy. He had the pneumonia and she was worried half to death because she couldn't keep him warm nor give him good food to eat. One day there's a knock on her door and when she opens up, she sees an orderly from the German hospital on the step. Without a peep, he hands her a vial of that sulfonamide, tips his cap, and walks away. He had stolen it from their dispensary for her. They caught him later, trying to steal some again, and they sent him off to prison in Germany—maybe hung him. We'd not be knowing which."

He glared at me again suddenly. "And I say that if some toffee-nosed Brit wants to call being human Collaboration, they'll need to talk to me and Mrs. Godfray first!"

I tried to protest, but Sam turned his back and walked away. I gathered Kit up and we came on home. Between the wilted flowers for Amelia and the coffee beans for Sam Withers, I felt I was beginning to know Kit's father—and why Elizabeth must have loved him.

Next week will bring Remy to Guernsey. Dawsey leaves for France on Tuesday to fetch her.

Love,
Juliet

From Juliet to Sophie

22nd July, 1946

Dear Sophie,

Burn this letter; I would not care to have it appear among your collected papers.

I've told you about Dawsey, of course. You know that he was the first here to write me; that he is fond of Charles Lamb; that he is helping to raise Kit; that she adores him.

What I haven't told you is that on the very first evening that I arrived on the Island, the moment Dawsey held out both his hands to me at the bottom of the gangplank, I felt an unaccountable jolt of excitement. Dawsey is so quiet and composed that I had no idea if it was only me, so I've struggled to be reasonable and casual and *usual* for the last two months. And I was doing very nicely—until tonight.

Dawsey came over to borrow a suitcase for his trip to Louviers—he is going to collect Remy and bring her here. What kind of man doesn't even own a suitcase? Kit was sound asleep, so we put my case in his cart and walked up to the headlands. The moon was coming up and the sky was colored in mother-of-pearl, like the inside of a shell. The sea for once was quiet, with only silvery ripples, barely moving. No wind. I have never heard the world be so silent before, and it dawned on me that Dawsey himself was exactly that silent too, walking beside me. I was as close to him as I've ever been, so I began to take particular note of his wrists and hands. I was wanting to touch them, and the thought made me light-headed. There was a knife-edgy feeling—you know the one—in the pit of my stomach.

All at once, Dawsey turned. His face was shadowed, but I could see his eyes—very dark eyes—watching me, waiting. Who knows what might have happened next—a kiss? A pat on the head? Nothing?—because in the next second we heard Wally Beall's horse-drawn carriage (that's our local taxi) pull up to my cottage, and Wally's passenger called out, "Surprise, darling!"

It was Mark—Markham V. Reynolds, Junior, resplendent in his exquisitely tailored suit, with a swath of red roses over his arm.

I truly wished him dead, Sophie.

But what could I do? I went to greet him—and when he kissed me all I could think of was *Don't! Not in front of Dawsey!* He deposited the roses on my arm and turned to Dawsey with his steely smile. So I introduced the two of them, wishing all the time I could crawl into a hole—I don't know why, exactly—and watched dumbly as Dawsey shook his hand, turned to me, shook my hand, said, "Thank you for the suitcase, Juliet. Good-night," climbed in his cart, and left. Left, without another word, without a backward glance.

I wanted to cry. Instead I invited Mark indoors and tried to seem like a woman who had just received a delightful surprise. The wagon and the introductions had awakened Kit, who looked suspiciously at Mark and wanted to know where Dawsey had gone—he hadn't kissed her good-night. Me neither, I thought to myself.

I put Kit back to bed and persuaded Mark that my reputation would be in tatters if he didn't go to the Royal Hotel at once. Which he did, with a very bad grace and many threats to appear on my doorstep this morning at six.

Then I sat down and chewed my fingernails for three hours. Should I take myself over to Dawsey's house and try to pick up where we left off? But where *did* we leave off? I'm not sure. I don't want to make a fool of myself. What if he looked at me with polite incomprehension—or worse yet, with pity?

And besides—what am I thinking? Mark is here. Mark, who is rich and debonair and wants to marry me. Mark, whom I was doing very well without. Why can't I stop thinking about Dawsey, who probably doesn't give a hoot about me. But maybe he does. Maybe I was about to find out what's on the other side of that silence.

Damn, damn, and damn.

It's two in the morning, I have not a fingernail to my name, and I look at least a hundred years old. Maybe Mark will be repulsed by my haggard mien when he sees me. Maybe he will spurn me. I don't know that I will be disappointed if he does.

Love,
Juliet

From Amelia to Juliet (left under Juliet's door)

23rd July, 1946

Dear Juliet,

My raspberries have come in with a vengeance. I am picking this morning and making pies this afternoon. Would you and Kit like to come for tea (pie) this afternoon?

Love,
Amelia

From Juliet to Amelia

23rd July, 1946

Dear Amelia—

I'm terribly sorry, I can't come. I have a guest.

Love,
Juliet

P.S. Kit is delivering this in hopes of getting some pie. Can you keep her for the afternoon?

From Juliet to Sophie

24th July, 1946

Dear Sophie,

You should probably burn this letter as well as the last one. I've refused Mark finally and irrevocably, and my elation is indecent. If I were a properly brought-up young lady, I'd draw the curtains and brood, but I can't. I'm *free*! Today I bounced out of bed feeling frisky as a lamb, and Kit and I spent the morning running races in the pasture. She won, but that's because she cheats.

Yesterday was a horror. You know how I felt when Mark appeared, but the next morning was even worse. He turned up at my door at seven, radiating confidence and certain that we'd have a wedding date set by noon. He wasn't the least bit interested in the Island, or the Occupation, or Elizabeth, or what I'd been doing since I arrived—didn't ask a single question about any of it. Then Kit came down to breakfast. That surprised him—he hadn't really registered her the night before. He had a nice way with her—they talked about dogs—but after a few minutes, it was obvious he was waiting for her to clear off. I suppose in his experience, nannies whisk the children away before they can annoy their parents. Of course, I tried to ignore his irritation and made Kit her breakfast as usual, but I could feel his displeasure billowing across the room.

At last Kit went outside to play, and the minute the door closed behind her, Mark said, "Your new friends must be damned smart—they've managed to saddle you with their responsibilities in less than two months." He shook his head—pitying me for being so gullible.

I just stared at him.

"She's a cute kid, but she's got no claim on you, Juliet, and you're going to have to be firm about it. Get her a nice dolly or something and say good-bye, before she starts thinking you're going to take care of her for the rest of her life."

Now I was so angry I couldn't talk. I stood there, gripping Kit's porridge bowl with white knuckles. I didn't throw it at him, but I was close to it. Finally, when I could speak again, I whispered, "Get out."

"Sorry?"

"I never want to see you again."

"Juliet?" He really had no idea what I was talking about.

So I explained. Feeling better by the minute, I told him that I would never marry him or anyone else who didn't love Kit and Guernsey and Charles Lamb.

"What the hell does Charles Lamb have to do with anything?" he yelped (as well he might).

I declined to elucidate. He tried to argue with me, then to coax me, then to kiss me, then to argue with me again, but—it was over, and even Mark knew it. For the first time in ages—since February, when I met him—I was completely sure that I had done the right thing. How could I ever have considered marrying him? One year as his wife, and I'd have become one of those abject, quaking women who look at their husbands when someone asks them a question. I've always despised that type, but I see how it happens now.

Two hours later, Mark was on his way to the airfield, never (I hope) to return. And I, disgracefully un-heartbroken, was gobbling raspberry pie at Amelia's. Last night, I slept the sleep of the innocent for ten blissful hours, and this morning I feel thirty-two again, instead of a hundred.

Kit and I are going to spend this afternoon at the beach, hunting for agates. What a beautiful, beautiful day.

Love,
Juliet

P.S. None of this means anything with regard to Dawsey. Charles Lamb just popped out of my mouth by coincidence. Dawsey didn't even come to say good-bye before he left. The more I think about it, the more convinced I am that he turned on the cliff to ask if he could borrow my umbrella.

From Juliet to Sidney

27th July, 1946

Dear Sidney,

I knew that Elizabeth had been arrested for sheltering a Todt worker, but I hadn't known she had an accomplice until a few days ago, when Eben happened to mention Peter Sawyer, "who was arrested with Elizabeth." "WHAT?" I screeched, and Eben said he'd let Peter tell me about it.

Peter is living now in a nursing home near Le Grand Havre in Vale, so I telephoned him, and he said he'd be very glad to see me—especially if I had a tot of brandy about me.

"Always," I said.

"Lovely. Come tomorrow," he replied, and rang off.

Peter is in a wheelchair, but what a driver he is! He races it around like a madman, cuts round corners and can turn on a six-pence. We went outside, sat under an arbor, and he tippled while he talked. This one time, Sidney, I took notes—I couldn't bear to lose a word.

Peter was already in the wheelchair, but still living in his home in St. Sampson's, when he found the Todt worker, Lud Jaruzki, a sixteen-year-old Polish boy.

Many of the Todt workers were permitted to leave their pens after dark to scrounge for food—as long as they came back. They were to return for work the next morning—and if they didn't, a hunt went up for them. This "parole" was one way the Germans had to see the workers didn't starve—without wasting too much of their own foodstuffs on them.

Almost every Islander had a vegetable garden—some had hen

houses and rabbit hutches—a rich harvest for foragers. And that is what the Todt slave workers were—foragers. Most Islanders kept watch over their gardens at night—armed with sticks or poles to defend their vegetables.

Peter stayed outside at night too, in the shadows of his hen house. No pole for him, but a big iron skillet and metal spoon to bang it with and sound the alarm for neighbors to come.

One night he heard—then saw—Lud crawl through a gap in his hedgerow. Peter waited; the boy tried to stand but fell down, he tried to get up again, but couldn't—he just lay there. Peter wheeled over and stared down at the boy.

"He was a child, Juliet. Just a child—lying faceup in the dirt. Thin, my God he was thin, wasted and filthy, in rags. He was covered with vermin; they came out from under his hair, crawled across his face, crawled over his eyelids. That poor boy didn't even feel them—no flicker, no nothing. All he'd wanted was a goddamned potato—and he didn't even have the strength to dig it up. To do this to boys!

"I tell you, I hated those Germans with all my heart. I couldn't bend down to see if he was breathing, but I got my feet off my chair pedals and managed to prod and poke him until I got his shoulders turned near me. Now, my arms are strong, and I pulled the boy halfway onto my lap. Somehow, I got us both up my ramp and into the kitchen—there, I let the boy fall on the floor. I built up my fire, got a blanket, heated water; I wiped his poor face and hands and drowned every louse and maggot I picked off him."

Peter couldn't ask his neighbors for help—they might report him to the Germans. The German Commandant had said anyone who sheltered a Todt worker would be sent to a concentration camp or shot where they stood.

Elizabeth was coming to Peter's house the next day—she was his Nursing Aid and she visited once a week, sometimes more.

He knew Elizabeth well enough to be pretty certain that she'd help him keep the boy alive and she'd keep quiet about it.

"She arrived around mid-morning next day. I met her by the door and said I had trouble waiting inside and if she didn't want trouble she shouldn't come in. She knew what I was trying to say, and she nodded and stepped right in. Her jaw clenched when she knelt by Lud on the floor—he smelled something fierce—but she got down to business. She cut off his clothes and burned them. She bathed him, shampooed his hair with tar soap—that was a jolly mess, we did laugh, if you can believe it. Either that or the cold water woke him up some. He was startled—scared till he saw who we were. Elizabeth, she kept speaking softly, not that he could understand a word she said, but he was soothed. We hauled him into my bedroom—we couldn't keep him in my kitchen, neighbors might come in and see him. Well, Elizabeth nursed him. There wasn't any medicine she could get—but she got soup bones for broth and real bread, on the Black Market. I had eggs, and bit by bit, day by day, he got his strength back. He slept a lot. Sometimes Elizabeth had to come after dark, but before curfew. It wouldn't do for anyone to see her coming to my house too often. People told on their neighbors, you know—trying to curry favor, or food, from the Germans.

"But someone did notice, and someone did tell—I don't know who it was. They told the Feldpolizei, and they came on that Tuesday night. Elizabeth had bought some chicken meat, stewed it, and was feeding Lud. I sat by his bedstead.

"They surrounded the house, all quiet until they busted in. Well—we was caught, fair and square. Taken that night, all of us, and God knows what they did to that boy. There wasn't any trial, and we was put on a boat to St. Malo the next day. That's the last I saw of Elizabeth, led into the boat by one of the guards from the prison. She looked so cold. I didn't see her after, when we got to France, and I didn't know where they sent her. They sent me to the federal prison in Coutances, but they didn't know what to do with a prisoner in a wheelchair, so they sent me home again after a week. They told me to be grateful for their leniency."

Peter said he knew Elizabeth had left Kit with Amelia whenever she came to his house. Nobody knew Elizabeth was helping with the Todt worker. He believes she let everyone think she had hospital duty.

Those are the bare bones, Sidney, but Peter asked if I would come back again. I said, yes, I'd love to—and he told me not to bring brandy—just myself. He did say he would like to see some picture magazines if I had any to hand. He wants to know who Rita Hayworth is.

Love,
Juliet

From Dawsey to Juliet

27th July, 1946

Dear Juliet,

It will soon be time for me to gather Remy from the hospice, but as I have a few minutes, I will use them to write to you.

Remy seems stronger now than she was last month, but she is very frail yet. Sister Touvier drew me aside to caution me—I must see to it that she gets enough to eat, that she stays warm, that she's not upset. She must be around people—cheerful people, if possible.

I've no doubt that Remy will get nourishing food, and Amelia will see to it that she's warm enough, but how am I to serve up good cheer? Joking and such is not natural to me. I didn't know what to say to the Sister, so I just nodded and tried to look jolly. I think I was not a success, for Sister glanced at me sharply.

Well, I will do my best, but you, blessed as you are with a sunny nature and light heart, would make a better companion for Remy than I. I don't doubt she will take to you as we all have, these last months, and you will do her good.

Give Kit a hug and kiss for me. I will see you both on Tuesday.

Dawsey

From Juliet to Sophie

29th July, 1946

Dear Sophie,

Please ignore everything I have ever said about Dawsey Adams.

I am an idiot.

I have just received a letter from Dawsey praising the medicinal qualities of my "sunny nature and light heart."

A sunny nature? A light heart? I have never been so insulted. Light-hearted is a short step from witless in my book. A cackling buffoon—that's what I am to Dawsey.

I am also humiliated—while I was feeling the knife-edge of attraction as we strolled through the moonlight, he was thinking about Remy and how my light-minded prattle would amuse her.

No, it's clear that I was deluded and Dawsey doesn't give two straws for me.

I am too irritated to write more now.

Love always,
Juliet

From Juliet to Sidney

1st August, 1946

Dear Sidney,

Remy is here at last. She is petite and terribly thin, with short black hair and eyes that are nearly black too. I had imagined that she would look wounded, but she doesn't, except for a little limp, which shows itself as a mere hesitancy in her walk, and a rather stiff way of moving her neck.

Now I've made her sound waiflike, and she isn't, really. You might think so from a distance, but never up close. There is a grave intensity in her that is almost unnerving. She is not cold and certainly not unfriendly, but she seems to be leery of spontaneity. I suppose if I had been through her experience, I would be the same—a bit removed from daily life.

You can cross out all of the above when Remy is with Kit. At first, she seemed inclined to follow Kit around with her eyes instead of talking to her, but that changed when Kit offered to teach her how to lisp. Remy looked startled, but she agreed to take lessons and they went off to Amelia's greenhouse together. Her lisp is hampered by her accent, but Kit doesn't hold that against her and has generously given her extra instructions.

Amelia had a small dinner party the evening Remy arrived. Everyone was on their best behavior—Isola arrived with a big bottle of tonic under her arm, but she thought better of it once she had a look at Remy. "Might kill her," she muttered to me in the kitchen, and stuffed it in her coat pocket. Eli shook her hand nervously and then retreated—I think he was afraid he'd hurt her accidentally. I was pleased to see that Remy was comfortable with Amelia—they will enjoy each other's company—but Dawsey is her favorite. When he came into the sitting room—he was a little later than the rest—she relaxed visibly and even smiled at him.

Yesterday was cold and foggy, but Remy and Kit and I built a sandcastle on Elizabeth's tiny beach. We spent a long time on its construction, and it was a fine, towering specimen. I had made a thermos of cocoa, and we sat drinking and waiting impatiently for the tide to come in and knock the castle down.

Kit ran up and down the shoreline, inciting the waters to rush in farther and faster. Remy touched my shoulder and smiled. "Elizabeth must have been like that once," she said, "the Empress of the seas." I felt as if she had given me a gift—even such a tiny gesture as a touch takes trust—and I was glad she felt safe with me.

While Kit danced in the waves, Remy spoke about Elizabeth. She had intended to keep her head down, conserve the strength she had left, and come home as quickly as she could after the war. "We thought it would be possible. We knew of the invasion, we saw all the Allied bombers flying over the camp. We knew what was happening in Berlin. The guards could not keep their fear from us. Each night we lay sleepless, waiting to hear the Allied tanks at the gates. We whispered that we could be free the next day. We did not believe we would die."

There didn't seem to be anything else to say after that—though I was thinking, if only Elizabeth could have held on for a few more weeks, she could have come home to Kit. Why, why, so close to the end, did she attack the overseer?

Remy watched the sea breathe in and out. Then she said, "It would have been better for her not to have such a heart."

Yes, but worse for the rest of us.

The tide came in then: cheers, screams, and no more castle.

Love,
Juliet

From Isola to Sidney

1st August, 1946

Dear Sidney,

I am the new Secretary of the Guernsey Literary and Potato Peel Pie Society. I thought you might like to see a sample of my first minutes, being as how you are interested in anything Juliet is interested in. Here they are:

30th July–1946–7:30 P.M.

Night cold. Ocean noisy. Will Thisbee was host. House dusted, but curtains need washing.

Mrs. Winslow Daubbs read a chapter from her autobiography, *The Life and Loves of Delilah Daubbs*. Audience attentive—but silent afterwards. Except for Winslow, who wants a divorce.

All were embarrassed, so Juliet and Amelia served the dessert they'd made earlier—a lovely ribbon cake, on real china plates—which we don't usually run to.

Miss Minor then rose to ask if we were going to start being our own authors, could she read from a book of her very own thoughts? Her text is called *The Common Place Book of Mary Margaret Minor.*

Everybody already knows what Mary Margaret thinks about everything, but we said "Aye" because we all like Mary Margaret. Will Thisbee ventured to say that perhaps Mary Margaret will edit herself in writing, as she has never done in talking, so it might not be so bad.

I moved we have a specially called meeting next week so I don't have to wait to talk about Jane Austen. Dawsey seconded! All said, "Aye." Meeting adjourned.

Miss Isola Pribby,
Official Secretary to the Guernsey Literary and Potato Peel Pie Society

Now that I'm Official Secretary, I could swear you in for a member if you'd like to be one. It's against the rules, because you're not an Islander, but I could do it in secret.

Your friend,
Isola

From Juliet to Sidney

3rd August, 1946

Dear Sidney,

Someone—and I can't imagine who—has sent Isola a present from Stephens & Stark. It was published in the mid-1800s and is named *The New Illustrated Self-Instructor in Phrenology and Psychiatry: with Size and Shape Tables and Over One-Hundred Illustrations.* If that is not enough, there's a sub-title: *Phrenology: the Science of Interpreting Bumps on the Head.*

Eben had Kit and me, Dawsey, Isola, Will, Amelia, and Remy over for supper last night. Isola arrived with tables, sketches, graph paper, a measuring tape, calipers, and a new notebook. Then she cleared her throat and read the advertisement on the first page: "You too can learn to read Head Bumps! Stun Your Friends, Confound Your Enemies with Indisputable Knowledge of Their Human Faculties or Lack of Them."

She thumped the book onto the table. "I'm going to become an adept," she announced, "in time for the Harvest Festival."

She has told Pastor Elstone she will no longer dress up in shawls and pretend to read palms. No, from now on she will see the future in a Scientific way, by reading head bumps! The church will make far more money from head bumps than Miss Sybil Beddoes does with her booth, WIN A KISS FROM SYBIL BEDDOES.

Will said she was exactly right; Miss Beddoes wasn't a good kisser and he for one was tired of kissing her, even for Sweet Charity's sake.

Sidney, do you realize what you have unleashed on Guernsey? Isola's already read the lumps on Mr. Singleton's head (his stall is next to hers at market) and told him his Love of Fellow Creatures Bump had a shallow trench right down the middle—which was probably why he didn't feed his dog enough.

Do you see where this could lead? Someday she'll find someone with a Latent Killer Knot, and he'll shoot her—if Miss Beddoes doesn't get her first.

One wonderful, unexpected thing did come from your present. After dessert Isola began to read the bumps on Eben's head—dictating the measurements for me to write down. I glanced over at Remy, wondering what she would make of Eben's hair standing on end, and Isola rummaging through it. Remy was trying to stifle a smile, but she couldn't manage it and burst out laughing. Dawsey and I stopped dead and stared at her!

She is so quiet, not a one of us could imagine such a laugh. It was like water. I hope I'll hear it again.

Dawsey and I have not been as easy with one another as we once were, though he still comes often to visit Kit, or to walk Remy over to see us. Hearing Remy laugh is the first time we've caught eyes for a fortnight. But perhaps he was only admiring how my sunny nature had rubbed off on her. I do, according to some people, have a sunny nature, Sidney. Did you know that?

Billee Bee sent a copy of *Screen Gems* magazine to Peter. There was a photo essay on Rita Hayworth—Peter was delighted, though surprised to see Miss Hayworth posing in her nightdress! Kneeling on a bed! What was the world coming to?

Sidney, isn't Billee Bee tired of being sent on personal errands for me?

Love,
Juliet

From Susan Scott to Juliet

5th August, 1946

Dear Juliet,

You know Sidney does not keep your letters clasped next to his heart; he leaves them open on his desk for anyone to see, so of course I read them.

I am writing to reassure you about Billee Bee's errand-running. Sidney doesn't ask her. She begs to perform any little service she can for him, or you, or "that dear child." She all but coos at him and I all but gag at her. She wears a little angora cap with a chin bow—the kind that Sonja Henie skates in. Need I say more?

Also, contrary to what Sidney thinks, she isn't an angel straight from Heaven, she's from an *employment agency*. Meant to be *temporary*, she has dug herself in—and is now indispensable and *permanent*. Can't you think of some living creature Kit would like to have from the Galapagos? Billee Bee would sail on the next tide for it—and be gone for months. Possibly forever, if some animal there would just eat her.

> All my best to you and Kit,
> Susan

From Isola to Sidney

5th August, 1946

Dear Sidney,

I know it was you who sent *The New Illustrated Self-Instructor in Phrenology and Psychiatry: with Size and Shape Tables and Over One-Hundred Illustrations.* It is a very useful book and I thank you for it. I've been studying hard, and I've got so I can finger through a whole headful of bumps without peeking into the book more than three or four times. I hope to make a mint for the church at the Harvest Festival, as who would not desire to have their innermost workings—good and rotten—revealed by the Science of Phrenology? No one, that's who.

It's a real lightning bolt, this Science of Phrenology. I've found out more in the last three days than I knew in my whole life before. Mrs. Guilbert has always been a nasty one, but now I know that she can't help it—she's got a big pit in her Benevolence spot. She fell in the quarry when she was a girl, and my guess is she cracked her Benevolence and was never the same since.

Even my own friends are full of surprises. Eben is Garrulous! I never would have thought it of him, but he's got bags under his eyes and there's no two ways about it. I broke it to him gently. Juliet didn't want to have her bumps read at first, but she agreed when I told her that she was standing in the way of Science. She's awash in Amativeness, is Juliet. Also Conjugal Love. I told her it was a wonder she wasn't married, with such great mounds.

Will cackles up, "Your Mr. Stark will be a lucky man, Juliet!" Juliet blushed red as a tomato, and I was tempted to say he didn't know much because Mr. Stark is a homosexual, but I recollected myself and kept your secret like I promised.

Dawsey up and left then, so I never got to his lumps, but I'll pin him down soon. I think I don't understand Dawsey sometimes. For a while there, he was downright chatty, but these days he doesn't have two words to rub together.

Thank you again for the fine book.

> Your friend,
> Isola

Telegram from Sidney to Juliet

6th August, 1946

BOUGHT A SMALL BAGPIPE FOR DOMINIC AT
GUNTHERS YESTERDAY. WOULD KIT LIKE ONE?
LET ME KNOW SOONEST AS THEY ONLY HAVE ONE
LEFT. HOW'S THE WRITING? LOVE TO YOU AND
KIT. SIDNEY

From Juliet to Sidney

7th August, 1946

Dear Sidney,

Kit would love a bagpipe. I would not.

I think the work is going splendidly, but I'd like to send you the first two chapters—I won't feel *settled* until you've read it. Do you have the time?

Every biography should be written within a generation of its subject's life, while he or she is still in living memory. Think what I could have done for Anne Brontë if I'd been able to speak to her neighbors. Perhaps she wasn't really meek and melancholy—perhaps she had a screaming temper and dashed the crockery to the floor regularly once a week.

Each day I learn something new about Elizabeth. How I wish I had known her myself! As I write, I catch myself thinking of her as a friend, remembering things she did as though I'd been there—she's so full of life that I have to remind myself she's dead, and then I feel the wrench of losing her again.

I heard a story about her today that made me want to lie down and weep. We had supper with Eben this evening, and afterward Eli and Kit went out to dig for earthworms (a chore best done by the light of the moon). Eben and I took our coffee outside, and for the first time he chose to talk about Elizabeth to me.

It happened at the school where Eli and the other children were waiting for the Evacuation ships to come. Eben was not there, because the families were not allowed, but Isola saw it happen, and she told him about it that night.

She said the room was full of children, and Elizabeth was buttoning up Eli's coat, when he told her he was scared about getting on the boat—going away from his mother and his home. If their ship *was* bombed, he asked, who would he say good-bye to? Isola said that Elizabeth took her time, like she was studying his question. Then she pulled up her sweater and took a pin off her blouse. It was her father's medal from the first war, and she always wore it.

She held it in her hand and explained to him that it was a magic badge, that nothing bad could happen to him while he wore it. Then she had Eli spit on it twice to call up the charm. Isola saw Eli's face over Elizabeth's shoulder and told Eben that it had that beautiful light children have before the Age of Reason gets at them.

Of all the things that happened during the war, this one—making your children go away to try to keep them safe—was surely the most terrible. I don't know how they endured it. It defies the animal instinct to protect your young. I see myself becoming bearlike around Kit. Even when I'm not actually watching her, I'm watching her. If she's in any sort of danger (which she often is, given her taste in climbing), my hackles rise—I didn't even know I *had* hackles before—and I run to rescue her. When her enemy, the parson's nephew, threw plums at her, I roared at him. And through some queer sort of intuition, I always know where she is, just as I know where my hands are—and if I didn't, I should be sick with worry. This is how the species survives, I suppose, but the war threw a wrench in all that. How did the mothers of Guernsey live, not knowing where their children were? I can't imagine.

Love,
Juliet

P.S. How about a flute?

From Juliet to Sophie

9th August, 1946

Darling Sophie,

What lovely news—a new baby! Wonderful! I do hope you won't have to eat dry biscuits and suck lemons this time. I know you two don't care which/what/who you have, but I would love a girl. To that end, I am knitting a tiny matinee jacket and cap in pink wool. Of course Alexander is delighted, but what about Dominic?

I told Isola your news, and I'm afraid she may send you a bottle of her Pre-Birthing Tonic. Sophie—please don't drink it and don't dispose of it where the dogs might find it. There may not be anything actually poisonous in her tonics, but I don't think you should take any chances.

Your inquiries about Dawsey are misdirected. Send them to Kit—or Remy. I scarcely see the man anymore, and when I do, he is silent. Not silent in a romantic, brooding way, like Mr. Rochester, but in a grave and sober way that indicates disapproval. I don't know what the trouble is, truly I don't. When I arrived in Guernsey, Dawsey was my friend. We talked about Charles Lamb and we walked all over the Island together—and I enjoyed his company as much as that of anyone I've ever known. Then, after that appalling night on the headlands, he stopped talking—to me, at any rate. It's been a terrible disappointment. I miss the feeling that we understood one another, but I begin to think that was only my delusion all along.

Not being silent myself, I am wildly curious about people who are. Since Dawsey doesn't talk about himself—doesn't talk at all, to me—I was reduced to questioning Isola about his head bumps to get information about his past life. But Isola is beginning to fear that the lumps may lie after all, and she offered as proof the fact that Dawsey's Violence-Prone Node isn't as big as it should be, given he almost beat Eddie Meares to death!!!!

Those exclamations are mine. Isola seemed to think nothing at all of it.

It seems Eddie Meares was big and mean and gave/traded/sold information to the German authorities for favors from them. Everyone knew, which didn't seem to bother him, since he'd go to a bar to brag and show off his new wealth: a loaf of white bread, cigarettes, and silk stockings—which, he said, any girl on the Island would surely be plenty grateful for.

A week after Elizabeth and Peter were arrested, he was showing off a silver cigarette case, hinting it was a reward for reporting some goings-on he'd seen at Peter Sawyer's house.

Dawsey heard of it and went to Crazy Ida's the next night. Apparently, he went in, walked up to Eddie Meares, grabbed him by the shirt collar, lifted him up off his bar stool, and began banging his head on the bar. He called Eddie a lousy little shit, pounding his head down between each word. Then he yanked Eddie off the stool and they set to it on the floor.

According to Isola, Dawsey was a mess: nose, mouth bleeding, one eye puffed shut, one rib cracked—but Eddie Meares was a bigger mess: two black eyes, two ribs broken, and stitches. The Court sentenced Dawsey to three months in the Guernsey jail, though they let him out in one. The Germans needed their jail space for more serious criminals—like Black Marketeers and the thieves who stole petrol from army lorries.

"And to this day, when Eddie Meares spies Dawsey coming through the door of Crazy Ida's, his eyes go shifty and his beer spills and not five minutes later, he's sidling out the back door," Isola concluded.

Naturally, I was agog and begged for more. Since she's disillusioned with bumps, Isola moved on to actual facts.

Dawsey did not have a very happy childhood. His father died when he was eleven, and Mrs. Adams, who'd always been poorly, grew odd. She became fearful, first of going into town, then of going into her own yard, and finally, she wouldn't leave the house at all. She would just sit in the kitchen, rocking and staring out at nothing Dawsey could ever see. She died shortly before the war began.

Isola said that what with all of this—his mother, farming, and stuttering so bad at one time—it came to pass that Dawsey was always shy and never, except for Eben, had any ready-made friends. Isola and Amelia were acquainted with him, but that was about all.

That was how matters stood until Elizabeth came—and made him be friends. Forced him, really, into the Literary Society. And then, Isola said, how he did blossom! Now he had books to talk about instead of swine fever—and friends to talk with. The more he talked, says Isola, the less he stuttered.

He's a mysterious creature, isn't he? Perhaps he *is* like Mr. Rochester, and has a secret sorrow. Or a mad wife down in his cellar. Anything is possible, I suppose, but it would have been difficult to feed a mad wife on one ration book during the war. Oh dear, I wish we were friends again (Dawsey and I, not the mad wife).

I meant to dispatch Dawsey in a terse sentence or two, but I see that he has taken several sheets. Now I must rush to make myself presentable for tonight's meeting of the Society. I have exactly one decent skirt to my name, and I have been feeling dowdy. Remy, for all she's so frail and thin, manages to look stylish at every turn. What is it about French women?

More anon.

Love,
Juliet

From Juliet to Sidney

11th August, 1946

Dear Sidney,

I am happy that you are happy with my progress on Elizabeth's biography. But more about that later—for I have something to tell you that simply cannot wait. I hardly dare believe it myself, but it's true. I saw it with my own eyes!

If, and mind you only if, I am correct, Stephens & Stark will have the publishing coup of the century. Papers will be written, degrees granted, and Isola will be pursued by every scholar, university, library, and filthy-rich private collector in the Western Hemisphere.

Here are the facts—Isola was to speak at last night's Society meeting on *Pride and Prejudice,* but Ariel ate her notes right before supper. So, in lieu of Jane, and in a desperate hurry, she grabbed up some letters written to her dear Granny Pheen (short for Josephine). They, the letters, made up a kind of a story.

She pulled the letters out of her pocket, and Will Thisbee, seeing them swathed in pink silk and tied with a satin bow, cried out, "Love letters, I'll be bound! Will there be secrets? Intimacies? Should gentlemen leave the room?"

Isola told him to hush up and sit down. She said they were letters to her Granny Pheen from a very kind man—a stranger—when she was but a little girl. Granny had kept them in a biscuit tin and had often read them to her, Isola, as a bedtime story.

Sidney, there were eight letters, and I'm not going to attempt to describe their contents to you—I'd fail miserably.

Isola told us that when Granny Pheen was nine years old, her father drowned her cat. Muffin had apparently climbed onto the table and licked the butter dish. That was enough for Pheen's beastly father—he thrust Muffin into a burlap bag, added some rocks, tied up the sack, and flung Muffin into the ocean. Then, meeting Pheen walking home from school, he told her what he'd done—and good riddance, too.

He then toddled off to the tavern and left Granny sitting plumb in the middle of the road, sobbing out her heart.

A carriage, driving far too fast, came within a whisker of running her down. The coachman rose from his seat and began to curse her, but his passenger—a very big man, in a dark coat with a fur collar, jumped out. He told the driver to be quiet, leaned over Pheen, and asked if he could help her.

Granny Pheen said no, no—she was beyond help. Her cat was

gone! Her Pa had drowned Muffin, and now Muffin was dead—dead and gone forever.

The man said, "Of course Muffin's not dead. You do know cats have nine lives, don't you?" When Pheen said yes, she had heard of such before, the man said, "Well, I happen to know your Muffin was only on her third life, so she has six lives left."

Pheen asked how he knew. He said he just did, He Always Knew—it was a gift he'd been born with. He didn't know how or why it happened, but cats would often appear in his mind and chat with him. Well, not in words of course, but in pictures.

Then he sat down in the road beside her and said for them to keep still—very still. He would see if Muffin wanted to visit with him. They sat in silence for several minutes, when suddenly the man grabbed Pheen's hand!

"Ah—yes! There she is! She's being born this minute! In a mansion—no, a castle. I think she's in France—yes, she's in France. There's a little boy petting her—stroking her fur. He loves her already, and he's going to name her—how strange, he is going to name her Solange. That's a strange name for a cat, but still. She is going to live a long, lovely venturesome life. This Solange has great spirit, great verve, I can tell already!"

Granny Pheen told Isola she was so rapt by Muffin's new fate, she quit crying. But she told the man she would still miss Muffin so much. The man lifted her to her feet and said of course she would—she *should* mourn for such a fine cat as Muffin had been and she would grieve for some time yet.

However, he said, he would call on Solange every once in a while and find out how she was faring and what she was up to. He asked Granny Pheen's name and the name of the farm where she lived. He wrote her answers down in a small notebook with a silver pencil, told her she'd be hearing from him, kissed her hand, got back into the carriage, and left.

Absurd as all this sounds, Sidney, Granny Pheen did receive letters. Eight long letters over a year—all about Muffin's life as the French cat Solange. She was, apparently, something of a feline Musketeer. She was no idle cat, lolling about on cushions, lapping up cream—she lived through one wild adventure after another—the only cat ever to be awarded the red rosette of the Legion of Honor.

What a story this man made up for Pheen—lively, witty, full of drama and suspense. I can only tell you the effect it had on me—on all of us. We sat enchanted—even Will was left speechless.

But here, at last, is why I need a sane head and sober counsel. When the program was over (and much applauded), I asked Isola if I could see the letters, and she handed them to me.

Sidney, the writer had signed his letters with a grand flourish:

Very Truly Yours,
O. F. O'F. W. W.

Sidney, do you suppose? Could it possibly be that Isola has inherited eight letters written by Oscar Wilde? Oh God, I am beside myself.

I believe it because I *want* to believe it, but is it recorded anywhere that Oscar Wilde ever set foot on Guernsey? Oh, bless Speranza, for giving her son such a preposterous name as Oscar Fingal O'Flahertie Wills Wilde.

In haste and love and please advise at once—I'm having difficulty breathing.

Juliet

Night Letter from Sidney to Juliet

13th August, 1946

Let's believe it! Billee did some research and discovered that Oscar Wilde visited Jersey for a week in 1893, so it's possible he went to Guernsey then. The noted graphologist Sir William Otis will arrive on Friday, armed with some borrowed letters of Oscar Wilde's from his university's collection. I've booked rooms for him at the Royal Hotel. He's a very dignified sort, and I doubt he'd want Zenobia roosting on his shoulder.

If Will Thisbee finds the Holy Grail in his junkyard, don't tell me. My heart can't stand much more.

Love to you and Kit and Isola,
Sidney

From Isola to Sidney

14th August, 1946

Dear Sidney,

Juliet says you're sending a hand-writing fellow to look at Granny Pheen's letters and decide if Mr. Oscar Wilde wrote them. I'll bet he did, and even if he didn't, I think you will admire Solange's story. I did, Kit did, and I know Granny Pheen did. She would twirl, happy in her grave, to have so many others know about that nice man and his funny ideas.

Juliet told me if Mr. Wilde did write the letters, many teachers and schools and libraries would want to own them and would offer me sums of money for them. They would be sure and keep them in a safe, dry, properly cooled place.

I say no to that! They are safe and dry and chilly now. Granny kept them in her biscuit tin, and in her biscuit tin they'll stay. Of course anyone who wants to come see them can visit me here, and I'll let them have a look. Juliet said lots of scholars would probably come, which would be nice for me and Zenobia—as we like company.

If you'd like the letters for a book, you can have them, though I hope you will let me write what Juliet calls the preface. I'd like to tell about Granny Pheen, and I have a picture of her and Muffin by the pump. Juliet told me about royalties and then I could buy me a motorcycle with a sidecar—there is a red one, second-hand, down at Lenoux's Garage.

Your friend,
Isola Pribby

From Juliet to Sidney

18th August, 1946

Dear Sidney,

Sir William has come and gone. Isola invited me to be present for the inspection, and of course I jumped at the chance. Promptly at nine, Sir William appeared on the kitchen steps; I panicked at the sight of him in his sober black suit—what if

Granny Pheen's letters were merely the work of some fanciful farmer? What would Sir William do to us—and you—for wasting his time?

He settled grimly among Isola's sheaves of hemlock and hyssop, dusted his fingers with a snowy handkerchief, fitted a little glass into one eye, and slowly removed the first letter from the biscuit tin.

A long silence followed. Isola and I looked at one another. Sir William took another letter from the biscuit tin. Isola and I held our breath. Sir William sighed. We twitched. "Hmmmm," he murmured. We nodded at him encouragingly, but it was no good—there was another silence. This one stretched on for several weeks.

Then he looked at us and nodded.

"Yes?" I said, hardly daring to breathe.

"I'm pleased to confirm that you are in possession of eight letters written by Oscar Wilde, madam," he said to Isola with a little bow.

"GLORY BE!" bellowed Isola, and she reached round the table and clutched Sir William into a hug. He looked somewhat startled at first, but then he smiled and patted her cautiously on the back.

He took one page back with him to get the corroboration of another Wilde scholar, but he told me that was purely for "show." He was certain he was correct.

He may not tell you that Isola took him for a test drive in Mr. Lenoux's motorcycle—Isola at the wheel, he in the sidecar, Zenobia on his shoulder. They got a citation for reckless driving, which Sir William assured Isola he would be "privileged to pay." As Isola says, for a noted graphologist, he's a good sport.

But he's no substitute for you. When are you going to come

see the letters—and, incidentally, me—for yourself? Kit will do a tap dance in your honor and I will stand on my head. I still can, you know.

Just to torment you, I won't tell any news. You'll have to come and find out for yourself.

Love,
Juliet

Telegram from Billee Bee to Juliet

20th August, 1946

DEAR MR. STARK CALLED SUDDENLY TO ROME.
ASKED ME TO COME AND COLLECT LETTERS THIS
THURSDAY. PLEASE WIRE IF THIS SUITS; LONGING
FOR PETITE VACANCE ON DARLING ISLAND.
BILLEE BEE JONES

Telegram from Juliet to Billee Bee

I'D BE DELIGHTED. PLEASE LET ME KNOW ARRIVAL
TIME, AND I'LL MEET YOU. JULIET.

From Juliet to Sophie

22nd August, 1946

Dear Sophie,

Your brother is becoming altogether too august for my taste—he has sent an emissary to retrieve Oscar Wilde's letters for him! Billee Bee arrived on the morning mail boat. It was a very rough voyage so she was shaky-legged and green-faced—but game! She couldn't manage lunch, but she rallied for dinner and made a lively guest at tonight's Literary Society meeting.

One awkward moment—Kit doesn't seem to like her. She backed away and said, "I don't kiss," when Billee attempted one. What do you do when Dominic is rude—chastise him on the spot, which seems embarrassing for everyone, or wait until later for privacy? Billee Bee covered beautifully, but that shows her good manners, not Kit's. I waited, but I'd like your opinion.

Ever since I learned that Elizabeth was dead and Kit an orphan, I have worried about her future—and about my own future without her. I think it would be unbearable. I'm going to make an appointment with Mr. Dilwyn when he and Mrs. Dilwyn return from their holiday. He is her legal guardian, and I want to discuss my possible guardianship/adoption/foster-parenting of Kit. Of course, I want outright adoption, but I'm not sure Mr. Dilwyn would consider a spinster lady of flexible income and no fixed abode a desirable parent.

I haven't said a word about this to anyone here, or to Sidney. There is so much to dither over—What would Amelia say? Would Kit like the idea? Is she old enough to decide? Where would we live? Can I take her away from the place she loves for

London? A restricted city life instead of going about in boats and playing tag in cemeteries? Kit would have you, me, and Sidney in England, but what about Dawsey and Amelia and all the family she has here? It would be impossible to replace or replicate them. Can you imagine a London nursery-school teacher with Isola's flair? Of course not.

I argue myself all the way to one end of the question and back again several times a day. One thing I am sure of, though, is that I want to take care of Kit forever.

Love,
Juliet

P.S. If Mr. Dilwyn says no, not possible—I might just grab Kit up and come hide out in your barn.

From Juliet to Sidney

23rd August, 1946

Dear Sidney,

Called suddenly to Rome, were you? Have you been elected Pope? It had better be something at least that pressing, to excuse your sending Billee Bee to collect the letters in your stead. And I don't know why copies won't do; Billee says you insist on seeing the originals. Isola would not countenance such a request from any other person on earth, but for you, she'll do it. Please do be awfully careful with them, Sidney—they are the pride of her heart. And see that you return them *in person*.

Not that we don't like Billee Bee. She's a very enthusiastic guest—she's outdoors sketching wildflowers this minute. I can see her little cap among the grasses. She thoroughly enjoyed her introduction to the Literary Society last night. She made a little speech at the end of the meeting and even asked Will Thisbee for the recipe of his delicious Apple Puff. This may have been carrying good manners too far—all we could see was a blob of dough that didn't rise, covering a yellowish substance in the middle and all peppered through with seeds.

I am sorry you weren't in attendance, for the evening's speaker was Augustus Sarre, and he spoke on your favorite book, *The Canterbury Tales*. He chose to read "The Parson's Tale" first because he knew what a Parson did for a living—not like those other fellows in the book: a Reeve, a Franklin, or a Summoner. "The Parson's Tale" disgusted him so much he could read no more.

Fortunately for you, I made careful mental notes, so I can give you the gist of his remarks. To wit: Augustus would never let a child of his read Chaucer, it would turn him against Life in general and God in particular. To hear the Parson tell it, life was a *cesspool* (or as near as), where a man must wade through the muck as best he could; evil ever seeking him out, and evil ever finding him. (Don't you think Augustus has a touch of the poet about him? I do.)

Poor old man must forever be doing penance or atoning or fasting or lashing himself with knotted ropes. All because he was Born in Sin—and there he'd stay until the last minute of his life, when he would receive God's Mercy.

"Think of it, friends," Augustus said, "a lifetime of misery with God not letting you draw one easy breath. Then in your last few minutes—POOF!—you'd get Mercy. Thanks for nothing, I say.

"That's not all, Friends: man must never think well of himself—that is called the sin of Pride. Friends, show me a man who hates himself, and I'll show you a man who hates his neighbors more! He'd have to—you'd not grant anyone else something you can't have for yourself—no love, no kindness, no respect! So I say, Shame on the Parson! Shame on Chaucer!" Augustus sat down with a thump.

Two hours of lively discussion on Original Sin and Predestination followed. Finally, Remy stood to speak—she'd never done so before, and the room fell silent. She said softly, "If there is Predestination, then God is the devil." No one could argue with that—what kind of God would intentionally design Ravensbrück?

Isola is having several of us to supper tonight, with Billee Bee as guest of honor. Isola said that though she doesn't like rifling through a stranger's hair, she will read Billee Bee's bumps, as a favor to her dear friend Sidney.

Love,
Juliet

Telegram from Susan Scott to Juliet

24th August, 1946

DEAR JULIET: AM APPALLED BILLEE BEE ON GUERNSEY TO COLLECT LETTERS. STOP! DO NOT— I REPEAT—DO NOT TRUST HER. DO NOT GIVE HER ANYTHING. IVOR, OUR NEW SUB-EDITOR, SAW BILLEE BEE AND GILLY GILBERT (HE OF THE *LONDON HUE AND CRY* AND LATE VICTIM OF YOUR TEAPOT THROWING) EXCHANGING LONG,

LOOSE-LIPPED KISSES IN THE PARK. THE TWO
OF THEM TOGETHER BODES ILL. SEND HER
PACKING, WITHOUT THE WILDE LETTERS.
LOVE, SUSAN

From Juliet to Susan

25th August, 1946
2:00 A.M.

Dear Susan,

You are a heroine! Isola herewith grants you an honorary
membership in the Guernsey Literary and Potato Peel Pie
Society, and Kit is making you a special present that involves
sand and paste (you'll want to open that parcel outdoors).

The telegram came in the nick of time. Isola and Kit had gone
out early to collect herbs, and Billee Bee and I were alone in the
house—I thought—when I read your telegram. I bolted up the
stairs and into her room—she was gone, her suitcase was gone,
her handbag was gone, and the letters were gone!

I was terrified. I ran downstairs and telephoned Dawsey to
come quick and help hunt for her. He did, but first he called
Booker and asked him to check the harbor. He was to stop Billee
Bee from leaving Guernsey—at any cost!

Dawsey arrived quickly and we hurried down the road toward
town.

I was half-trotting along behind him, looking in hedgerows
and behind bushes. We had drawn even with Isola's farm when
Dawsey suddenly stopped short and began to laugh.

There, sitting on the ground in front of Isola's smokehouse, were Kit and Isola. Kit was holding her new quilted ferret (a gift from Billee Bee) and a big brown envelope. Isola was sitting on Billee Bee's suitcase—a Portrait of Innocence, the both of them—while an awful squawking was coming from inside the smokehouse.

I rushed to hug Kit *and* the envelope to me, while Dawsey undid the wooden peg from the smokehouse hasp. There, crouched in a corner, cursing and flailing, was Billee Bee—Isola's parrot, Zenobia, flapping around her. She had already snatched off Billee Bee's little cap, and pieces of angora wool were floating through the air.

Dawsey lifted her up and brought her outside—Billee Bee screaming all the while. She'd been set upon by a crazed witch. Assaulted by her Familiar, a child—clearly one of the Devil's Own! We'd regret it! There'd be lawsuits, arrests, prison for the lot of us! We'd not see daylight again!

"It's you who won't see daylight, you sneak! Robber! Ingrate!" shouted Isola.

"You stole those letters," I screamed. "You stole them from Isola's biscuit tin and tried to sneak off with them! What were you and Gilly Gilbert going to do with them?"

Billee Bee shrieked, "None of your business! Wait till I tell him what you've done to me!"

"You do that little thing!" I snapped. "Tell the world about you and Gilly. I can see the headlines now—'Gilly Gilbert Seduces Girl to Life of Crime!' 'From Love-Nest to Lock-up! See Page Three!'"

That shushed her for a moment and then, with the exquisite timing and presence of a great actor, Booker arrived, looking huge and vaguely official in an old army coat. Remy was with him, carrying a hoe! Booker viewed the scene and glared so fiercely at Billee Bee, I was almost sorry for her.

He took her arm and said, "Now, you'll collect your rightful belongings and take your leave. I'll not arrest you—not this time! I will escort you to the harbor and personally put you aboard the next boat to England."

Billee Bee stumbled forward and gathered up her suitcase and handbag—then she made a lunge for Kit and yanked the quilted ferret out of her arms. "I'm sorry I ever gave it to you, you little brat."

How I wanted to slap her! So I did—and I feel sure it jarred her back teeth loose. I don't know but what island living is getting to me.

My eyes are falling shut on me, but I must tell you the reason for Kit and Isola's early-morning herb collecting. Isola felt Billee Bee's head bumps last night and didn't like her reading at all. B.B.'s Duplicitous Bump was big as a goose egg. Then—Kit told her she'd seen Billee Bee in her kitchen, prowling through the shelves. That was enough for Isola, and they set their surveillance plan in motion. They would shadow Billee Bee today and *see what they would see*!

They rose early, skulked behind bushes, and saw Billee Bee tiptoeing out of my back door with a big envelope. They followed her a bit, until she passed by Isola's farm. Isola pounced and manhandled her into the smokehouse. Kit gathered all of Billee Bee's possessions from the dirt, and Isola went to get her claustrophobic parrot, Zenobia, and threw her into the smokehouse with Billee Bee.

But, Susan, what on earth were she and Gilly Gilbert going to do with the letters? Weren't they worried about being arrested for thieving?

I am so grateful to you and Ivor. Please thank him for everything: his keen eyesight, his suspicious mind, and his good sense. Better yet, kiss him for me. He's wonderful! Shouldn't Sidney promote him from Sub-Editor to Editor-in-Chief?

Love,
Juliet

From Susan to Juliet

26th August, 1946

Dear Juliet,

Yes, Ivor is wonderful and I have told him so. I kissed him for you, and then again for myself! Sidney did promote him—not to Editor-in-Chief, but I imagine he's well on his way.

What did Billee Bee and Gilly plan to do? You and I weren't in London when the "teapot incident" broke into the headlines—we missed the uproar it caused. Every journalist and publisher who loathes Gilly Gilbert and *The London Hue and Cry*—and there are plenty—was delighted.

They thought it was hilarious and Sidney's statement to the press didn't do much to soothe matters—just whipped them into fresh fits of laughter. Well, neither Gilly nor the *LH&C* believes in forgiveness. Their motto is get even—be quiet, be patient, and wait for the day of vengeance to come, as it surely will!

Billee Bee, poor besotted booby and Gilly's mistress, felt the shame even more keenly. Can't you see Billee Bee and Gilly huddled together, plotting their revenge? Billee Bee was to insinuate herself into Stephens & Stark, and find anything, anything at all, that would hurt you and Sidney, or better yet, turn you into laughingstocks.

You know how rumors run like wildfire around the publishing world. Everyone knows you're in Guernsey writing a book about the Occupation, and in the last two weeks, people have begun to whisper that you've discovered a new Oscar Wilde work there (Sir William may be distinguished, but he's not discreet).

It was too good for Gilly to resist. Billee Bee was to steal the letters, *The London Hue and Cry* would publish them, and you and Sidney would be scooped. What fun they'd have! They'd worry about lawsuits later. And of course, never mind what it would do to Isola.

It makes me sick to my stomach to think how close they came to succeeding. Thank God for Ivor and Isola—and Billee Bee's Duplicitous Bump.

Ivor will fly over to *copy* the letters on Tuesday. He has found a yellow velvet ferret, with emerald-green feral eyes and ivory fangs, for Kit. I think she'll want to kiss him for it. You can too—but keep it short. I make no threats, Juliet—*but Ivor is mine!*

Love,
Susan

Telegram from Sidney to Juliet

26th August, 1946

I'LL NEVER LEAVE TOWN AGAIN. ISOLA AND
KIT DESERVE A MEDAL, AND SO DO YOU.
LOVE, SIDNEY

From Juliet to Sophie

29th August, 1946

Dear Sophie,

Ivor has come and gone, and Oscar Wilde's letters are back safe in Isola's biscuit tin. I've settled down as much as I can until Sidney reads them—I'm wild to know what he thinks of them.

I was very calm on the day of our adventure. It was only later, after Kit was in bed, that I started to feel skittish and nervous—and began to pace.

Then there was a knock at the door. I was amazed—and a little flustered—to see Dawsey through the window. I threw the door open to greet him—and found him *and* Remy on my front step. They had come to see how I was. How kind. How flat.

I wonder if Remy shouldn't be getting homesick for France by now? I have been reading an article by a woman named Giselle Pelletier, a political prisoner held at Ravensbrück for five years. She writes about how difficult it is for you to get on with your life as a camp survivor. No one in France—not friends, not family—wants to know anything about your life in the camps, and they think that the sooner you put it out of your mind—and out of their hearing—the happier you'll be.

According to Miss Pelletier, it is not that you want to belabor anyone with details, but it *did happen to you* and you cannot pretend it didn't. "Let's put everything behind us" seems to be France's cry. "Everything—the war, the Vichy, the Milice, Drancy, the Jews—it's all over now. After all, everyone suffered, not just you." In the face of this institutional amnesia, she writes, the only help is talking with fellow survivors. They know what life in the camps was. You speak, and they can speak back. They talk, they rail, they cry, they tell one story after another—some tragic, some absurd. Sometimes they can even laugh together. The relief is enormous, she says.

Perhaps communication with other survivors would be a better cure for Remy's distress than bucolic island life. She is physically stronger now—she's not so shockingly thin as she was—but she still seems haunted.

Mr. Dilwyn is back from his holiday, and I must make an appointment to talk to him about Kit soon. I keep putting it off—I'm so dreadfully afraid that he'll refuse to consider it. I wish I looked more motherly—perhaps I should buy a fichu. If he requests character witnesses, will you be one? Does Dominic know his letters yet? If so, he can print out this:

Dear Mr. Dilwyn,

Juliet Dryhurst Ashton is a very nice lady—sober, clean, and responsible. You should let Kit McKenna have her for a mother.

> Yours sincerely,
> James Dominic Strachan

I didn't tell you, did I, about Mr. Dilwyn's plans for Kit's heritage on Guernsey? He has engaged Dawsey, and a crew Dawsey is to select, to restore the Big House: banisters replaced; graffiti removed from the walls and paintings; torn-out plumbing replaced with new; windows replaced; chimneys and flues cleaned; wiring checked and terrace paving stones repointed—or whatever it is you do to old stones. Mr. Dilwyn is not yet certain what can be done with the wooden paneling in the library—it had a beautiful carved frieze of fruit and ribbons, which the Germans used for target practice.

Since no one will want to go on holiday to Europe itself for the next few years, Mr. Dilwyn is hoping the Channel Islands might become a tourist haven again—and Kit's house could make a wonderful holiday house for families to rent.

But on to stranger events: the Benoit sisters asked me and Kit for tea this afternoon. I had never met them, and it was quite an odd invitation; they asked if Kit had "a steady eye and good aim? Does she like rituals?"

Bewildered, I asked Eben if he knew of the Benoit sisters. Were they sane? Was it safe to take Kit there? Eben roared with laughter and said yes, the sisters were safe and sane. He said Jane and Elizabeth had visited them every summer for five years; the girls always wore starched pinafores, polished court shoes, and little lace gloves. We would have a fine time, he said, and he was glad to see the old traditions were coming back. We would have a lavish tea, with entertainment afterwards, and we should go.

None of which told me what to expect. They are identical twins, in their eighties. So very prim and ladylike, dressed in ankle-length gowns of black georgette, larded with jet beads at bosom and hem, their white hair piled like swirls of whipped cream atop their heads. So charming, Sophie. We did have a sinful tea, and I'd barely put my cup down when Yvonne (older by ten minutes) said, "Sister, I do believe Elizabeth's child is too small yet." Yvette said, "I believe you're right, Sister. Perhaps Miss Ashton would favor us?"

I think it was very brave of me to say, "I'd be delighted," when I had no idea what they were proposing.

"So kind if you would, Miss Ashton. We denied ourselves during the war—so disloyal to the Crown, somehow. Our arthritis has grown very much worse: we cannot even join you in the rites. It will be our pleasure to watch!"

Yvette went to a drawer in the sideboard, while Yvonne slid out one side of the pocket doors between their drawing room and dining room. Taped to the previously hidden panel was a full-page, full-length newspaper rotogravure portrait in sepia of the Duchess of Windsor, *Mrs. Wallis Simpson as was.* Cut out, I gather, from the society pages of the *Baltimore Sun* in the late '30s.

Yvette handed me four silver-tipped, finely balanced, evil-looking darts.

"Go for the eyes, dear," she said. So I did.

"Splendid! Three-for-four, Sister. Almost as good as dear Jane! Elizabeth always fumbled at the last moment! Shall you want to try again next year?"

It's a simple story, but sad. Yvette and Yvonne adored the Prince of Wales. "So darling in his little plus fours." "How the man could waltz!" "How debonair in evening dress!" So fine, so royal—until that hussy got hold of him. "Snatched him from the throne! His crown—gone!" It broke their hearts. Kit was enthralled with it all—as well she might be. I am going to practice my aim—four-for-four being my new goal in life.

Don't you wish we had known the Benoit sisters while we were growing up?

Love and XXX,
Juliet

From Juliet to Sidney

2nd September, 1946

Dear Sidney,

Something happened this afternoon; while it ended well, it was disturbing, and I am having trouble going to sleep. I am writing to you, instead of Sophie, because she's pregnant and you're not. You don't have a delicate condition to be upset in, and Sophie does—I am losing my grip on grammar.

Kit was with Isola, making gingerbread men. Remy and I needed some ink and Dawsey needed some kind of putty for the Big House, so we all walked together into St. Peter Port.

We took the cliff walk by Fermain Bay. It's a beautiful walk, with a rugged path that wanders up and around the headlands. I was a little ahead of Remy and Dawsey because the path had narrowed.

A tall red-headed woman walked around the large boulder at the path's turning and came toward us. She had a dog with her, an Alsatian, and a big one. He was not on a leash and he was overjoyed to see me. I was laughing at his antics and the woman called out, "Don't worry. He never bites." His paws came up on my shoulders, attempting a big, slobbering kiss.

Then, behind me, I heard a noise—an awful gulping gasp: a deep gagging that went on and on. I can't describe it. I turned and saw that it was Remy; she was bent over almost double and vomiting. Dawsey had caught her and was holding her as she kept on vomiting, deep spasms of it, over both of them. It was terrible to see and hear.

Dawsey yelled, "Get that dog away, Juliet! Now!"

I frantically pushed the dog away. The woman was crying and apologizing, almost hysterical herself. I held on to the dog's collar and kept saying, "It's all right! It's all right! It's not your fault. Please go. Go!" She finally did, hauling her poor, confused pet along by his collar.

Remy was quiet then, only gasping for breath. Dawsey looked over her head and said, "Let's get her to your house, Juliet. It's closest." He picked her up and carried her—me trailing behind, helpless and scared.

Remy was cold and shaking, so I drew a bath for her, and after she was warm again, put her into bed. She was already half-asleep, so I gathered her clothes into a bundle, and went downstairs. Dawsey was standing by the window, looking out.

Without turning, he said, "She told me once that those guards used big dogs. Riled them up and loosed them deliberately on the lines of women standing for roll call—just to watch the fun. *Christ!* I've been ignorant, Juliet. I thought being here with us could help her forget.

"Good will isn't enough, is it, Juliet? Not nearly enough."

"No," I said, "it isn't." He didn't say anything more; he just nodded to me and left. I telephoned Amelia to tell her where Remy was and why and started the laundry. Isola returned Kit; we had supper and played Snap till bedtime.

But I can't sleep.

I am so ashamed of myself. Had I actually thought Remy well enough to return home—or did I just want her to go? Did I think it was past time for her to go back to France—to just get on with *IT,* whatever *IT* might be? I did—and it's sickening.

Love,
Juliet

P.S. As long as I'm confessing, I might as well tell you something else. Bad as it was to stand there holding Remy's awful clothes and smelling Dawsey's ruined ones, all I could think of was, *he said "good will . . . good will isn't enough, is it?"* Does that mean that is all he feels toward her? I've chewed over that errant thought all evening.

4th September, 1946

Dear Juliet, All that errant thought means is that you're in love with Dawsey yourself. Surprised? I'm not. Don't know what took you so long to fall to it—sea air is supposed to clear your head. I want to come and see you and Oscar's letters for myself, but I can't get away till the 13th. All right? Love, Sidney

---

5th September, 1946

DEAR SIDNEY—YOU'RE INSUFFERABLE, ESPECIALLY WHEN YOU'RE RIGHT. LOVELY TO SEE YOU ANYHOW ON THE 13TH. LOVE, JULIET

6th September, 1946

Dear Sidney,

Juliet says you're going to come look at Granny Pheen's letters with your own eyes, and I say it's about time. Not that I minded

Ivor; he was a nice fellow, though he should leave off wearing those little hairbow ties. I told him they didn't do much for him, but he was more interested to hear about my suspicions of Billee Bee Jones, how I shadowed her and locked her up in the smokehouse. He said it was a fine piece of detective work and Miss Marple couldn't have done better herself!

Miss Marple is not a friend of his, she is a lady detective in fiction books, who uses all she knows about HUMAN NATURE to figure out mysteries and solve crimes that the police can't.

He set me to thinking about how fine it would be to solve mysteries myself. If only I knew of any.

Ivor said skullduggery is everywhere, and with my fine instincts, I could train myself to become another Miss Marple. "You clearly have excellent observation skills. All you need now is practice. Note everything and write it down."

I went to Amelia's and borrowed a few books with Miss Marple in them. She's a caution, isn't she? Just sitting there quietly, knitting away; seeing things everybody else misses. I could keep my ears open for what doesn't listen right, see things from the sides of my eyes. Mind you, we don't have any unsolved mysteries on Guernsey, but that's not to say we won't one day—and when we do, I'll be ready.

I still savor the head bump book you sent me and I hope your feelings are not hurt that I want to turn to another calling. I still trust the truth of lumps; it's just that I've read the head bumps of everyone I care for, except yours, and it can get tedious.

Juliet says you'll come next Friday. I can meet your plane and ride you to Juliet's. Eben is having a beach party the next night, and he says you are most welcome. Eben hardly ever gives parties, but he said this one is to make a happy announcement to us all. A celebration! But of What? Does he mean to announce nuptials? But whose? I hope he is not getting married hisself;

wives don't generally let husbands out by themselves of an evening and I would miss Eben's company.

Your friend,
Isola

From Juliet to Sophie

7th September, 1946

Dear Sophie,

Finally, I mustered my courage and told Amelia that I wanted to adopt Kit. Her opinion means a great deal to me—she loved Elizabeth so dearly; she knows Kit so well—and me, almost well enough. I was anxious to have her approval—and terrified that I wouldn't get it. I choked on my tea but in the end managed to get the words out. Her relief was so visible, I was shocked. I hadn't realized how worried she'd been about Kit's future.

She started to say, "If I could have one—" then stopped and started again, "I think it would be a wonderful thing for both of you. It would be the best possible thing—" Then she broke off and pulled out her handkerchief. And then, of course, I pulled out my handkerchief.

After we were finished crying, we plotted. Amelia will go with me to see Mr. Dilwyn. "I have known him since he was in short pants," she said. "He won't dare refuse me." Having Amelia on your side is like having the Third Army at your back.

But something wonderful—even more wonderful than having Amelia's approval—has happened. My last doubt has shrunk to less than pinpoint size.

Do you remember my telling you about the little box Kit often carried with her, all tied up in string? The one I thought might hold a dead ferret? She came into my room this morning, and patted my face until I woke up. She was carrying her box.

Without a word, she began undoing the string and took the lid off—parted the tissue paper and gave the box to me. Sophie—she stood back and watched my face as I turned the things in the box over, and then lifted them all out on the coverlet. The articles were: a tiny, eyelet-covered baby pillow; a small snapshot of Elizabeth, digging in her garden and laughing up at Dawsey; a woman's linen handkerchief, smelling faintly of jasmine; a man's signet ring; and a small leather book of Rilke's poetry with the inscription, *For Elizabeth—who turns darkness into light, Christian.*

Tucked into the book was a much-folded scrap of paper. Kit nodded, so I carefully opened it and read, "Amelia—Kiss her for me when she wakes up. I'll be back by six. Elizabeth. P.S. Doesn't she have the most beautiful feet?"

Underneath this was Kit's grandfather's WWI medal, the magic badge Elizabeth had pinned on Eli when he was being evacuated to England. Bless Eli's heart—he must have given it to her.

She was showing me her treasures, Sophie—her eyes did not leave my face once. We were both so solemn, and I, for once, didn't start crying; I just held out my arms. She climbed right into them, and under the covers with me—and went sound asleep. Not me! I couldn't. I was too happy planning the rest of our lives.

I don't care about living in London—I love Guernsey and want to stay here, even after finishing Elizabeth's book. I can't imagine Kit living in London, having to wear shoes all the time, having to walk instead of run, having no pigs to visit. No fishing with Eben and Eli, no visits with Amelia, no potion-mixing with Isola, and most of all, no walks, no days, no visits, with Dawsey.

I think, if I become Kit's guardian, we can continue to live in

Elizabeth's cottage and save the Big House as a holiday home for the idle rich. I could take my vast profits from *Izzy* and buy a flat for Kit and me to stay in when we visit London.

Her home is here, and mine can be. Writers can write on Guernsey—look at Victor Hugo. The only thing I'd truly miss about London are Sidney and Susan, the nearness to Scotland, new plays, and Harrods Food Hall.

Pray for Mr. Dilwyn's good sense. I know he has it, I know he likes me, I know he knows Kit is happy living with me, and that I am solvent enough for two at the moment—and who can say better than that in these decadent times? Amelia thinks that if he does say no adoption without a husband, he will still gladly grant her guardianship to me.

Sidney is coming to Guernsey again next week. I wish you were coming too—I miss you.

Love,
Juliet

From Juliet to Sidney

8th September, 1946

Dear Sidney,

Kit and I took a picnic out to the meadow to watch Dawsey start to rebuild Elizabeth's fallen-down stone wall. It was a wonderful excuse to spy on Dawsey and his way of going at things. He studied each rock, felt the heft of it, brooded, and placed it on the wall. Smiled if it accorded with the picture in his head.

Took it off if it didn't and searched out a different stone. He is very calming to the spirit.

He grew so accustomed to our admiring gazes that he issued an unprecedented invitation to supper. Kit had a prior engagement—with Amelia—but I accepted with unbecoming haste and then fell into an absurd twitter about being alone with him. We were both a bit awkward when I arrived, but he, at least, had the cooking to occupy him and retired to the kitchen, refusing help. I took the opportunity to snoop through his books. He hasn't very many, but his taste is superior—Dickens, Mark Twain, Balzac, Boswell, and dear old Leigh Hunt. *The Sir Roger de Coverley Papers,* Anne Brontë's novels (I wonder why he had those) and my biography of her. I didn't know he owned that; he never said a word—maybe he loathed it.

Over supper, we discussed Jonathan Swift, pigs, and the trials in Nuremberg. Doesn't that reveal a breathtaking range of interests? I think it does. We talked easily enough, but neither of us ate much—even though he made a delicious sorrel soup (much better than I could). After coffee, we strolled down to his barn for a pig viewing. Grown pigs don't improve upon acquaintance, but piglets are a different matter—Dawsey's are spotted and frisky and sly. Each day they dig a new hole under his fence, ostensibly to escape, but really just for the amusement of watching Dawsey fill in the gap. You should have seen them grin as he approached the fence.

Dawsey's barn is exceedingly clean. He also stacks his hay beautifully.

I believe I am becoming pathetic.

I'll go further. I believe that I am in love with a flower-growing, wood-carving quarry-man/carpenter/pig farmer. In fact, I know I am. Maybe tomorrow I will become entirely miserable at the thought that he doesn't love me back—may, even, care for Remy—but right this very moment, I am succumbing to euphoria. My head and stomach feel quite odd.

See you on Friday—you may go ahead and give yourself airs for discovering I love Dawsey. You may even preen in my presence—this one time, but never again.

Love and XXXX
Juliet

Telegram from Juliet to Sidney

11th September, 1946

AM ENTIRELY MISERABLE. SAW DAWSEY IN ST. PETER PORT THIS AFTERNOON, BUYING SUITCASE WITH REMY ON HIS ARM, BOTH WREATHED IN SMILES. IS IT FOR THEIR HONEYMOON? WHAT A FOOL I AM. I BLAME YOU. WRETCHEDLY, JULIET

DETECTION NOTES OF MISS ISOLA PRIBBY
PRIVATE: NOT TO BE READ, EVEN AFTER DEATH!

SUNDAY

This book with lines in it is from my friend Sidney
Stark. It came to me in the mail yesterday. It had
PENSÉES written in gold on the cover, but I scratched
it off, because that's French for Thoughts and I am only
going to write down FACTS. Facts gleaned from keen
eyes and ears. I don't expect too much of myself at
first—I must learn to be more observant.

Here are some of the observations I made today. Kit
loves to be in Juliet's company—she looks peaceful
when Juliet comes in the room and she doesn't make
faces behind people's backs anymore. Also she can wig-
gle her ears now—which she couldn't before Juliet came.

My friend Sidney is coming to read Oscar's letters.
He will stay with Juliet this time, because she's cleaned
out Elizabeth's storage room and put a bed in it for him.

Saw Daphne Post digging a big hole under Mr. Ferre's
elm tree. She always does it by the dark of the moon.
I think we should all go together and buy her a silver
teapot so she can quit and stay home nights.

MONDAY

Mrs. Taylor has a rash on her arms. What, or who,
from? Tomatoes or her husband? Look into further.

Tuesday

Nothing noteworthy today.

Wednesday

Nothing again.

Thursday

Remy came to see me today—she gives me the stamps from her French letters—they are more colorful than English ones, so I paste them up. She had a letter in a brown envelope with a little open window in it, from the FRENCH GOVERNMENT. This is the fourth one she's gotten—what do they want of her? Find out.

I did start to observe something today—behind Mr. Salles's market stall, but they stopped when they saw me. Never mind, Eben is having his beach picnic on Saturday—so I am sure to have something to observe there.

I have been looking at a book about artists and how they size up a picture they want to paint. Say they want to concentrate on an orange—do they study the shape direct? No, they don't. They fool their eyes and stare at the banana beside it, or look at it upside down, between their legs. They see the orange in a brand-new way. It's called getting perspective. So, I am going to try a new way of looking—not upside down between my legs, but by not staring at anything direct or straight ahead. I can move my eyes slyly if I keep my lids lowered a bit. Practice this!!!

FRIDAY

It works—not staring head-long works. I went with Dawsey, Juliet, Remy, and Kit in Dawsey's cart to the air-field to meet dear Sidney.

Here is what I observed: Juliet hugged him to her, and he swung her around like a brother would. He was pleased to meet Remy, and I could tell he was watching her sideways, like I was doing. Dawsey shook Sidney's hand, but he did not come in for apple cake when we got to Juliet's house. It was a little sunk in the middle, but tasted fine.

I had to put drops in my eyeballs before bed—it is a strain, always having to skitter them sideways. My lids ache from having to keep them half-way down too.

SATURDAY

Remy, Kit, and Juliet came with me down to the beach to gather firewood for this evening's picnic. Amelia was out in the sun too. She looks more rested and I am happy to see her so. Dawsey, Sidney, and Eli carried Eben's big iron caul-dron down between themselves. Dawsey is always nice and polite to Sidney, and Sidney is pleasant as can be to Dawsey, but he seems to stare at him in a wondering sort of way. Why is that?

Remy left the firewood and went over to talk to Eben, and he patted her on the shoulder. Why? Eben was never one to pat much. Then they talked awhile—but sadly out of my earshot.

When it was time to go home for lunch, Eli went off

beach-combing. Juliet and Sidney each took ahold of one of Kit's hands, and they walked her up the cliff path, playing that game of "One Step. Two Step. Three Steps—LIFT UP!"

Dawsey watched them go up the path, but he did not follow. No, he walked down to the shore and just stood there, looking out over the water. It suddenly struck me that Dawsey is a lonesome person. I think it may be that he has always been lonely, but he didn't mind before, and now he minds. Why now?

SATURDAY NIGHT

I did see something at the picnic, something important—and like dear Miss Marple, I must act upon it. It was a brisk night and the sky looked moody. But that was fine—all of us bundled up in sweaters and jackets, eating lobster, and laughing at Booker. He stood on a rock and gave an oration, pretending to be that Roman he's so crazy about. I worry about Booker, he needs to read a new book. I think I will lend him Jane Austen.

I was sitting, senses alert, by the bonfire with Sidney, Kit, Juliet, and Amelia. We were poking sticks in the fire, when Dawsey and Remy walked together toward Eben and the lobster pot. Remy whispered to Eben, he smiled, and picked up his big spoon and banged on the pot.

"Attention All," Eben yelled, "I have something to tell you."

All were silent, except for Juliet, who drew in her breath so hard I heard her. She didn't let it out again, and went all over rigid—even her jaw. What could be the matter? I was so worried for her, having once been toppled by appendix myself, that I missed Eben's first few words.

". . . and so tonight is a farewell party for Remy. She is leaving us next Tuesday for her new home in Paris. She will share rooms with friends and is apprenticed to the famous confectioner Raoul Guillemaux, in Paris. She has promised that she will come back to Guernsey and that her second home will be with me and Eli, so we may all rejoice in her good fortune."

What an outpouring of cheers from the rest of us! Everyone ran to gather around Remy and congratulate her. Everyone except Juliet—she let out her breath in a whoosh and flopped backward onto the sand, like a gaffed fish!

I peered around, thinking I should observe Dawsey. He wasn't hovering over Remy at all—but how sad he looked. All of a sudden, IT CAME TO ME! I HAD IT! Dawsey didn't want Remy to go, he feared she'd never come back. He was in love with Remy, and too shy in his nature to tell her so.

Well, I'm not. I could tell her of his affections, and then she, being *French,* would know what to do. She would let him know she'd find favor in his suit. Then they could marry, and she would not need to go off to Paris and live. What a blessing that I have no imagination and am able to see things clearly.

Sidney came up to Juliet and prodded her with his foot. "Feel better?" he asked, and Juliet said yes, so I quit worrying about her. Then he walked her over to make her manners to Remy. Kit was asleep in my lap, so I stayed where I was by the fire and thought carefully.

Remy, like most Frenchwomen, is practical. She would

want evidence of Dawsey's feelings for her, before she changed her plans willy-nilly. I would have to find the proof she'd need.

A bit later, when wine was opened and drunk in toasts, I walked up to Dawsey and said, "Daws, I noticed your kitchen floor is dirty. I want to come and scrub it for you. Will Monday suit?"

He looked a little surprised, but he said yes. "It's an early Christmas present," I said. "So you mustn't think of paying me. Leave the door open for me."

And so it was settled, and I said good-night to all.

SUNDAY

I laid my plans for tomorrow. I am nervous.

I will sweep and scrub Dawsey's house, keeping a watch out for evidence that he cares for Remy. Maybe a poem "Ode to Remy," all scrunched up and in his wastepaper basket? Or doodles of her name, scribbled all over his grocery list? Proof that Dawsey cares for Remy must (or almost must) be in plain sight. Miss Marple never really snooped so I won't either—I will not force locks.

But once I give proof of his devotion to Remy, she'll not get on the aeroplane to Paris on Tuesday morning. She will know what to do, and then Dawsey will be happy.

ALL DAY MONDAY:
A SERIOUS ERROR, A JOYOUS NIGHT

I woke up too early and had to fiddle around with my hens till the hour I knew Dawsey had left for work up at the Big House. Then, I cut along to his farm, checking every tree trunk for carved hearts. None.

With Dawsey gone, I went in his back door with my mop, bucket, and rags. For two hours I swept, scrubbed, dusted, and waxed—and found nothing. I was beginning to despair, when I thought of books—the books on his shelves. I began to clap dust out of them, but no loose papers fell to the floor. I was fair along when suddenly I saw his little red book on Charles Lamb's life. What was it doing here? I had seen him put it in the wooden treasure box Eli carved for his birthday present. But if the red book was here on the shelf, what was in his treasure box? And where was it? I tapped the walls. No hollow sounds anywhere. I thrust my arm down his flour bin—nothing but flour. Would he keep it in the barn? For rats to chew on? Never. What was left? His bed, under his bed!

I ran to his bedroom, fished under the bed, and pulled the treasure box out. I lifted the lid and glanced inside. Nothing met my eye, so I was forced to dump everything out on the bed—still nothing: not a note from Remy, not a photograph of her, no cinema ticket stubs for *Gone With the Wind,* though I knew he'd taken her to see it. What had he done with them? No handkerchief with the initial *R* in the corner. There was one, but it was one of Juliet's scented ones and had a *J* embroidered on it. He must have forgotten to return it to her. Other things were in there, but *nothing of Remy's.*

I put everything back in the box and straightened up the bed. My mission had failed! Remy would get on that aeroplane tomorrow, and Dawsey would stay lonely. I was heart-sore. I gathered up my mops and bucket.

I was trudging home when I saw Amelia and Kit—they were going bird-watching. They asked me to come along, but I knew that not even bird-song could cheer me up.

But I thought Juliet could cheer me—she usually does. I'd not stay long and bother her writing, but maybe she would ask me in for a cup of coffee. Sidney had left this morning, so maybe she'd be feeling bereft too. I hurried down the road to her house.

I found Juliet at home, papers awhirl on her desk, but she wasn't doing anything, just sitting there, staring out the window.

"Isola!" she said. "Just when I've been wanting company!" She started to get up when she saw my mops and pails. "Have you come to clean my house? Forget that and come have some coffee with me."

Then, she got a good look at my face and said, "Whatever is the matter? Are you ill? Come sit down."

The kindness was too much for my broken spirits, and I—I admit it—I started to bawl. I said, "No, no, I'm not sick. I have failed—failed in my mission. And now Dawsey will stay unhappy."

Juliet took me over to her sofa. She patted my hand. I always get the hiccups when I cry, so she ran and got me a glass of water for her fail-safe cure—you pinch your nose shut with your two thumbs, and plug up both ears with your fingers, while a friend pours a glass of water down your throat without let. You stomp your foot when you are close to drowning, and your friend takes the glass away. It works every time—a miracle—no more hiccups.

"Now tell me, what was your mission? And why do you think you failed?"

So I told her all about it—my idea that Dawsey was in

love with Remy, and how I'd cleaned his house, looking for proof. If I'd have found any I'd have told Remy he loved her, and then she'd want to stay—maybe even confess her love for him first, to soothe the way.

"He is so shy, Juliet. He always has been—I don't think anybody's ever been in love with him, or him with anybody before, so he'd not know the right thing to do about it. It'd be just like him to hide away mementos and never say a word. I despair for him, I do."

Juliet said, "A lot of men don't keep mementos, Isola. Don't want keepsakes. That doesn't necessarily mean a thing. What on earth were you looking *for*?"

"Evidence, like Miss Marple does. But no, not even a picture of her. There's lots of pictures of you and Kit, and several of you by yourself. One of you wrapped up in that lace curtain, being a Dead Bride. He's kept all your letters, tied up in that blue hair ribbon—the one you thought you'd lost. I know he wrote Remy at the hospice, and she must have written him back—but no, nary a letter from Remy. Not even her handkerchief—oh, he found one of yours. You might want it back, it's a pretty thing."

She got up and went over to her desk. She stood there awhile, then she picked up that crystal thing with Latin, *Carpe Diem,* or some such, etched on the top. She studied it.

" 'Seize the Day,' " she said. "That's an inspiring thought, isn't it, Isola?"

"I suppose so," I said, "if you like being goaded by a bit of rock."

Juliet did surprise me then—she turned around to me and gave me that grin she has, the one that made me first like her so much. "Where is Dawsey? Up at the Big House, isn't he?"

At my nodding, she bounded out the door, and raced up the drive to the Big House.

Oh wonderful Juliet! She was going to give Dawsey a piece of her mind for shirking his feelings for Remy.

Miss Marple never runs anywhere, she follows after slowly, like the old lady she is. So I did too. Juliet was inside the house by the time I got there.

I went on tippy-toes to the terrace and pressed myself into the wall by the library. The French windows were open.

I heard Juliet open the door to the library. "Good morning, gentlemen," she said. I could hear Teddy Heckwith (he's a plasterer) and Chester (he's a joiner) say, "Good morning, Miss Ashton."

Dawsey said, "Hello, Juliet." He was on top of the big stepladder. I found that out later when he made so much noise coming down it.

Juliet said she would like a word with Dawsey, if the gentlemen could give her a minute.

They said certainly, and left the room. Dawsey said, "Is something wrong, Juliet? Is Kit all right?"

"Kit's fine. It's me—I want to ask you something."

Oh, I thought, she's going to tell him not to be a sissy. Tell him he must stir himself up and go propose to Remy at once.

But she didn't. What she said was, "Would you like to marry me?"

I liked to die where I stood.

There was quiet—complete quiet. Nothing! And on and on it went, not a word, not a sound.

But, Juliet went on undisturbed. Her voice steady—and me, I could not get so much as a breath of air into my chest.

"I'm in love with you, so I thought I'd ask."

And then, Dawsey, dear Dawsey, swore. He took the Lord's name in vain. "My God, yes," he cried, and clattered down that stepladder, only his heels hit the rungs, which is how he sprained his ankle.

I kept to my scruples and did not look inside the room, tempted though I was. I waited. It was quiet in there, so I came on home to think.

What good was training my eyes if I could not see things rightly? I had got everything wrong. Everything. It came out Happy, so happy, in the end, but no thanks to me. I don't have Miss Marple's insight into the cavities of the human mind. That is sad, but best to admit it now.

Sir William told me there were Motorcycle Races in England—silver cups given for speed, rough riding, and not falling off. Perhaps I should train for that—I already have my bike. All I'd need would be a helmet—maybe goggles.

For now, I will ask Kit over for supper and to spend the night with me so that Juliet and Dawsey can have the freedom of the shrubbery—just like Mr. Darcy and Elizabeth Bennet.

From Juliet to Sidney

17th September, 1946

Dear Sidney,

Terribly sorry to make you turn around and come right back across the Channel, but I require your presence—at my wedding. I have seized the day, and the night too. Can you come and give me away in Amelia's back garden on Saturday? Eben to be Best Man, Isola to be Maid of Honor (she is manufacturing a gown for the occasion), Kit to throw rose petals.

Dawsey to be Groom.

Are you surprised? Probably not—but I am. I am in a constant state of surprise these days. Actually, now that I calculate, I've been betrothed only one full day, but it seems like my whole life has come into being in the last twenty-four hours. Think of it! We could have gone on longing for one another and pretending not to notice *forever*. This obsession with dignity can ruin your life if you let it.

Is it unseemly to get married so quickly? I don't want to wait—I want to begin at once. All my life I thought that the story was over when the hero and heroine were safely engaged— after all, what's good enough for Jane Austen ought to be good enough for anyone. But it's a lie. The story is about to begin, and every day will be a new piece of the plot. Perhaps my next book will be about a fascinating married couple and all the things they learn about one another over time. Are you impressed by the beneficial effect of engagement on my writing?

Dawsey has just come down from the Big House and is demanding my immediate attention. His much-vaunted shyness has evaporated completely—I think it was a ploy to arouse my sympathies.

Love,
Juliet

P.S. I ran into Adelaide Addison in St. Peter Port today. By way of congratulation, she said "I hear you and that pig-farmer are going to regularize your connection. Praise the Lord!"

Acknowledgments

The seed for this book was planted quite by accident. I had traveled to England to research another book and while there learned of the German Occupation of the Channel Islands. On a whim, I flew to Guernsey and was fascinated by my brief glimpse of the island's history and beauty. From that visit came this book, albeit many years later.

Unfortunately, books don't spring fully formed from their authors' foreheads. This one required years of research and writing, and, above all, the patience and support of my husband, Dick Shaffer, and my daughters, Liz and Morgan, who tell me that *they* never doubted I would finish this book, even if I did. Besides believing in my writing, they insisted that I actually sit down at the computer and type, and it was these twin forces at my back that propelled the book into existence.

In addition to this small cluster of supporters at home, there was a much larger group out in the world. First and in some ways most important were my friends and fellow-writers Sara Loyster and Julia Poppy, who demanded and beguiled and cajoled—and read every word of the first five drafts. This book truly would not have been written without them. Pat Arrigoni's enthusiasm and editorial savoir-faire were also instrumental in the early stages of writing. My sister Cynnie followed lifelong tradition in urging me to buckle down to work, and, in this case, I appreciate it.

I am grateful to Lisa Drew for directing my manuscript to my agent, Liza Dawson, who combines kindness, patience, editorial wisdom, and publishing know-how to a degree I would not have believed possible. Her colleague Anna Olswanger was a source of a number of excellent ideas, for which I am in her debt. Thanks to them, my manuscript found its way to the desk of the amazing Susan Kamil, an editor both profoundly intelligent and deeply humane. I am also grateful to Chandler Crawford, who brought the book first to Bloomsbury Publishing in England and then turned it into a worldwide phenomenon, with editions in ten countries.

I must tender special thanks to my niece Annie, who stepped in to finish this book when unexpected health issues interrupted my ability to work shortly after the manuscript was sold. Without blinking an eye, she put down the book she was writing, pushed up her sleeves, and set to work on my manuscript. It was my great good luck to have a writer like her in the family, and this book could not have been done without her.

If nothing else, I hope these characters and their story shed some light on the sufferings and strength of the people of the Channel Islands during the German Occupation. I hope, too, that my book will illuminate my belief that love of art—be it poetry, storytelling, painting, sculpture, or music—enables people to transcend any barrier man has yet devised.

Mary Ann Shaffer
December 2007

It was my good fortune to enter into this project armed with a lifetime of my aunt Mary Ann's stories and the editorial acumen of Susan Kamil. Susan's strength of vision was essential in making the book what it wanted to be, and I am truly privileged to have worked with her. I salute her invaluable assistant editor, Noah Eaker, as well.

I am grateful, too, to the team at Bloomsbury Publishing. There, Alexandra Pringle has been a paragon of patience and good humor, as well as a font of information about how to address a duke's offspring. I particularly appreciate Mary Morris, who dealt gracefully with a gorgon, and the marvelous Antonia Till, without whom British characters would be wearing pants, driving wagons, and eating candy. In Guernsey, Lynne Ashton at the Guernsey Museum and Art Gallery, was most helpful, as was Clare Ogier.

Finally, I extend very special thanks to Liza Dawson, who made it all work.

Annie Barrows
December 2007

The Guernsey Literary
and Potato Peel Pie Society

MARY ANN SHAFFER
& ANNIE BARROWS

A Reader's Guide

Afterword
by Annie Barrows

I grew up in a family of storytellers. In my family, there is no such thing as a yes-or-no question, a simple answer, or a bald fact. You can't even ask someone to pass the butter without incurring a story, and major holidays always end with the women gathered around the table, weeping with laughter, while our husbands sit in the next room, holding their heads.

Obviously, with so much practice, my family is rich in fine storytellers, but my aunt Mary Ann Shaffer was the jewel in our crown. What was it about Mary Ann turning a tale? She was one of the wittiest people I ever met, but wit wasn't the essence of her gift. Her language was lustrous, her timing was exquisite, her delivery was a thing of beauty and a joy forever, but none of these reaches to the center of her charm. That, it seems to me, was her willingness to be delighted by people—their phrases, their frailties, and their fleeting moments of grandeur. Together with her delight was the impulse to share it; she told stories so that the rest of us, listening, could be delighted with her, and, time and again, she succeeded.

To tell is one thing, to commit to paper is another. For as long as I can remember, Mary Ann was always working on something, but she never completed a book to her own satisfaction, at least not until she embarked upon *The Guernsey Literary and Potato Peel Pie Society*.

The story of that embarkation began in 1980, when Mary

Ann was in the throes of a fascination with Kathleen Scott, wife of the polar explorer Robert Falcon Scott. In order to write her biography, Mary Ann traveled to Cambridge, England, where her subject's papers were archived. But when she reached her destination, Mary Ann discovered that the archive consisted primarily of aged bits and notes, illegibly scrawled in pencil. Thoroughly disgusted, Mary Ann threw the project over, but she was not yet ready to return home. Instead, for reasons that will always be obscure, she decided to visit the island of Guernsey, far in the nethermost reaches of the English Channel.

Mary Ann flew there, and, of course, drama followed. As her plane landed, what she described as "a terrible fog" arose from the sea and enshrouded the island in gloom. The ferry service came to a halt; the airplanes were grounded. With the dismal clank of a drawbridge pulling to, the last taxi rattled off, leaving her in the Guernsey airport, immured, isolated, and chilled to the bone. (Are you getting the sense of how Mary Ann told a story?) There, as the hours ticked by, she hunkered in the feeble heat of the hand-dryer in the men's restroom (the hand-dryer in the women's restroom was broken), struggling to sustain the flickering flame of life. The flickering flame of life required not only bodily nourishment (candy from vending machines), but spiritual aliment, that is, books. Mary Ann could no more endure a day without reading than she could grow feathers, so she helped herself to the offerings at the Guernsey airport bookstore. In 1980, this bookstore was evidently a major outlet for writings on the occupation of the island by the Germans during World War II. Thus, when the fog lifted, Mary Ann left the island, having seen nothing that could be considered a sight, with an armload of books and an abiding interest in Guernsey's wartime experiences.

Some twenty years passed before Mary Ann, goaded by her writing group, began *The Guernsey Literary and Potato Peel Pie Society*. As the members of the Literary Society found during their ordeal, companionship can help us surmount nearly any barrier, imposed, self-imposed, or imagined. Likewise, Mary Ann's writing group, by cajoling, critiquing, admiring, and demanding, sustained her through the obstacle course of creation and across the finish line to her first completed manuscript.

"All I wanted," Mary Ann once said, "was to write a book that someone would like enough to publish." She got what she wanted—and more—for publishers from around the world flocked to buy her book. It was a triumph, of course for her, but for the rest of us longtime Mary Ann listeners as well. Finally we had proof of what we had known all along—our own personal Scheherazade could beguile the world. We swelled with pride.

But then, just as if we were in some horrible retributive folk tale, the triumph turned, because Mary Ann's health began to fail. When, shortly thereafter, the book's editor requested some changes that required substantial rewriting, Mary Ann knew that she did not have the stamina to undertake the work, and she asked me if I would do it, on the grounds that I was the other writer in the family.

Of course I said yes. Writers are rarely the solution to anyone's problems, and this was a unique occasion to help someone I loved. But to myself I whispered that it was impossible—impossible for me to take on my aunt's voice, her characters, the rhythm of her plot.

However, there was no help for it; I had to begin. And once I began, I discovered something: It was easy. It was easy because I had grown up on Mary Ann's tales—they didn't just

come with the butter, they *were* the butter. They were nourishment. All those years and years when her stories were the
wallpaper of my life, when just passing through the dining
room would garner me an odd expression or an obscure fact,
Mary Ann's idea of narrative was becoming mine. In the same
way that people acquire accents and politics from their sur-
roundings, I acquired stories.

Working on the book, then, was like sitting down with
Mary Ann—her characters were people I knew (sometimes
literally) and their most irrational actions had a certain familiar logic to me. When Mary Ann passed away, in early
2008, the book was a comfort, because it held her within it.
The Guernsey Literary and Potato Peel Pie Society is a testa-
ment to Mary Ann's talent, to be sure, but in the truest way
it's also the embodiment of her generosity. In it she offers, for
our enjoyment, a catalog of her delights—the oddities that
enchanted her, the expressions that entertained her, and,
above all, the books that she adored.

I think that Mary Ann knew, before she died, that her
book was going to be well received, but no one could ever be
entirely prepared for the avalanche of acclaim that greeted its
publication. As first the booksellers, then the reviewers, and
finally actual readers got their hands on the book, we noticed
that their praise often took the same form—the book was
quirky, unlike anything else, charming, vivid, witty. . . . In
other words, it was like Mary Ann herself. Suddenly, the rest
of the world had a seat at the table where I had been feasting
my whole life, and, as with any family party, they clustered
around Mary Ann, weeping with laughter—or sorrow—as
her stories billowed forth

The only flaw in the feast is that it ends. If I could have
anything I wanted, I would choose story without end, and it

seems that I have lots of company in that. I have received many, many letters from readers all over the world bemoaning the fact that the book comes to an end. "I want it to go on forever," they say. "I want to go to Guernsey and join a book club." "I want to be a member of the Society." The good news is that as long as we don't get too caught up in the space-time continuum, the book *does* still go on, every time a reader talks about it with another reader. The membership of the Guernsey Literary and Potato Peel Pie Society increases each time the book is read and enjoyed. The wonderful thing about books—and the thing that made them such a refuge for the islanders during the occupation—is that they take us out of our time and place and understanding, and transport us not just into the world of the story, but into the world of our fellow readers, who have stories of their own.

In the months since the book was published, I have heard from readers who were reminded of their own wartime experiences. One Guernsey native told me of his evacuation to England, along with hundreds of other children, the week before the Germans invaded. The most thrilling moment, he said, was his first glimpse of a black cow. He hadn't known that cows came in black. Another woman, a child in Germany during the war, told of bringing food to the French soldier hiding in her attic—she was the only member of the family small enough to squeeze through the trapdoor. It's not all war stories, either. I've heard from people who want to know if Mary Lamb really stabbed her mother with a carving knife (yes!) and people who want to make potato peel pie (I advise against this) and people who want to read another book written in letters (*Daddy Long Legs*).

This profusion of questions, exclamations, and tales is the new version of the Society. Its members are spread all over the world, but they are joined by their love of books, of talking about books, and of their fellow readers. We are transformed—magically—into the literary society each time we pass a book along, each time we ask a question about it, each time we say, "If you liked that, I bet you'd like *this*." Whenever we are willing to be delighted and share our delight, as Mary Ann did, we are part of the ongoing story of *The Guernsey Literary and Potato Peel Pie Society*.

Questions and Topics
for Discussion

1. What was it like to read a novel composed entirely of letters? What do letters offer that no other form of writing (not even emails) can convey?

2. What makes Sidney and Sophie ideal friends for Juliet? What common ground do they share? Who has been a similar advocate in your life?

3. Dawsey first wrote to Juliet because books, on Charles Lamb or otherwise, were so difficult to obtain on Guernsey in the aftermath of the war. What differences did you note between bookselling in the novel and bookselling in your world? What makes book lovers unique, across all generations?

4. What were your first impressions of Dawsey? How was he different from the other men Juliet had known?

5. Discuss the poets, novelists, biographers, and other writers who capture the hearts of the members of the Guernsey Literary and Potato Peel Pie Society. What does a reader's taste in books say about his or her personality? Whose lives were changed the most by membership in the society?

6. Juliet occasionally receives mean-spirited correspondence from strangers, accusing both Elizabeth and Juliet of being immoral. What accounts for these judgmental letters?

7. In what ways were Juliet and Elizabeth kindred spirits? What

did Elizabeth's spontaneous invention of the society, as well as her brave final act, say about her approach to life?

8. Numerous Guernsey residents give Juliet access to their private memories of the occupation. Which voices were most memorable for you? What was the effect of reading a variety of responses to a shared tragedy?

9. Kit and Juliet complete each other in many ways. What did they need from each other? What qualities make Juliet an unconventional, excellent mother?

10. How did Remy's presence enhance the lives of those on Guernsey? Through her survival, what recollections, hopes, and lessons also survived?

11. Juliet rejects marriage proposals from a man who is a stereotypical "great catch." How would you have handled Juliet's romantic entanglement? What truly makes someone a "great catch"?

12. What was the effect of reading a novel about an author's experiences with writing, editing, and getting published? Did this enhance the book's realism, though Juliet's experience is a bit different from that of debut novelist Mary Ann Shaffer and her niece, children's book author Annie Barrows?

13. What historical facts about life in England during World War II were you especially surprised to discover? What traits, such as remarkable stamina, are captured in a detail such as potato peel pie? In what ways does fiction provide a means for more fully understanding a non-fiction truth?

14. Which of the members of the Society is your favorite? Whose literary opinions are most like your own?

15. Do you agree with Isola that "reading good books ruins you for enjoying bad ones"?